Werner
KRAUSS

German Film and Theatre Actor,
Nazi Propaganda Collaborator

A Fictional Re-imagining of his Life

This book is dedicated to Mum and Dad
Julie and Donald Watts
who have encouraged and supported me in
everything I have ever done

GARETH WATTS

Werner
KRAUSS

German Film and Theatre Actor, Nazi Propaganda Collaborator

A Fictional Re-imagining of his Life

sussex
ACADEMIC
PRESS
Brighton • Portland • Toronto

2 4 6 8 10 9 7 5 3 1

First published in Great Britain in 2017 by
SUSSEX ACADEMIC PRESS
PO Box 139, Eastbourne BN24 9BP

and in the United States of America by
SUSSEX ACADEMIC PRESS
International Specialized Book Services
920 NE 58th Ave #300
Portland, Oregon 97213

British Library Cataloguing in Publication Data
A CIP catalogue record for this book is available from the British Library.

Library of Congress Cataloging-in-Publication Data
Names: Watts, Gareth, 1982– author.
Title: Werner Krauss : German film and theatre actor, Nazi propaganda
  collaborator : a fictional re-imagining of his life / Gareth Watts.
Description: Portland, OR : Sussex Academic Press, 2017. | Includes
  bibliographical references.
Identifiers: LCCN 2017013472 | ISBN 9781845198985 (pbk : alk.
  paper)
Subjects: LCSH: Krauss, Werner, 1884–1959—Fiction. | World War,
1939–1945—Collaborationists—Germany—Fiction. | National
  socialism—Fiction. | Antisemitism—Fiction. | LCGFT: Biographical
fiction
Classification: LCC PR6073.A8795 W47 2017 | DDC 823/.92—dc23
LC record available at https://lccn.loc.gov/2017013472

Typeset & designed by Sussex Academic Press, Brighton & Eastbourne.

Contents

Acknowledgements

The author and publisher gratefully acknowledge the following for permission to reproduce copyright material:

Excerpts from John London, 'Non-German Drama in the Third Reich', from *Theatre Under The Nazis* (ed. Jack London), (Manchester: Manchester University Press, 2000), courtesy of Manchester University Press.

William R. Elwood, 'Werner Krauss and the Third Reich', from *Theatre in the Third Reich, The Prewar Years* (ed. by Glen W. Gadberry), (London: Greenwood, 1995); excerpts from pp. 92, p. 94, p. 95 and p. 96. Permission to reproduce granted via ABC Clio through Copyright.com.

Material from Werner Krauss, *Das Schauspiel Meines Lebens* (Stuttgart: Henry Goverts Verlag, 1958). The Author and Publisher have made extensive efforts to track down the rights-holder for this work, but without success.

George Bernard Shaw letters, quoted in Werner Krauss, *Das Schauspiel Meines Lebens*. Permission to reproduce granted by the Estate of George Bernard Shaw.

Excerpts from Hayden White, 'Figural Realism in Witness Literature', from *Parallax*, vol. 10, no. 1 (London: Taylor & Francis, 2004). Permission to reproduce granted by Taylor & Francis.

Excerpts from Brian Cheyette, 'The Uncertain Certainty of *Schindler's List*', *Spielberg's Holocaust; Critical Perspectives on Schindler's List* (ed. Yosefa Loshitzky), (Indianapolis: Indiana University Press, 1997). Permission to reproduce granted by Indiana University Press.

The cover illustration, Das Cabinet des Dr. Caligari, is reproduced courtesy of Mirnau Stiftung, Wiesbaden, Germany.

The publishers apologize for any errors or omissions in the above list and would be grateful to be notified of any corrections that should be incorporated in the next edition or reprint of this book.

Many thanks to everyone at the Department of English and Drama, Loughborough University. Particular gratitude must go to John Schad for his role in securing my three-year Departmental Studentship and Elaine Hobby for offering me (highly enjoyable) teaching work – crucially, your faith and trust made this project financially viable. My Directors of Research, Clare Hanson and Gabriel Egan, gave a timely 'second opinion', insight and a welcome sense of perspective.

As my second Supervisor, Julian Wolfreys guided me through the final twelve months of this project with lucid insight, encouragement and timely reassurance. It was a pleasure to work with him during the testing 'write-up' process.

Thank you to my fellow PhD students: James Holden, Gemma Twitchen, Lindsey Croft, Steph Foster, Jenni Ramone and particularly Vicky Smith. Thanks also to my Critical Studies students – teaching really is the best form of learning.

Thanks to the librarians at The Pilkington Library, Loughborough University, particularly Laurie Salemohamed, and also to those at the University of Leicester Library. The staff at the film archive at the Imperial War Museum were warm and accommodating, as were the staff at The Wiener Library, Devonshire Street, London, who gave me access to a wealth of crucially important primary source material. Also thanks to Jo Fox, of the University of Durham, for her informative email correspondence and to Aaron Hulme, for his help with some of the more difficult German translation.

Jonathan Taylor is a Supervisor, mentor and friend, whose tireless support and willingness to help was simply invaluable. Throughout my MA and PhD projects, his assistance has been thorough and astute.

Finally, special thanks go to Charlotte Watts, without whose love, patience, smile, jokes and songs, this project would have been impossible.

Introduction

'It felt as though writing to satisfy a particular agenda wasn't really writing at all – just a series of unconvincing answers to a set of impossible questions.'[1]

Shylock, Krauss and the Genesis of 'Never Felt It Till Now'

The initial idea for this book arose in 2002, as a response to an essay assignment I was set as an English undergraduate. The essay question was: 'Should *The Merchant of Venice* still be staged in light of the Holocaust?' While researching the essay, I turned my attention to particular productions of the play, intrigued to know if it had ever actually been staged by the Nazis and, if so, how effective it was as a propaganda tool.

The Merchant of Venice was shown regularly throughout Nazi-occupied Europe. In one performance, directed by Paul Rose in 1942, extras were planted amongst the audience, 'hurling abuse as soon as Shylock appeared'.[2] Another notorious production was staged in 1943 at the Vienna Bergtheater, starring Werner Krauss as Shylock. This staging was blatant in its intentions, and one contemporary reviewer claimed that Krauss encapsulated 'the pathological picture of the Eastern European racial type in all his internal and external dirtiness, emphasizing danger through humour'.[3] Another declared: 'Words are inadequate to describe the linguistic and mimic variety of Werner Krauss' Shylock [. . .] Every fibre of his body seems impregnated with Jewish blood; he mumbles, slavers, gurgles, grunts and squawks with alarming authenticity . . . '[4]

I was simultaneously appalled and fascinated by these discoveries, for it seemed that such productions were used to convince the German theatregoer that the Nazi 'struggle' against the Jews was a historic one, and one tacitly supported by William Shakespeare. Although I appreciated that the Jewish characterisation in *The Merchant of Venice* was inherently problematic, I was nonetheless astonished at just how blatantly the play was being used by the Nazis in a barbaric propaganda campaign, almost four hundred years after its first performance.

The hideousness of this notion stayed with me, long after completing the assignment, and I started to become interested by instances of misinterpretation and distortions of historical details in more contemporary works. It occurred to me that the very aspects of reading fiction which I found most appealing: extended metaphors, ironic turns of phrase, the freedom of authors to represent morally dubious points-of-view, were, in fact, the very aspects which allowed for, or even invited, misinterpretation and the distortion of historical facts. I was left with an intriguing dichotomy: I enjoyed the freedoms afforded to the artist, and yet I was frustrated by the apparent moral anarchy, which such freedoms relied upon.

My specific interest in anti-Semitic portrayals in *The Merchant of Venice*, coupled with a passion for contemporary novels, soon led me to read works whereby, in differing forms, the Holocaust itself was represented. These works included Thomas Keneally's *Schindler's Ark*, William Styron's *Sophie's Choice* and Martin Amis' *Time's Arrow*. I chose to study these works in more detail, examining precisely how each author had attempted to combine the academic rigour necessary to represent such an appalling, systematic atrocity; one of the most inhumane acts in history, with the novelistic impulse towards the use of fictive devices in plotting and maintaining a narrative. I was especially interested in the extent to which each author displayed a humanising tendency in their representation of Nazi actions, and attempted to identify how, if at all, the 'entertainment function' was being employed in such a bleak historical setting.

I wrote a series of essays on these novels, (one of which is revisited here) and concluded in each instance that such texts omitted to explore the underlying reasons for the Nazi rise, and fundamentally neglected to ask *why* their policies were supported and enacted by ordinary Germans. I am not suggesting that this was a failing of these works *per se*, rather that my subjective, individual curiosities were not being addressed in these works of fiction.

Indeed, I was interested in the questions: '*how* could it (the Nazi rise) happen?' and '*why* did it happen?' and wondered how such impossibly broad concerns might be explored in a work of fiction. I contemplated composing my own experimental, fictional piece as a way to test this problem. As a result, the focus of my research altered, as I shifted my attention away from 'Holocaust Fiction' to more factual accounts of the Nazi ascent, the history of German anti-Semitism, the failings of the Weimar Republic and the state of Germany in the wake of the Treaty of Versailles.

One significant finding concerned the unemployed population of

Weimar Germany. Richard Bessel asserts that mass unemployment 'provided one of the conditions for the destruction of democracy and the triumph of National Socialism.'[5] Yet, although one might assume that the unemployed had formed a key constituent in voting for the Nazis – whose vilification of flourishing Jewish businesses provided a perfect scapegoat for the 'indigenous' unemployed – statistical research in this area actually suggests otherwise. Although the numbers of unemployed 'increased to more than five million in the winter of 1930–1, and six million in 1931–2 [. . .] By January 1932 it was estimated that the unemployed, with their dependents, made up about a fifth of the entire population, some 12.86 million people,'[6] Jürgen Falter's studies into voting patterns of the time, actually suggest that:

> There is a *negative* statistical correlation between the level of unemployment and the electoral successes of the Nazis: 'In the Reichstag elections of 1932 and 1933. In terms of both its absolute strength and the growth of its support, the NSDAP [Nazi Party] tended to be more successful in areas where unemployment was below the Reich average, and less successful where it was above it.[7]

Indeed, it was the Nazis main opponents, the Communist Party, who 'gained most from the political mobilisation of the jobless. As the unemployment rate rose through 1930, 1931 and 1932, so too did the Communist vote.'[8] As such, it appeared that even the most logical assumptions about the appeal of the Nazis to German voters, were not necessarily supported by the historical record.

Similarly, one might be tempted to focus upon the extent of Jewish success in securing desirable roles under the Weimar regime – as doctors, lawyers and prominent retailers – in provoking jealousy, resentment and a Nazi-led backlash. Yet in his detailed study of the Jewish place in Weimar society, *The Jews in Weimar Germany*, Donald L. Niewyk disputes any such simplistic, cause-and-effect analysis:

> No consideration of the Jews' conduct and role should suggest that different behaviour during the Weimar years would have altered the outcome in any significant way. By 1919 the "mythical Jew" was already an established figure in the minds of those who chose to believe in him. Had the Jews succeeded in attaining perfection itself, they would only have been denounced for yet another demonic plot.[9]

Therefore, any attempt to explore the grounds for Nazi success should not be addressed by singular, linear analytical means. Rather, one should adopt an open-minded approach, allowing for a multiplicity of reasons and complex, underlying factors. Following this logic, it occurred to me that a fictional novel should be a wholly appropriate platform upon which these issues could be explored. Indeed, as Niewyk concludes: 'An understanding of German anti-Semitism requires appreciation both of the psychological torments produced by a troubled society and of the vulnerable position that the Jews held in it.'[10] It was in this combination, between insights into the individual psychological process, with that of a society as a whole, which I felt would provide a particularly apt starting-point for a creative response.

Another aspect of my research was to investigate what the alternative to a Nazi Dictatorship really was for the German people. In summary, it seemed that the political climate had become polarised, and the choice for the average member of the public started to become the choice between Communism and Nazism, extreme left or extreme right. As John Willett asserts: 'The middle-of-the-road parties were squeezed into ineffectiveness while the extreme Right and the extreme Left gathered strength, and of these two it was clear which was gathering it quicker.'[11] Perhaps in their revulsion for one extreme ideology, the German people felt compelled to subscribe to another. Peter D. Stachura shows in his study of younger voters, it was only these extreme parties that appealed most directly to youthful desires for radical change and for a more alluring national aesthetic:

> In their relentless campaign to destroy the Weimar Republic the anti-democratic, totalitarian movements of National Socialism and Communism both successfully styled themselves as 'parties of youth'. They appealed in their different ways to a sense of heroic idealism, militancy, excitement and novelty as well as to German youth's longing for a feeling of belonging and purpose behind a cause; they both aggressively sought to act out the much discussed, dramatic theme of a 'mission of youth' (*Sendung der jungen Generation*).[12]

In *The New Sobriety*, John Willett reflects that this polarisation between left and right was also evident in the artistic and cultural production of the late Weimar-era Germany: 'Pending the arrival of this (as it proved) Armageddon there was a cultural tug-of-war in which gains were made on both sides.'[13] In considering the appeal of a political party to younger voters and the effect of cultural factors, I felt compelled to ask the question of 'why' to myself, and in doing so, discovered exactly what it was that I was searching for from this project. I asked myself why *I* have ever, or would ever subscribe to a particular political point of view. The answer was quite simple: I am influenced by art, artists, writers, novels, plays, poems, musicians, actors, comedians, critics, commentators, academics, friends, family, sportspeople – almost *anyone other than politicians themselves*. Upon realising this, I found the focus of my thesis, because I wanted to apply this worldview to Nazi Germany, and find out exactly what role the arts and media played in the Nazi rise to power. And given my previous insight into a particular staging of *The Merchant of Venice*, this production, and the people involved in it, provided an ideal focal point for my curiosity.

Having found this focus, it was not long before I started to realise the cultural importance of one of the actors involved – the man giving the morally dubious portrayal of Shylock already mentioned – Werner Krauss. I discovered that, just as he is regarded with contempt for his Nazi affiliations, Krauss is simultaneously revered for his performance in a silent film (which has since acquired 'cult' status amongst film aficionados) *The Cabinet of Dr. Caligari*. I became fascinated by this man, and felt compelled to write about a life that had obviously experienced such incredible professional high-points as well as demonstrating such an apparent lack of judgement by aligning himself with the Nazi cause.

Initial research into Krauss' personal life revealed that he was married three times, firstly to Paula Saenger from 1908 until 1930, with whom he had a child, Egon, in 1913. Whilst still married, he started an affair with the actress Maria Bard, and was so blatantly passionate onstage with Bard at a show where his wife was in attendance, that his wife immediately returned home and committed suicide.[14] He married Maria Bard in 1931, and they divorced in 1940. Bard's story is also of interest, as she went on to marry another actor, Hannes Stelzer and then she too committed suicide in 1944. Krauss' third marriage was to Liselotte Graf, with whom he had a child, Gregory, in 1945.[15]

Armed with such details of Krauss' life, it became clear that it would be interesting to investigate the extent to which his personal affairs might have influenced his political and professional decision-making. Indeed, my instinct was to find metaphors in his personal life, such as his public gesture of infidelity and his inability to commit to a monogamous relationship, for the actions he took professionally. Further research found differing interpretations of Krauss' career, with some commentators emphasising the duress that he was placed under by the Party, with others condemning him as simply a Fascist sympathiser and Nazi collaborator. However, Krauss is almost unanimously labelled 'opportunistic', 'conceited' and 'difficult', descriptions that I felt could be applied to his personal life just as they could to his professional career. Wolfgang Goetz described Krauss as 'aloof': 'He apparently did not have many friends, was subject to depressions, and periodically felt depressed in daily life'.[16] William R. Elwood, who also notes Krauss' depressive tendencies, supports this notion: 'His shyness, according to some, was a result of his feelings of low self-esteem.'[17]

The historical fact that I felt to be most telling of Krauss' attitude was his public request in 1940, that although he was playing several Jewish roles in the propaganda film *Jud Süss*, he was not actually a Jew. According to Elwood, 'He was thought so true to (stereo)type in these roles "that he asked Goebbels to announce publicly that he was not Jewish, but a loyal Aryan merely playing a part as an actor in the service of the state"'.[18] Indeed, Elwood goes on to say: 'Although Krauss does not bear sole responsibility for the effects of the film on the Jews, *Jud Süss* has been linked to the Nazi terror: there is documented evidence that the film inspired violence against the Jews.'[19] As such, it seemed that Krauss was at the heart of the Nazi propaganda efforts, and that his actions on stage and screen had real-life consequences.

It became apparent that Krauss' life could be represented in three distinct acts, set in three distinct political and cultural contexts for Germany. The first major phase of his career culminates in a starring role in *The Cabinet of Doctor Caligari*, produced in the early years of government for the Weimar Republic. Siegfried Kracauer interprets this film as being metaphorical for the stifling and futile nature of the previous German administration, describing it as 'stigmatis[ing] the omnipotence of a state authority manifesting itself in universal conscription and declarations of war. The German war government seemed to the authors the prototype of such voracious authority'.[20] This sense of disillusionment and futility seems to have been pervasive in the early Weimar era. Indeed, the filming of *Das Cabinet* in Berlin occurred at the same time as great civil unrest, culminating in the 'Kapp Putsch' of 1920, an uprising which is often viewed as a precursor to the Nazi seizing of power, over a decade later.

Another important figure in contextualising this period of Krauss' life, is Max Reinhardt, the Jewish film and theatre director who 'discovered' Krauss, taking him from touring provincial theatres into successive stints at the national *Staatstheater*. John Willett reflects upon how Reinhardt proved to be an extremely important figure in German cultural life, and laments 'it is a sad indictment [. . .] that this great director's role in German – indeed in world – theatre should, nowadays be so underrated.'[21] Willett goes on to describe Reinhardt's impact, and outlines the theatrical output of the time:

> Such were the varied talents and interests of the man who took the Deutsches Theater to its peak of fame before the First World War, setting the standards against which German theatre was to be measured till Hitler made unpersons of him and many of his colleagues. [. . .] In the repertoire itself there was no great change; it simply expanded along the lines already set, that is to say, primarily Shakespeare and the German classics; the Scandanavian and German naturalists; Nestroy, Aristophanes and Goldoni for light relief; and finally modern plays by such as Wedekind, Shaw, Schnitzler, and Hofmannsthal. The acting talent expanded to match, [. . .] Werner Krauss joined the earlier nucleus, with Albert Bassermann too, coming over from the Lessing Theater and Kainz himself appearing as a guest in 1909.[22]

The second act, for Krauss, is crystallised by his controversial role as Shylock in *The Merchant of Venice* and his apparent collaboration during the Nazi years. It was quite common for Shakespeare plays to be performed on the Nazi stage. Indeed, according to John London, 'Shakespeare was the dramatist most performed in Nazi Germany after Schiller'.[23] Furthermore, it is interesting to note how little the theatrical output had changed since the Reinhardt years, in terms of how frequently 'foreign' plays were staged:

> Far from proclaiming a blanket xenophobia, spokesmen for the Third Reich were keen to assert the receptive, European nature of German culture. Weeks after the Theater Chamber had been founded in 1933, its president, Otto Laubinger, declared that 'Shakespeare, Calderon, and Moliere, just like the great Nordic-Germanic writers Ibsen, Bjornson, Hamsun etc.' were 'part of the permanent property of German theatre.[24]

As such, the rate of influence upon Krauss' professional life of the new Nazi regime was initially gradual. It was only later in their reign, when he was co-opted into official propaganda films, such as *Jud Süss*, and other dubious Jewish portrayals, that their impact became more pronounced and problematic.

The final act of Krauss' story involved his becoming ostracised from the theatrical fraternity, and his de-Nazification trial in the setting of post-war West Germany. William R. Elwood describes the chain of events that characterised the end of his career:

> In 1945 Krauss was brought before the Allied authorities on charges that he was a Nazi *Mitlaufer* (fellow traveller). In that year the authorities levied an *Arbeitsverbot* (work ban) on him. He was required to leave Austria in 1946. Three times he was brought before the courts to clarify his relationship with the Nazis. Such leading theatre figures as Carl Zuckmayer, Kathe Dorsch and George Bernard Shaw spoke on his behalf. In 1948 he was fined heavily and allowed to work, but at first no German Intendant would hire him.[25]

Having conducted this initial research on Germany and on Krauss, I felt compelled to tell his story, but strived to do so in a way that was consciously informed by my critique of the 'Holocaust fiction' I had previously scrutinised. The recurring themes of my investigation included: The absence of the question, 'why?' in 'Holocaust fiction', the 'presence' of the author in these works, and the use of novelistic devices in factual accounts. I was determined to establish exactly what I had found so problematic with such texts, and felt that by creating my own novel I could learn at first-hand the extent to which an author is bound by the historical record, as well as the extent to which an author can indulge their novelistic flair for fiction, within a factual context.

'To Avoid All Fiction' – *Never Felt It Till Now* in Response to *Schindler's Ark*

> The novel's techniques seem suited for a character of such ambiguity and magnitude as Oskar [Schindler]. I have attempted to avoid all fiction, though, since fiction would debase the record, and to distinguish between reality and the myths which are likely to attach themselves to a man of Oskar's stature.[26]
>
> THOMAS KENNEALLY, 'Author's Note'

Although my fictional re-imagining of Werner Krauss' life *Never Felt It Till Now* was not written in direct response to *Schindler's Ark*, it is reasonable to assume that this was the novel most influential in provoking my fascination with the genre 'Holocaust fiction'; the novel that I found to be both the most affecting, as well as the most problematic. As such, I shall re-visit my initial responses to Thomas Keneally's text, in the light of completing *Never Felt It Till Now*.

Schindler's Ark is the story of Oskar Schindler, a Czech industrialist who saved over a thousand of his Jewish factory workers from the Nazi concentration camps. Upon publication in 1982, it became an extremely popular novel, which was awarded the Booker Prize for fiction and was subsequently adapted into an award-winning and commercially successful film, directed by Steven Spielberg. As such, I suggest that it may be Keneally's text, above all others of the past twenty-five years, which has shaped the public consciousness and awareness of the events of the Holocaust. The popularity of *Schindler's Ark*, and its subsequent film adaptation, seems difficult to ignore in our retrospective criticism of it; inaccuracies or embellishments on Keneally's part could be said to have extremely significant consequences. However, *Schindler's Ark* is not an attempt to create a 'Holocaust text' that is in any way definitive. Rather, it focuses mainly upon various accounts of the actions of one man, and his rescue of hundreds of Jews from the Nazi concentration camps.

Likewise, with *Never Felt It Till Now*, it was my intention to focus almost entirely on the lifestyle and actions of one man. With the exception of the inclusion of fictional suicide notes from Maria Bard, which are nevertheless addressed to him, Werner Krauss dominates the novel. One of the reasons for this was to induce a sense of claustrophobia into the narrative, to deliberately make the reading experience uncomfortable. The reader's access to Krauss' life becomes intense and intimate – we are with him when he wakes up, when he urinates, even when he sleeps – and as such we are painfully aware of his humanity and his vulnerability.

I intended to focus on Krauss, not at the expense of representing the wider cultural climate, but rather because he was a figure who was both influenced by the prevailing Nazi ideology and, in turn, influential in manipulating the perceptions of film and theatre audiences. The defining example of his influence, within the novel, can be found in the scene when he is attacked by a gang of youths, mistaking him for a Jew as he is still in costume as Shylock.

Werner caught a glimpse of his own reflection in a shop window. He saw an old Jew, staggering along, as if imbalanced by the weight of his hooked beak. "Father hates Jews, doesn't he?" said one boy. The other, shorter but stockier, grunted in agreement. And with that, they charged. (GW)

As mentioned earlier, there is documented evidence to support the view that at least one of Krauss' roles (in the anti-Semitic propaganda film, *Jud Süss*) actually inspired violence against Jews. As such, I hope that by solely focusing on this one individual, I might also be highlighting the wider implications of the work of him and others in perpetuating Nazi propaganda.

The literary genre of *Schindler's Ark* is difficult to classify in any conventional sense, as it eludes singular generic descriptions, such as history, fiction or biography – rather, it is a combination of these. Injecting a sense of historical reliability into the text, Keneally regularly highlights his use of documentary evidence, making it clear when a part of the narrative is directly influenced by a specific source: 'There are photographs of Oskar sitting with them at expensive tables, everyone smiling urbanely at the camera, everyone well fed, generously liquored, and the officers elegantly uniformed' (78). However, Keneally also regularly *alludes* to documentary evidence, without being as specific about the type of source or its contents. Early in the novel he writes: 'But the narrative depends also on documentary and other information supplied by those few wartime associates of Oskar's who can still be reached, as well as by the large body of his postwar friends'. (13) The boundaries between actual historical records, and the author's interpretation of them, become blurred. Consequently, the reader is invited to simply trust Keneally, who provides no direct references or footnotes to his text.

Although *Never Felt It Till Now* also omits to punctuate its prose with footnotes, it is far more direct in its use of anterior texts. For example, Krauss' letter to George Bernard Shaw is replicated verbatim:

> I take it that my name is not quite unknown to you, because I have acted in many of your plays in German Theaters. During my stay in London in the year 1933 I had the pleasure on the 5th October to be your guest together with Siegfried Trebitsch and Maria Bard.[27]

The inclusion of primary sources in this way gives the reader direct access to historical documents, providing them with the opportunity to draw their own moral conclusions about Krauss' character, and in turn make their own judgments about the adjacent, fictional prose.

With regard to *Schindler's Ark*, this notion of 'access' to the historical record is complicated by a very knowing, self-aware narrative voice, which is especially apparent at the beginning and the end of the novel – effectively 'framing' the historical revelations held within. For instance, the Prologue presents a 'snapshot' of the kind nature of Oscar Schindler, who is sympathetic to the plight of the Jewish servant, Helen Hirsch. Although in this passage the reader can enjoy the flamboyance of the novel's protagonist, it is also the first example of the controlling sensibilities of the narrator, who seeks to reassure the reader as to his reasons for opening the story in this way. 'Not to stretch belief so early, the story begins with a quotidian act of kindness, a kiss, a soft voice, a sugared bar' (32). Such narrative insecurity could be said to reinforce the *fictional* nature of the story itself. It is significant that these primarily aesthetic, artificial concerns are so highlighted in an apparently 'factual' book. Carmel Gaffney defends such a pre-occupation, arguing that this opening is necessary to aid the reader's understanding of Keneally's 'factual' intentions: 'Statements of this kind are the rhetorical techniques of a master craftsman who assumes the various roles of historian, critical listener and demythologiser in order to present an Oscar Schindler re-fashioned through the profundity of his perception'.[28]

With *Never Felt It Till Now*, I aimed to provide a narrative voice that was far less intrusive. Throughout the novel, the narrator experiences events at the same time as Krauss, and as such, hopefully avoids the glib rhetoric of the narrator of *Schindler's Ark*. Occasionally, the narrator interjects with brief summaries and commentaries, but only in order to counter the otherwise fast-pace of the plot: 'Sat alone in the waiting room, Werner tried to make sense of the day. He remembered feeling determined to make it up to Maria this morning. And despite having the attention of all of those nurses in the café, he really was looking forward to getting home to her. How did things go so wrong?' (GW 111). Frequent, lengthy passages of dialogue were also included in order to add to the pace and 'real-time' feel of the novel – further emphasising the fact that often decisions are made 'in the moment', and that Krauss was as vulnerable to peer pressure and seductive influences as anyone:

> The actor had no intention of becoming a clandestine drinker by candlelight, yet here he was, caught up in Otto's ritual. Otto swigged straight from the bottle, and, as he caught his breath, passed it on, encouraging his friend to do the same. In a gruff voice, he said: "down the hatch, we haven't got all day." The actor assented, and gulped. (GW 103)

Hayden White suggests that, irrespective of generic conventions, it is the 'truth-value' of a text that is of most interest to a critical reader: 'The theoretical question has to do with the truth-value of a text which promises in its preface that "none of the facts has been invented" but whose meaning resides in large measure in the extent to which it copies the plot-structure of a poetic fiction'.[29] Of particular note, in a text that retells such horrific Nazi actions, is the author's use of novelistic techniques such as humour or bathos. Lars Sauerberg comments on such novelistic assimilation in *Schindler's Ark*:

> Keneally's approach, the combination of documentary and novel, allows him to integrate references to fact, since this is in the traditional nature of the novel, but at the risk of upgrading by his chosen format the entertainment function. By adopting the novelistic format he hopes, however, to be better able to draw a correct picture of the historical person Herr Schindler.[30]

The word 'entertainment' is important here, because, however earnestly this book was written and however well researched, it will still be subjected to the same *reading* patterns as any other 'entertaining' novel. The author may feel a responsibility, however unwittingly, to relieve the tension of a section of the novel, by digressing from the wide-ranging cruelty and suffering to more relatively light-hearted, individual anecdotes and experiences. In doing so, the author emphasises the human qualities of the Jewish population he describes, such as their ability to joke and laugh, rather than simply re-iterating how horrible and tragic their plight was. Also, one cannot ignore the commercial appeal of the 'entertaining' sections of the novel, as the more witty or sensational aspects of the text undoubtedly broaden its market appeal.

An example of Keneally's 'fictional' strategy that reinforces this authorial duty to the general reader lies in the way he structures the chapters of the novel. On several occasions, a chapter ends on a very bleak note and the subsequent chapter opens on a completely different, less serious subject. One example occurs between chapters four and five. As chapter four ends, 'They shot him first and shot the rest anyway and set fire to the place, making a shell of the oldest of all Polish synagogues', chapter five begins 'Victoria Klonowska, a Polish secretary, was the beauty of Oskar's front office, and he immediately began a long affair with her' (68–69). Another similar device is employed as the events of the novel are often described in relation to the date of Oskar's birthday. Such a technique serves both to illustrate this sense of renewed hope, but it also provides a factual basis which documents the chronology of the events. In this way, Keneally is often able to combine the demands of novelist and historian, with apparent ease.

The trend in *Never Felt It Till Now* is to produce the reverse effect of Keneally's 'hopeful' structure – reminders of Krauss' fallibility and lack of judgement immediately undercut joyous or positive moments, with dark humour. For example, in the revelatory passage in part two, where Krauss resolves to help his son and his Jewish fiancée, he decides to take a definite moral position: 'Now, it felt as though he had actually committed to something, and taken a stand. He thought about the way those boys had behaved – the vile, loathsome looks on their young faces and their foul language' (GW 144). This admirable realisation is followed, on the very next page, by Krauss discovering the result of his request to a newspaper:

THIS IS A SPECIAL ANNOUNCEMENT, REGARDING ONE OF THE REICH'S MOST RESPECTED AND ESTEEMED ACTORS. DESPITE HIS SKILFUL AND ACCURATE PORTRAYAL OF DESPICABLE JEWISH CHARACTERS, WERNER KRAUSS, THE ACTOR, IS *NOT* A JEW. (GW 145)

As such, I hoped to ground the humorous, 'entertainment' function of *Never Felt It Till Now* within the dark reality of its context; as readers we can enjoy the irony of Krauss' inner idealism without necessarily enjoying his hypocrisy.

Despite Keneally's largely effective use of humour and bathos in *Schindler's Ark*, there are passages where the narration is not so subtle, and can seem intrusive or even patronising. For instance, after having described Oskar Schindler's early life, the narrator claims to be able to anticipate the reader's desires: 'Oskar's later history seems to call out for some set piece in his childhood. The young Oskar should defend some bullied Jewish boy on the way home from school. It is a safe bet it didn't happen, and we are happier not knowing, since the event would seem too pat' (37). This invites us to question why this idea was mentioned at all. Dangerously, such a statement implies that the novel itself does not contain any elements that could be described as 'pat'. Such implications resonate elsewhere in the novel, as Bryan Cheyette notes:

Where the facts of Schindler's exploits are unclear, such as his purported visit to Auschwitz to liberate the three hundred women destined for Brinnlitz, Keneally makes explicit such lack of knowledge. But these lapses in knowledge also indicate that his seductive narrative is, in the end, absolutely sure of itself.[31]

Indeed, surely this demonstrates that, rather than *avoiding* fiction, Keneally is actually *providing* a fiction which he invites us to avoid. In this sense, Keneally 'over-reaches' in establishing his role as fictional author and historian. By foregrounding the dilemmas that face the author, he over-contextualizes the novel. Despite already outlining his intentions in the author's note and in the lengthy, self-reflective prologue, Keneally continues to remind the reader of his own insecurities throughout the narrative. This does not serve a relevant purpose in the novel – the reader does not need such glib metaphors as a heroic child-Oskar. Indeed, such digressions simply serve to distract the reader from the real testimony that is being divulged, and they invite us to indulge in Keneally's pre-occupation of noting the 'fictional' qualities of Oskar Schindler's story. Cheyette reflects upon these insecurities, comparing *Schindler's Ark* with non-fictional works by the Italian Auschwitz survivor Primo Levi: 'Whereas Levi is concerned with the dangers of reducing the Holocaust to a Manichaean allegory, both Spielberg and Keneally generate a representational uncertainty with regard to the "certainty" of its supposed documentary form'.[32]

Perhaps to re-inforce the 'entertainment function', mentioned earlier, this uncertainty invites a sense of familiarity between the reader and the narrator, at the expense of our faith in the author as a historian. An example of such uncertainty can be found in the lines: 'A number of Schindler's friends would claim later – though it is not possible to prove it – that Oskar had gone looking for the dispossessed family at their lodgings in Podgorze . . . ' (57). Here, the uncertainty of the author is positively promoted. As such, it is this uncertainty that provides the basis for a substantial sub-plot in *Schindler's Ark* – that of the author's struggle to represent the 'raw materials', the historical sources at his disposal. It is *this* sub-plot that most confuses the notions of fact and fiction in the text, as it reveals a pre-occupation with fictional devices in a factual context.

In *Never Felt It Till Now*, I attempted to dispense with such uncertainty whenever possible, both by providing the reader with direct access to primary sources, such as newspaper articles, reviews, interviews and script extracts, and by giving a voice to strong characters, prepared to challenge *Krauss'* certainty – particularly its three main female characters: Paula, Maria and Peta. For example, Maria's letters constantly question the wisdom of his party affiliations:

> *People like Conrad – they could have stayed to become a hero for the government, a stooping, snivelling National Socialist icon like you. But they gave it up, because they knew what they*

believed in, knew exactly what they wanted. Did you know what you wanted, Werner? Or did you just drift from one state of affairs to the next, from one set of rules, from one luxury apartment, from one day, one drink, one fucking girl – *to the next?* (GW 136)

As such, I hope to have provided a range of materials and viewpoints from which the reader can form their own judgement. This sense of an attempted, though imperfect, narratorial 'neutrality' is especially evident in the postscript of the novel, whereby actual newspaper stories, which were written towards the end of Krauss' life, are reproduced in their entirety.

When reading *Schinndler's Ark*, I was troubled by the imbalance between these two 'codes', of history and fiction. As Cheyette notes: 'Keneally claims the truth of history to give his fiction more authority. The omniscient and self-confident narrative voice in Keneally's novel is, however, only rarely troubled about facilely recreating the most intimate details of the past'.[33] This self-confidence is especially apparent in lines such as: 'Yet even with his order book wide open and his pencil flying, Oskar – in the months in 1938 before the German divisions entered the Sudeten – also felt a sense of a grand shift in history, and was seduced by the itch to be party to it' (42). Here, there is a dangerous blend of historical information and retrospective inference. David Lowenthal defines Keneally's 'confident' narrative style as 'pretentious omniscience':

> To deny that history and fiction are either mutually exclusive or utterly indistinguishable routes to the past, however, is not to condone a compromise that claims the virtues of both while accepting the limitations of neither. What is called 'faction' imitates much new fiction and some new history in smudging the distinction between them, but displays a pretentious omniscience that traduces both approaches.[34]

If we are to interpret Keneally's approach as one of 'compromise', we could apply his work to Michel Foucault's assertion that: 'A certain number of notions that are intended to replace the privileged position of the author actually seem to preserve that privilege and suppress the real meaning of his disappearance.[35] In this case, Keneally's familiar tone, which could be seen to replace the cold detachment of a traditional narrator, actually preserves his 'privileged' role as author – his presence in *Schindler's Ark* is explicit and inescapable.

In *Never Felt It Till Now*, the question of authorial intention is itself highlighted within the text, particularly towards the end of the novel, as Krauss attempts to write his autobiography: 'He knew he had the perfect answer to her question, but by describing an isolated example of his resistance to the Nazi regime, was he somehow highlighting its exceptional nature? He poured a small glass of *Rottwein*, and set about describing his most public affront to the Hitler Reich' (GW 185). The passages that Krauss goes on to 'write' are actually translations from his autobiography, *Das Schauspiel Meines Lebens*. Importantly, within the composition of these passages, the nature of writing is itself scrutinised: in some sections, Krauss' thoughts are shown to be interpreted and articulated by Peta, and he also decides what to include based on the forthcoming De-Nazification trials: 'Re-reading his scribbles, he wondered if it might actually be wise to await the outcome of Harlan's trial before writing any more about him. Without necessarily trying to, he seemed to be simultaneously defending and attacking the director' (GW 216). As such, although the mediating influences that can impinge on writers are highlighted, the reader is invited to draw their own conclusions about the reliability of Krauss' words.

Although Keneally's claim to have attempted to 'avoid all fiction' relates in this case to his treatment of the historical sources at his disposal, it is his use of fictional techniques, such as prolepsis, in conveying what he interprets as 'facts', that has a significant effect on the experience of the reader, and in turn the reader's impression of the 'facts' being represented. Keneally reveals that Oskar Schindler eventually 'performs acts of outrageous rescue' (14) to save the *SchindlerJuden* (as his Jewish workers are referred to in the novel) in the opening of the novel. This gives the reader the sense that, however distressing this novel is, they are assured of a 'happy ending' of sorts. As Schwarz writes, 'From the outset, the novel's narrator does not hide that Schindler will help Jews, but rather anticipates it'.[36] This is the most obvious example of Keneally deliberately accommodating a general readership, as it fundamentally undermines the reader's understanding of the feelings and actions of the people he represents. In this sense, there is a form of dramatic irony at work – as readers we know that the 'main characters', such as Leopold Pfefferberg, will survive. This device counteracts the natural rhythm of the events that are being documented, and Keneally could, therefore, be accused of 'fictionalising' the plights of the people involved in a more disturbing way. The reader's knowledge of their eventual survival may undermine their empathy for the situation, and the reader does indeed begin to view them as *characters* or *protagonists* rather than people. For example, the thrilling description of

Pffeferberg's daring escape from Amon Goeth echoes the style of generic crime-fiction:

> Pffeferberg began to run, not looking back, and it would not have surprised him if he had been felled from behind. Running, he got to the corner of Wegierska and rounded it, past the hospital yard where some hours ago he had been a witness. The dark came down as he neared the gate, and the ghetto's last familiar alleys faded. (206)

Such a description, coupled with the knowledge that Pfefferberg *will* survive, invites the reader to enjoy the novelistic flair of the book, rather than to engender a true sense of empathy with the real people being described.

Keneally does, however, allude to this retrospective view of history: 'To write these things now is to state the commonplaces of history. But to find them out in 1942, to have them break upon you from a June sky, was to suffer a fundamental shock, a derangement in that area of the brain in which stable ideas about humankind and its possibilities are kept' (137). Readers may have been more morally repelled if the novel *had* opted to use the eventual plight of the individuals as 'mysteries'. If this had been the case, the thrust of the novel would have encouraged us to discover whether or not the characters actually survived, and cheapen the actual events, being described on each page. Keneally, at least, avoids the *fetishisation* of death in his book by frankly revealing which characters will survive in this way.

The chronology of *Never Felt It Till Now* is principally linear, yet does feature flashbacks and a prologue, which 'frames' the story in a similar fashion to that of *Schindler's Ark*. The function of the prologue was to immediately reveal the results of Krauss' actions, therefore encouraging the reader to ask the question 'why?' when reading the story that follows. The question of 'why?' was fundamental to my reasons for embarking on this project, and I hoped to engender a similar sense of curiosity in the reader. By describing the negative consequences of Krauss' actions, at the very beginning of the novel, I also hoped to undermine any latent sense of glamour or charm, which might have accompanied Krauss' philandering. I was determined to do my best to ensure there was nothing 'heroic' about the depiction of Krauss' lying and misogyny, by contriving to show that many of his attempts to deceive his wife are thwarted immediately:

> "It's the truth." He grabbed her hand. "Darling . . . " She pulled away.

"And last night?"

"I stayed with Freund, I told you, remember?"

"You did, didn't you? In fact, according to Freund, you're still there."

"What do you mean?"

"'He can't come to the phone now, Maria, he's taking a bath.' It's actually quite sweet, how many of your pathetic minions will lie for you . . . " (GW 141)

Likewise, perhaps the most common criticism of *Schindler's Ark* in terms of its fictional sensibilities lies in its treatment of Oskar Schindler as a 'hero'. Sauerberg highlights the pitfalls of the author elevating his main protagonist in this way: '*Schindler's Ark* threatens to make Herr Schindler into a hero figure, in the light of which the text may easily be experienced as a Romance kind of narrative with melodramatic overtones'.[37] Again, this can have the effect of desensitising the reader to the fear and uncertainty experienced by the people involved in Schindler's 'story'. The reader is afforded a sense of reassurance by the focalisation upon Schindler, to the extent that the events surrounding him seem unimaginable, or mere digressions from the Schindler 'tale'. Sauerberg feels that this is inevitable in any text that has novelistic pretensions: 'There is in the realistic novel a tendency, which is a function of the limited cast required to carry through a minimum action of conflict, to elevate the protagonist, and, in consequence, to make him or her into an interesting figure'.[38] Keneally demonstrates his awareness of this danger in the Prologue: 'Fatal human malice is the staple of narrators, original sin the mother-fluid of historians. But it is a risky enterprise to have to write of virtue'. (15) He goes on to claim that, as a drinker and womaniser, Oskar's 'virtue' exists in a 'narrow interpretation of morality'.

Theodor Adorno writes of the danger of perpetuating this hero-function in a Holocaust text, noting that our sympathy for an individual can often be at the expense of our understanding of a totality:

I was told of the story of a woman who, upset after seeing a dramatisation of *The Diary of Anne Frank*, said: "yes, but *that* girl at least should have been allowed to live." To be sure even that was good as a first step toward understanding. But the individual case, which should stand for, and raise awareness about, the terrifying totality, by its very individuation became an alibi for the totality the woman forgot.[39]

Such an analogy could easily be applied to *Schindler's Ark*, which is dominated by the story of an individual. However, Adorno also concedes that: 'The perplexing thing about such observations remain that even on their account one can not advise against productions of the Anne Frank play and the like, because their effect nonetheless feeds into the potential for improvement'.[40] Indeed, it could be argued that the Schindler story provides an accessible way for people to learn of the Holocaust, and Keneally's familiar narrative style complements such a sense of accessibility.

Daniel Schwarz is not so generous, highlighting examples of Keneally's insensitivity, claiming that:

> While Keneally's narrator is sympathetic to the Jews from the outset, he misses some important implications of the story he tells. In rendering Schindler's final speech, does Keneally realise how Germanic Schindler's stress on "order" – repeated twice – and "discipline" (terms resonant of Nazi proclamations) is and how Schindler's words are for this reason out of touch with the Jewish sensibility of those who had survived, including the women who had spent some weeks in Auschwitz?[41]

In *Never Felt It Till Now*, Werner Krauss is not characterised as a hero, nor is he necessarily portrayed as being villainous. Rather, I attempted to depict a flawed, opportunistic, pragmatic human – but a human nonetheless. For I believe very strongly, that to de-humanise Krauss, in response to his collaboration with the Nazis, would be to fall into the trap of employing the uncivilised, reactionary tactics of the Nazis themselves. Krauss' characterisation is relentlessly ambiguous. For instance, even when he gives a morally reprehensible statement to a reporter: '"It's one of my favourite Shakespeare plays, and I'm sure you'd agree, the theme of the greedy, viscous Jew has never been more relevant to an audience"' (GW 124). It is instantly followed with the qualifier: 'He had remembered that line from one of the early reviews' (GW 124). This does not excuse his actions, but serves to place them in a wider context, as well as showing how the 'fiction' of the review Krauss speaks of, influences his world view.

There are instances of ambiguity and attempted irony in Keneally's language that fail, due to the 'uncertainty' of his fictional form. For instance, note the use of the term 'subhuman' in the following extract: 'But Madagascar, too, would look ridiculous once means were discovered to make substantial inroads into the subhuman population of Central Europe' (67). Although the informed reader may be aware that Keneally is assimilating the contemporary language of the Nazi Party – a curious literary device – as historical writing such a statement is wholly inappropriate, as the playfulness of the language may not seem so apparent over the course of time. As such, the freedom afforded by the novel format can serve to undermine the credibility of the language being used. Similarly, Keneally invents a conversation between two German officers that reveals a dark humour relating to the use of the word 'concentration' in the name 'concentration camps': "'They call it,' said Toffel, "*concentration. That's the word you find in the documents. Concentration. I call it bloody obsession*"' (72). Schwarz notes 'the irony is weak and lacks the felt empathy of someone who knows the culture he writes about'.[42] These serve as examples where the fictional novel should be read in context, and should not purport to reflect a reliable choice of words that portrays a definitive version of events. This is especially important, given the global popularity of the text. On a broader note, perhaps Keneally's *realism* undermines the conviction of his attempt to create a *documentary*.

In *Never Felt It Till Now*, there is an undeniable resonance to the term 'aktion'. Often used in the early part of the novel, shouted by a director to indicate the commencement of a film scene; the term 'aktion' has come to be known in the context of the Holocaust to refer to the mass exterminations conducted by SS troopers. In doing so, I may have left myself open to accusations of insensitivity, similar to those levelled at Keneally. However, I was intrigued by the fact that these two meanings – which relate both directly and indirectly to Krauss' career – are encapsulated by the same word. In this sense, the term served as a cautionary reminder, early on in the novel, of the *results* of Krauss' early success, that his 'actions' eventually provoked reactions in perpetuating the Nazi propaganda message.

This notion relates to further weaknesses in Keneally's text. Indeed, although the author goes to great lengths to contextualise his own struggle with the subject matter, *Schindler's Ark* suffers from a lack of contextual information, in terms of how these horrific events were allowed to happen and the extent to which ordinary Germans or Poles were implicated in allowing the Holocaust to take place. Indeed, Keneally largely fails to question the role of the soldiers who were more directly involved. As Schwarz writes: 'Has, we might ask, Keneally shown us the degree to which the Germans – wearing SS uniforms, or guarding concentration camps, or shepherding people to the gas chambers – were complicit?'[43] He argues that such ellipses are the result of a lack of detailed understanding and an absence of clear definitions in the text:

Keneally's narrator is amazed at the Nazi stupidity of diverting, "in the midst of a desperate battle," human and technological resources from the European war to what he calls an "extermination" that has not a military or economic meaning but only a "psychological" meaning (148). Does Keneally fully understand that the war against the Jews was the *principle* campaign of the National Socialists? Does he not realise that ingrained hatred of the Jews motivates Germans and that an entire country had to be infected with the virus of fanaticism for the Holocaust to succeed?[44]

I suggest that such controversial *facts*, in relation to the compliance of the non-Jews in these atrocities, would serve to undermine the neatness and the comfort of Keneally's *fiction*. It was this need to understand the everyday context and underlying motivations of the Nazi actions that inspired *Never Felt It Till Now*, and serves to explain the fundamental difference in tone between my novel and *Schindler's Ark*. Indeed, by setting my novel in urban Berlin and Stuttgart, in this quest for contextual information, rather than in the ghettos and concentration camps of Poland, I suggest that *Never Felt It Till Now* is not, in fact, 'Holocaust Fiction'. Unlike *Schindler's Ark*, it does not attempt to depict the Nazi actions, but rather, to represent the society in which they were allowed to happen.

Hayden White asks us to consider the Holocaust as a unique historic event, and suggests that this is why any attempts at representation are problematic.

> I believe that events like the Final Solution had been 'unimaginable' as late as the nineteenth century, when different social arrangements and cultural expectations prevailed. To be sure, cases of genocide were known in the nineteenth century, in the Belgian Congo and in German West Africa, but were not registered in public consciousness with the same degree of shock as the Holocaust. The Holocaust is a different matter. This is why not only witness literature but other kinds of documentation of its occurrence raise so many theoretical as well as practical questions.[45]

This concept of 'witness literature' highlights another assumption held throughout Keneally's text, regarding the reliability of the witness testimony he uses. Early in the text he writes: 'This account of Oskar's astonishing history is based in the first place on interviews with fifty Schindler survivors from seven nations – Australia, Israel, West

Germany, Austria, the United States, Argentina and Brazil' (13). Yet in the course of the novel he fails to question the reliability of such sources, implicitly encouraging the reader to share his uncritical approach towards oral testimony. Hayden White notes the unique and often fragile nature of Holocaust testimony:

> But witnesses to the Holocaust have typically testified under the fear that they had to relate facts that were intrinsically 'unbelievable', that the events which they had endured were so bizarre, so 'unspeakable', that many despaired of ever finding a voice or manner of writing that could compel belief in the veracity of what they had to say. And indeed so fraught with emotion, suffering, and pain has been the greater part of survivor testimony that some have recommended classifying it as 'traumatic in nature and consigning it to psychoanalytical and/or anthropological techniques of analysis for its proper understanding. Thus, Holocaust testimony is at once confirmed as an index of the events about which it speaks (like a scar or a bruise) and pathologized as a product of a wounded consciousness which requires not so much understanding as, rather, treatment of a medical or psychological kind.[46]

In this sense, Keneally could be commended for not 'pathologizing' the witnesses of whom he writes; rather they are regarded as 'ordinary' human beings. However, the sense of 'trauma' that White speaks of is barely even acknowledged by Keneally, who portrays the witnesses in his novel as jovial storytellers. For instance, he humorously introduces Leopold Pffeferberg as: 'another Cracow Jew who gives an account of meeting Schindler that Autumn of 1939 as well as coming close to killing him' (55). I suggest that such a portrayal, whilst serving to entertain the reader, ultimately undermines the reliability of the testimony, as well as being insensitive to the complicated and traumatic nature of the testimony itself. Interestingly, in the light of the success of Spielberg's film, Keneally's book was re-issued and re-packaged to include a collection of photographs from the Yad Vesham museum and from Pfefferberg's private collection. Daniel Schwarz proposes that this revised edition 'not only bridges the gap between film and book, but gives the story some further journalistic authenticity'.[47] This explicit use of historical sources does indeed appear to reinforce the 'authentic' nature of the text, yet it is also another example of historical evidence being presented uncritically by the author. Whilst Keneally's restraint, in refusing to dwell upon the negative effects that the Holocaust has had upon his witnesses, is admirable, his inability to scrutinise historical evidence serves to undermine the reliability of the claims he makes.

It could be argued, however, that it is his disregard for such strict historical scrutiny that has enabled Keneally to create a popular novel, which conveys the story of Oskar Schindler and his rescue mission, so successfully. This use of individual storytelling by such figures as Pfefferberg, is perhaps the most appropriate response to such a horrific event as the Holocaust. Hayden White notes this quality in the works of Primo Levi:

> The most vivid scenes of the horrors of life in the camps produced by Levi consist less of the delineation of "facts" as conventionally conceived than of the sequences of figures he creates by which to endow the facts with passion, his own feelings about and the value he therefore attaches to them.[48]

Indeed, Bennett and Royle suggest that we must not dismiss the notion of 'fictionality', when reading any text which purports to be 'factual'. They argue that often it is fictional devices which shape an individual's understanding of real-world events anyway: 'The word 'person', then, is bound up with questions of fictionality, disguise, representation and mask . . . . In this respect, the notion of a person is inseparable from the literary'.[49] This idea is supported by Barbara Foley, who suggests that any sort of storytelling, by definition, blurs the distinctions between fact and fiction: 'narrative eradicates the borderline between the two (fiction and non-fiction) by an admission of the fictionality of reality'.[50] Such an eradication of this fundamental 'borderline' places a text such as *Schindler's Ark* in both a very privileged, and a potentially dangerous position. Richard Johnstone playfully summarises the book by quoting Truman Capote, asserting that 'the point is not whether the story is 'true' – an impossible term to define – but that it is told as though it were'.[51] I suggest that this is to ignore the moral universe that such texts are created in, and that surely any sort of focalisation upon the events of the Holocaust invite some sort of moral reaction. David Irving's denial of many of the widely-accepted facts concerning the events of the Holocaust in his book, *Hitler's War*, is 'told as though it were' true. And yet a high-profile court case found that many of his sources were fabricated and that his book was created specifically with a fascist agenda in mind. Ironically, Irving's text purported to be a work of 'history' in the traditional sense of the term, and as such serves as an extreme example that illustrates the danger of approaching any text, whatever its genre, in a moral vacuum.

On this notion of historical 'truth', Keneally distinguishes between the factual records of events, of documentary and numerical evidence, with the 'truth' that is derived from less stable sources. He argues that it is the latter which is of more value to him as a novelist: 'For the thing about a myth is not whether it is true or not, nor whether it *should* be true, but that it is somehow truer than truth itself' (250). Carmel Gaffney detects the contradiction here, noting the shift in the importance that Keneally places upon the facts: 'Having sifted myth and fable to find facts and to appreciate the truth beyond myth, Keneally now uses facts to support this partial insight into a truth'.[52] Perhaps it is *this* audacity, or at least this pragmatism, that has enabled Keneally to create such a popular novel. By refusing to bow to the received academic or generic constraints that we might expect to be thrust upon his work, the author is able simply to tell a story, and in doing so he uses the language and the techniques most appropriate to the scene, and most accessible to the reader.

I suggest that it is Keneally's disregard for such strict definitions that has allowed him to connect with such a large audience – the narrative voice is so confident that the reader is invited simply to accept what is being claimed, and to enjoy the book for its literary and its emotive merits. In this sense at least, his 'avoidance' of the 'fiction' of prescribed academic methodology, is successful.

In a sense, it was these aspects of Keneally's work that I found particularly inspiring. Indeed, during the writing process of *Never Felt It Till Now*, I initially felt constrained by the burden of trying to represent such varied and monumental historical events, and made several, abortive attempts to tell Krauss' story. It was only when I resolved to focus on the *fictional* aspects of his life – his personal relationships, his everyday routines – that I was able to eventually include factual details of his career and his Nazi affiliations. This may well be due to my individual approach, but perhaps it is symptomatic of the storyteller's obligation to provide a traditional narrative arc, which dictates that the shape and style of the novel are ordered, in the first instance, by fictional pre-occupations.

In the strictest sense of the word, Thomas Keneally has not avoided all fiction. Rather, he has drawn attention to the fictional context of his work. *Schindler's Ark* lacks the conviction of a thorough biography or a historical study, and often its author hides behind his novelistic skills, rather than attempting any sort of profound historical analysis. I suggest that although this novel utilises documentary evidence within a fictional framework, to apply the definition 'documentary fiction' would be to mislead, as the omniscience of the fictional narrator far outweighs the impact of the few documentary sources that are presented.

Never Felt It Till Now: Influences and Contemporaries

When I first embarked upon *Never Felt It Till Now*, I was not aware of many, similar novels set in Nazi-occupied Berlin. This may have been due to my initial focus on 'Holocaust Fiction', i.e. novels that actually represent the events at concentration camps, such as *Schindler's Ark, Sophie's Choice* and *Time's Arrow*. However, one novel, which dealt with many of the themes and issues that interested me, was *Mephisto* by Klaus Mann. In a thinly veiled attack on one of Krauss' contemporaries, Gustaf Grundgens, Mann's novel tells the story of Hendrik Hofgen, who in his pursuit to becoming a famous actor, leaves his wife and friends and denounces his Communist past. Hofgen's performances as Mephistopheles in *Faust* garner Nazi party approval, and he becomes the darling of the party elite, specifically Hermann Goering. Although this novel featured similar tropes to those I wanted to explore in *Never Felt It Till Now*, in terms of its setting and plot, I felt that it lacked the particularly Jewish emphasis that I was keen to investigate. Another influence was *The Tin Drum* by Gunter Grass, not in any particular technical sense, but in the way in which it demonstrated the value of focusing exclusively on one character in order to tell the wider story of the Nazi era.

Goodbye to Berlin by Christopher Isherwood provided an enlightening, contemporary fictional account of Weimar Berlin, written in English, and *Berlin Noir*, a collection of three crime thrillers by Phillip Kerr (*March Violets, The Pale Criminal* and *A German Requiem*) was a useful reference in that it featured a protagonist who neither liked, nor particularly rebelled against, the Nazi regime. Like Krauss, Bernie Gunther concentrates on his career, (as a private investigator) adapting to the political climate in a single-minded, pragmatic way.

A major theme of my novel in terms of its characterisation of Krauss' personal life is that of masculinity. The three parts of *Never Felt It Till Now* represent three distinct stages of a struggle with his gender and sexual identity. In this sense, the novels of Martin Amis, and in particular, *Money*, influenced my work. In *Money*, the protagonist, John Self, is a deluded misogynist: rapacious, and utterly incapable of resisting drink, drugs or prostitutes, in spite of the fact that each of his relationships is little more than a financial transaction. In parts two and three of my novel; I attempted to imbue Krauss with a similarly unrewarding sexual appetite, whereby his instinctive objectification of women actually prevents him from forming meaningful relationships. For example, in part three he is crass and bawdy when he first meets Peta: 'There was a knock. He limped to the door, and opened it to find *those* legs' (GW 177). and his eventual, revolting treatment of her leads him to self-realisation, only when it is too late, that he has ruined their friendship: 'Yet at precisely the moment he felt confident about the trial, he also realised precisely why he was being tried at all. With Peta, as with much else in his life, he had *assumed too much*, and jumped to the conclusions that were easiest' (GW 218).

Further influences were drawn from television and film. As well as film adaptations of the texts already mentioned, such as Istvan Szabo's *Mephisto*, I was influenced by less obvious sources, such as television shows *The Sopranos* and *Extras*. What I found particularly beguiling about *The Sopranos*, was the way in which several characters can lie incessantly, and yet the viewer is trusted to be able to appreciate the various plot strands and deceptions, without each scene having to be explained with unnecessary exposition. In *Never Felt It Till Now*, I was keen to create similar 'webs' of deception, whereby Krauss' very identity starts to become eroded by his compulsion to lie. Comedy shows such as *Extras* were influential in my use of dark humour to further convey this problematising of Krauss' identity. Opting for the laughter of embarrassment, of finding comedy in social *faux pas* rather than contrived, 'set-piece' scenarios, shows such as *Extras* influenced the way I wanted to characterise Krauss. For example, early on in the novel, he is asked for his autograph by a young fan:

> "Hey! Weren't you the Cripple in '*A Dance of Death*'?" the boy asked.
> "I played that part . . . "
> "Can I have your autograph?"
> "Of course," [. . .] Werner started to scribble on the ticket [. . .]
> "Excuse me, what does this actually *say?*"
> "It says 'Werner Krauss', that's my real name."
> "Oh," said the boy, "I'll write 'Cripple' underneath later, just so I remember who you are." (GW 46)

As well as being a fairly straightforward joke, this sequence demonstrates the change that has occurred in which language choices are considered acceptable by society. The term 'Cripple' was actually the official name given for Krauss' part in *Totentanz*, aka *A Dance of Death*,[53] and, as such, reflects the fact that terms we would find extremely dubious now, were seen as acceptable during Krauss' lifetime. Therefore, although the existence of such a problematic linguistic register in no way excuses the election of the Nazis to power, it may, in some small way, provide one explanation as to why German society started to allow Nazi propaganda and persecution.

As mentioned earlier, it was this search to understand the under-lying causes – the mundane, everyday motivations of Krauss and his contemporaries – that guided my work on *Never Felt It Till Now*. Predictably, there were no easy answers, nor did I uncover any singular explanations as to why people like Krauss behaved in the way that they did. However, I do feel that I have told his story from a refresh-ingly humanistic standpoint, whereby his decisions are given scrutiny, context and consequence. There are obvious difficulties in trying to ascertain a place in 'the market' for a novel such as *Never Felt It Till Now*, yet it was always my intention to write with a pace and tone which is accessible to the general reader. For if there is one strength of *Schindler's Ark* above all others, it is the novel's ability to reach out to a wide audience, and inform a generation of readers about the horrors of the Nazi actions. Indeed, to re-visit Adorno's quotation, the effect of works like *Schindler's Ark* 'nonetheless feeds into the poten-tial for improvement'.[54] Though obviously not anticipating the extraordinary success of Keneally's novel, I do however hope to have created something equally accessible and informative.

Notes

1   Gareth Watts, Never Felt It Till Now, p. 216. All subsequent references to this text will be given in parenthesis, along with the initials 'GW'.
2   John London, 'Non-German Drama in the Third Reich', from *Theatre Under The Nazis*, (ed. by Jack London), (Manchester: Manchester University Press, 2000), p. 246.
3   Ibid., p. 245.
4   William R. Elwood, 'Werner Krauss and the Third Reich', from *Theatre in the Third Reich, The Prewar Years* (ed. by Glen W. Gadberry), (London: Greenwood, 1995), p. 96 *Quotation from:* Otto Horny review in Richard Geehr, *Karl Lueger, Mayor of Fin de Siècle Vienna* (Detroit, 1990), p. 361, n. 122.
5   Richard Bessel, 'Unemployment and Demobilisation in Germany After the First World War', from *The German Unemployed* (ed. by Richard J. Evans and Dick Geary), (London: Croom Helm, 1987), pp. 38–39.
6   Richard J. Evans, 'Introduction: The Experience of Unemployment in the Weimar Republic', from *The German Unemployed* (ed. by Richard J. Evans and Dick Geary), (London: Croom Helm, 1987), p. 6.
7   Jürgen Falter *et al.*, 'Arbeitslosigkeit und Nationalsozialismum. Eine empirische Analyse des Beitrags der Massnerwerbslosgkeit zu den Wahlerfolgen der NSDAP 1932 und 1933', from *Kolner Zeitschrift fur Soziologie und Sozialpsychologie 35* (1983), 525–54 quotation from Evans, 'Introduction . . . ', p. 16.
8   Richard J. Evans, 'Introduction: The Experience of Unemployment in the

Weimar Republic', from *The German Unemployed* (ed. by Richard J. Evans and Dick Geary), (London: Croom Helm, 1987), pp. 16–17.

9   Donald L. Niewyk, *The Jews in Weimar Germany* (Manchester: Manchester University Press, 1980) pp. 45–46.

10 Donald L. Niewyk, *The Jews in Weimar Germany* (Manchester: Manchester University Press, 1980), p. 45.

11 John Willett, *The New Sobriety: Art and Politics in the Weimar Period 1917–33* (London: Thames and Hudson, 1978), p. 202.

12 Peter D. Stachura *The Weimar Republic and the Younger Proletariat: An Economic and Social Analysis*, (London: Macmillan, 1989), p. 155.

13 John Willett, *The New Sobriety: Art and Politics in the Weimar Period 1917–33* (London: Thames and Hudson, 1978), p. 204.

14 Thomas Staedeli, 'Portrait of the actress Maria Bard', website: http://www.cyranos.ch/smbass-e.htm. Accessed: 08/11/2004.

15 Thomas Staedeli, 'Portrait of the actor Werner Krauss', website: http://www.cyranos.ch/smkrau-e.htm. Accessed 08/11/2004.

16 Wolfgang Goetz, *Werner Krauss* (Hamburg, 1954), pp. 189–190.

17 William R. Elwood, 'Werner Krauss and the Third Reich', from *Theatre in the Third Reich, the Prewar Years* (ed. by Glen W. Gadberry), (London: Greenwood Press,1995) p. 92.

18 William R. Elwood, 'Werner Krauss and the Third Reich', from *Theatre in the Third Reich, The Prewar Years* (ed. by Glen W. Gadberry), (London: Greenwood, 1995), p. 95 *Quotation from: David Welch, Propaganda and the German Cinema 1933–1945* (Oxford, 1983), p. 291. [Elwood's Note] Since this statement is rather significant, I cite Welch's source: W.A. Boelcke, *Kriegspropaganda 1939–41. Geheime Ministerkonferenzen im Reichspropagandaministerium* (Stuttgart, 1966).

19 William R. Elwood, 'Werner Krauss and the Third Reich', from *Theatre in the Third Reich, The Prewar Years* (ed. by Glen W. Gadberry), (London: Greenwood, 1995), p. 95. Since this statement is also significant, I cite Gadberry's source: Joseph Wulf, *Theater und Film in Dritten Reich* (Gutersloh, 1964),p. 447.

20 Siegfried Kracauer, *From Caligari to Hitler; A Psychological History of the German Film,* (Princeton: Princeton University Press, 1974), p. 64.

21 John Willett, *The Theatre of the Weimar Republic* (London: Holmes and Meier, 1988), p. 33.

22 John Willett, *The Theatre of the Weimar Republic* (London: Holmes and Meier, 1988), pp. 44–45.

23 John London, 'Non-German Drama in the Third Reich', from *Theatre Under The Nazis* (ed. by Jack London), (Manchester: Manchester University Press, 2000), p. 223.

24 John London, 'Non-German Drama in the Third Reich', from *Theatre Under The Nazis* (ed. by Jack London), (Manchester: Manchester University Press, 2000), p. 222.

25 William R. Elwood, 'Werner Krauss and the Third Reich', from *Theatre*

in the Third Reich, The Prewar Years (ed. by Glen W. Gadberry), (London: Greenwood, 1995), p. 94.

26 Thomas Keneally, 'Author's Note' to *Schindler's Ark* (London: Hodder & Stoughton, 1982), pp. 13–14. *All further references to this text will be given in parenthesis.*

27 Quotation from *Never Felt It Till Now.* Original source: Werner Krauss, *Das Schauspiel Meines Lebens* (Stuttgart: Henry Goverts Verlag, 1958), p. 228.

28 Carmel Gaffney, 'Keneally's Faction: Schindler's Ark', *Quadrant 29* (1985, Vol. 7, PT 213) p. 77.

29 Hayden White, 'Figural Realsim in Witness Literature', from *Parallax*, Vol. 10, No. 1 (London: Taylor and Francis, 2004), p. 113.

30 Lars Sauerberg, 'Fact into Fiction; Documentary Realism in the contemporary novel' (London: Macmillan, 1991), p. 106.

31 Brian Cheyette, 'the Uncertain Certainty of *Schindler's List*', *Spielberg's Holocaust; Critical Perspectives on Schindler's List* (ed. by Yosefa Loshitzky), (Indianapolis: Indiana University Press, 1997), p. 228.

32 Ibid.

33 Ibid.

34 David Lowenthal. *The Past is a Foreign Country* (Cambridge: CUP 1985), pp. 224–231.

35 Michel Foucault, 'What is an Author' in *The Foucault Reader* (ed. by Paul Rabinow), (London: Penguin, 1984), p. 103.

36 Daniel R. Schwarz, *Imagining the Holocaust* (New York: St. Martin's Griffin, 1999), p. 212.

37 Sauerberg, 'Fact into fiction', p. 115.

38 Ibid.

39 Theodor W. Adorno, 'Working through the Past' in *Can One Live After Auschwitz?* (ed. by Rolf Tiedemann), (Stanford: Stanford University Press, 2003), p. 16.

40 Ibid., p. 16.

41 Schwarz, *Imagining the Holocaust*, p. 213.

42 Ibid., p. 216.

43 Ibid., p. 214.

44 Ibid., pp. 215–216.

45 Hayden White, 'Figural Realsim in Witness Literature', p. 113.

46 Ibid.

47 Schwarz, *Imagining the Holocaust*, p. 210.

48 White, 'Figural Realsim in Witness Literature', p. 124.

49 Andrew Bennett *et al.*, *An Introduction to Literature, Criticism and Theory* (London: Prentice Hall, 1995), p. 52.

50 Barbara Foley, *Telling the Truth: The Theory and Practice of Documentary Fiction* (New York: Cornell, 1986), p. 10.

51 Richard Johnstone "The Rise of Faction" in *Quadrant*, Vol. 24, No. 4, April 1985, p. 78.

52 Carmel Gaffney, "Keneally's Faction: *Schindler's Ark*," in *Quadrant*, Vol. 29, No. 7, July 1985, p. 77.
53 The Internet Movie Database (IMDB), *Werner Krauss*, website: http://www.imdb.com/name/nm0470328 accessed 14/03/2006.
54 Theodor W. Adorno, 'Working through the Past' in *Can One Live After Auschwitz?* (ed. by Rolf Tiedemann), (Stanford: Stanford University Press, 2003), p. 16.

Never Felt It Till Now

By Gareth Watts

How rash to assert that man shapes his own destiny. All he can do is determine his inner responses. You cannot know another's inner life from his circumstances. To know that you must know his dreams, his relationships, his moods, his sickness, and his death.

ETTY HILLESUM

Prologue

But how to communicate with the future?

Lifting the collar of his overcoat, Werner Krauss ducked his head and walked quickly. Each step seemed to mimic the pace of his heart. Why was he doing this? He was a free man, after all.

On waking that morning, he'd ambled into the kitchen of his Stuttgart residence and taken a bottle of *Asbach Uralt* from the cupboard. Grabbing a dirty wine glass from the draining-board, he poured carelessly, overflowing the stemmed glass. Preparing himself for a shock, he gulped it down. Tears rolled from his eyes, but he resisted the urge to vomit. He took a cigarette from the box which had been to bed with him, and, with an unsteady hand, placed it in his mouth. Sinking to his knees, he lit it using the gas flame of the oven hob, which had been burning all night. He stole an hour of sleep, there on the kitchen floor, with the cigarette butt still in his mouth. Waking with a start, he dressed thoughtlessly, and, realising he was too late to arrange a ride, headed for the court on foot.

For months he had been preparing for this day – memorising anecdotes about a compassionate, sensitive man. But these monologues now seemed to be slipping away, and all he could think of was his sore ankle.

As the State Court building came into view, so too did the sizeable and angry crowd.

'There he is – traitor, TRAITOR!'

The noise grew, and individual insults rang out.

'Fascist . . . '

'Hitler's friend, he was Hitler's friend!' – a Jew, unmistakeably.

'Murderer!'

That last one echoed in his ear. His cheeks burned. As the crowd got closer, Werner noticed there was no sign of the special security that he had requested. His name obviously didn't carry the same weight in Stuttgart as it had before. He swallowed hard, and started to run, or rather, limp, at the crowd, head-on. He fought his way through, almost reaching the court door, and relative safety. Then it happened. A placard bearing the words *NAZI COWARD* crashed down on his forehead. He fell to the ground amid kicks, punches and insults.

Sat now in the corridor outside the courtroom, he gazed at a grey wall for some time, trying to piece together the speech in his mind, and forget the morning's unexpected nightmare. He reached into his jacket

for a notebook and pen. Wanting to commit words to the page, he
would remind himself of his humanity:

Somewhere, there is salvation. A place to feel alive even when
they line the streets, calling for your death . . .

Werner knew he was exaggerating, but for a moment at least he
enjoyed the melodrama and continued to dwell on the 'tragedy' of his
situation:

. . . I am not a murderer and yet they try me like one. They want
me dead as an example to all. In the pages of the pauper-press I
am demonised for doing my duty, performing my tasks, being
true and being artistic. Hath a Jew not eyes?

He smiled as he scrawled that last question mark. For a moment he
considered incorporating these notes in his memoirs. 'It could be
included in the prologue,' he thought. Laughing to himself, he tore the
page from his notebook and put it into his pocket. He must be careful
not to allow his sense of humour to be used against him. Fear started
to grip the face of the man who had worn so many masks. Being
nervous was natural though, he decided, and the court must not
suspect a performance – they must see a human – a man, not an actor.
He should talk only of circumstance, of coincidence. He could talk
about Maria. He could talk about his son.

With those thoughts in mind, Werner was led into the courtroom
and asked to confirm his name. The presiding officer was a young,
slither of a man who hid behind a pair of spectacles. This infuriated
Werner. 'So where were you in the Weimar years?' he wanted to shout.
He fantasised about smashing this man's spectacles into his face, using
a nearby chair. At least then, he thought, he could have a reason for
remorse, a reason to be tried.

Werner let out a quiet, though not inaudible, belch. The brandy was
rising from his stomach and he felt sick. But he could not leave the
courtroom and attract more attention. He swallowed hard, and tried
to concentrate on the question the presiding officer had begun to ask:

"Herr Krauss, how would you define your role in Hitler's Reich?"

Part One

1

Werner woke unusually early. He was due at the film-set at 9 a.m. – the same time his two children had to be at school – and he didn't want to get caught in the morning chaos of searching for uniforms and arguing over who ate the last piece of bread. He dressed quickly, and walked to the Bernau-Friedenstal station to catch the first train. The carriage was fairly empty, and his gamble of not buying a ticket for the fare came off, with no inspectors in sight. He emerged at Weißensee where he found a café. He only had the money for a coffee, and not breakfast as he had hoped, but was pleased to see they already had a copy of *Deutsche Zeitung*. He flipped quickly to the arts section, and was thrilled to discover a journalist describing the opening of *King Lear* later in the week as 'eagerly anticipated'. As was happening more and more often of late, Werner was balancing film commitments with theatre work and had been given special dispensation from the director of *Lear* to miss some rehearsals in order to complete filming. He only had a supporting role in the play, and was fairly confident of his lines, having performed it several times, most recently a couple of years ago, in Dresden.

Within the small preview feature about the play was the name 'Maria Bard'. Just reading those two words together made Werner's stomach loop from excitement to trepidation, and back again.

He opened his battered leather briefcase and looked over his directions for the day's filming. Work on *Das Cabinet des Dr. Caligari*, had gone particularly well so far. Werner had to admit, it was a thrill to be playing the eponymous Doctor, and finally have a claim to being the 'star' of a film (despite the fact that Conrad Veidt, who played Cesare the Somnambulist, had just as much screen-time). It certainly felt like things were changing for Werner, who for many years had struggled to find work and support his young family. There was a time when he and his wife, Paula, lived in complete poverty, relying on the pittance she earned while he did awful extra work and bit-parts in feature films. Now, the offers of work were fairly constant, and with any luck he would soon be able to buy breakfast whenever he chose.

He finished his coffee and walked the short distance to the set.

"*Guten Morgen*, Herr Krauss."

It was satisfying finally to be acknowledged by the security guard. On all the other films he'd worked on, Werner had to suffer the rigmarole of repeating his name while the staff searched lists and memos before he was finally admitted to the studio.

The schedule for the day was quite intense, due largely to the fact they were filming many of the supposedly outdoor scenes, requiring a large number of extras and a great many scene changes. When he emerged from the make-up room, an assistant helped him with the cumbersome grey wig, before carefully fitting his imposing black top hat. It was apparently too early in the morning for anyone to indulge in much conversation, but Werner's spirits were high, and he whistled while those around him grumpily went about their business.

When everything was ready, he was ushered onto the set. "*Anfangen!*" was yelled, but Werner waited, 'a thousand and one, a thousand and two, a thousand and three.' He climbed the steps up the large platform, and entered the shot. A great many extras were milling around the set, befitting the carnival atmosphere. As Caligari, Werner mingled with them next to the extraordinary carousel, perched (like most of the props) at a peculiar, diagonal angle. In turn, the extras visited a sideshow – an elderly actor was holding up a monkey, which was wearing a waistcoat, to wave at them. He gave a knowing look at, though not directly into, the camera, announcing his arrival into the festival mayhem. He staggered around at the front of the platform, gurning mischievously. One of the extras was a dwarf, brought in, no doubt, to add to the queasiness of the dimensions. Already hunched, Caligari bent down to get a better look at him, and smiled.

"*Halt*! Splendid, Werner, splendid! We can move straight on to the next sequence." Weine, the director, liked to work fast.

"You look terrifying, Herr Krauss," the dwarf chatted to Werner as they left the set, "make-up have added about thirty years!"

"It takes a lot to age these boyish good looks." Werner winked and the dwarf smiled. He headed back to the changing room as the extras were ushered into a neighbouring studio. Werner was fussed over for a while by the make-up girl until he was recalled to the set.

The façade of a small marquee had been erected on top of another platform. Weine yelled "*aktion*" again and Caligari emerged from the marquee, carrying a bell and a large scroll-chart. A tight camera angle was being used as he slowly, deliberately observed the crowds. Violently, he started to ring the bell.

"*Halt*! Now to the wide-shot – everyone in position . . . Okay, Werner, whenever you're ready . . . "

A crowd gathered around the platform. Caligari stood with his arms wide open, beckoning them to his show. He positioned the scroll-chart and pulled down the scroll, which read:

"Step up! Step up! See
the amazing CESARE,
the SOMNAMBULIST!"

He beat the scroll with his cane, then held the cane aloft. He repeated this action several times as the crowds gathered.

"*Halt*! Good work, let's take a break."

He left the set and asked for coffee.

"Is that really a good idea, Herr Krauss?" the assistant asked. She pointed to his face – the Dr. Caligari character was heavily made-up, with thick white powder and deep black eye shadow.

"I'll take my chances, I can always get a touch-up later, thanks."

"Fine. Oh, and there's someone at reception to see you . . . a Maria somebody, shall I send her through?"

"I don't know a Maria," he lied, " . . . but send her through anyway, I'm intrigued."

The assistant laughed. "No problem, Herr Krauss."

He felt grateful for the ghoulish make-up, which concealed his embarrassment. Maria appeared at the far side of the set. She slowly negotiated the chunky, bizarre props – the triangular bushes and square trees, which cluttered the place. She was tall and slim and looked especially delicate amongst the over-sized scenery.

"What are you doing here?" Werner asked.

"Rehearsals finished early over at *Konigstraße* so I thought I'd come and see you."

"It's not a good idea. Sorry, but until I've spoken properly with Paula, we have to be careful."

"You don't want to see me . . . that's fine."

"Of course I want to see you, but it's is a busy set, people talk."

"You're ashamed, you think I'm just some dumb little girl who . . . "

"Not now," he interrupted. His assistant had appeared behind Maria, waiting with the coffee. "Thanks, dear – just watch me ruin this make-up now," he joked.

"Enjoy, Herr Krauss." The assistant left them, with a smile.

"How long do you think *she* was there? You see, she'll be telling everyone about us now."

"And why does that matter? I don't believe you sometimes, Werner. I'm not a stupid little girl you know . . . and I'm not going to wait around for you forever."

"Don't say that. Leave me to finish this scene, go off and book a table at any restaurant you like. I'll call you, and we can have dinner tonight. Together. Okay?"

"What about the cost?"

"Don't worry, I'll take care of it. We'll go anywhere you like, it's fine, I promise!"

"Oh Werner, that'll be lovely, thank you!" She grabbed him and gave him a hug. Clumsily, she pulled tightly on his neck, forcing his face into the crevice of her lean shoulder. He emerged, to find he'd left a white powder stain on her dress. She yelped with embarrassment.

"Sorry, sorry, I'm so sorry!" She said.

"It's all right, calm down." Others on the set had stopped what they were doing. They were staring at Werner and Maria. "You'd better get going, I need to sort myself out."

"I'm sorry." Maria wiped a tear from her cheek. "See you tonight?" she asked. Werner nodded, and she marched back through the set, leaving through a fire exit. He sipped meekly at his coffee. His assistant re-appeared.

"I'll get someone over here right away."

"Thanks," he said, and nodded towards the space Maria had left behind. "A friend of my wife – she's having a few problems."

"You've got a nerve, Werner, I'll say that for you. The way you've been behaving . . . " Conrad was indignant. He vigorously scraped the greasepaint from his face.

"I'm still the Werner you know and love. It's my *method*, Conny, you know that." Werner gently punched his co-star in the ribs.

"*Method?* Let's see now: petulance, irritability, you're completely irrational . . . "

"Enough."

"And now you're asking for money?"

"It's only until next week. Come on, it's for Egon, he needs new shoes for school and until we get paid I . . . "

"Three marks, it's all I've got." Veidt reached into his pocket.

"Make it five? Please?"

"Unbelievable!" He passed the money over to Werner.

"Excellent. You won't regret this, Conny. It's worth it, believe me."

"Those shoes must be really great."

Werner smiled. "They are."

"Come on, I want to know – I won't be jealous, I promise, I'm just interested." Their bottle of wine was half empty, and Werner hadn't touched a drop. It had been years since he had been to a restaurant and he couldn't help but feel irritated by the unnecessary opulence of the place, the excess.

"You want to know how I met my wife? Sounds like it could end in tears . . . "

"It won't, I promise. Please?"

"You owe me one."

"Sounds interesting . . . "

He smiled, took a breath and began the story. "We were a lot younger – obviously. We grew up in the same town, living just a few streets away from each other, in fact. Our parents knew each other and both our families got together often . . . "

"Stop, Werner. Please stop." Maria was laughing.

"Why? What's the matter?"

"If you don't want to tell me, fine. But there's no need to lie, and so badly . . . " she started to impersonate him, "'we grew up in the same town and our families were so close.' You should hear yourself!"

"I'm sorry," he said. "It's personal. And we *are* still living together."

"I understand, darling." Maria poured the remaining wine.

"You know, I think you're wonderful. I've never met anyone like you before," he said.

"Are you still lying?"

"I'm serious – everything you do, everything you say. You're enchanting to me, Maria." He took her hand and held it tight. "With most girls – you just tell them what they want to hear . . . "

"Is that so, Herr Krauss?" she interrupted.

"But you're different. You know the *real* me."

"Good. I'm glad. I was worried that, because you're . . . " she paused,

" . . . older – you can say the word – because I'm older."

"I was worried that because you're a *bit* older, you might just think I was a silly little girl. Young, stupid, impressionable . . . " he reached for her hand across the table.

"The kind of silly girl who gets my make-up all over her dress?" he laughed. For a moment they just stared at each other. It was this moment, Werner thought, this *particular* moment which made him sure he was doing the right thing. There might be a thousand obstacles to overcome, if they were to make their relationship official, but he should always remember the way he felt at *this* moment, and it would all be worthwhile.

"Werner, if you want to . . . tonight we could, you know," beneath the table, her bare foot slid up the inside of his calf, " . . . we don't *have* to wait."

"I'll bear that in mind," he said, and smiled. "But I think you've had a little too much to drink. We need to get back."

"Never! The night is still young," she said.

"But I'm not!" he said. "Filming started at an unearthly hour this morning, I could sleep for a week."

"We can go now, *if* you promise you'll tuck me into bed?"

He dropped the five marks on the table. He had planned to wait for the change, but wanted to get back to Maria's apartment as quickly as he could.

Lying on her small single bed, they ate chocolates and kissed.

"So when will it all be over, Werner? All this creeping around?"

"Soon, just give me time. She already knows it's finished between us – just not in so many words."

"I know, and I promise I'll stop asking. It's just that . . . " she took his hand and pressed it to the inside of her thigh, " . . . I really can't wait."

"Neither can I, darling," he said. "But, you know, I think we should," he removed his hand from her thigh, and stroked the hair away from her face, tucking it behind her ear. "I want to show you I *can* wait. I don't want you to think I'm just a dirty old man who's trying to get you into bed."

"You've got me *onto* bed," she laughed.

"You know what I mean."

"Werner, I love you," she said, and they embraced. He thought of that perfect moment in the restaurant earlier, and how this came pretty close. He shuffled his lower body away from her on the bed, doing his best to keep a discreet distance. Lying there, he continued to stroke her hair until eventually she fell asleep. Quietly, he shuffled out of her apartment and began the long, dark, cold walk home.

He needed to get to the railway station quickly, so took a shortcut through the industrial area of town. A piercingly bright sun was beating down on him. It seemed that no matter how fast he tried to run, his surroundings still passed him slowly, as if it were merely scenery, being pedalled by a lethargic stagehand. Each footstep was

heavy, each breath gasping and desperate. He heard an argument emanating from a large mouldings factory:

"Go on then, put all that away and let's do it."

"If that's what you want?"

"It is. Come on, let's go."

Their shouting got louder and louder, and no matter how hard he tried to run, it seemed as though he couldn't get away from them.

Eventually he stopped, turned around, and noticed the two men had left the factory. Both wearing dirty blue overalls, they were each holding planks of wood, and appeared to be hitting each other hard. One of them fell, and the other continued to strike him. Slowly, Werner approached them. The standing man dropped to his knees, while still hitting the other man or, appearing to hit him. Werner couldn't be sure – some of the strikes seemed to miss, deliberately.

He pinned down the other man's arms. As Werner got closer, he noticed the person lying on the ground was, in fact, a woman. Werner was disgusted – the man seemed to be positioning himself to rape her.

"That's enough. Stop it, stop now!" his voice sounded feeble. The two factory workers stopped, looked at each other, then looked at Werner, and started to laugh.

"Don't mind him, he's probably just found out about Richard and Ann-Marie!" They laughed again. Richard was his father's name – what were they talking about? He'd never heard of anyone called Anne-Marie. Was his father having an affair? He tried to speak, but nothing would come out. He couldn't turn away, he couldn't move. A dollop of thick creamy liquid landed on his right foot. Then another. He felt the warm gunk start to slide down his neck and drip onto his shirt. It was his face. Slowly, he was melting in the heat. He tried to scream.

"Werner, for God's sake what's wrong?" Paula and their son Rudi were in his room. They had been sharing the double bed since Werner and Paula had decided to sleep apart months earlier. He had obviously woken them. His mouth was dry, his eyes crusty and blurred.

"It was a nightmare, I'm sorry."

"What happened? Why were you screaming?"

"I needed to catch a train and . . . " as he spoke, his recollections began to fade. All he could think was that his father was having an affair. But he didn't know *why* he thought that, "doesn't matter. I can't remember."

"Well what do you expect when you come home so late? Every night. Come on, Rudi, back to bed." She seemed to spit words at her husband. They left, but Werner was too anxious to return to sleep.

Although he couldn't remember the details of his dream, its impact was somehow vivid. He noticed the transistor radio on his son's bedside table. Carefully, he turned the dial, hoping he could have it on quietly and let the music distract him. But all that came out of the radio was a loud buzz.

"You've got to be joking!" Paula shouted from across the hallway.

"Sorry, sorry!" Werner yelled back, and fumbled with the dial until the noise went. A rush of sweat soaked his back and gave him a piercing chill. He got up and wandered downstairs. He lit a candle and noticed some scissors on the dining table. He decided to trim his toenails. Doing so made him feel old, as he noticed his pitted hands, his feet, his legs – they all reminded him of how his father had looked, when he was a teenager. That was how he looked to Maria. Would he really do this to her? Would he become an embarrassment or a burden? A joke? Finishing the last toe, he collected the clippings and emptied them into the dustbin. He wasn't tired, so he lay down on the floor, and slowly, painfully began to perform sit-ups. Peering over his stomach, he kept count, and upon completing twenty agonising crunches, he collapsed. Sweating and shaking, he got up and returned to bed.

2

He woke to find the house empty. There was no filming today, just a rehearsal in the evening – this was a rare chance to relax. Slipping out of bed, he noticed his naked body in the mirror: his chest, his stomach, his chin and its twin – he hated the way he looked. His abdominal muscles ached and shuddered at the memory of the previous night's tentative workout. Perhaps he could follow-up with some press-ups if he found time later on. He made some coffee, and found his copy of the script for *King Lear*. The role of the Duke of Kent was a step-down for Werner, having played Lear himself over in Dresden. But work was work, and he'd been desperate to perform with Maria again since they first met.

A knave, a rascal, an eater of broken meats;
a base, proud, shallow, beggarly, three-suited,
hundred-pound, filthy, worsted-stocking knave;
a lily-liver'd, action-taking, whoreson, glass-
gazing, superserviceable, finical rogue; one-
trunk-inheriting slave; one that wouldst be a
bawd in way of good service, and art nothing

but the composition of a knave, beggar, coward,
pander, and the son and heir of a mongrel bitch;
one whom I will beat into clamorous whining, if
thou deny'st the least syllable of thy addition.

Werner couldn't concentrate. He kept thinking of that dream. And
his father. He couldn't remember actually seeing his father in the
dream, but the *thought* of him was so stark. He had rarely thought of
his father since the last time he saw him, over twenty years ago.

It had been a scorching hot Summer afternoon in Gestungshausen,
and young Werner had the house to himself. His father was over at
the church conducting a funeral, where his mother played organ, usher
and anything else her husband was too important for. At this tender
age, Werner was already obsessed with drama. It was the only thing
that interested him at school: mathematics, history or geography just
seemed so empty, so dull. He loved reading play-scripts, especially
Goethe, some of whose work he had perfectly memorised. Pacing
around the empty house that afternoon, he felt liberated: having the
space to perform and make some noise.

"Use well your time! It flies so swiftly from us; But time through
order may be won, I promise," he roared.

He bounded upstairs and pranced across the hallway . . .

"I'm tired enough of this dry tone, – Must play the Devil again, and
fully,"

. . . opened the door to his parents bedroom and leapt up onto the
double bed . . .

"Your mind will shortly be set aright, When you have learned, all
things reducing, To classify them for your using."

. . . as if bouncing on a trampoline, he let his legs give way and
landed on his back. These few hours he got to spend alone over the
Summer were precious. When his father was around, everything was
ordered, everything routine. Without even being asked, Werner had
been signed-up to volunteer schemes helping the elderly in their
gardens – this was supposed to be holiday time. But lying there, on
that enormous bed, it was bliss. He noticed a small wooden box on
his mother's bedside table. Without thinking, he opened the box and
found some eye-liner, rouge, some blue eye shadow and a tube of
lipstick. Werner was surprised, his father didn't approve of make-up.
He felt a pang of sorrow for his mother. He had discovered her treasure trove, her enchanting secret. As silly as it seemed, he had always
assumed he knew everything about his mother, yet this was a blind
spot in his knowledge. The make-up seemed so glamorous, so other-
worldly. He started by dabbing a little rouge onto his cheeks. He

pouted and posed into his mother's mirror. It felt like an epiphany –
as if a million doors had opened to him all at once. He was so excited.
He added some eye shadow, then made a mess with the eye-liner –
being too scared to use it on his inner eyelid, his shaking hand clumsily stroked the pencil over the base of his lashes. But it didn't matter.
He felt elated.

"I feel his presence like something ill / I've else, for all, a kindly
will,"

Acting into the mirror, he was in his element. This was an escape.
He knew he would have to wash it all off before his parents returned,
but there was one more thing he wanted to try. Frantically, he started
to rummage through his mother's wardrobe.

"A man who with thee goes, thy mate, Within my deepest, inmost
soul I hate."

He emerged with a plain cream dress, which he threw over his head
and tugged down over his shirt and trousers. It was far too tight, but
he didn't care.

"My heart is gone. My peace is sore: I never shall find it, Ah never-
more!"

He moved back to the mirror, to check his eye make-up. It was like
looking at someone else – he was thrilled.

"What are you doing up there, Werner?" the familiar, disapproving
tone came from downstairs. He hadn't heard his parents arrive.
Hastily he tried to remove the dress, but it got caught on one of his
shirt buttons, and he couldn't get it back over his head.

"What on earth are you doing, boy? In my dress? Get that off at
once!" his mother's voice reached a scream. Werner stood still. It felt
as though time had slowed down. The dress finally came off, revealing
his made-up face. His mother slapped him. His father appeared,
dragged him to the bathroom sink, turned on the cold water and
pushed his neck down, so that his face was immersed in the running
water. He couldn't breathe, and made the most terrifying panting
noises.

"Make sure all that filth is off your face – what sort of boy *are*
you?"

Soaking wet, and shuddering, he was dragged back into his parents'
room. His father had removed his belt and Werner knew what to do.
He pulled down his trousers and with no delay, felt the first crack of
leather across his thighs. He counted each smack, expecting the pain
to be over on five. Then ten. But his father carried on and on, until
after the seventeenth strike he couldn't take any more and doubled-
over, shielding his legs and getting hit on the back. "If you force me
like this, I'll beat the sinful streak from you. Do you understand?"

Werner didn't know exactly when – he had lost count – but eventually the beating stopped, and his father left the room. It was the last time he ever saw him.

His tears were starting to seep into the script. He needed to get out of the house. Rehearsals for *King Lear* didn't begin until six p.m., but he could head into town early and try to occupy his thoughts. He grabbed his coat and the script, and was searching for his keys when he heard a knock at the door. He fitted the security chain and opened the door a couple of inches. It was a man with a long nose, wearing thick-rimmed glasses, clutching a clipboard. It could only be a Communist Party activist – they seemed to be calling every other day.

"*Guten Morgen*, is Frau Krauss at home today?"

"No, sorry, I think she's at her mother's. Can I help at all?" Werner asked. The Commie sighed and shrugged.

"Er.. no, thank you . . . good day to you, sir," he said, and started to walk away.

"Do I not even get a leaflet?" called Werner, mischievously.

"Of course, sorry sir . . . " he turned around, fumbled in the top pocket of his jacket and handed Werner a leaflet, "there we go, sir. It's time for the oppressed *Deutsche Arbeiterklasse*, like yourself, to overthrow this feeble Weimar regime." His speech seemed a little half-hearted. Werner started to close the door.

"*Danke* Comrade – I'm sure you'll call again!" He smiled and pushed the door shut. Obviously Paula had charmed the local Commie on a previous visit. He read the back of the leaflet: 'YOUR PARTY REPRESENTATIVE: KAMERADE KOHL'.

He took the train into town. The sky was cloudy and threatening, so he ducked into the pictures for a matinee. They were showing the Chaplin film, '*A Day's Pleasure*'. Chaplin takes a trip on a steamboat, on which some Negroes are playing in a band. The sea is turbulent, so he is constantly crashing into the other passengers. Werner loved the way Chaplin managed to involve almost everyone around him. Extras, just blending into the background, are suddenly thrust into the action. It takes real poise, real presence to do that well, he thought. The rocking boat is perfect for all the silly walks and pratfalls – a perfect Chaplin vehicle, you might say. Werner chuckled, and wondered if he could ever perform in similar roles. Could he be a whole-hearted, comic actor like that? Could he ever be such a physical actor, such a clown, a fool? He had played comic roles before, but nothing distinctive, not like Chaplin. He laughed out loud when Charlie and the band of Negroes start to feel seasick. The back and forth motion of the trumpet player starts to mesmerise Charlie, who feels more and more nauseous until he can take no more, snatches the trumpet from the black man, and hurls it into the sea. No one else in the cinema seemed to find this funny – laughing instead when Chaplin struggled with a faulty deckchair. Werner had seen that all before: the public obviously responded best to the broad, cheap jokes. As usual, the scene descended in to fighting and chaos, and the audience cheered.

Werner slipped out of the cinema into the pouring rain and ran across the road to find a bar. The film had been a good distraction. Now he could discover a quiet table, and become engrossed with *King Lear* again. He didn't drink alcohol, so ordered a small soda, which he sipped slowly as he tried to let the play dribble back into his consciousness. The Duke of Kent has the very first line in the play, and it was always a thrill to be the first actor the audience sees. Under his breath, he muttered each word quietly so as not to attract attention.

> I thought the King had more affected the
> Duke of Albany than Cornwall . . .

He managed to get through three acts and two sodas. There was something quite special about reading in a public place. There were just as many distractions as there were at home, but somehow there was a pressure to concentrate, to *appear* to be engaged with the book or script, even if you're not. Werner was diligent when it came to memorising his lines – he did so much film work these days that it was a relief to get on stage and actually be heard. Just feeling the words in his mouth, the flow, the conflict, the rhythm – it was a joy. He paid his bar tab and wandered out into the dusk. A film showing must've just finished, because a hoard of people emerged from the cinema and rushed towards him. A spotty-faced boy approached:

"Hey! Weren't you the Cripple in '*A Dance of Death*'?" the boy asked.

"I played that part . . . "

"Can I have your autograph?"

"Of course," he said. The boy rummaged around in his satchel. Werner checked his watch, he only had a few minutes before rehearsals began, over in Konigstraße. "Did you enjoy the film?" Werner asked, but the boy ignored him, concentrating instead on his search for a pen. Eventually, he handed Werner his cinema ticket and a blunt pencil.

"There, you can use that . . . " Werner started to scribble on the ticket, " . . . you look a lot older in real life, you know."

"That's acting I suppose," said Werner. He handed the signed ticket back to the boy, and turned towards the station.

"Excuse me, what does this actually *say?*"

"It says 'Werner Krauss', that's my real name."

"Oh," said the boy, "I'll write 'Cripple' underneath later, just so I remember who you are."

I pray you, father, being weak, seem so.
If, till the expiration of your month,
You will return and sojourn with my sister,
Dismissing half your train, come then to me.
I am now from home, and out of that provision
Which shall be needful for your entertainment.

Maria was playing Regan beautifully. She had a delicate, under-stated way of delivering her lines. Most actresses Werner had seen were overblown – too eager to please. But Maria had a quiet confidence. He noticed the sweet way in which she rubbed her thumb and index finger together whenever she spoke.

"Quite a girl, eh Krauss?" Hessler whispered to him. Hessler was the odious young rascal playing Oswald, he had sidled up to Werner in the front row.

"She acts well – direct . . . but graceful." Werner knew Hessler was prying. Gossip was a currency among some of the actors, and Werner wasn't prepared to invest.

"You know what I mean . . . she's nice."

"I suppose so."

"Come on, Krauss . . . you can do better than that. Bet you'd love to get your hands on those tits, eh?"

"Show some fucking respect!" The action onstage stopped, everyone was looking at him. "Sorry about that. Carry on . . . please."

"Are you okay, Werner?" Maria asked from the stage.

"Fine. I'm fine, please carry on." The action resumed.

"I'm sorry Werner. Didn't realise I was touching such a nerve," Hessler whispered. Werner turned to him:

"You, young man, will be lucky if you still have a part in this play by tomorrow. Do you understand?" Hessler didn't reply. He got up and stropped out of the rehearsal studio. Werner had no idea where this threat had come from, or if he really did have sufficient influence to get someone fired anyway. He was just sick of the insolence, the *nerve* of these younger men. All they ever talked about – *thought about* – was sex, and they assumed everyone else was the same. In a way, Werner was glad he wasn't like that anymore – always chasing girls and trying to act tough. He wanted to start a new life with the wonderful young woman performing in front of him, and these bastards shouldn't be allowed to make it difficult.

At the end of the session, he approached the director.

"So sorry about that, Herr Wengel. It's just that boy, Hessler. Talk about impertinence . . . "

"Not a problem, Werner. I understand. In fact, you're not the first person he's irritated."

"Maybe you could . . . just . . . " Werner didn't really know the correct parlance, " . . . let him go?"

"We open Friday, Werner dear. Sorry, but there's no way."

"Fine, of course, I understand."

"Not like you to get so uptight though – he must've really got to you."

"He was being rude about some of the girls. Needs to think before he opens his mouth, that one."

"I hear you, dear. Just try to let it go, eh? Like most scoundrels – Hessler's a fine actor." Wengel winked at Werner and gave a little smile. Werner smiled back, but he felt lousy. He'd made a fool of himself – now Hessler and his gang would be worse – his threat had been empty. The only possible good that could come of this would be Maria's reaction to his public defence of her honour.

"Ready to go, my sweet?" She took him by the arm. "You can walk me home and tell me what you're getting all upset about.

"You're thirty-five, Werner, not ancient."

"I know . . . it just feels like they're a different generation. They've got absolutely no respect." They held hands as they walked through the *Tiergarten*.

"It's very sweet of you, darling, but boys are just being boys, you shouldn't let it get to you . . . "

"You didn't hear what he said."

"Then tell me. Go on, I'm a big girl, I can take it."

"Alright," Werner was annoyed at having to prove his chivalry – why couldn't she just take his word for it? "He said: 'I bet you'd love to get hold of her tits.' Happy?"

"And would you, Werner?"

"Would I what?"

"Would you like to get hold of them?"

"Maria!" He feigned outrage. They laughed, and he kissed her on the cheek.

"Now it's time for you to listen to me," she said, "my day's been horrendous." Maria's mother had been in hospital for a couple of months now. Werner had completely forgotten to ask how she was. "The specialist was supposed to see her at nine a.m. – guess what time he showed up?"

Werner shrugged.

"Four in the afternoon! Can you believe it? What's worse is we were both ready for him early – we'd prepared a list of questions for him, about her heart, when she could get out of hospital and what would happen next *etcetera*. But by the time he turned up our nerves were shot. We were so worried, so tired of waiting – neither of us could concentrate. He was this little weasel-faced Jew. He mumbled something about medication and we nodded like dumb animals. We both forgot about the list and the questions. It'll probably be months before she gets to see someone like him again. It's so frustrating – makes you feel useless." She leaned her head against his shoulder.

"One day it won't be like that you know," Werner said, improvising re-assurance.

"What do you mean?"

"Obviously I can't make any guarantees, but I've heard big things are happening with this film, *Das Cabinet*."

"What big things?"

"America's interested. The producers are in touch with Hollywood studios – this could really be a big break for me, for *us*."

"Oh Werner, that's wonderful . . . " Maria said, stroking his stomach as they walked, "but what's it got to do with Mother?"

"We could get her the best treatment. Private doctors, physicians, the best people, real *German* specialists."

"Does this mean . . . " Maria stopped. "You're . . . really *serious* about me?"

"I suppose it does, yes," he said. It was undeniably alluring to speak so powerfully, with such control. It was true; there had been talk of Hollywood on the set of *Das Cabinet*. But then again, there was *always* talk of Hollywood, on every film he'd ever worked on. Why should this one be any different?

"Well this *is* a dubious honour. What are you doing home?" Paula was sat at the dining table in her nightdress. She was reading *Deutsche Zeitung*.

"Not now, please. I'm tired. Are the children awake?"

"They've just gone up. Don't disturb them now, will you?"

"Are they okay?"

"Moody, selfish, bad-mannered – they're fine." She tossed the sheet of newspaper over.

"Friend of yours called this morning. He was canvassing for the Commies."

"I don't know what you mean." Paula kept her eyes fixed on the newspaper.

"Well he asked for you . . . " Werner pulled the leaflet from his trouser pocket, " . . . Comrade Kohl, our local representative." He slapped the leaflet down on top of her newspaper. She took a brief glance.

"Never heard of him," she said. "Do you want a coffee?"

"Yes. Thanks."

She got up and walked towards the kitchen. "Hope there'll be no screaming from you tonight . . . "

"So do I. Sorry about that," he said.

"What do you think it was? Guilty conscience?"

Werner raised his eyebrows. Paula smiled. "The problem with me is I just can't *remember* dreams – they seem to fade the second I wake."

"Try some exercises before you go to bed – it'll wear your body out, help you sleep properly."

"I might. Thanks, Paula." It was rare for them to have a civilised conversation like this. It felt rewarding – like talking to a friend. Paula poured two coffees and they both sat down at the table. She turned back to the newspaper.

"Have you read what this Wolfgang Kapp character is saying? Arrogant swine. Look . . . " she searched the newspaper article with her index finger,

" . . . 'Deutschland needs a new leader, a strong warrior, not feeble diplomats. Nothing ever gets achieved by windbag committees. Deutschland needs a different path, and that path will begin here in Berlin . . . '"

"Sounds like he's onto something to me." Werner slurped at the hot coffee.

"Sure, it's just what we need: more upheaval, more fighting."

"Then what do *you* suggest? Give power to your Commie friend? Think that'd bring prosperity, do you?"

"You can be a real prick sometimes, Werner. You know that?" Paula folded the newspaper and tossed it aside.

"I'm sorry. Really," Werner said. He hadn't wanted to argue. "To be honest, I don't take enough of an interest." Brooding, Paula didn't reply. Werner tried to tickle her under her arms, "Come on, there's no need to hate me all your life . . . "

"Get off! Werner, I mean it."

"Just give me a smile and I'll stop."

Eventually, she burst into fits of laughter. "You're a monster, Werner, get off!" He stopped, and for a moment they stared at each other. They were both red-faced and panting after the struggle.

"I'd better get up to bed," Werner said. "Early start in the morning."

"You know . . . I could come with you – help you get to sleep. We *are* married, after all. It's what married people do."

3

"Five marks says you haven't even got the guts to try."

Egged-on by the other boys, Karl slid the green note towards Werner. It was a lot of money to a sixteen year old. Stupidly, Werner had spent his first months with the travelling company exaggerating to Karl: about how tough he was, how much alcohol he drank and about his experience with women. Even more stupidly, he had started the conversation with his friends as they took their seats in a busy café in Bonn. Pointing out of the window to a street prostitute, he said:

"I bet I could get her to do it with *me* for free."

It was, of course, just a joke. But now the gauntlet had been laid down, and the excitement amongst the small gang of boys was almost tangible.

"Yeah, go on then, Krauss. Put your money where your mouth is."

"Talk to her then, if you're so big."

He thought about it for a moment, and decided that the worst thing that could happen would be she'd shout at him and tell him where to go. At five marks, that was a good deal. Plus, he liked the idea of acting the clown and doing the dare – it made him feel like he belonged, as if he had a place amongst these grubby misfits. This was the first day off they'd had for weeks, and Werner was determined to make the most of it. Seizing upon the theatrical potential of the moment, he snatched the note and stood to attention. His wooden chair scraped along the floor as he stood.

"She won't know what hit her!"

He left the café. The cold wind chilled his bones as well as his bravado. What on earth was he doing? He couldn't bear even to look towards the prostitute. He kept his head down, taking his time to cross the road. Mercifully, each time he went to cross, another vehicle appeared. He turned back to look at his friends through the café window – they were pointing and laughing, willing him on. Eventually he crossed, and started to walk in her direction. From the café, all he had noticed about the prostitute was that she was quite tall, and that the way she had her arms folded made her breasts look big. Approaching her now, though, his heart sank. She couldn't have been much older than him. He could smell the vodka seeping through her skin before he even got close. And she looked so cold, so fragile. He stood next to her; she looked him up and down, and sneered. He swallowed hard. How do you start a conversation with a prostitute, he wondered?

"Hello there, my name's Werner."

She didn't reply. She was shivering. Her skin looked so grey, and she had sores all over her face and neck. Werner felt awful to be using her as part of a joke, a silly dare.

"You look freezing. Would you like to go somewhere for a drink?"

"Got money?" she asked, and Werner nodded. "Let me see."

He opened his fist and unravelled the note.

"Come on then."

As he escorted her away, the playground instinct within him demanded that he looked back towards his friends. The scene didn't disappoint. Karl and the others were in raptures – punching the air with their fists and laughing. But he didn't feel good about this, and decided he would try to help the girl. She led him to a dark, dingy café. It was full of old men, smoking and talking loudly. Werner suspected that most of them were homeless, the way they huddled together and cradled their drinks.

"So did you want a drink, or shall I sort out a room?"

"A drink. Please. Just coffee," he spluttered. She stood and stared until he realised what she wanted. "Sorry, the money, of course." He found an empty table at the back, and sat down. He realised she could quite easily disappear with the money, but, then again, she was probably hoping he had more to spend. She returned with two mugs of steaming hot coffee, and to Werner's surprise, dropped his change on the table.

"I'm going to be honest with you," he said, "I was with some friends back there and they dared me to talk to you."

She shrugged.

"What I mean is, I don't actually want to . . . *you know* . . . with you."

Again, she didn't respond. She seemed to be enjoying the feeling of hot steam from the coffee on her face.

"But anyway, this place is . . . nice."

She looked at Werner as if he had just blasphemed. "You think this is *nice?*"

"Well . . . no. Sorry. It's horrible. Just something to say though, isn't it? And you're not exactly talkative, so . . . "

"Sorry," she said, and looked him in the eye for the first time, "Just so cold . . . "

"Here," Werner took off his jacket. He got up, and wandered around the table to drape it over her shoulders, but she snatched it from him and put it on.

"Thanks. I'll give it back in a minute . . . " she said. "So tell me about this dare then." As she spoke, Werner noticed her teeth were brown and rotten.

"It's really stupid, just boys messing about – they bet me that five marks I wouldn't go and talk to you."

"Easy money. I suppose they all think we're doing it now, do they?"

"Probably. But I'll tell them we didn't . . . if you want?" She didn't answer. "I know it's none of my business, but aren't you a bit young to be . . . "

"When exactly is a good age, then?" She peered at him over her mug.

"You're right. Sorry. Just that you seem nice. You know, *too* nice. For this."

"Thanks," she said, sarcastically.

"I take it you've ran away from home then, or something?"

"Never really had a home. Just go from place to place, with Hirsch. He takes care of me."

"So where's Hirsch now?"

"God knows. He has different businesses and sometimes hooks me up."

"I ran away from home you see." Werner couldn't remember ever saying those words before – so why was he opening up to this girl? "Couldn't take it there any more. Luckily I got adopted by this acting company. We go from town to town performing shows – it's like a family. They don't pay properly though . . . so, I can't give you any money. Or anything. Sorry."

"It's okay. I guessed. At least I'm getting warm. It's good to talk to someone for a change. Most men don't have much to say to me, obviously."

"I'm glad. It's good – *great* – talking to you too." Werner smiled at the girl. He was amazed at how confidently he was performing, how relaxed he must seem. This was probably the longest conversation he'd ever had with a girl, and he had his new acting abilities to thank for it.

"Do you mind if I ask something personal?" he said.

"You're paying for the coffee."

"Don't you want to *stop* doing this? I mean, how much longer are you going to . . . you know . . . with strange men. Don't you want anything else?"

"Didn't have much choice." Again, she was silent for what seemed an eternity, slowly sipping her drink. "Eventually I'll get married though, and get a proper place to live. I just need to do this for a few years until . . . "

"Until what?"

"Don't know. Until someone wants to marry me, I suppose." Werner felt so hopeless. Who would want to marry a prostitute, someone who'd slept with all those men – someone whose life was over before it had even begun? Just as he was formulating the next question in his mind, she got up to leave. "Thanks for the drink. Oh, and the coat." She took his coat off, handed it back and shivered in the chill.

"That's okay. I'm probably going to be in town for a couple of weeks so . . . would it be okay to see you again?"

"You know where I am, right?"

He woke alone to the sound of Paula and the children clattering around downstairs. For a brief moment, he couldn't remember what had happened the previous night. It was a blissful, innocent fragment of amnesia. Then he remembered. He remembered suddenly having a rush of good feeling for Paula. Not love, or even lust, just a feeling of warmth, of a shared instinct. She was so different to the people he saw all day – free of the vanity and self-interest – in that moment it just felt right. Like when they were younger, they crept up the stairs together, hand-in-hand. They had to be careful not to wake the children, and confuse them any more with their strange arrangement. Paula had joined him in their son's bed. She disappeared under the sheets and used her lips and tongue. Werner had closed his eyes and gently stroked her hair. It was such a thrill – so audacious – Paula hadn't behaved like this for years. It was all over in a few minutes. She didn't even stay to cuddle him or to talk, she just slipped out of the room without saying a word.

"What happens now?" he thought. "What about Maria?"

He got up, washed, dressed, and grabbed his briefcase. He dashed downstairs to find Paula and the children around the dining table.

"Sorry. Running late. See you tonight," he said.

"Say goodbye to your father," Paula instructed, but no response came from the two boys. Again, he took the train to *Weißensee* and dashed up the *Lixie-Altelier* to the studio. He was late arriving onto the set, but luckily they had started work on one of the scenes that he wasn't involved with.

Heavily made-up in gothic splendour, Conrad looked terrifying, scampering around the set:

"There is something
frightful in our midst!"

Werner couldn't help but feel envious of his younger, thinner compatriot. He looked especially striking with those darkened eyes and pale, perfectly sculpted features.

"It'll be a miracle if we get you in and out of make-up on time." His assistant was flustered. He sat down at the counter, and she talked to him via the mirror. "Late night, was it?"

"No . . . " Werner hated taking responsibility for his lateness – it was something he deplored in others – "actually Egon wasn't feeling well this morning, and I had to stay behind and . . . "

"Oh dear, poor thing." She gently massaged the tops of his shoulders. "What's wrong with him?"

"I think it's a virus or something, you know what kids can be like."

"So where is he now? Is someone at home with him?"

He wasn't prepared to flesh-out his lie any further. "Can we just get on with this please? I've got enough to deal with." The massage stopped and the assistant left, only to return a moment later. She slammed down a cup of coffee.

"I've got to check on Conrad. Do you need anything else?"

He put the drink to his lips to find it was stone cold. He swallowed anyway. "Nothing thanks, I'm fine."

The studio was packed with people. This was Caligari's moment – presenting his Somnambulist to the crowd.

"Everything should be big, Werner! Big! Big! Big!" Weine was keen to use wide shots wherever possible, to gauge the crowd's reaction. This involved a degree of exaggeration on Werner's part, to add to the spectacle.

"No problem."

"Just let yourself go – if we need to reign you in, we'll redo the take. Give it everything."

He appeared to the crowd, removed his top hat and took a bow. He then produced a wand, which he waved wildly. He simply touched the curtain and it lifted. The props supervisor was perched on a ledge high above him, frantically pulling the cord. The cabinet was revealed.

It was a peculiar, rock-like shape. He pulled the two doors apart, revealing Cesare the Somnambulist, standing perfectly still, as though rigor mortise had set in. Gesticulating with the wand and his cane, Caligari presented him to the crowd,

"*Halt!* I think we're all happy with that, Werner. We'll move in for some close work."

Together with Conrad, he was led to his mark in front of the camera. This was to be the scene in which the audience first see his grotesque, gruesome appearance close-up.

"*Und . . . aktion!*"

Peering over his spectacles like a professor, his eyes scuttled from left to right. He shook his cane in front of the Somnambulist.

"Wake up, Cesare!
I, Caligari, your master,
Command you!"

The camera dwelled on Cesare's ghostly face. Slowly he blinked and eventually his eyes opened. His bottom lip dropped as he took a desperate gasp for air. Werner had to admit, it was a masterful performance. He stared directly into the camera, as if to accuse the viewer, as if the world were responsible for his fate. His eyebrows rose – he was disgusted by what he saw.

"Marvellous, marvellous, gentlemen. We're on a roll now so let's get set up straight away for the emergence."

Caligari waved his wand, and the Somnambulist started to walk.

"*Halt!* No, no I'm sorry. We need to try it slow, moody, tense – okay Werner?"

"I thought you wanted big?"

"We did 'big,' old boy, it was marvellous. Now for *slow* . . . deliberate."

With a sigh and a shrug, Werner nodded.

"*Und . . . Aktion!*"

This time, Caligari held the wand firmly, and slowly moved it up and down the Somnambulist's legs. Stiffly, awkwardly, he moved his right leg and took a step, then followed with his left. As he walked, Caligari backed away, like Frankenstein in awe of his creation. With an outstretched palm, he introduced his monster to the crowd. He moved his spectacles, so they sat at a strange angle on his forehead, away from his eyes. He removed his hat, and took a curtsy-like bow.

"Ladies and gentlemen!
Cesare knows all secrets!

**Ask him to look into
Your future."**

"*Halt!* Wonderful work again – let's have a round of applause everyone!" The massed ranks of extras started to clap. It was a peculiar feeling – a moment of appreciation in the most contrived, intense circumstances. Werner felt quite embarrassed.

"You're all *far* too kind . . . and you don't get extra money for being sycophantic – I should know, I've been doing it for years!" Mercifully the crowd all laughed, and again they applauded. Surely it was a sign of a good film, to have such a feeling on the set.

"Alright now let's get on. Proceeding from that point, Hans should emerge from the crowd and ask his question. All quiet on set please."

"This clown was pathetic in rehearsal," Conrad whispered to Werner.

"Thank God no one will hear him then."

"Ready, *und . . . aktion!*"

The student strode towards the Somnambulist, but Caligari firmly held out his cane, to restrain him.

"How long shall I live?"

The Somnambulist stared back at him with icy distain. He opened his mouth and growled terrifyingly:

**"The time is short.
You die at dawn!"**

The student gasped and panted, then smiled. He turned to his friend and they laughed hysterically.

"Good, good. Well done, gentlemen. We'll go again, let's get a slower, more sustained response from you, Hans. You *should* laugh, but it's a laugh of disbelief, of fear. Nervous, not so . . . comedic."

"I never thought it'd get to this stage. But she's so much worse. I think after the disappointment of yesterday – the stupid Jew quack that did nothing – she's just given up. I needed to help her to . . . you know, go to the toilet today. Everything she said was down. Down, down, down. 'There's no hope for me,' she'd say, 'not long left now.' Honestly, I don't know what I'd do if I didn't have you, Werner." He said nothing. "Are you even listening to me?"

He could hear Maria, but all he could think about was his wife. He wondered if there would be a repeat of last night. Perhaps he should take the initiative and lead her up to bed when he got home. He knew this wasn't right, that he should be focusing his attention on Maria, and trying to split with Paula for good. But there was something almost nostalgic about the way he felt for Paula, something comforting and secure.

"I'm sorry. I just need to get home and have an early night."

"But you said we could do something – I came all the way from *Charlottenburg* to see you. I could have stayed with mother."

"I know, I know, sorry." He remembered his story from earlier. "Egon's not been too well. It's only fair that I go home, you know, help out."

"Poor little thing. I'm sorry, Werner – no wonder you were distracted. Can't I come with you – see if there's anything I can do?"

"I think you know that's not a good idea. Anyway, how is your mother?"

He took the train back to *Bernau*. He knew Maria had every right to be annoyed, but acting hysterically, like she did, only made him want his wife more. He bought some tulips from a street vendor outside the station, and practically jogged the rest of the way home. Like when they first met – he couldn't wait to see her again. He found Rudi waiting on the doorstep.

"Can't go in yet, *Vater*."

"What do you mean?"

"It's the rule – we're not allowed in until six-thirty."

Werner checked his watch – it was almost six o'clock.

"Nonsense, you'll freeze to death out here." Rudi shrugged. Werner took out his keys, unlocked the door and they entered.

"Guess who got back early!" he shouted, but there was no reply. They went into the front room to find a familiar looking jacket folded neatly on the settee. On the dining table he found a clipboard, and a pile of leaflets. It was the Commie. Werner felt sick. He was stupid for allowing himself to start feeling for her again – so much had changed, they'd both moved on. Indulging his curiosity, he carefully climbed the stairs without making a sound, and listened. Sure enough, he could hear his wife whispering and shuffling around. He crept back downstairs and took Rudi by the hand.

"Don't tell your mother I was here. Do you understand?"

Rudi nodded.

"Good boy." Werner searched in his pockets for some coins to give to his son, but found nothing. "Next time I see you I'll have a lovely treat, okay?" He left. He couldn't believe that pathetic, slimy Commie was with his wife. In *his* house. He headed straight back to *Bahnhof Bernau-Friedenstal* and caught the next train. He knew he had to end it properly now. He should save some money to give to Paula, to take care of the children, and then he'd get out of there. The train reached *Alexanderplatz*, and he made the short walk to Maria's apartment block.

"They're beautiful! Oh, Werner I could never stay mad at you for long!" He hadn't realised he was still clutching the bunch of flowers. She pulled him into the small lounge. "How's Egon? I thought you had to look after him?"

"Fast asleep. We think it could be an allergy . . . " he chuckled, "he's been allergic to school lately. Little rascal, there's not much wrong with him."

"Don't be too hard on him. We all had days like that when we were younger."

"I had whole *years* like that . . . "

"You see. Now I was just about to open a bottle of wine, lie on the sofa and think about how much I hated you and how selfish and ignorant you were." She smiled. "Want to join me?"

"Sure. Oh but don't . . . "

"I know what you're going to say," she interrupted, "'don't pour any wine for me, I don't drink.' Maybe you should have a glass with me. Relax. *Maybe* I'll insist . . . " She stood close, so he could feel her breasts up against him. He held her waist in his hands.

"Okay. And then we get to talk about my selfishness, right? I hate it when anyone else is the topic of conversation."

Maria poured him a large glass of white wine. For so many years and for so many reasons, he had abstained. But maybe it was time to let go. He was already paranoid about being too old, *acting* too old. Perhaps this would be a way to claw back some of his youth. First he sipped, and then he gulped. His throat burned and he wheezed.

"*Prost!*" he said.

"*Prost!*" Maria responded. She sipped from her glass, and kissed his cheek.

"I want to tell you something, Maria. It's not news, as such, and I don't know if you'll agree, but . . . "

"Spit it out, Werner! You can say anything to me."

"You know I'm serious about you."

"Fairly serious . . . "

"Well this time I am, this time I mean it. As soon as I get the chance, I'll tell Paula I'm leaving . . . "

"That's wonderful, Werner!"

" . . . but obviously I need somewhere to stay, so I wanted to ask if I could live here with you? I know it's not ideal."

"It *is*. It is ideal. You don't know how happy this makes me!"

"Good. I'm serious, Maria. You're everything I want in my life."

They hugged. He swallowed hard, feeling relieved he had placated her, but still confused and upset about his wife. All he could do was throw himself into this new life.

"Bedroom . . . " she whispered, "it's more comfortable."

They lay on the bed kissing passionately. Maria started to unbutton Werner's trousers.

"I thought we agreed . . . "

"Shh!" She interrupted. She put her hand down into his underpants and started to stroke. "I want this *now*." She moved his hand up her skirt. He knew he wouldn't be able to stop himself. She removed his trousers and pants, gripped him and stroked vigorously. In fact, *too* vigorously. She was clumsy, and he tried to writhe away from her. His eyes started to water.

"You like that?"

He grunted in response. Werner realised his contorted expression was being mistaken for a look of ecstasy. He felt no desire, just . . . *agony*. She gripped and pulled harder, closing her eyes in concentration, as if carrying out an act of manual labour.

"Stop! Stop! Please stop for God's sake!"

Maria stared back at him in wide-eyed shock. A first tear started to crawl down her red face.

"Sorry, I didn't mean it like that. You were hurting me and . . . "

She got up, stormed out of the room and slammed the door. He could hear her loud, wailing cry coming from the bathroom. How did this happen? He laid back, and tentatively checked himself. He was numb and sore, but didn't think there was any real damage. Why couldn't he have just kept quiet?

"Maria, please, let me explain?" he called. "We were having a good time, please don't let it be spoiled?"

4

He tried to visit the girl each day that week. Sometimes she would be waiting for him, sometimes he would have to spend a few hours in the café opposite, wondering when she would return from whoever she was with. He didn't mind. He always carried a copy of Goethe's *Werther* and found it easy to lose himself in it, wherever he was. Their meeting usually consisted of him buying hot drinks and lending her his coat. Werner would chatter on about his role in the play, the friends he had made, and what it was like living 'on the road'. Although, as a virgin, he was desperate to sleep with pretty much anyone, he didn't *think* he felt anything sexual for this girl. Mainly, he felt a sense of responsibility, that he should do all he could while he was here, to make her life a little better.

Saturday was his last day in Bonn. As he approached the *Grunaer Straße*, he wondered how he would say '*auf Wiedersehen*' to her. Running away from home the way he did, had obviously taken '*auf Wiedersehen*' out of the equation back then, and he didn't quite know what to say now. He thought he would miss having someone like her to talk to. Meeting the way they had, he felt no inclination to hide the truth from her, or exaggerate. And he knew he would miss being able to operate with such honesty. Would he try to kiss her, he wondered? Despite her cracked lips and brown teeth, he would *like* a kiss. It had been months since he had kissed a girl, and given the amount of coffee he'd bought her, she at least owed him . . . no. 'Stop it,' he thought. Such thoughts made him no better than one of her men. There was no way she would kiss him. She probably wouldn't notice if he never came back anyway.

"I'm glad you're here." She had been running. Breathless, she grabbed him by the shoulder and held him tightly. "He's left me . . . he's just gone and left . . . "

"Take your time. What do you mean – who has left you?"

She was still panting. Werner noticed her make-up was smudged, leaving a black stain sleeping under each eye.

"Hirsch. Said he doesn't need girls no more, bad for his image . . . "

"What? Why? What sort of image . . . what does he do anyway?"

"He's being promoted to head of something-or-other in the Nationalists. They said he had to clean up his act. He just *left* me."

"He's a politician?" Werner practically spat the word at the girl.

"I don't know, politician, ambassador, it doesn't matter now, does it? What am I going to do?"

He took off his coat, and carefully draped it around her shoulders. He felt pretty powerless to help. He led her around the corner to the grotty café, where they found their regular table.

"He was the only reason, you know."

"The only reason for what?"

"What do you think? For doing this, what I do . . . "

Werner was confused. What the hell had he got involved with? And all because of his stupid joke . . .

"He told me he loved me – that in a few years we could get married and move away. He said this was only temporary. I knew he was rich, so . . . "

"Let me get some coffee. Stay there. And try to relax . . . or something."

He was relieved to have a moment to think at the counter. He knew nothing about Bonn, except that the cafés were miserable and the audiences weren't easy to please. This girl needed everything: a home, a job, or else . . . what? She could die – was he going to let her die?

"Pot of coffee again, is it?"

"Please. And a slice of toast."

The greasy-looking waiter leaned-in. "You know, most men don't go to all this effort. Just tell her what you want and she'll do it. From what I've heard . . . "

"Toast and coffee will be fine, thanks."

"You know best. But remember, they're only girls, my friend, just girls . . . "

He woke, shivering in the relentless cold, on a strange sofa. He was still wearing the clothes he'd been in last night. At first, he was disorientated, and then he remembered where he was. Maria hadn't spoken to him after what had happened. She simply handed him a blanket and a pillow, and pointed to the small settee. His aching back, and the horrible warm spit in his mouth, forced him to rise early. He poured a glass of water and sipped. 'How many other men could go from having two women one day, to no women the next?' he thought. He smiled. Things weren't so bad. If he was honest, Maria's obvious inexperience with men made him feel more strongly for her. He was to be her first, and she deserved to be treated well. Poking around in the unfamiliar kitchen, he gathered what ingredients he could find, and started to prepare breakfast for her. After clattering around and making a mess of the place, he emerged with some toast, ham and a poached egg. He wrote a note for Maria, and together with the plate of food, placed it on a tray.

"You're sorry you love me? What?" She tried to read the note with one eye open. Still slumped on her pillow, her face was blotchy – she had obviously been crying for most of the night.

"No! No, darling, it says 'I'm sorry *and* I love you.'"

"Oh, okay. Thank you." She said, and buried her head in the pillow once more.

"I've made you breakfast, too."

Reluctantly, she slowly propped the pillows against her headboard, and sat up. He placed the tray on her lap and kissed her cheek.

"I *am* sorry, darling."

"It's all right, honestly. There'll be plenty of chances for me to get better at it, won't there?" She smiled.

"Of course, of course – if you still *want* an old fool like me?"

She put the uneaten breakfast to one side, and they snuggled together in the single bed.

Werner woke alone for the second time, and ambled into the kitchen. It was immaculately clean. Maria was tidying away her detergents, lining them up precisely in the cupboard.

"Sorry about the mess."

"Don't be, it's fine. It was lovely to have breakfast brought to me."

"I'm going to have to get to the studio. Better leave soon so I don't miss the train."

"Oh, I thought I might come with you, if that's alright? And that we could . . . cycle? Together. If you want? It's such a nice day, it'd be a shame for you to be cooped up in a train." Maria looked nervous as she made her suggestion.

"Been a few years since I sat on a bicycle, but I think I can just about remember how it's done." Werner didn't quite know how to take this. Was it a sign of things to come – her compulsive cleaning and exercise? Or was she trying to tell him something? He knew he should be doing a few sit-ups and press-ups . . . but cycling?

They arrived at the studio and he waved her '*auf Wiedersehen*' at the security office.

"No way for a film star to travel is it, Herr Krauss?" The security guard was grinning like a hyena. Werner gave a wry smile back. He liked being called 'a star'.

"You never know, it might catch on!"

**"When the shadows
lay darkest . . . "**

Creeping down the winding corridor, he hunched over and peeped through the keyhole. First he paused. "One thousand and one, one thousand and two . . . " Then he forced his way into the room.

"*Halt!* Lovely Werner, let's move straight on."

The overcoat and wig were stiflingly hot. He was already sweating from the bike ride. He hadn't known anyone to work like Weine, so quickly and without hesitation. It was as if the film was being created in real time.

"The room's set up. Keep it sprightly, Werner, maintain that element of mystery."

"No problem, Robert."

"Let's go then. Lights are set, *und . . . aktion!*"

He started to stir at the creamy porridge in the pot. Next, he lifted the two wooden doors simultaneously, and opened the casket. He grabbed Cesare by the shoulders to lift him. The tall, thin figure sat upright – perfectly still and perfectly straight. Caligari grabbed the porridge and started to feed his captive guest, spoonful after spoonful.

"Cut! That's great, gentlemen."

Conrad spat the porridge out, all over the interior of his wooden coffin.

"Argh! How many spoonfuls were you going to give me, Werner?"

Werner laughed. "You're a growing boy, you need building-up a bit."

" . . . to be a fat bastard like you?" Conrad mumbled.

"Okay we're ready again. Remember you've just heard a knock at the door. The police have caught up with you . . . all ready . . . *aktion!*"

Caligari slammed Cesare back down. His shoulders shuddered against the hard wooden casket. He slammed the two flaps shut and gingerly crept to the front door.

"And cut!"

"Christ, Werner, what's your problem?" The voice from the coffin was incensed. Eventually a flap was pushed open, and Conrad peered over at his co-star.

"Sorry, sorry, Con. Just got a bit carried away, that's all." Werner tried to disguise his smile. "Fat bastards like me can get distracted this close to lunchtime."

Conrad wasn't laughing. "You've got real problems, Krauss."

He found Maria waiting for him outside the studio. She was sat on her bicycle, leaning against a far wall. Werner had forgotten all about the damn bicycles. He longed for a seat in a busy train carriage.

"Thought I'd surprise you! We could go somewhere to eat together before rehearsal."

"I can't, darling, they want me in early to do that interview – remember?"

"No. I'd forgotten. Can't I come with you though? I am *in* the play."

Werner thought for a moment. She was already following him around like a puppy. And if they gave the interview together, would people suspect they *were* together?

"Sure, why not? To be honest I don't know why they want to talk to me anyway. Must be the first Duke of Kent to ever get press . . . "

"I think you know why, Werner. You're in films – people are starting to recognise you."

"I don't know about that," he said, "anyone who saw my purse wouldn't think I was famous."

"But that's going to change – you said so yourself . . . "

Werner found his bicycle.

"You can lead the way."

"Scared I'll overtake you?"

"No. I just like watching your bottom wiggle."

They met Muller in a café next door to the theatre. Muller had offered to pay, so Werner ordered coffee, some sandwiches and several slices of cake.

"I thought it would be good for Maria to join us. I'm convinced her portrayal of Regan can really take the theatre world by storm!"

"I'll write the headlines, if it's all the same to you, Herr Krauss? Now, you're playing Kent in this production – many theatregoers would expect you to play Lear himself. Why accept the role?"

"When I saw the cast that had been assembled, I was really excited. Maria here, for instance . . . "

"But why take a lesser role?"

"You say it's a lesser role – that's your opinion. I love *King Lear*, and have played the role of Lear before and thought this would be a new challenge. Plus, I'm also in the middle of a busy filming schedule and couldn't really dedicate the time to a lead role."

"Doesn't that undermine Jacobson, who *is* playing Lear? You're saying the role would be yours if only you had the time . . . "

"No, I didn't say that – you pushed me for an answer, and . . . "

"Tell me about this film project you're working on. Must be pretty important if it forces you to turn down roles at the Staatstheater?"

"It is actually a very interesting project. It's a film called *Das Cabinet des Doctor Caligari* . . . "

"And what role do you play in that?"

"I play the Doctor. Doctor Caligari . . . "

"Ah, so you *are* the lead in the film – that's why you're not really bothering with the play . . . "

"No, I think the play will be great. You asked me . . . "

"And you've promised to get some exposure for your girlfriend here?"

"No – this is Maria Bard – a real talent for the future . . . "

"So why should people come to see this play?"

"It's a great production. There's some wonderful, fresh acting talent, a superb director. The costumes and sets are different, there's an expressionist feel, giving the play a contemporary setting . . . "

"So they shouldn't wait until you're less busy and playing a proper role?"

"I really object, now you're just being rude."

"Sorry, sorry." Muller leaned back in his chair, and sighed. "It's just that this job's so mind-numbing. All they want me to do is say how 'exciting' the play is; about how much you're looking forward to it and how good the cast is. Don't worry, that *is* what I'll write . . . "

"But . . . "

"Didn't you know one of the producers owns our paper?

"No, I . . . "

"Just that sometimes it's good fun to cut to the chase – get to the truth – don't you agree?"

"I suppose."

"You *are* probably more concerned about the film – this play's just to line your pockets for a few weeks. Fair enough – who could blame you for that? But that would never get written would it?"

"I certainly hope . . . "

"I've really got to go. Don't worry it'll be a good old puff piece – you're quite safe. Herr Krauss, Sofia . . . " he nodded at them both in turn.

"Her name's *Maria* . . . "

"Thanks for your time – have a good evening." He got up, dropped some money onto the table, and left.

They entered the theatre together. All the actors were complaining about the fit of their costumes. Some of the women were making their own adjustments – sitting on the theatre seats wielding their needle-and-thread. Hessler caught Werner's eye straight away. He was smiling.

"I promise you, if he says *one* word out of place . . . "

"Just leave it," Maria interrupted, "rise above it. You're not children in a playground."

After trying on their costumes, they found each other again and sat together, chatting and laughing. It was only after around ten minutes, when Wengel asked to get started, that Werner realised how open he was being, how *familiar* the pair of them must look together.

> Faith, he is posted hence on serious matter.
> It was great ignorance, Gloucester's eyes being out,
> To let him live; where he arrives he moves
> All hearts against us. Edmund, I think, is gone
> In pity of his misery, to dispatch
> His knighted life; moreover , to descry
> The strength o' th' enemy.

Sat again watching Maria's delightful Regan, Werner noticed some shuffling around in the seats next to him. It was Hessler.

"Whatever it is, I don't want to hear it." Werner said.

"No, no, I understand. I just wanted to say '*Danke*'. That's all." Hessler whispered.

Werner didn't respond. Was this a trick, an ironic gesture? Hessler *looked* earnest, at least.

"What're you thanking me for?"

"Wengel told me . . . about what you said. About how he was ready to throw me out of the play, but you said I should have one more chance. You're a good man, Werner, a real inspiration."

Werner knew old Wengel was a canny devil, but this was brilliant.

"Everyone deserves a second chance. Just mind your mouth in future, and concentrate on the performance."

"Yes, Werner. Thank you, Werner." Hessler took his hand and shook vigorously. "I can learn a lot from someone like you."

It was almost midnight when the dress rehearsal was over. Emerging from the dressing room, Werner bounded over to Wengel straight away. "Thank you, for what you did, talking to Hessler. I can't begin to tell you what a relief it was."

"Hardly be doing my job if I couldn't keep my big *movie* star happy, now, would I?"

"Stop it." Werner said, embarrassed. "But you should have seen him creeping up to me earlier, his face was a treat to behold. Like he'd seen a ghost."

"Any time, Werner, just remember me when you're walking down the red carpet in Hollywood, okay?"

Werner laughed, but was confused by the director's tone.

"I'll bear that in mind," he said.

"Oh, and Werner . . . it would be a good idea if you could meet up with Hessler, properly. Have a talk with him, give him some advice. He's just a kid, he needs some looking after."

"You really think that's a good idea?"

"I do. Even you were young once, Werner, I'm sure a few people gave you a chance."

"If you arrange it, I'll be there . . . " he said, and wandered back to Maria.

"Excellent show, dear." He kissed her on each cheek, as if she were merely an acquaintance.

"Onto a bar, darling? We deserve a drink and I won't take no for an answer." Determined not to indulge his act any more, she took him by the arm, and led him past their colleagues to the door.

"It's very late . . . " he said.

"And we're very young!" she smiled. They found a bar that was open on the Torstraße. He ordered a bottle of *Weißwein*.

"It was strange talking to Wengel earlier. Kept calling me a 'big star' and talking about going down the red carpet in Hollywood."

"So, what's wrong with that?"

"Where did he get that idea from? He's not usually prone to innuendo."

"Maybe . . . " she stopped herself. "I might have mentioned something." She bit her bottom lip, and searched his eyes for a reaction. "I knew you were worried about Hessler and thought it would help if I told the director how well *Das Cabinet* was doing. About how there was interest from the big studios in the States."

He knew this was his fault, but couldn't hide his anger from Maria.

"That's fine. Don't worry."

"You're mad at me, aren't you?"

"No. I said: 'it's fine'. Don't make me repeat myself."

"Why do I always get it wrong?" Her face was crimson.

"You haven't got anything wrong. Just that I think I might stay at home tonight. I need to see the children."

"At this time of night?"

"No," he thought for a moment, "but I can see them in the morning. It might also give me the chance to tell Paula I'm moving out." He didn't know where that idea came from. He just wanted to get away from Maria, he couldn't believe she'd been gossiping – she was making a fool out of him.

"Are you sure? You still want to live with me?" Was she going to cry again?

"Of course I do." He kissed her cheek, "but I have to go."

The room was white. Blindingly, glowingly, white. Werner had a vague sense of motion – that he was walking forward, that he should walk forward, whatever the consequences. No matter how far he tried to walk or at what pace, he remained in this white room. Exhausted, he stopped and stooped to clutch his knees and regain his breath. He looked up, and noticed the white get brighter. It was beginning to hurt his eyes so he shut them tightly. As he did so, it felt as though, somehow, his teeth were relaxing. They no longer felt like gravestones, deeply embedded in his gums. They felt loose and rapidly decaying. Panicking, he opened his eyes and tried to call: "Help!" But he couldn't hear a sound.

He decided to walk on, still trying: "Help! Please, somebody?" until eventually a dark figure became visible in the light. The figure seemed to walk strangely, waddling towards him. The figure was swinging a cane, twirling it around his fingers. After a few minutes, he was close enough to see his face. The man was pale and stern looking. He had a small moustache resting on his top lip. "Please help – my mouth . . . " Werner tried to say, but again no words would emerge. The pale figure put his finger to his lips. He dropped his cane, picked it up, then dropped it again. Then, he began to rummage around in his oversized trouser pockets. What was he searching for? Werner was afraid, the man had made no gesture of friendship, there was absolutely nothing warm about him. Eventually, he produced a pin. He held the pin out and nodded, urging Werner to take it. Werner obliged and gripped the pin between his thumb and index finger. The figure started to point at Werner's face, then he gestured to his own mouth. "You want me to put the pin in my mouth?" Werner couldn't hear himself speak, but the figure started to nod vehemently. Again, he pointed to Werner's face. Werner held the pin tightly, and slowly pushed it into one of his teeth – the lower incisor on his right side. All the pain from his mouth seemed to dissipate immediately, replaced by this one, sharp pain being caused by the pin.

As if to rejoice, the figure tossed his cane into the air and gave a salute. He turned on his heels and – rather than waddling as before – confidently marched with perfect military timing, back into the light, and disappeared. The pain in his mouth was gone . . . he held onto the pin . . . the throbbing sensation in that particular tooth felt soothing, gently beating, gently beating . . .

"Chaplin!" He thought, "Chaplin came to me in a dream – how wonderful!" As usual, the details of the dream were slipping away. He remembered the colour white, and the word Chaplin. But gradually the reason for either memory slipped away. Nevertheless, he felt elated. This must *mean* something. Maybe he would meet Chaplin, work with him, or even be *bigger* than him?

"Please?"

"But what does she *do*?"

"She'll do anything – help out around the place – make drinks, help with the props and costume."

"But, Werner . . . "

"Yes! That's it, *costumes*." Werner was working on the assumption that all girls knew about clothes. "She's terrific at sewing and turning worn-out old rags into wonderful new garments."

"Stop! Werner, please. We can't take anyone on. I'm sorry. You know how cramped things are for us already. We make our own clothes *and* our own drinks – you know that!"

"Please, Herr Holtkamp I think she could be in danger."

"There's nothing for her here . . . I'll make a few calls. I'm friendly with a man called Steinberg – he runs a company that tours military camps, they always need people. It's not easy, and the conditions aren't great. But if your friend needs to get away, she could do a lot worse."

Werner's stomach was churning. On the one hand he was ecstatic to be helping her. On the other, he hated the thought of sending her away and maybe never seeing her again. And what would happen if there was war?

"You're sure there's nothing she could do for us?"

"Werner!"

"Sorry. Thank you – please ask your friend if he can take her on. I'll go and tell her straight away."

Despite being wrapped in Werner's coat, the girl was still shivering. She rocked to and fro in her seat in the theatre auditorium.

"Let me guess: 'thanks but no thanks'?"

"There's nothing going with our company . . . "

"What a surprise . . . "

"But he's got a friend who can help you. They tour military bases all over. Is that all right?"

"Of course, of course, oh – thank you thank you!" She leapt up, held Werner tightly and kissed him three times.

"Nothing's for sure yet, but Herr Holtkamp is a good man, he'll do all he can."

5

Werner woke to the sound of his wife screaming. One of the children must have done something wrong. He got dressed with great deliberation, hoping that Paula could hear he was awake, and that his arrival might bring about some calm. Gingerly he entered the front room. "So are you going to tell your father? Or shall I?" She was shouting at Egon, who was silent. "This little monster has been stealing!"

"Is it true?" Werner tried to remain calm. He knew that Paula's anger would soon be directed at him, and he didn't want to provoke her further. "I'm talking to you young man . . . " Egon nodded. His face was red and blotchy from a morning of yelling and tears.

"Look at this – can you believe it?" She held up a small brass pocket-watch. "I found it in his room. He won't tell me where he got it."

"Let me look." Werner took the watch. It was heavy, and he unclasped it to reveal the Meylan clock face and a delicate Swiss mechanism. "Egon, go to your room. Take a few minutes to think carefully about what you've done – you've been stealing, and I will call the police if you don't tell your mother and I exactly how you got this watch. Do you understand?" Again, he nodded, and dashed up the stairs.

"Can't say I'm surprised. What do you expect, when his father's never around? He thinks he can do what he likes . . . " Paula was collecting the plates from the dining table. " . . . and he treats this place like a hotel – where do you think he gets that from?"

"I don't have time for this, Paula. I'm sorry I wasn't home the other night, let's just leave it at that for now, shall we?"

"That would be *so* much easier, wouldn't it? If I just kept quiet. I wonder – did you go for drinks with Maria Bard after rehearsal? You make quite a pair according to this morning's paper."

This was as much as he could take.

"Yes, we did, as it happens. Did Comrade Kohl call again?"

"No. Why? What is that supposed to mean?"

"Nothing, just wondered." Werner resisted a smile.

"Anyway, what're you going to do about your son? You'd better punish him – I have to live with these children of yours . . . "

"They're your children too. And I will – after I've found out where this damn watch came from."

"You'll be lucky. He won't tell me a thing."

"Egon!" Werner shouted, "Time's up, come down now." Egon plodded down each step slowly, eventually appearing in the front room. "Sit down," Werner told him. "I want the truth."

"There's a boy at school called Matthais. He's a real bore, he always says these stupid things and gets on everyone's nerves and . . . "

"And what?"

"I don't know how it happened. A few of us . . . we just started taking his money."

Paula made a lunge for her son, but Werner held her back. "You nasty piece of work – how could you?"

"He's being honest with us," Werner turned to Egon, "you're doing the right thing now." Werner took his wife by the arm and led her across the room. He whispered. "Leave us to it. He's started talking – I'll deal with it. Please?"

"Fine," she said, and went through to the kitchen, slamming the door behind her. Werner joined his son on the sofa.

"So you take money from this boy. How long has it been going on?"

"It's not just me, it's Josef as well. It started a few months ago."

"And how does all this relate to the watch?"

"Last week, when we . . . " he paused.

"When you were stealing money?"

"He didn't *have* any money, with him, at school, and Jo said we should follow him home. So that's what we did. We told him to get us money from home."

"Why the hell do you want all this money anyway?" Werner raised his voice. "What do you need it for?"

"Because I never get any money, from you, or mother. It's not fair."

Werner slapped his son across the face. "That's no excuse. You might not be rich like some of the others, but you've never been hungry. Your mother and I always do the best we can for you."

Egon started to cry. "I'm sorry."

"So this boy gave you a watch, did he?"

Egon replied, but was barely audible beneath his sniffling. "It was his Grandpa's. He took it from his Grandpa."

"And gave it to you. Well, when you've been punished, we'll go there straight away to return it – do you understand?"

"We can't. His Grandpa died a few weeks ago and Matthais has left school. No one has seen him for weeks."

Werner didn't want to punish his son now. Poor Egon's face was sore, it was sopping wet with tears and his high-pitched pleading was nauseating. But he knew he must appease Paula and set an example. As his father unbuckled his belt, Egon ran for the door. Werner grabbed him by the shirt and snatched him backwards.

"If you resist, it's ten lashes. If not – just five." Sobbing, Egon nodded and stood still. "Now take down your trousers." The boy removed his trousers while Werner prepared the leather belt. Folding it in half, he cracked the belt to give a terrifying snap. Egon winced. Standing, shivering in his underpants, he cut a pretty pathetic figure, and Werner just wanted to give him a hug.

"I'm not enjoying this, you know. Your Grandpa used to do this when I stepped out of line. I know how it feels." He lashed out with the belt, striking his son's legs. Egon gave an almighty scream. Werner felt his eye twitch nervously, and lashed out again, without looking. He followed-up quickly, with his eyes closed, but failed to connect. He opened his eyes and realised Egon had backed away from him, leaving a small pool of urine between them. Werner couldn't stand any more, and dropped the belt.

"Wipe all that up and get ready for school."

Without saying '*auf Wiedersehen*', Werner left the house and headed straight for the station. There had been no chance to talk seriously to Paula this morning, and he had left poor Maria crying at the theatre last night. He needed to start making some proper decisions, and acting upon them – he should stop making empty promises and false threats. He took a small notepad from his briefcase and started to scribble some names and numbers. The numbers didn't add up, and seeing the names on paper was heartbreaking. The seed of an idea was beginning to grow, but he might have to do some terrible things to make it work.

The train ground to a halt at the station and he walked purposefully to the studios.

"No bicycle today, Herr Krauss?"

He tried desperately to think of a witty riposte – he enjoyed having friendly banter with the security staff – but nothing came to mind. "Not today." Whistling, he bounded along the grubby corridors, and entered the dressing room. "And how are you, dear?" the assistant looked like she had even more problems than Werner.

"I'm fine. We're having to go with the other cloak – don't ask me why – there's no hot water for drinks so don't ask . . . Weine wants to re-shoot a couple of scenes, he said "nothing personal", something about angles and editing . . . oh, and that Maria woman already called three times to see if you were here. We can fob her off if you like . . . unless you want to call her?"

Werner thought for a moment. Usually he would just go along with things, "get rid of her," he would say. But he thought of the notes he composed on the train, and his determination to start doing the right thing.

"I'll call her back. I didn't leave things on good terms last night. My fault, as you might expect."

"Oh?" the assistant looked genuinely surprised, "I thought she was a friend of your . . . "

"A friend of my wife's?" he interrupted. "Let's say that was one of my little *untruths*."

"Well, it's none of my business, of course. There's a telephone in the office you can use."

"Thank you." Werner couldn't help but smile. Honesty felt incredibly liberating. It was somehow subversive, wicked even. He hoped the feeling would become addictive.

"Darling, I've had some time to think, and . . . I didn't get the chance, sorry it . . . we had some problems with Egon this morning . . . it's the *truth*! Honestly . . . of course I want to see you . . . in fact . . . oh, okay that's fine. I hope she feels better . . . well not exactly *better* then, but you know what I mean . . . Maria, please, I wanted to tell you . . . no, that's fine. See you at rehearsal? . . . Bye, then darling . . . bye."

"Everything all right, Herr Krauss?" His assistant began combing his hair flat, in order to correctly fit his wig and hat.

"I can never seem to get it right, you know? Sometimes she's all over me – cheerful, affectionate, and easy-going – then *I'm* not in the mood. But when I want to talk, or I feel *good* about something . . . well, you can guess . . . "

"You're talking about . . . Maria?"

"Yes, of course."

"What about your wife?"

Werner just stared at his assistant, via the mirror. This honesty mask was already starting to feel uncomfortable.

"We've not really been together *properly* for ages, dear. We're good friends and we've helped each other out a lot over the years. A lot. More like a brother and sister, you know? But the marriage? Not really a marriage . . . " he fell silent. Why was he talking like this? He couldn't even remember this woman's name, yet he was giving her his life story.

"Perhaps you'll never really get things right with this . . . Maria . . . " she hesitated,

"Go on . . . "

"While you're still married. But, like I said, it's none of my business."

"No, you're right. Completely. It's exactly what I was thinking. So easy, just *talking* about these things though, eh? So difficult trying to do them . . . "

Waiting with Conrad while the lighting rigs were repositioned, Werner wanted to continue in this spirit of honesty. It was starting to feel like an experiment.

"Sorry I was out-of-order yesterday, Con . . . "

"It's okay. Sorry I called you a fat bastard. You're not fat . . . "

"It's fine – don't worry. Friends?" He held out his hand.

"Of course." Conrad shook firmly. "Though I still haven't forgotten the money . . . "

"What money?"

"You owe me – five marks. Remember?"

"Oh.. yes . . . I'll get it to you next week."

"Nice shoes were they?"

"What shoes?"

"The shoes you needed the money for – shoes for your son – remember?"

"Oh, yes. They were fine. Leather. Good fit. Thank you."

Conrad climbed into the casket and lay down.

"Everyone ready? We're going to try this a few times. Happy, Werner?"

"Always happy when you're around, Robert . . . "

"Here we go then . . . *und aktion*!"

The policemen burst into the room. Caligari stood perfectly still. The officers opened the casket and did all they could to revive the Somnambulist. Caligari's eyes snaked from left to right. He seemed cold, quietly enraged by the police presence.

"Wake him!"

He twisted his neck, and looked on with distain. More policemen entered. They began to dart around the room frantically. One of them grabbed a newspaper.

HOLSTENWALL
MURDERER
CAUGHT

―――――――

*Attempts third
killing*

Removing his top hat, Caligari took a lunging, sarcastic bow.

"Cut! Werner – great work. Well done everyone. Stay where you are, Werner, we want some reactions on a close shot. Moving straight on, okay?"

"Just the eyes, Robert?"

" . . . and a grimace, we still want the *threat*. Let's imply menace."

"You got it."

"*Aktion!*"

"I'm looking for Frau Bard – am I in the right place?"

"And you are?"

"I'm here to see her daughter, Maria. My name is . . . "

"Well this *is* an honour. You must be Herr Krauss – we've all heard lots about you. Come this way." The nurse strode away from Werner briskly. "I'm afraid she's been complaining a lot recently. And with good reason. She's in a lot of pain. Her daughter's been an absolute angel though – you're a very lucky man."

"I am, you're right."

"Wait until I tell the others, they'll all want to see you. Will you be signing autographs?"

"Another time, maybe. This is just a quick visit."

The nurse stopped.

"Fine. Of course. You'll find them on your left, in the ward at the far end of this corridor. Is there anything I can do?"

"No. Thanks for your help."

Performing an about-turn, she marched back towards the reception. It was only now, approaching the ward that Werner realised what the various smells were. They got stronger and stronger – a pungent smell of bleach, overwhelmed by the stench of urine and faeces. This was where Maria was spending most of her days, and she hardly complained.

"Werner, what a surprise – what are you doing here?"

"Could we talk for a moment?"

"Aren't you going to say '*hallo*' to mother? She's been longing to meet you."

"*Guten Tag* Frau Bard . . . " he peered over to find a surprisingly young woman lying there. Her breathing was heavy. "Please, I just need a few minutes?"

"You can do your talking here. It's nothing I haven't heard before." Frau Bard's voice was grating and reedy.

"Maria, please?"

"Alright!" She turned to the bed. "Mother, I'll be back soon, okay?"

They found a seat in the waiting room.

"I just wanted to say 'sorry', Maria."

"What are you sorry for?"

"The way I've been acting. The way I treated you last night. I just wanted to tell you, I've been thinking, and you *are* the most important thing to me. I'm serious."

"You've said this before, Werner. You were moving in with me, remember? Then a day later you're back at home with your wife . . . So, what's changed this time?"

"What's changed is that I haven't been doing things properly. I just drifted, from one day to the next, not really focusing on what's important."

"So? What are you going to do?"

"Just trust me, okay? I have a plan to sort everything out, once and for all."

"Let's say I believe you . . . " She smiled. "Are you staying with me then, until we cycle to rehearsal?"

"No, I actually need to go home now . . . so I'll meet you there. And don't worry, it's all part of the plan . . . "

He took the train home, not knowing exactly what he was going to say. He just wanted to be honest – 'be guided by honesty', he thought.

She kissed and kissed and kissed. "Thank you! No one's ever been as nice to me as you before." Holtkamp had got the girl straight in with the military touring company. She would be assigned to menial jobs like washing, mending clothes, and cleaning the living quarters.

"You're welcome!" Werner couldn't remember feeling this happy before. When he had been given *his* big chance, all he could feel was nervousness and relief. "But now you have to do something for me . . . "

"Anything!"

"Promise that you'll write to me whenever you can?"

"Sorry . . . I'd love to, but . . . "

" . . . you can't write?" She shook her head. "Well, that's okay, it's something you can learn while you're away. I learned loads of things I'd have never known otherwise."

" . . . like how to talk to street girls?"

Werner blushed.

"Yes, that. Anyway, maybe you could ask someone to write for you?"

"Good idea, I'll do my best." She hugged him again. "You know what the best thing is about all this?"

"What?"

"I can start doing something about my drinking. Come on, you must've noticed?"

"Not really," he lied.

"I usually drink half a bottle of vodka in the morning, just to get me through the day. Just so I don't *feel* anything . . . "

"I think I understand."

"I don't even like it – makes me look and smell *awful*. Hopefully this chance will help me to give up."

"I hope so too."

"And I've got you to thank!" Again, she kissed and kissed him. He wondered if things might go further. All of this contact was definitely causing adolescent stirrings . . .

"You're such a sweetie. Honestly, if there's anything I can do?"

Did she mean *anything*? Werner started to panic.

"What's going to happen with Hirsch, then? Won't he want to know where you are? And what about your . . . you know . . . *Klienten*?"

"Ha, you're funny! *Klienten*! I couldn't care less about any of them – ugly, desperate bastards. As for Hirsch, who knows? Maybe one day he'll get off his high horse and try to find me again. But I don't care anymore, I'll be long gone . . . "

"You're not frightened?"

"Not now. I'm pretty excited. Don't get me wrong, though, a couple of days sober and I'll be petrified!"

For a moment there was silence between them. Werner felt a lump in his throat, he really liked her, he really would miss her.

"You know what's weird?" He said.

"No, what?"

"I never once asked your name . . . "

"What are you doing home at this time of day?"

Werner pushed past his wife and entered the front room. He cleared his throat.

"We need to talk. There are things that have to be said." He was clutching the notebook in his left hand. He had tucked his index finger inside the book, to mark the page headed '*Paula, marriage, etc.*'

"You'll just have to say them another time. I can't have you here now."

She clasped his shoulder as if to usher him out. He pushed her arm away.

"For God's sake, this *is* my house. You *are* my wife."

Paula cackled sarcastically. "You could've fooled me. Whatever it is, come back tonight, okay? Please Werner, let's not fight about this."

"You're not joking, are you? I just came all the way from Weißensee. I wanted to sort things out between us. This is a fucking farce!"

"You said it, Werner."

He shoved past Paula and out of the door.

Werner sat alone on a wooden bench on the platform. Having spent so long pursuing Maria like a salivating dachshund, jumping from the studio to the theatre, chasing money and fame, he truly hadn't realised exactly how much Paula had changed. She seemed so distant now. It was quite a trick she'd pulled off: to make a man feel like an intruder in his own home – a stranger to his own children. He wiped his eyes: it wasn't her fault, *he* was the one that changed – all she had done was to adapt. She was a survivor – one of the reasons he had fallen for her all those years ago. She had the ability to move-on and show strength, be positive. After all she had gone through when she was younger, he never thought he would be adding to her problems, joining the list of despicable men who had used her. *Had* he used her?

His train blustered into the station, but he wasn't ready to leave. He watched it come and go. Perhaps he would find an *Autobus* to take him to the theatre, or catch the next train. Looking back, perhaps Paula had arrived in his life at the time he needed a strong woman. Although when he first ran away, he had felt angry towards her, bitter and guilty, above all he simply *missed* his mother. For those first few days, Paula became someone he could confide in, and look up to. Then when Reinhardt had taken him on, and insisted he got a wife, "lest, people think you're a dandy-boy, Werner . . . " she was there for him then, too.

But why was he worrying about *her*? Shouldn't he stop feeling so guilty – wasn't *she* was the one servicing the *charming* Herr Kohl every afternoon? *She* was the one who had confused things between them the other night, slipping in and out of the dark like a gloriously baffling dream. And *she* was the one who couldn't even spare a minute for him to talk seriously to her, and try to convey what he was thinking. He turned to his notebook – perhaps his plans should change. He scribbled one word. Stared at it a moment, then added a question mark.

Revenge?

"Werner, where have you been? Wengel is frantic – said he needs to see you right away."

"I know, I know, sorry." He tried to plant a kiss on Maria's cheek, but in his haste caught the edge of her ear.

"Don't apologise to me. How did the plan go? Did you speak to your wife?"

"Not exactly . . . we'll have to talk later."

"We'll go for a drink then?"

"Yes," he strode away from her, "definitely!"

As he charged across the auditorium, trying to find Wengel, he could hear snatches of conversations between the other actors:

"I'm telling you, he tried to kiss her . . . "

"They were together yesterday, *and* the day before . . . "

It was a bizarre sensation for Werner – having his personal life discussed and having no control over what was said. He'd read interviews with other, older actors complaining about the gossip that appeared in newspapers and magazines, and thought they should stop complaining and get on with it. A fairly harmless side effect, he assumed. But now it was happening to him and he loathed it. What business was it of theirs? Didn't they have their own lives to get on with?

"Werner, finally! Can we have a word, dear?" Wengel grabbed him by the wrist, and took him backstage.

"I'm really sorry, lateness is unforgivable, I know . . . "

"Don't worry, you're here now, that's what matters. Actually, I wanted to talk to you about that interview you gave."

"Right, I completely forgot to look in the paper for it – is it okay?"

"The interview's fine – should make a splendid advert for the play. No, it was the interview*er* I was interested in."

"Okay . . . " Werner said slowly, " . . . what about him?"

"You didn't notice anything strange? Was he maybe a bit . . . down, a bit depressed?"

"I don't know about that. He was certainly odd. Spent the whole interview trying to argue with me, contradicting, interrupting, then got up and said 'don't worry, I won't write any of that, the interview will be fine,' So I just took his word for it."

"Sounds about right," he leaned in to whisper, "he's dead, Werner. That's why I've been looking for you. The police were here earlier."

"God, that's terrible."

"Isn't it?"

"So it was . . . " Werner didn't want to say the word.

"Suicide? Yes. His wife found him in the bath this morning with his wrists gashed open. He had three children too."

"What makes someone *do* that?"

Wengel just shrugged. "So anyway, you might have to give a statement. Your interview was the last thing he submitted to the paper."

"I can't believe it. I mean, he was *strange*, but not sombre. In fact, he was pretty manic, kind of menacing, you know?"

"Probably knew he was going to do it, then. Was relieved – didn't care what he said to you."

They both stood silently for a moment, staring at the crimson carpet beneath them.

"Right, well we'd better get on with it, Werner."

"Sure. Oh, and sorry for being late. Few problems with the kids this morning."

"I'll forgive you if you give a great performance." He smiled, "*And* if you turn up to the date I've arranged for you tonight . . . "

"Date? What date?"

"You and Hessler – remember our deal?"

"Werner, you can't afford this . . . " Maria whispered behind her menu,

"Shh! It'll be okay." He knew it was stupid pride, but Werner had got them a table at the *Adlon*, one of the best hotels in Berlin. "Hope you're hungry, Hessler?"

"I don't know what to say, Herr Krauss. I've certainly never been anywhere like this before. Don't take this the wrong way, but it almost feels *too* splendid, you know, excessive."

"Call me Werner, please," he couldn't quite remember if he'd successfully maintained his honesty policy throughout the day, but decided this would be a good time to try it out again. "And that's exactly what I was thinking. Makes you feel sick, doesn't it? All this food going to waste when the rest of the country's in the state it's in."

"So . . . why did you bring us here then?"

"Hopeless pride – ridiculous vanity!" He adopted his upper-class English accent: "one does what one can, old boy!" Hessler and Maria laughed heartily. He started to click his fingers at the waiter, "What oh, old boy, come on now, chop, chop, chop, what, what, what!"

"Stop it, Werner!" Blushing, Maria's smile shrunk. "He's actually coming over . . . "

The waiter's suit looked more expensive than Werner's.

"Everything satisfactory, sir?"

"Marvellous, thank you! We just need a few more minutes to decide . . . "

"Very good, sir."

Like two naughty school children, Werner's small audience was in hysterics.

"I had you all wrong, Krauss . . . sorry . . . Werner. You're hilarious."

"He's not always like this you know . . . " Maria said.

"Really? Do tell, sweet Maria!"

They laughed again. Werner was pleased he'd somehow made the date-from-hell into a reasonably enjoyable night.

"So why did you want me here then, in all seriousness?" Hessler asked.

"To be completely honest, I didn't . . . "

"Go on . . . "

"Wengel pretty much forced me. Thinks you're a precocious talent – whatever that means. But I'm glad you're here now – we can talk about absolutely anything." Hessler was quiet. Perhaps Werner had hurt his feelings. "Go on, ask anything."

"Alright then. How did *you* get into films – you know, the first time?"

"Ah, you see I had a guardian angel. And, I actually *started* in films, more or less . . . "

"Have you heard of Max Reinhardt?" Maria interrupted.

"Of course . . . "

"It was him! He plucked Werner out of obscurity . . . "

"There was nothing obscure about the Gestunghausen travelling players," Werner joked.

"But you know what I mean . . . " she continued, "He just saw Werner perform one day, down in Breslau, and that was it – took him under his wing – put him straight into a film. Isn't that wonderful?"

"More luck than anything, dear," Werner said.

"So Reinhardt acted as your mentor – used his influence, pulled some strings – because he believed in you?"

"I suppose so, yes." Werner could see where Hessler was heading with this . . .

"And out of the blue, *you* asked *me* to dinner with you . . . "

"Under duress, remember?" He interrupted. "Let's not get ahead of ourselves. Presumption isn't becoming of you."

Hessler laughed. "Of course, I know. I understand. But I probably *do* need help – when I first started, the opportunities came flooding in, the roles just got bigger and bigger, until a couple of years ago . . . things seemed to have reached . . . "

"A plateau?" Maria interrupted.

"Exactly. And I don't know what to do. I don't want to end up as some bit-player. Don't want to just be an onlooker . . . "

"If you want me to be completely straight with you . . . "

"Please do . . . "

"I guess you're seen as a bit of a risk – you've got to admit, you do go against the grain a little. Producers are out there that probably *want* to cast you, but they don't want the headaches that come with it."

"What headaches? Come on, Werner, I'm not that bad."

"I can only go by what I hear on the grapevine. But what about that business between you and Ziegler's wife?"

"That was nothing, a bit of harmless, friendly . . . chitchat."

"You know they split up after that?"

"Not my fault. Honestly. He was screwing every young actress that came his way – and his wife knew it."

"You don't have to tell me. The point is, other actors – *leading men* – don't get involved in such things – they just keep themselves to themselves. Think of Marian, or Conrad who I'm working with at the moment. A bit of shyness doesn't hurt, you know? If you're causing a scene and getting under people's skins all the time offstage what's left for them to see *on* the stage?"

"I get it. Thanks, Werner."

They ate *Cancarneau* with asparagus and Werner was surprised how much he had enjoyed the evening. Being around Hessler actually made him feel younger – like an older brother rather than the ranting grandfather he thought he'd become. The three of them stepped out into the Berlin chill.

"I really can't thank you enough, Werner." They shook hands firmly.

"It's nothing, really. Been good to get to know you properly – shouldn't believe everything you hear about people, eh?"

"You said it."

"In fact, I was thinking, if it's a film you want, I could maybe have a chat to Wiede and Pommer when I go in for some re-shoots tomorrow. Knowing them, they're probably thinking two films in advance of the one they're on anyway, so they might have something for you."

"Werner, what can I say?"

"Don't say anything. Just start keeping your nose clean and out of other people's business." They both smiled. Hessler held out his hand again, and when Werner took it to shake, Hessler pulled him into an embrace.

"I won't forget this, Werner. Thank you."

Back at Maria's apartment, they opened a bottle to celebrate their evening of reconciliation.

"You see, I told you he wasn't that bad."

"I know, I know. You were right as always . . . "

"Your problem is you think all younger people are out to undermine you. All Hessler needed was a bit of advice."

"Come here." Maria joined him on the sofa, they embraced and kissed. He tried to think of the right words to say to her. It was part of his plan, to be honest with her, and tell her how much he loved her. But he was so tired, his back ached and his head was spinning with problems and ideas.

"You're great, you know." he could barely keep his eyes open.

"That's very sweet of you, Werner."

"And whatever happens, just remember, I love you."

She took him by the hand and led him upstairs to her bedroom. He quickly undressed and slid into the single bed. He wanted to watch her undress: her long, supple legs, her perfect breasts and slender waist. But as his head hit the pillow, he struggled to concentrate. He felt her squeeze in beside him, held out his hand and stroked her back. She was talking but he couldn't really hear . . .

He looked at his watch again and again. He wasn't sure exactly when his audition was, but he felt as though it was five minutes away. The second hand on his watch seemed to crawl slowly. He wondered why nobody else was waiting to be seen, and why he didn't have a script. "It must be a done-deal," he thought, "a formality". Everyone wants the wondrous Herr Krauss in their film. Everyone. Was it a film, or a play? It didn't matter. He looked at his watch again – had any time passed? He tried to take in his surroundings. This waiting room was better kept, much more formal than any he had been used to. And the doors along the adjoining corridor, they looked like the doors to offices, not studios. What was going on?

'Calm down, Werner,' he thought. You don't get nervous. You're Werner Krauss, after all. They're probably nervous waiting for you. He looked at his watch again, but didn't really take any notice of the hands or numbers. Why was he waiting? Why did they want him?

Then, a door opened. A white light burst from the door, and a figure emerged. He looked familiar, with a satisfied grin sliced into his face. Was it Conrad? Weine? Hessler? He couldn't tell – his eyes were stinging so he had to close them. There was a sour, warm taste in his mouth, which made him want to spit, but he couldn't spit in these genteel surroundings.

"Herr Krauss, we'll see you now."

He stepped into the light and passed into the room. He saw a long table, behind which sat three people: one woman and two men.

"Please be seated, Herr Krauss."

He found a solitary chair at the other side of the room, and dragged it over to the table.

"I'm not too sure why I'm here," he said. The three strangers just laughed.

"Very good, Herr Krauss, very funny indeed. Now, I'd like you to start by telling us why you'd like the job . . . "

It was the woman and she seemed incredibly serious. He felt so confused. What should he say?

"I have worked as an actor for several years, in films and theatre shows, working with some of the finest directors and . . . "

"With all due respect, Herr Krauss," one of the men interrupted, "we'd like to know about your work experience. Please let us know what real work you've done. For instance, presumably you served in the war?"

"Actually, no. Although I performed in several fund-raising shows and benefit concerts. We even went to the front-line with a travelling company for a few months . . . "

The woman sighed noisily.

"But what about work experience?" she enunciated each word harshly, as though talking to an imbecile. "Don't you have children? And a wife? Surely you should be providing for them with some real work, something tangible?"

"Acting does provide, it is real work. Last year I earned . . . "

"Please, carry on."

"The point is, I earn enough. And I'm in a very good film which promises to be successful."

"I think we've probably heard enough, Herr Krauss. You can be on your way now."

"What about the job?"

"We'll let you know," said the woman.

"Yes, we'll let you know," the two men chimed in unison.

"Thank you." Werner said, and stood. He wanted to spit. He wanted to shout. But he shook each of their hands, in spite of their disapproving, smug expressions. "Thank you," he said again, "thank you."

"Werner, please!" Maria was shaking him. "I'm so tired, and it's the big day tomorrow."

"What, sorry, what's wrong?"

"You keep shuffling around and kicking me. It really hurts . . . "

"I'm sorry, I'm really sorry." He lay flat on his back. The bed sheets were drenched in his sweat. Already, the memories of his dream were fading – he felt so frustrated, so damn *guilty*. "I have these really bad dreams sometimes . . . I'm going to get a drink. Do you want anything?"

"No," she kissed his forehead, "just for you to calm down and get some sleep, poor thing. You know how long I waited for us to be able to sleep together like this?"

He crept out of the bedroom, and did his best to feel his way to the kitchen in the dark. The glasses were perfectly arranged in the cupboard – he felt guilty just taking one out of its place. He gulped one glass of water, then re-filled.

"Werner! Darling, come back to bed . . . "

"I'll be there in a minute . . . " he started to sip.

"No. Get in here now!"

He threw the remaining water in the sink, and felt his way back to the bedroom. Maria cast aside the bed sheets.

"You've woke me up now, and I'm not taking 'no' for an answer . . . "

She looked stunning. "Darling, we should wait . . . "

"Stop worrying," she said, and stroked the small space next to her on the bed.

6

He could hear Maria fussing around in the adjoining room.

"Darling, what're you doing?" he asked.

"Just some tidying. I'll bring your breakfast in soon."

"Can't you come in now, just for a minute?"

She came straight in. "What is it, Werner? I'm just trying to get my jobs done."

"I know. Sorry." He felt like a spoilt child who was being reprimanded. "I just wanted a quick cuddle. I can't believe how *sexy* you were last night. I never knew you . . . "

"Stop it, Werner!" She interrupted, and kissed him on his forehead, "I'll be in soon with breakfast."

As he lay there, he had an aching, guilty feeling. If his plan was to work, he had *so* much to do today – he had no time for snoozing and breakfast. He found his clothes folded neatly next to the bed, reached insider his trouser pocket, and consulted his notebook. "Don't worry about breakfast, darling." He said, and rolled out of bed.

"Why not? I've told you I'll bring it in a minute . . . "

"No, it's fine. Let's meet up for lunch though. In *Alexanderplatz*, okay?"

"Whatever you say. I'm sure it's all part of your . . . "

"It's all part of my plan."

Naked, he wandered into her meticulously kept bathroom, and filled the sink with water. Rubbing his body with her perfumed soap, yet again he felt a pang of inferiority. How could she find *this* body even remotely attractive? He noticed the snaking veins on his calves and his sagging, womanly chest. Why didn't she want to be with someone young, like Hessler? Using a flannel, he began to wipe away the foamy residue, and sheepishly looked at himself in the mirror. He really *had* to start exercising regularly, otherwise he would start to feel like this every day, in the company of this beautiful young girl.

On the train journey, he opened his notebook and started to make alterations to the page headed 'Opening Night.' Yet again, his sums didn't add up, and he considered asking Pommer, the producer, for an advance on his wages for *Dr. Caligari*.

'Too *gauche*?' he wrote.

He needed a way to find money fast. Maybe he could ask Conrad, he thought. But – *Scheiße* – he already owed him money as it was.

"So what's brought this on then, Werner?" As he had feared, Paula was suspicious. It had been over two years since he had taken her to a performance, when he had played Guildenstern back in Graz. "What's so special about tonight's show that you want *me* to come along all of a sudden?"

"No one's forcing you to come. It would just be good if you did. Would give us a chance to talk afterwards. That's all." He grabbed his coat, gave Rudi a kiss and left. Somehow he knew she would come.

The bright glow of the jewellery counter strip-light stung Werner's eyes, like a light of interrogation. He swallowed hard. Apart from this counter, the room was dark and gloomy. He had never entered a pawnbroker's before, having assumed they were just a haven for the gamblers and criminals who needed quick money and no questions. It was a couple of minutes before the owner appeared from behind the security caging; he was an old Jew, wearing a young man's suit.

"Hello my friend. Buying, selling, neither, either or both?"

Werner smiled. You had to give these Jews credit – they knew how to do business.

"Both actually. I need to buy a ring, and thought this might help me pay." He produced the pocket watch and slid it across the counter.

"Nice, very nice indeed. Anything you ought to tell me about it?"

"No. Not really . . . " he hesitated, "other than it's pretty valuable." Inwardly, he cringed. The Jew smiled.

"Is that so? Well, why don't you take a look at some rings while I inspect this lovely piece of yours?"

He turned and took the watch into a back room. Werner's stomach was dancing with guilt as he tried to concentrate on the rings. Each probably told its own story: of desperate widowers, bitter divorcees, or of thieves like his son. He knew Maria preferred silver, but there were hardly any suitable silver rings here. They were mostly thick gold bands – garish and jewel encrusted. One of these would have to do. From the little he knew about the pawnbroker's, he knew you got a better deal with an exchange; there was still a distrust of the value of cash around town. A small ruby, sat atop a modest but pretty gold band caught his eye. It would suit Maria's delicate hand, he thought.

"Seen one you like, my friend?" The Jew was back. "I think we can definitely do some business Herr . . . ?"

"Caligari, Werner Caligari." The Jew had slipped his hand through the small opening in the cage. Werner shook it limply, dreading the imminent bartering session.

"Who's the lucky girl then, Herr Caligari, anyone I know?" The Jew's friendly conversation was disarming.

"I don't think so. She's not from around here, she's lives in Cologne . . . "

"Long-distance love. How charming."

"Yes. I was quite interested in this one, actually." Werner pointed at the ruby ring.

"A shrewd choice, Herr Caligari." The Jew began fumbling with a bunch of keys behind the counter. He unlocked the cabinet and slid out the tray of jewellery. "This is eighteen carat, Herr Caligari, with a sizeable jewel, a splendid ring if ever I saw one."

"So what about the pocket watch?"

"It's nice, very nice. It would fetch around . . . twenty marks."

"And the ring?"

"The ring is worth fifty at least."

Werner said nothing. It was an uncomfortable, agonising silence. He hoped the Jew would suggest a deal, an alternative, something. But he didn't. The Jew seemed happy with the silence – he was in control.

"But this is all I have," he volunteered, and immediately felt stupid for doing so.

"Most unfortunate, Herr Caligari . . . and such a nice ring." The silence returned. Again, the Jew smiled. Werner wanted to get out of there, but he knew he must get rid of the watch as soon as he could. Eventually, the Jew spoke again:

"Excuse my impertinence, Herr Caligari. But may I ask about the ring on *your* finger? It is unusual for a man to have a ring before his bride, is it not?"

Werner stretched out the fingers on his left hand, and surveyed his thick gold wedding ring. As if trying to offload stolen goods wasn't embarrassing enough – now the old Jew was quizzing him. Annoyed, he held his hand up to the cage:

"Alright, what about it then? I'll give you this *and* the watch, for the ring and . . . and fifteen marks."

Again, the silence resumed, but Werner was pleased with himself for being so assertive. The Jew pressed his face up against the caging to inspect the ring.

"Interesting. Let me take a closer look."

Werner struggled to prise it off his finger, where it had been for the last seven years. When it eventually came off, a red dent was left at the base of his finger.

"Give me your hand, Herr Caligari."

Tentatively, Werner pushed his hand through the small gap in the cage. The Jew cupped it firmly.

"I know you must be in a bit of trouble here. But I am an honest man and I'll be honest with you." He began to whisper, as if in prayer, and shook Werner's hand as he did so. "This ring you've shown me is very nice indeed. I will agree to this exchange. The ring and fifteen marks – it's yours. But you must promise you will come back to me again next time . . . " the whisper became barely audible, " . . . and I will give you a special deal. Special prices for you from now on, Herr Caligari".

Werner felt foolish. He knew this meant his ring must've been worth a fortune. He'd never bothered to ask Paula where she had got it from, or what it was worth. But he knew it would have had to go eventually, and he needed a ring for Maria if his plan was to work. He had to concede – the Jew had charmed him: "It's a deal."

"Werner . . . you remember what we did . . . last night?"

"Pretty difficult to forget . . . "

"Well, you know that means you *have* to sort it all out now . . . don't you?"

"I will, I will – I have a plan, remember?"

"I've told you . . . I can't do this forever."

"And I've told you . . . you won't have to. It'll be all over, and sooner than you think."

"Really? What are you going to do? Are you going to tell her it's me you're with? Or won't you mention that part?"

"You want it done, and it will get done."

"Always so secretive. I suppose you think I wouldn't understand. I'm just a girl, after all."

"You *are* just a girl I'm afraid, my darling . . . but I, for one, won't hold it against you."

She gave a rueful smile. They kissed and he left the café. Werner knew this was by no means ideal. In fact, he knew it was a pretty lousy thing to do. The children were old enough to understand exactly how he had left their mother, and they would probably think it unforgivable. But at least he could put an end to the lies and suspicion. He needed to do this now and make a clean break, before *Das Cabinet* was in the cinemas, and his private life might begin to interest people. If the rumours were to be believed, the film really was going to be big, in *Deutschland* and beyond. If this was true, Werner needed to be prepared. He could employ an agent full-time, and get a new place in the centre of Berlin. Paula and the family were holding him back, but Maria was energetic and ambitious, like him. Together they could take on the world.

The ritual had begun many years ago, as a practical joke. Werner had only been with the travelling company for a couple of weeks, when one of the older boys, Karl, had given him some advice.

"Want to know the best thing to do if you want to be a good actor? You know, *really* good?"

Werner shook his head.

"Trust me, if you want to be relaxed and confident when you get onstage, you should . . . you know . . . clean your pipes just before you go on."

"Which pipes? What are you talking about?"

"You know, play with yourself – have a wank. I do it all the time, gets rid of all that tension and helps you focus."

"That's disgusting." Werner said. "Is it honestly what you do?"

"Always. Especially if I'm in a romantic scene, with one of the girls.

You don't want the whole audience to see you get a stiffy, do you?"

Werner had to admit, there was a peculiar logic to this advice. He did think that some of the girls were fantastically attractive, which had made him slightly reluctant to volunteer for romantic scenes.

"Thanks Karl, I'll bear it in mind."

The next day, before the first workshop began, Karl approached Werner again:

"So, you gonna do it?"

"There's nowhere *to* do it."

"Sure there is – just slip into the toilet there for ten minutes. We all do it. Trust me."

Werner shrugged and headed to the lavatory. He didn't usually like being so easily led, but Karl was one of the really popular boys, and he seemed pretty smart. Werner locked the cubicle door and pulled down his trousers. The pungent smell and damp flooring were anything but arousing. Nevertheless, he pulled down his underwear and closed his eyes, trying to remember one of the few encounters with girls he had had up to that point. He thought of Emily, a girl he had left back in Gestunghausen. They had kissed once or twice, and she had let him feel her breasts a few weeks before he had ran away. He imagined ripping off her dress and getting to grips with her voluptuous body. Now things were happening. He stretched out in the cubicle, flexing his neck muscles; he opened his eyes and stared at the ceiling. Relaxing again, he looked down, and noticed something taped to the cistern. It was a photograph of a naked African tribeswoman. She had huge, sagging bosoms, and was balancing a basket on top of her head. Underneath the photograph was some scrawled handwriting: 'something to get you going, Werner'. He felt breathless with embarrassment. He knew he had already been in the toilet too long to pretend he hadn't done anything, but he certainly couldn't carry on. He felt sick, and quickly got re-dressed, doing his best to hide his semi-erection.

He left the lavatory to find Karl and his friends, pointing and laughing.

"Did it do the trick, Werner?"

"Did the photo of the negro help you out?"

Despite this humiliation, Werner tried Karl's 'method' again when he left the travelling company. He enjoyed the danger of it, the audacity. The grim surroundings of a toilet cubicle or an empty dressing room certainly demanded an adventurous imagination. And what better way for an actor to prepare, than to fire up his imagination? Some of his colleagues through the years had wondered why he disappeared so close to stage time, assuming he had adopted some form of exotic meditation. They were most impressed, especially as he would always emerge calm and relaxed in time for the performance.

Fifteen minutes before stage time at the Staatstheater, Werner was alone in the gents' toilets. Despite his wife's suspicions, he still hadn't actually *made love* with Maria, as such. Now, thoughts of their few sensual encounters were running through his mind. Alone at the party where they first met, and the feel of her lips on him last night. Just the thought of her young body drove him to distraction.

"*You* knock!"

"*I'm* not knocking. He knows you – he won't mind."

Dani and Thomas, who were playing Albany and Cornwall, were arguing outside the lavatory. Werner pulled up his trousers.

"You're such a child. Get out the way."

There was a knock at the toilet door. Werner tried to compose himself.

"I said I wasn't to be disturbed – what is it?"

"Herr Krauss, I'm very sorry. There's someone here to see you."

"Tell them there's only ten fucking minutes until we're on!"

"It's your wife, Herr Krauss."

He washed his hands, checked himself in the mirror and emerged from the lavatory. Thomas led him to the outside door at the rear of the theatre.

"Thanks. Find Herr Wengler and tell him we might need ten minutes."

"Yes, of course."

Outside, Paula was arm-in-arm with Kohl. They were huddling in the cold, smoking cigarettes. Werner couldn't deny he was shocked to see them together, especially in public.

"What's going on?" he said.

"Werner, this is Julius. Now I don't know exactly why you insisted I came here tonight, but I've got something to tell you."

"I'd say that was pretty obvious. You do know I should be onstage now?"

"It won't take long. I'm leaving you, Werner. I'm taking the children and we're going to live with Julius. Don't try to stop me." Kohl pulled her even closer. Werner couldn't believe his luck.

"Alright. Fine . . . " he said. "But I get to visit the children, okay? I'm still their father. You both understand that?"

Kohl grunted his assent. This was so easy.

"Great, well that's sorted then."

"And you're not in the least bit bothered? I'm talking about our marriage, Werner. Finished! *Kaputt!*"

"We both know there's not *been* a marriage, for years. I'm happy for you both, honestly."

"If that's how you feel – fine. Come on, Julius, let's get back."

"No. No, stay for tonight's show, please? There's no reason for us to be uncivilised, now, is there? I'll arrange an extra seat for Herr Kohl."

Meantime we shall express our darker purpose.

The curtain fell and Werner began jockeying for position. He was supposed to take his bow between Thomas and Dani, as they were in the final scene with him. Nevertheless, he firmly pulled the boys out of the way, securing his place next to Maria. He grabbed her hand, and they bowed for a warm applause as the curtain rose for the first time. As the curtain fell, he embraced her. "Trust me – it's all sorted" he said, closed his eyes and started to kiss her. As they kissed the curtain rose, he heard the crowd coo, and he knew his wife would be among them. He opened his eyes. Maria was red and seemed incredibly embarrassed. She turned back to the audience and gave a polite smile, then scampered off the stage. Werner stayed for the final curtain, pouting for the appreciative crowd. He noticed Paula and Kohl, sidestepping along their row to the aisle, and the exit.

He could hear the other actors talking about him as they left the stage:

"Didn't you say his wife was in tonight?"

"I told you there was something funny going on between those two."

He descended the rickety wooden steps into the backstage area, grabbed a gown and made his way to the small, communal dressing room. There was no sign of Maria. He fumbled through his pile of possessions until he found the briefcase. He opened it, and grabbed the jewellery box containing the ring. Knowing it was the only other place she could be, he turned back and headed for the female toilets. His fellow actors hushed to an awkward silence.

"Go get her, Werner. You only live once, old boy!" It was Hessler.

"A bit less of the 'old' if you don't mind." He couldn't help but smile. To think he'd had the nerve to lecture Hessler about settling down. As he pushed open the door to the lavatory, someone said:

"You can't go in there."

He ignored them, and went in. "Maria. Maria are you here?" he asked, in an unintentionally jovial way. There was no response, but he heard a sharp intake of breath and a sniffle come from one of the cubicles. "Maria, let me in, please? You don't understand – things have changed." Eventually, the cubicle door swung open. Weeping, Maria had curled up on top of the lavatory seat, clutching her knees in a foetal position.

"So that was your plan? That was your way of sorting things out?" she said, still crying. "You're a monster!"

"No – *she's* left *me*. She left me and got together with this . . . Kohl character, honestly. She told me before the show – that was why I was late starting. I just couldn't *wait* to kiss you . . . now we can set things straight once and for all. Maria, I'm sorry. But I did it because of you." Why *did* he do it that way? Did he always have to be so damn dramatic?

"Because of me? You humiliated that poor woman in front of everyone – that wasn't what I wanted. Why, Werner? Why did you have to do that in front of everyone?"

"What can I say? It's done now. Doesn't it make you happy?"

"I don't know, Werner. I don't know. If this is what you're capable of then . . . I can't help thinking . . . "

"Can't help thinking what?"

"That it's exactly how you'll be treating me, in a few years, when someone younger – and prettier – comes along."

"That won't happen, Maria – I love you."

"How can you be sure, Werner? How can *I* be sure?"

"I'm crazy about you, you know that, and . . . " he fumbled around in the pocket of his gown, pulled out the jewellery box and sunk to one knee, " . . . I know it's not the ideal place for this . . . " Maria laughed through her tears, " . . . but you'd make me the happiest man alive . . . if you'd say you'll marry me?" He opened the box.

Part Two

1

'"Words are inadequate to describe the linguistic and mimic variety of Werner Krauss' Shylock . . . "' He held a copy of the *Volkischer Beobachter* aloft like a script, away from his chest. "Listen to this: 'Every fibre of his body seems impregnated with Jewish blood; he mumbles, slavers, gurgles, grunts and squawks with alarming authenticity . . . '" He threw the official Party paper onto the bed, narrowly missing his wife's face. "How many times? '*Alarming* authenticity' indeed. This has to stop."

"Don't you think you're being a bit over-sensitive? It's a *good* review, Werner, good – encouraging – positive! Isn't that what you want?" Maria sat up, and lit a cigarette.

"I know it *looks* good – but I want to know what they're *implying*."

He waited for a response, but she remained impassive, tapping her cigarette against an ivory ashtray – a gift from the Party. Eventually she replied: "Did you read the whole piece?" and turned her attention to the review itself. "It goes on to say: 'everything demonic . . . little ghetto usurer . . . blah, blah . . . ah – here we are 'he becomes a *caricature*, especially together with the no less realistic Tubal of Ferdinand Maierhofer. An infernal puppet show.' See, it's quite clear you're not actually a Jew!"

"I suppose you're right. But I still want to do something about it." He stooped across the bed to kiss her, "One of the producers is holding a party tonight, at his house. I could go along to see what he thinks."

"Sounds good, it's been ages since we went to a party." They kissed, she slipped out of bed, and walked towards the long mirror at the far end of the room.

"I thought it might be for the best if I went alone," he said, nervously. "It'll just be a quick drink, you won't even know I've gone."

Maria fiercely combed through the tangles in her hair. "And why, exactly, would that be 'for the best?'"

"You know what the doctor said, Maria. You're not well enough, and you need time to get better."

"I'm fine and you know it." She began to shout, "You'd just rather I wasn't there, embarrassing you." She grabbed a dressing gown.

"Don't be silly . . . " he said. But she charged out of the bedroom, slamming the door behind her. The actor sighed, and started to undress. "Til thou canst rail the seal from off my bond – thou but offend'st thy lungs to speak so loud." He smiled at himself in the mirror. "Hath not a Jew hands, organs, dimensions, senses, affections, passions?"

He could hear Lothar talking to his wife in the kitchen. His driver always arrived early – Werner insisted upon it – but in truth he would rather he just waited outside in the car. These days, more often than not, he was walking into an argument or a crisis of some sort. It was embarrassing. Werner could picture him in the bar after his shift, gossiping to whoever would listen: "The great Werner Krauss obviously isn't so great in the bedroom – she was crying again today. She always makes me a coffee when I arrive, gives me a smile and a slice of cake. He just grunts and grabs his coat."

These people think it's so easy, thought Werner, they don't know the half of it.

"Good morning, Lothar. And how the devil are you today?"

"Very good, thank you, Herr Krauss."

"Can I get you anything? A soda, coffee, something a little stronger, perhaps?"

"Your good lady is making tea, thank you sir."

"Such a sweetie, isn't she?" He put his arm around Maria, and kissed her forehead. "I've told her she should get someone in to do all this, but she won't listen."

"I live to serve." She sounded sarcastic, but he was determined to avoid another argument.

"So, Lothar, how's your wife? And the children?"

"They're fine . . . thank you, Herr Krauss. My youngest starts school next week, so . . . " The driver sounded nervous.

"Don't bother him with silly questions, Werner." Maria handed Lothar his tea. "Let him enjoy his drink in peace."

"Don't they grow up so fast – the time just flies by. My eldest actually got engaged recently – my little Egon, can you believe it?" Lothar just shrugged. Werner realised he probably hadn't even mentioned his children before. "Doesn't seem like more than five minutes ago, he was still wetting the bed."

"Well, he'll have to do something about *that* before he gets married," Maria chirped in. Lothar sniggered.

"Ha! Quite a sense of humour this one, I tell you."

"Don't over-do it, Werner." She said.

As they arrived at the rehearsal building, a security guard dashed from his cabin to open Werner's door.

"Good journey, Herr Krauss?"

"It was fine, thank you." He slipped ten marks into the guard's jacket, as was customary. Although he had heard a rumour that Marian was now tipping twenty.

"Thank you, Herr Krauss. If there's anything I can do, just let me know."

The guard walked him through the corridor and into the rehearsal room.

"Werner, dear! You're looking splendid as ever – can we get you anything?" The director, Muthel, grabbed each of Werner's arms just below the shoulder and looked him up and down.

"A coffee would be good, I suppose."

Muthel clicked his fingers. "Let's get a coffee, over here *now*!" he yelled,

"Honestly, you have to beg for proper treatment these days . . . "

Werner laughed. "I suppose so. I don't really like to make a fuss."

"But you *must*. You really must, Werner, let them know who's boss."

"I'll bear that in mind."

"Alright you lot, you know why you're all here. There are still parts that need rehearsing and there are some changes that have been . . . sent from above, let's say . . . so shall we get on with it? You could all take a leaf from this man's book." He turned to Werner, "Werner didn't *have* to be here – his time is precious – but *he* wants to see you all get it right, and so do I, do you all understand?" The company of actors groaned in assent. "If any of you aren't sure – watch this man. *He's* the master."

The huddle of actors disbanded, and everyone found their position.

"What changes now then? Who's been sniffing around the script?"

"The *big* man, if you know what I mean . . . "

"Again? You'd think he'd have better things to do . . . "

"'This is *not* how Jew vermin behaves,' he said." Muthel's Goebbels impression was scarily accurate – it was high and whiny. Werner was trying not to laugh too hard, in case they were overheard. "'This speech, 'Hath a Jew not eyes', it is not essential in the story. It gives a misleading impression about their humanity!' The dwarf thinks he knows better than the Bard, now."

"So that speech is gone, really?"

"It's looking that way. He didn't ban it completely, in so many words, but I'm willing to bet there'll be a memo to that effect . . . "

"And the papers are already describing my performance as 'caricatured'."

"I know. *His* papers, Werner, don't forget, *his* papers."

Werner's first meeting with Goebbels was on the film set for *Hundert Tage*. Werner was in costume as Napoleon at the time, and somehow had the nerve to joke with the Minister.

"I would shake your hand, sir, but as you can see – " he gestured towards his right arm, which was tucked inside his jacket.

"Most amusing, Herr Krauss." Little Joseph seemed bewildered by this break with the customary etiquette. His three burly security men looked positively appalled.

"Pleasure to meet you, sir," he said, and quickly whipped his arm out of the jacket, to shake the Minister's hand firmly.

"I'm going to have to keep an eye on you, Krauss, I can tell." Laughing, Goebbels put his arm around Werner, and allowed him to conduct a tour of the set. Everyone breathed a sigh of relief, as Werner did his best to break the ice and continued to crack a few jokes. For some reason, he didn't feel as intimidated as those around him. Since the phenomenal success of *Das Cabinet des Dr. Caligari*, Werner had become used to meeting important people, and he knew better than anyone that they were just ordinary human beings. Everyone likes a joke, even the 'Little Gnome'. Werner simply couldn't understand the dread on the faces of those around him. "If you've done nothing wrong, you've nothing to worry about," he always said.

After the rehearsal, which now featured what Muthel regarded as 'barbaric' re-writes, Werner went for lunch with Ferdinand Marian, his co-star.

"So how are things, Werner? Life treating you well?"

"Splendidly thank you – I can't complain."

"Apart from having to re-learn half the play, you mean."

"Don't exaggerate, Ferdy, it's not so bad." Werner said.

Marian lit a cigarette, then offered another to his co-star. "You know what, soon everyone will be calling you 'Toes' Krauss, and not Werner."

Werner took the cigarette, and leaned in to share a light. "What, why on earth would anyone call me 'toes'?"

"Because you're so far up Goebbels' arse, it's all that we can still see of you!"

Obligingly, Werner laughed. "Okay, okay . . . so I like the easy life – it doesn't pay to make too many waves."

"Not everything comes down to 'paying', Werner. There's more to life than money . . . "

"Really, like what?" Again, they shared a smile. Werner ordered a bottle of *Rottwein*. "Not often we get a day off, eh? Might as well make the most of it."

"Doesn't Frau Krauss mind you drinking during the day?"

"Maria? No, of course not."

"And everything's all right . . . with her, is it?"

"She's fine – why do you ask?"

"No reason, really. Just that I haven't seen her in anything recently. There was a time when you couldn't go anywhere without seeing the name 'Maria Bard' in lights."

"All the more reason to take a break, wouldn't you say? She's being careful – doing her best not to become *over* exposed. It's a different business for women than for us." Werner felt quite pleased with his off-the-cuff rationale.

"That doesn't make sense, Werner. Since the war started, opportunities for women are everywhere."

Ferdy was starting to get irritating, "Well, *you* tell her that then. She can work in a hundred films a year for all I care."

"Sorry, Werner, I didn't mean to . . . I mean, it's none of my business . . . "

"No, *I'm* sorry. I shouldn't have snapped like that. She's not been feeling too well if you must know, so . . . "

"Nothing serious, I hope."

"No, no, she'll be fine. So anyway, tell me about you . . . are you still with . . . "

"Clara?"

"Clara, yes, of course . . . "

"Yes, we're still together. In fact, we're having a few friends around for dinner on Thursday night – we'd be thrilled if you and Maria could come along?"

"Just try to stop us! Sounds great, Ferdy, count us in." Werner clicked his fingers, trying to get the waiter's attention. "Another bottle!"

As instructed, Lothar arrived outside the restaurant to collect Werner, armed with a clean jacket and a breath-freshening spray. Lately, Maria had been complaining about his drinking. She didn't realise it was just a bit of sociable fun. Werner climbed into the back seat of his Mercedes.

"You're too good to me, Lothar," he said, "a life saver,"

"I do what I can, sir. Would you like me to take the jacket you're wearing, get it dry-cleaned?"

"Why not – splendid idea! Turning into a military operation this, isn't it, old chum?"

"I didn't realise you were in the military, sir?"

"Figure of speech, old boy. Get your foot down."

Stepping into the apartment, he was overcome by the smell of detergents and furniture polish. He started to sneeze.

"You've got a bright red face and you've been out for lunch, Werner. Now that's a surprise . . . "

"What's that suppose to mean? If my face is red it's a reaction to this stupid *stuff* you use. The house is already clean, you don't have to . . . " Catching sight of her face, he stopped talking. "Sorry. But if you're implying that I'm drunk, then you're wrong."

Otto Weitner answered the door with a bottle of port lodged in his armpit. He pulled the actor in, and slapped him on the shoulder: "Knew you'd come to one of my shindigs in the end, Werner, you old *Hund*."

He smiled. Otto was so difficult to work with anywhere near a theatre, yet in home surroundings he was quite charming.

"Still a stickler for the *Rotwein?*" Otto bashed his guest on the shoulder again.

"Please. Make it large."

"Good man, that's what I like to hear."

Otto's ground floor apartment was heaving with guests, most of them unknown to Werner. It was a warm July evening and he felt uncomfortable. It seemed years since he had attended a gathering like this on his own. As he poured the wine, Otto continued to joke about alcohol, about how it was the cure of all life's ills and the cause of none, etc. etc.

But the actor wasn't concentrating. He had noticed a short, blonde girl staring at him from across the room, and he gave her an embarrassed smile. She turned away, at which point he realised that Otto had just asked a question.

"Well . . . I've not offended you have I?"

He had no idea what Otto was talking about, "No, of course, not at all."

"Good, old boy. Now I must mingle, but help yourself to the Holy Water."

"Amen, Otto." He was pleased to be left alone, and made his way to the back of the room, hoping he wouldn't have to start any meaningless conversations with strangers. He would ask Otto about the

Jewishness of his Shylock, and go. Leaning against the bookshelves, away from the cluster of chattering drinkers, he wondered if he really had been missing out much. Being away from Maria and amongst these back-slapping drunks – it wasn't the glamorous adventure he had imagined.

"It must be hard work – you're very physical on the stage." It was the blonde. She was standing close.

"It is," he said.

"So do you take regular exercise?"

"Not as much as I used to. As I should. You enjoy the show?"

"*The Merchant* isn't one of my favourites, I'm afraid. Your Shylock is wonderful though – the reason for turning up, I should say." She fingered the lower button on his suit jacket.

"You're too kind. And what about you, are you involved with theatre?"

"No, though you could say I'm part of the scenery." She smiled. Werner fell silent. Staring into his glass of wine, he wondered where this might lead, and thought of Maria. The blonde was still staring up at him, probably expecting some theatrical words of wisdom, but he had none to impart. Otto returned and placed an arm around the blonde's waist. Werner backed away from them.

"So, you've finally met Herr Krauss, your hero. My little girl is something of a fan of yours, Werner. I do hope she's not boring you with too many questions?"

He smiled, "It's fine, of course. Though actually, I still don't know your daughter's name."

"My name's *actually* Sofia. And I'm not a little girl any more." She walked off.

"Petulant as ever. And I've told her to sort that hair out – she'll get me shot, looking so decadent."

"I didn't know you *had* a daughter, Otto?"

"Neither did I, till a couple of years ago, old boy!" Otto took a swig from his glass of wine. "Her mother was part of a touring company that worked with me in Dresden, back in my days in the Provincials. We met a few times, had a little *tête-à-tête*, and I thought no more about it. Sixteen years later, this creature turns up on my doorstep. Her mother got caught in some . . . cross-fire . . . shall we say? I took her in, naturally."

Werner stared across at Sofia once more. "And she's happy?"

"Seems to be, old boy. Of course, I'm hardly around much, but she's old enough to look after herself. All I have to do is keep my eye on the randy *Kaninchen*, claiming to have important business here.

"Young actors, I'd guess?"

"No, the ones chasing my girl are old, jaded buggers like me actually – directors, the money-men – insatiable, the lot of us."

The actor chuckled politely, and returned to the subject Otto was most comfortable with:

"My glass is empty, Otto. What kind of party is this?"

"Perhaps we should move on to something stronger then, my friend. You don't have to ask me twice. Come down to the cellar."

He followed Otto, but was stopped in his tracks by Sofia, who was clutching a scrap of paper and a pen.

"Daddy, I wonder if I could trouble Herr Krauss for his autograph?"

"Go on then – I'll meet you downstairs, Werner." Otto pushed his way past a group of guests, "I shall return with untold riches and fine refreshment!"

"Hurrah!" said the actor, half-heartedly. It seemed that everyone else was ignoring their genial host. He smiled at Sofia, took the pen and paper from her, and signed: '*Dear Sofia, delightful to meet you – best wishes, Werner Krauss.*'

"And do you want mine?" she asked, waving another piece of paper.

"By all means – it would make a nice change." As Sofia scribbled, she looked up into his eyes, as if she had rehearsed this quirky seduction. When she stopped writing, she folded the paper and slipped it into his jacket pocket.

"You're not allowed to read it until tomorrow," she said, and rubbed his chest where the note was lying. He wondered if he was to join the group of illustrious old buggers fighting for her affections. She wasn't much younger than Maria, of course. He gave his excuses, left her in the lounge and made his way through the crowd into the kitchen, where he found the cellar door, and, he hoped, something to take his mind off his host's daughter.

"Think I've found just the thing, old boy." Otto waved a peculiar, prism-shaped bottle high above his head. "Now I'm not *really* supposed to have this, but that shouldn't trouble a couple of wily old cats like us, eh, Werner?" Somehow, the actor felt obliged to play along with this macho game. He thought it might be easier to bring up the delicate subject of the greedy Jew, if they were both drunk.

"Not a problem, my man. What is it? Gin?"

"Not a chance, it's Absinthe, old boy. That American Hemingway swears by it." Otto ushered him down into the cellar, and closed the hatch behind him. The actor had no intention of becoming a clandestine drinker by candlelight, yet here he was, caught up in Otto's ritual. Otto swigged straight from the bottle, and, as he caught his breath, passed it on, encouraging his friend to do the same. In a gruff voice, he said: "down the hatch, we haven't got all day." The actor assented, and gulped.

"Good, old boy. Now, out of this confined space before people talk. There are some *special* guests I want you to meet."

DEAREST WERNER,
A thousand smiths' hammers are beating in my head!
It's almost midnight and you're not home. You're making your feelings clear, so I'll do the same with mine. Do you think this is 'for the best'? Being stuck alone, in a room with only dear old Emily Bronte for company? You might brood and mumble, my Heathcliff, but you're taking my best years.

I lie here every night, Werner, as you snore and gurgle, slobber and drool . . .
I'm in danger of being seriously ill – I wish it may prove true. He has startled and distressed me shockingly! I want to frighten him. *And don't think I haven't noticed. I was there, Werner, remember. It was me you used to sneak off to meet. Almost every night. You'd give your excuses: 'there's an after-show party', 'there's a gala reception' and we'd come back to my place. You knew I felt so guilty for that poor woman, but you promised you'd leave her, promised and promised. Until finally it happened. Publicly. Werner Krauss doesn't do things by halves. He must make it plain for all to see.*

He might come and begin a string of abuse, or complainings; I'm certain I should recriminate, and God knows where we should end! *Excuses, excuses. The excuses you're feeding me! This party that conveniently happens to be taking place tonight. I'm no fool, Werner. You won't do it to me – I'm stronger than you, Werner – I'll do it to myself.*

Yours,
Maria x

2

Waking early, he opened his eyes to find dark, oak roof beams hovering above him. As he lay there with his eyes closed again, he felt a dull, throbbing pain in his head. 'I've been poisoned' he thought, and turned onto his side, determined to bury his head deep into the silky pillows. As he did so, he felt a lean, female arm collapse into his ribcage.

"Sorry, Shy-lock" said a voice. It was a Munich accent – nothing like Maria. Realising he was in bed with another woman seemed almost logical – another pain in the head. He closed his eyes tightly, and tried to remember something of what had happened. He remembered Sofia, and briefly fantasised about lying in bed with her. A grin cracked into his pale face. 'Seducing Weitner's daughter,' he thought, 'right under his nose'. This momentary excitement made him aware of his body, of the fact that he was naked. He hadn't slept naked for years.

Tentatively, he opened his eyes again, and traced the arm resting on his side to a naked torso. He lifted his head to find that she had long, brown hair and a peaceful smile. He could feel her soft breath on his shoulder. He laid down his head and closed his eyes once more, struck by the absurdity of the situation. Though she seemed vaguely familiar, he had no recollection of sex with this girl, and took comfort in the fact. He would remember, wouldn't he? Otto had literally poured drinks down everyone's necks last night, and nobody was capable of getting home. Perhaps he had paired-up his guests to share the beds, and putting Werner together with this young woman obviously appealed to Otto's 'unique' sense of humour. Unless he received information to the contrary, if he left this house without disturbing anybody, this was a story he could believe, and for all intents and purposes, therefore, this was what *had* happened.

He carefully slipped out of bed to find his clothes scattered around on the floor, along with those of his sleeping partner. He realised their nudity rendered his version of events less plausible, but he had no desire to consider the alternatives. He picked up her silk blouse and found his own underwear, dressed as quietly as he could, and when he was fully clothed, took a final look at the girl, and left the room.

"Goodbye Shy-lock," she called after him, but he ignored her, clumsily ambling down the stairs and out of Otto's house.

He was surprised to find Maria asleep, as he tip-toed into their bedroom. He took a final sip from his glass of water and began to change into his cotton pyjamas. The fresh smell and crisp creases in his bedclothes made his heart ache – somehow they emphasised just how reckless he had been.

Removing the book that she had left on his pillow, he lay down next to Maria, placed a hand on her hip, and closed his eyes. He thought he could sleep for years.

"Damn nerve," she said, and cast his hand aside. The actor sighed and explained, unintelligibly:

"Otto wouldn't let us. We wanted to, we all wanted to go and he just kept making us." He smacked his lips together, as if to settle down again.

"You'd have to, wouldn't you?" Maria said. The actor knew the question was directed at him, but somehow he felt like an observer – about to witness another theatrical show. "You'd have to snore and make noises now – as if it wasn't enough, going out drinking with every whore in Berlin!"

The word 'whore' echoed in his ear, providing him with another interpretation of the previous night's events. Had he slept with one of Otto's *whores*?

"Are you listening?" Maria's voice grew in volume. "Are you even listening?" She rolled out of bed and sat at the dressing table. Staring at his lifeless body in the mirror, she continued: "So are you going to tell me what happened? Or aren't I important enough to know?" He remained silent. "No, I didn't think so. Not important enough now you're on *the scene*, on *the prowl* with Weitner. It's what you've always wanted, isn't it? 'Werner Krauss – everyone's second-best friend.' I hope it's made you happy."

"What do you want me to say?" His eyes were still closed.

"You've absolutely no idea, have you? So long as there's money in the bank and gin in the cabinet, you're happy. I could be out there too, Werner – ever thought of that? I get offers, all kinds, but I stay here with you – *for* you. 'What do you want me to say, Maria?' well what have you *got* to say for yourself?"

He sat up, and in his drunken haze he sobbed loudly, "I'm sorry. I'm so sorry." He wasn't sure exactly what he was apologising for: going to a party alone? Getting drunk? Fantasising about his producer's daughter? Sleeping with a whore? Snoring? All he knew was that, for once, Maria was probably justified. "I'm sorry, I didn't know how to stop – it all went too far. You can forgive me can't you?"

Maria climbed back onto the bed and straddled him, pressing his head to her chest. His tears and snot stained her floral nightgown – it came as a relief, finally to share in his wife's hysteria.

"Say you still love me."

"Of course I do, I love . . . "

"And you'll love me forever?"

"Yes."

"Even if a thousand girls wanted you . . . ?"

"Yes, even . . . "

" . . . at a thousand opening nights?"

"Yes, Maria, yes."

As they embraced, Maria slapped her hand down hard on his back. They rocked together there, both sobbing, as though their tears could wash away the hundred questions that needed to be answered. They lay down, stroking each other's faces and sinking into the rhythm of their unified breath. Werner actually thought they might make love, he wanted to summon the energy to kiss his wife, touch her lovingly, prove his loyalty and cement their partnership, he wanted to tell her . . .

So the other day I went up to a beautiful woman I saw in the theatre, and I said to her, "I've lost my wife in here and I would be very happy if you could find some time to talk to me for a few minutes." The woman asked, "Why on earth do you want me to do that?" And I replied, "Because every time I talk to a gorgeous woman, my wife appears out of nowhere . . . "

They laughed and laughed. He recognised some of their faces. They seemed to be laughing at everything he said.

"Stop it, please . . . really . . . "

Their nostrils flared, their brows furrowed.

"Tell another one, Werner . . . " *someone shouted,*

"No, no, they're stupid jokes, I . . . "

"Come on, give us another . . . "

"Okay – last one – these two Rabbis are discussing the decline of morals in the modern world . . . " *he gave his best Jewish accent,* "'I didn't sleep with my wife before I was married' said one of them, self-righteously, 'did you?'"

They all laughed. The anticipation was almost tangible.

"'I don't know' said the other Rabbi. 'What was her Maiden name?'"

*Again, they laughed and laughed. But why exactly were they laughing? Surely, everyone has heard these jokes hundreds of times, haven't they? He knew he was good at delivering jokes, but was it really so funny? Were wives or damn Rabbis really so hilarious? No, there could only be one explanation: they were scared. Scared how he would react if they didn't laugh. Scared about the friends he had now, the people he knew. This wasn't entertainment, it was bullying . . . *

"Stop laughing now, please!"

They though that this was part of the act, that he was being cute with them.

"Really, I don't like it . . . "

The roar got louder, the nostrils flared, the brows furrowed. When would they stop? Why wouldn't they stop?

He woke alone, his face burning in the afternoon sun. His throat was dry and his back felt stiff. On realising the time of day, he decided not to work against his hangover – rather, he would work with it, and pour himself a small brandy. His clothes had been neatly folded at the end of the bed, alongside a note from Maria.

A note for your growing collection. Remember you're meeting Willem today. I'd ask you not to be late, but what would be the point? – M

He had no time to decode her cryptic message. Hadn't they made up last night? Anyway, he had to rush if he were to keep his appointment with Willem at the *Altwienerhof*. His first theatrical agent, Willem was someone he could confide in about his rather delicate problem. Willem had been the subject of some gossip and suspicion himself, until he surprised everyone by marrying a young Austrian girl in the Spring. He could be annoying; pretty frenzied and irritating, at times – but if anyone could help, it was Willem. The actor washed, dressed, called for Lothar and gulped the brandy, hoping to achieve a level of numbness befitting the day.

"So you put yourself out on a limb. You said 'yes' so many times, 'yes, yes, yes, yes' to the Party, 'yes' to the censors, 'yes' to all those *wonderful* Goebbels men, darling, you forgot *why* you were doing it in the first place." Willem lit his second cigarette and knocked back his third schnapps. He gestured to the barman for another. The actor had hardly troubled his glass of Burgundy '22, but was keen to hear what his friend thought of his idea, and consented to the barman's polite gesturing:

"On my tab as well, Willem here is my guest . . . " He was eager for Willem to drink plenty, and so be vague with the information being revealed. In his experience, it was better for people to be inebriated, unsure of specific details, if ever questioned. Nowadays, he was wary of trusting even his closest friends.

"You might be right," he conceded, "but that's really not the point. You'll probably laugh, but I feel that I'm, as the English say: 'cutting off the nose to spite the face.'" He thought his English was near perfect, but Willem just stared.

"What's your point? You have a lovely big nose, dear!" he laughed, but the actor was unamused. "You're worried that you're too *good*? *Dramatic*? *Flamboyant*? Audiences love you, Werner, what's the problem?" He remained silent. "They paying you enough?" Willem laughed again, blowing smoke out the side of his mouth in a way that irritated his host.

"I don't want them thinking I'm a Jew!" he said. Regretting raising his voice, he checked over his shoulder. The café was empty, except for a group of nurses chatting at the front window. He moved in closer to Willem, who had allowed a grin to crack the lines of his reddening face. "You might laugh, but I'm thinking of requesting an announcement, in the theatre, the cinema, the programme – the damn radio if I have to . . . " He began to whisper, prodding his finger on the table: "Werner Krauss is an actor, an Aryan, not a Jew. Simply an actor, serving his art and his country." Saliva burst from the corners of Willem's tight lips.

"You want an announcement like that . . . " He laughed, knocking back the dregs of his schnapps, "and you're worried about what the *Party* will say?"

"Is it so hilarious? I could write to Goebbels himself if I have to. But is it a good move?"

"Werner . . . dearest Werner, listen to what you're saying! You want the Party to announce that the Reich's most celebrated acting talent is *so* disgusted by the thought of being mistaken for a Jew, that he wishes to assure everyone of his Aryan credentials?"

"In a manner, of speaking, I suppose . . . "

"Darling, they'll be *delighted* to indulge you. Can you think of a more perfect propaganda opportunity than that? Goebbels will shout it from the rooftops!"

The actor had to accept that his friend had a point, and he started to relax. Matching Willem in his intake of Schnapps, he invited the nurses to join them, and bought drinks for everyone. One of the nurses (he didn't ask her name) sat close.

"I recognise you," she said, excitedly, "you're Shylock – I'm sitting with Shylock!"

"He *plays* Shylock dear," Willem interrupted, "a real Jew would never buy a round of drinks!" They all laughed, and the actor felt grateful to his friend for his sense of perspective. Perhaps he was starting to lose touch a little. The nurses flirted, telling him they'd do *anything* for his autograph. He signed a napkin and said there was no charge, so long as they were nice to his friend. He winked at Willem, who shrank back in his chair with embarrassment. The actor explained that he was happily married, and was looking forward to going home to his beautiful wife. Willem's cynical eyes mocked, but it felt good, actually saying those words, and the nurses all responded with a motherly "aww." He showed them the photograph of Maria in his wallet, and they all twittered on about how pretty she looked, and how they wanted to find a man who was just as kind and faithful. Revelling in this new role as 'caring husband', he bought another round of drinks and proposed a toast, "to the Reich and her wonderful nursing staff."

Eventually, he staggered out of the café and ordered Lothar to take him home.

"Want me to get the other jacket, sir?"

"I think we've got passed the jacket stage, old boy." Werner laughed. "You know this was supposed to be a quick meeting? How long was I in there for?"

"Around five hours, sir. I was actually questioned by a *soldat* – he accused me of spying . . . "

Werner burst into fits of laughter again. "And what did you say?"

"I told them I was waiting for you. I gave them your agent's number and they said they'd check it out. That was about an hour ago, and they've not been back, so . . . "

Werner continued to laugh. "Well thank God you didn't need me to bail you out of jail – you'd have been there until Christmas!"

"Yes sir, I suppose you're right, sir."

He arrived to find Maria sat at the dining table, waiting for him. He leaned across to kiss her but she turned away, offering instead a cheek.

"Drunk again. How novel of you." She said.

"Welcome home, Werner. How was your day?" he slurred, and pulled up a chair. Sitting down, he focused on the bowl in front of him. It was empty, but for a scrap of paper.

"What's this – some sort of joke?"

"As if you don't know! Why don't you read it out to me?" Her voice had a sarcastic lilt, which seemed to pierce Werner's eardrums. How could she make him feel so angry? He unfolded the paper and read it to himself.

DEAREST WERNER,
Daddy's away all this week. I'll be in this big house all on my own, unless . . . ?

Sofia xx

"I've never seen this before . . . "

"Save your lies for the *Quadriga* or wherever you go – with Weitner – and *her*."

With tears in her eyes, Maria lent across the table and tried to take the paper away from him, but he grabbed it and held it down.

"Honestly, I know nothing about this," he said.

"But you know who it's from . . . "

"Some silly girl at the party, a kid Otto didn't know he had – she just wanted an autograph."

"That's convenient."

"It's the truth!"

"You said you remembered nothing about last night. Or have you forgotten you said that?"

"Don't talk to me like that." He stood, and hovered over Maria. "I arrived at the party, a girl wanted my autograph and that's it. End of story. So I got drunk with Otto – it's not a crime – I knew this would be my last day-off for a few weeks and went a bit overboard." He smiled to himself as a lie emerged from his lips: "I gave my jacket to Otto . . . she must've gone to the cloakroom and put the note in my pocket."

At this, Maria jumped from her seat and lashed out, grabbing his hair.

"Always an excuse, isn't there?" He pushed her away, and as he stood to hit her, she grabbed a fork and pointed it at his face. "Not this time." For a moment, their heavy breathing was again in unison. He grabbed at the fork but she pulled back, and plunged it deep into the top of her own thigh. As she yelled in pain, he held her by the hair.

"Look what you've done! What the hell are you thinking?"

Yelling and screaming, she put her arms around his neck.

"It's all right – we'll get it out."

He dragged her to a space on the floor, leaving a trail of blood to seep into the carpet, and laid her down. Impressed by his own clear-headedness, he fetched towels, and told her to hold them tight to her thigh. As she yelled in pain, he told her to close her eyes. He felt his chest begin to tighten, and grabbed the silver handle. It seemed to bend in the palm of his shaking hand. Desperately, he pulled hard, and tried to end the pain in one quick motion.

"We're really grateful, Lothar, doing this for us – and out of hours too."

On the back seat of the speeding Mercedes, Werner was still gripping the towel to his wife's leg.

"It's no problem, really. We just got the children off to bed, so . . . "

"Such a bizarre accident too, you know I told Maria, 'we should get someone to help with the dish-washing', but she always says 'no'."

"Werner, he's not an idiot, he knows it was no accident," Maria groaned.

"Please, it's none of my business . . . " said Lothar.

"Don't worry, Lothar. We are really grateful – we'll make sure you're paid properly for this."

Sat alone in the waiting room, Werner tried to make sense of the day. He remembered feeling determined to make it up to Maria this morning. And despite having the attention of all of those nurses in the café, he really was looking forward to getting home to her. How did things go so wrong? She thought he was drinking too much – but this was *his day off*. He just wanted to unwind – he'd be lucky to make time for the odd glass of wine in the evening when the theatre-run started in earnest. If a man can't enjoy a drink every once in a while . . .

Aided by the greying matron in blue uniform, Maria hobbled along the corridor towards him.

"You know there are people who really need our help: soldiers, *heroes*, without this kind of nonsense," said the matron. Werner wasn't quite sure if this lecture was directed at his wife or him. He nodded obediently anyway, and promised it wouldn't happen again.

They didn't speak in the taxi home, which suited Werner as he could feel a terrible headache developing. And to think he had to perform tomorrow. Thank God for old Shylock's make-up and prosthetics – at least he didn't have to *look* good. They both quietly got changed into their nightclothes and slipped into bed simultaneously. A pillow and the security of his soft bed came as quite a relief.

"So is that it, then? Nothing to be said, sweep it all under the carpet?"

Werner lay in silence for a couple of minutes, trying to summon an appropriate response.

"If you want to, we can talk about everything: me being out last night, this afternoon, the hospital, the fucking *note* – anything." He took a breath. "But even if we do I don't think I can give you the answers you're looking for . . . "

"What's that supposed to mean?"

"Deep down I don't think you'll believe me. What's more . . . " he pulled his knees close to his chest, curling up like a foetus, "I don't think you really believe in anything." He smacked his lips together and closed his eyes. He expected a scream, a rant, a reaction, but none came.

"You're probably right" she said. "Well done, Werner."

It took a moment for him to digest her sarcasm. He lay there with his back to her, wishing it were all a bad dream. He kept his eyes closed.

"Come on then, tell me what you do want, what you *do* believe in. Or have you given up completely? When was the last time you went to an audition? Or met up with friends?"

"Don't do this now, Werner . . . "

"No, come on, I want to know. It's so easy to blame me for everything – what are *you* doing about it?"

She didn't reply. He wondered what he could say next. He wanted to show her he was interested, that she was important to him. But sometimes she had a way of saying things that made him so angry – it clouded his judgement, and he'd forget the point he was trying to make. Maybe he should talk about the drinking, maybe make some promises . . . but he felt so tired. He could feel her shuffling around behind him. She put on her lamp and was reading her book . . . he could hear her scribbling and underlining certain words . . . she was reading a lot these days, at least that was something . . .

DEAR WERNER,
The truth is, I'm beginning to think you're right about me. God knows, it's not easy to admit, but it is as if I have given up. I don't see my friends, I don't try-out for parts. It all seems too much. Just getting through the day is enough of a struggle: eating, tidying, sleeping . . . it's as though I've forgotten how to sleep. I lie here, reading the same books, writing about the same things. Where does it . . .

"Horses!" said Werner.

"What? Are you sleep-talking again?" Maria quickly shoved her papers into her bedside drawer.

"No . . . I've had an idea! I was trying to think of something we could do together – to take your mind off things and relax a little."

"And . . . "

"And I've got a friend over in Oderburg who has stables. He's always said we should visit. We could go horse riding together. Tomorrow if you like. Just me and you."

"But I've never ridden a horse before in my life!"

He rolled over to face her, "Neither have I! It could be a fabulous disaster – but so what? We'll be together." Werner did his best to muster enthusiasm.

"What do you say?"

She smiled. "Do you mean it?"

"Of course!"

"Well, not tomorrow. But Thursday, maybe . . . "

"Good, it's settled then!" He kissed her cheek and lay down again on his back. "We'll get through this together you know. The old Maria will be back in no time – just you wait and see . . . "

. . . end? Such a sweet idea, dear Werner. And such a pity I won't be around. I've always wanted to ride a horse, but it'll take more than that to make me happy. You pig, you've had enough chances . . .

Why do I do this? Such a lovely man. Maybe you really do care. For once I wasn't lying awake alone . . . you were lying there . . . and thinking about me.

But no endings are perfect, and if I waited until we'd had a nice day together? Well, I'd feel better for a day or two, but what then? More drinking, more late nights, more women. It's pointless – I'd be wasting your time too, dear Werner.

I remember when we met – it was so exciting just to be around you. You made me feel like I was the only thing that mattered. Even when you made mistakes, I thought that really, deep down, you cared . . .

<u>3</u>

He woke with a terrible pain in his head and an erection. He was surprised to find Maria snoozing quite contentedly beside him – he couldn't remember the last time he had seen her asleep. It was rare for her to look so peaceful and serene. He slipped out of bed carefully and managed to get dressed without waking her. He remembered his promise to take her horse riding, and how it had finally placated her. He scribbled the word 'horses' on his hand to remind him to talk to Schumann. They hadn't been on the best terms the last time they met (something to do with an argument he had with Ziegler from the Staatstheater), but he would do all he could to keep his promise. Checking his watch, he realised it was still quite early, and he locked himself in the bathroom. He thought of Sofia, the strange blonde girl from the party the other night. She had quite a nerve, writing him that note. He wondered if she meant what she had written – about having the house to herself – or if it was just a childish game. Irrespective, he pictured her naked, begging to make love to the 'famous Shylock'. After a few minutes, he was done, and his head felt much better.

"Herr Krauss, I don't want to alarm you. But I've noticed the same car following us over the last few days."

Werner instantly turned his head to take a look at the black Volkswagen.

"Probably better not to look straight at them, sir."

"I shouldn't worry, old boy. You said they were asking you questions outside the café?"

"Yes, sir . . . "

"They're probably just doing their job, following up on you."

"I'm sure you're right, sir." Lothar was visibly embarrassed, and obviously felt compelled to change the subject.

"So how is your wife, Herr Krauss, if you don't mind me asking?"

Werner had forgotten about Lothar's involvement in last night's debacle. "She's better, thank you . . . " He said, reached into his jacket pocket, and opened his wallet.

"Listen, I know I don't have to talk to you about discretion . . . "

"Of course not, Herr Krauss, as I said, it's none of my . . . "

"I know" he interrupted. "But on this occasion you need to be particularly careful." He dropped a selection of notes onto the passenger seat.

"But, Herr Krauss, I . . . "

"The fact is, Lothar, that Maria's going through a bit of a *strange* time in her life – she's an actress, I've seen it all before with actresses – and these things will happen from time to time."

"Happens to women in general, eh, sir!"

"Yes, indeed." He forced a smile. "What you have to realise is that if any of this got out, if the Party or any of the papers heard . . . things could get very difficult for you, as well as me . . . do you understand?"

"I didn't even know he *had* a daughter . . . " Werner was sat in his agent's office for their weekly meeting. His agent, Stefan, was a short, hirsute man with notorious body odour. "And they say that secrets are things of the past."

"So, are you going to go round? Must have quite a body on her at that age, eh?"

Werner laughed. "She's just some silly kid. Besides, I'm a married man."

"And a fine husband you are too, Werner." Stefan raised his eyebrows.

"Enough. So what's on the menu today, my friend?"

Recently, Werner had started to wonder if Stefan was really cut out for the job – there was little variation in the roles he was securing, and he seemed particularly weak when it came to increasing Party pressures.

"There are a few different interviews lined-up for *The Merchant*, plus . . . word around the campfire . . . "

"Go on . . . "

"Nothing's confirmed, but I've heard there's a chance that 'various entertainers' will be requested to attend the state visit of Mussolini in a few days . . . " Stefan leaned back in his chair and with a knowing grin.

"How likely do you think it is, honestly?" Werner's heart raced at the prospect.

"Well, don't pack your bags, but . . . be ready. I can't think who else they would want, especially as your Shylock gets the full seal of approval."

"I see. So you think I should go?"

"You don't get a choice, Werner, you know that. All I'm saying is, be prepared – with the war and the security situation, I've heard they can make requests like this literally at the last minute . . . "

"I understand. Thanks, Stefan."

"Anything else?"

"Yes, smooth things over for me with Schumann, will you? I've promised to take Maria horse-riding . . . "

"Might be a problem with that, old boy."

"Why? That silly business with Ziegler?"

"That and the fact that he's dead!"

"You're joking?"

"Don't you know anything about what goes on in this town, Werner?"

"No, I really must get one of those . . . what are they called now? Agents! Yes *agents*, I really ought to get one of them to keep me up-to-date . . . "

"Touché, Werner. Well, I'm telling you now – Schumann is dead."

"But why? When did it happen?"

"Few months ago. Official reason was suicide . . . "

"Meaning?"

"You saw how much fuss he was making about the portrayals in *Don Carlos* and their interfering."

"Not a reason to *kill* him though. Come on, Stefan, who's spinning these yarns?"

"You're right, not a reason for killing him. But I heard things escalated . . . in the end they probably killed him just because he wasn't taking their threats seriously. Thought he was too important . . . "

Werner couldn't believe it. Surely there should be an investigation?

Someone should get to the bottom of this. For a man to *die*, over a stupid *show*?

"In that case, get me the number of a nice horse sanctuary . . . "

He returned home to find Maria breaking small pieces of chocolate into a bowl. She seemed blasé about his news.

"So why the conspiracy theory? He could have just killed himself . . . like people sometimes do."

"'Like people *do*'?" Werner tried to gauge her expression, but she was concentrating too intently on the chocolate. "What people? Anyway, that's what *I* said, but Stefan's convinced it's higher powers at work. Makes you think . . . doesn't it?"

"Makes *me* think you ought to be more careful who you mix with and what you say. You should bear it in mind the next time you're invited to a party . . . "

"Point made, Maria." He said.

"By the way, Egon called, said he can't believe you still haven't made the time to meet his new fiancée."

"*Scheiße*, what was her name again?"

"It's Hannah. He said they're in town this afternoon – they'll be at the café on *Rochstraße* at three if you can make it."

"I'm supposed to have a press interview, and I wanted to take a nap, I'm still exhausted from yesterday."

"He's your son, Werner."

"I'll call Lothar now."

Werner arrived at the café early. When the waiter asked for his order, he panicked a little. He knew he should cut back on alcohol, if he was to avoid Maria's hysterical performance each night. But he really didn't *want* a soft drink, he wanted to sip at a brandy and relax, before he had to face his son.

"Sir?" The barman seemed impatient. "I can come back to you if you need a moment?"

"Give me a beer, please. Oh, and when a young man joins me with his girl – their drinks are on me too."

"Very good, sir."

He found a table at the back of the bar, and immediately wished he'd brought something to read. It had been a few months since he had last seen Egon, and even then, they simply exchanged pleasantries, Werner wrote a cheque and his son went on his way. This time he should make more effort, he thought; make this girl feel at ease with her future father-in-law. Egon was a good kid really – he had turned out surprisingly well.

"Father, I'd like you to meet Hannah." He looked up and saw a beautiful, tall, dark-haired girl, holding hands with his son.

"Hannah, how lovely to meet you!" He held out his hand, which she shook and smiled. "Hannah, Hannah, I wish my name were a palindrome too . . . as it is, it would be . . . Renrew, I suppose."

They both smiled politely. He clicked his fingers at the waiter.

"Over here, please," he turned to Egon and Hannah, "order anything you want, it's on me. And sit down for goodness sake, relax!"

As Hannah removed her coat, Werner thought he noticed something on her arm.

"So how's your mother? Well, I hope?"

"She's fine."

"And what's-his-name?"

"You know perfectly well his name's Julius. He actually hasn't been around for a while now . . . we think he's gone into hiding, Mum won't say, of course . . . "

"That is a shame. Such a tricky business, politics . . . more trouble than it's worth if you ask me . . . "

"*Tricky business*? His life is in danger, Dad. Have a heart for once?"

He could see it quite clearly. Over one arm of her pale blue shirt, she was wearing an armband with the yellow Star of David on it. This had to be a joke . . .

"Dad, are you listening to me?"

A Jew? A fucking Jew? Exactly what was he trying to prove?

"Fine, come on, Hannah, he's gone into a sulk . . . we might as well leave."

They both stood.

"No, stay please. I'm sorry, sit down. I was just a bit distracted by your . . . "

They sat down. Hannah pointed to her armband.

"By this?"

"So are you a . . . "

"Yes, she's Jewish, Dad, why? Can't you say the word? '*Jud*' go on, try . . . "

"Don't talk to me like that." He could feel froth starting to gather in the corners of his lips. "Just a bit of a surprise, that's all. I'm allowed to be surprised, aren't I?"

"I suppose so."

They sat in silence for what seemed like an eternity. Part of Werner wanted to defy his son's expectations, be pleasant to this girl and try to ignore the fact she was a Jew. But he felt such an overwhelming sense of . . . dread. As though Egon had identified his father's one weakness – the way he was regarded by the Party and the way in which he had . . . played-up to their expectations . . . Did Egon even *know* what the implications were?

"So have you set a date for the big day?" Werner's voiced cracked as his asked the question.

"As soon as possible. Hannah's family are trying to move to the United States, and we want to do it while they're still around . . . "

"Right . . . but you're both . . . "

"Staying in Berlin? Of course. For as long as we possibly can, anyway. There's no way I'm leaving Mother behind, while we can still help it . . . "

"No, of course, of course."

He just couldn't face this any longer – he felt sick. Maybe he could give Egon a call later, when he had calmed down.

"I have to go, there are a few things we still need to go over with the script before tonight's performance. It was nice meeting you, Hannah . . . " they shook hands again, and Werner left some cash to pay for the drinks, "now I don't want any arguments." He took his chequebook from his jacket.

"Dad, I don't want your money."

"If you don't take it I'll give it to the waiter . . . "

His son cracked a smile. Werner wrote a cheque for one thousand marks, the most he'd ever given his son. The thought of never seeing him again flashed across his mind . . .

"That's far too much."

He ripped it from his chequebook and forced it into his son's hand. He clasped his hand tightly.

"Be careful, Egon" he turned to Hannah, "both of you . . . you know where I am if you need me."

He felt his eyes welling-up, and rushed out into the street as quickly as he could. He tried to swallow but it was impossible, his throat was so dry. His Egon, his poor little boy – with that Jew . . . what was he thinking? Of course, she did *seem* like a nice girl, but don't they all?

He walked quickly through the streets, he couldn't contain himself any longer – he whined and cried openly – what was he going to do? What if he packed them off to America? Or London? He'd heard about refuges in Stockholm . . . maybe they'd be safe there until the war was over. Should he tell anyone about this? Perhaps he could use his influence . . . but then again, would he *have* any influence after they found out? He thought about what had happened to Schumann, a Party man, a popular man – dead for no good reason, dead for a fucking play – what the hell was he going to do?

"Please, I don't have time for sarcasm . . . Alright then 'how are you, Paula?', happy now? . . . ah, yes, sorry to hear about that, you must be quite upset . . . so it's my fault, is it? I told him to be a raving Commy lunatic, did I? . . . Of course I don't *know* anything, who do you think I am? . . . Nice, Paula, nice – you read it in the paper, so it must be true – you can't talk about things like that over the phone, anyway . . . I've met them, alright, *met* them, believe it or not they don't consult me on domestic policy . . . I suppose so, I'm pretty busy but I don't see why not, come down to the Staatstheater one afternoon . . . Look, the reason I called was to talk about Egon . . . yes, she's *lovely* – accept no one *warned* me about her . . . about who she was, *what* she was . . . great! Are you deaf, I just said, you have to be discreet on the phone – yes, I'm referring to *that* . . . Jesus, Paula, I know he's my son – that's the problem . . . you know I didn't mean it like that . . . I suppose I just wanted to know how it happened . . . Do you think they'll definitely *get* married?"

"Sorry to bother you, Herr Krauss – Muthel wants us to start now."
"In a fucking minute! Can't you see I'm on the phone?"

"Sorry, Paula, what was I saying? . . . so how did they meet, *where* did they meet? . . . I might have known – your fucking husband . . . I get the picture – you've stood by and watched that Commy scumbag put our son's life in danger . . . I'll say what I like on the fucking phone! And to think I was calling *you* for advice! I can see it now – good old Commy Kohl giving a safe haven for the Yids . . . Paula? Are you there?"

"Alright everyone, let's not beat around the bush, we only have a couple of hours this afternoon before you have to start getting ready . . . I know some of you think you have *better* things to do, but for the rest of us this play is important so can we get a move on, please? Chop, chop . . .

Werner went over to Muthel immediately.

"Bit of a family crisis, I had to use the telephone and I was disturbed at just the wrong time."

"Just tread carefully, Krauss, okay? It's difficult enough trying to assert some authority with this lot."

"It won't happen again."

I have possess'd your Grace of what I purpose
And by our holy Sabbath have I sworn
To have the due and forfeit of my bond.
If you deny it let the danger light

He could, of course, be strong, and openly aid his son in his time of need . . .

Upon your charter and your city's freedom.
You'll as me why I rather choose to have
A weight of carrion flesh than to receive
Three thousand ducats. I'll not answer that,
But say it is my humour – is it answer'd?

. . . but he couldn't help thinking that for some reason Egon had done this on purpose. Perhaps he had never forgiven him for what he'd done to his mother . . .

What if my house be troubled with a rat,
And I be pleas'd to give ten thousand ducats
To have it ban'd? What, are you answer'd yet?
Some men there are love not a gaping pig;
Some that are mad if they behold a cat;
And others, when the bagpipe sings I' th' nose,
Cannot contain their urine; for affection,

. . . it was his little boy, his first-born son. Werner watched as Paula gave birth to him, on the kitchen floor of their first apartment in Austria . . .

Mistress of passion, sways it to the mood
Of what it like or loathes. Now, for your answer:
As there is no firm reason to be rend'red
Why he cannot abide a gaping pig;
Why he, a harmless necessary cat;
Why he, a woollen bagpipe, but of force
Must yield to such inevitable shame

. . . surely Egon wasn't the problem. All he had done was fall in love, with a girl who was, admittedly, quite beautiful. If she had turned up to meet Werner after a show, and suggested they got a room, he would certainly find it hard to say 'no.' But for the armband, he would never have known . . .

As to offend, himself being offended;
So can I give no reason, nor I will not,
More than a lodg'd hate and a certain loathing
I bear Antonio, that I follow thus
A losing suit against him. Are you answered?

"Stop! Stop . . . come on, Werner *with feeling*. We're at a pivotal moment here, you don't need me to tell you this."
"Can I try it again?"
"Why don't we all take ten minutes, okay? Take a proper look at the script, Werner, think about what it means, think about what's happening."
"No problem, was just a blip . . . "
"Perhaps you could spend a little more time on the script in future – a little less on the damn telephone!"

Muthel was right, the *ad hoc* rehearsal was dreadful – he just couldn't concentrate. Trying to stalk the stage as the scheming Semite villain, after the day he'd had, was impossible. He needed someone to talk to, someone he could trust.

"Hello darling . . . no particular reason, I just wanted to hear your voice . . . terrible, it was terrible – I'm pretty fed-up with it to be honest . . . well, it's farcical having the script changed every five minutes . . . what does it matter? Let them listen – they should have better things to do – it's a play for God's sake, just a play! . . . Believe me, I've never been more sober . . . no, seriously, darling, I am . . . so what have you been up to? . . . and have you eaten properly today? . . . all right, all right, I won't ask. Listen, Maria, why don't you come along tonight? . . . don't worry about that, I'll send Lothar . . . I was thinking we could go to a nice restaurant, maybe check-in to a hotel . . . please darling, just say 'yes', I really need you tonight, honestly, I've had a hell of a day . . . think about it, for me? . . . I mean it, . . . okay bye then. Bye . . . "

Having somehow sensed Werner's tension, the young make-up girl pampered and preened him for two hours before the show started. She rubbed his shoulders and massaged his head, which made him feel much better. At one point he was actually drooling, yet without a word the spittle was calmly wiped from his lips with a tissue, and never mentioned. After a coffee and some apple juice, he savoured a large glass of *Weitwein* as he was having his prosthetic nose and bushy whiskers applied.

"Must feel pretty strange, wearing this stuff." said the girl.

"You get used to it – it's better than some costumes I've had to wear, believe me."

"I bet it is . . . " she said. "This might be a stupid question . . . "

"Let me be the judge of that, dear."

"But is this really what a Jew looks like?" she asked.

"Surely you've *seen* a Jew before?"

"Funny isn't it? I don't think I have, anyway. I know they've all got these big noses – and Daddy said they're faces are all screwed up, like rats – but I've never actually seen one."

"I'm sure you probably have, you just don't know it. They're every-where. Some of the pictures you see in films and on posters, they do exaggerate a bit."

"So I might have gone past one in the street and not known about it?" The girl was horrified.

"Afraid so . . . " he said.

"Was never really a problem where I come from, you see, down in Augsburg. We never had any of them – a few gypsies was the worst we saw."

Half an hour before show time and Werner felt good. He sat in his robe, ate fruit and carefully read over the new parts of the script, doing his best to imagine them in performance. He was just starting to contemplate going to the lavatory for his pre-show ritual, when a knock came at the door.

"Who is it?" he called.

"Why not open up and find out?" came the reply.

He opened the door. It was the girl from the party.

"What a nice surprise!" he said. "Sofia, isn't it?"

"You remembered my name."

"An actor needs a good memory."

"Aren't you going to invite me in?"

"Yes, of course." he pulled the door open and she entered. Her eyes quickly searched around his room.

"Is all of this just for you?" she asked.

"I'm pretty lucky," he said.

"But don't you get lonely, being here on your own all the time?" Eyeing him up and down, she rushed towards him and threw her arms around his neck.

"What are you doing?" His voice was high-pitched and anything but assured.

"I know it's what you want, Herr Shylock."

It was ludicrous, even if he wanted to kiss her, there was a three-inch nose strapped to his face.

"Stop it! Please . . . I'm on in a few minutes . . . "

"Come on, just relax," she said. She dropped to her knees and started to unbutton his trousers. He stroked her head, wondering if they could get away with it. Then, there was another knock at the door.

"Fuck! Fuck . . . " he whispered.

"Just ignore it . . . "

"Don't be stupid, they know I'm in here." He pushed her away from him and re-buttoned his trousers. "Just a moment!" he shouted, and tried to compose himself. With a sigh, he pulled open the door.

"Terribly sorry to bother you, Herr Krauss . . . " it was a tall, skinny boy standing with his arm outstretched, "Michael Schmidt, here for the article . . . "

Werner took the man's hand.

"Aren't you a bit young?"

"Judge me on my writing, Herr Krauss . . . "

"Well, it's good to meet you, all the same. You do realise it's only a few minutes until stage time?"

"Yes, of course, I am terribly sorry – must have been a breakdown in communications or something – we were supposed to meet this afternoon . . . perhaps your agent didn't pass on the message?"

"No, he didn't," Werner lied.

"And we *were* promised a piece on *The Merchant* for the morning edition. Just give me two minutes – I can fill out the rest . . . "

"Very well then, *one* minute . . . "

"Great! Before we start, a quick photograph . . . "

The gangly rookie fumbled with his camera for a while, until eventually turning it in Werner's direction. It snapped and flashed without warning. Werner thought he would probably look like a startled animal when they were developed.

"So what is it about *The Merchant of Venice* that attracted you?"

Werner just couldn't think. The boy hadn't even acknowledged Sofia's presence in the room. Perhaps he thought she was an assistant or something.

"It's one of my favourite Shakespeare plays, and I'm sure you'd agree, the theme of the greedy, viscous Jew has never been more relevant to an audience."

He had remembered that line from one of the early reviews.

"Indeed, and if I may say so, your performance is particularly convincing . . . "

"One does one's best to immerse one's self in a role, in a character. No matter how despicable, it is the actor's job to portray the devilish as well as the angelic."

"And is that one of . . . "

"But," Werner interrupted, "your readers have to remember, it *is* just acting. I am not a Jew, after all . . . simply an actor."

"I'm sure that goes without saying, Herr Krauss."

"You'd be surprised, Michael. Unfortunately the line between fact and fiction grows ever more thin, like my hair. You can use that – it might make a good headline."

"I'll bear that in mind."

"Head-line, get it?" Sofia giggled behind him.

"Now as I was saying, is . . . "

"Sorry, time's up. You'll just have to be creative with the rest." Werner took the journalist by the arm and ushered him to the door.

"Well, it was an honour to meet you . . . and thanks again."

"No problem," said Werner, "any time." He closed the door and looked towards Sofia. He felt exhausted – why did these things always happen to him?

"Now, where were we?" she asked.

"We were nowhere," he said, "come on, out now, I should be onstage."

"Fine." She said, and stamped her heels. As she brushed past him on her way to the door she whispered. "You'll want it eventually; I know you will."

After the performance, Werner was pleased to find someone else in his dressing room, waiting for him.

"Darling, you came!" They embraced. "I really *need* you, Maria, I'm just so confused . . . "

"Why, darling? What's wrong?"

"A million things – Egon, Paula, *this damn play* . . . "

"Shh . . . " she stroked his hair reassuringly, "we'll find somewhere to go, and you can tell me all about it."

"It's so good to see you, darling," he said. With his head pressed against her chest, he noticed the bulk in her skirt where the bandage covered her thigh. "I'm so sorry darling, I never wanted you to be hurt . . . never."

He looked into her eyes, and moved in to kiss her.

"Werner, dear, you really pulled it off tonight – wonderful!" It was Muthel. He was clutching a bouquet of flowers and a bottle of champagne.

"Thank you, we couldn't have done it without you."

"Is this a bad time, Werner?"

He stroked his wife's hair.

"Not at all. Just been a bit of an emotional day, I'm sure you'll agree."

Muthel laughed, and gestured towards the champagne, "Are you going to open that thing or what?"

"I thought we were leaving early, Werner?" Maria squeezed his arm.

"Surely one celebratory drink can't do any harm."

"*Werner!*"

"Fine, fine . . . " he said, "we need to leave I'm afraid. We're going to get a room at the Quadriga – treat ourselves. You understand?"

"Of course, enjoy yourselves, you've earned it." Muthel held out the bottle. "Take this, with my compliments."

"Thank you." said Werner. He pulled his wife close, and placed an arm around her. "Same time again tomorrow?" he joked.

"I'm not busy, Werner, why not?"

They slipped into bed together at the hotel room. Maria wore her floral nightdress as usual, but Werner was naked. He rubbed her back, and started to pull at the gown.

"I was hoping you wouldn't need this," he said.

"I thought you wanted to talk, remember?"

"Can't it wait?"

"'Oh Maria, I'm so confused about everything, I need you to be there for me', well here I am, don't tell me this was all a ploy just for you to . . . you know . . . "

"Fine!" he said, and sighed. He sat up, and reached for the champagne. "Egon's wife . . . "

"His fiancée . . . "

"Whatever she is – she's a fucking . . . " he hushed his tone to a whisper, " . . . she's a fucking Jew." The cork popped, and he reached for a glass. "Some friend of that bastard Kohl who lives with Paula . . . "

"I see." She rubbed his arm sympathetically. "Perhaps you'd better pour me a glass." As they both sipped champagne, Werner couldn't help but notice a rather smug, knowing look on his wife's face.

"Anything to say on the matter, then?"

"You know what I think, Werner . . . "

"No," he interrupted, "enlighten me."

"I always said you were likely to get your fingers burnt."

"Go on."

"You don't want to hear this – you're angry with me, I can tell."

"I'm angry – yes – but not with you. Please, I would like to know your opinion."

"Well," she took a deep breath, "I really don't think Egon is the problem here, as such."

"Of course he's the fucking problem!"

"No . . . let me finish . . . I don't think he's the problem *per se*. Be honest, you're not altogether bothered who he marries, are you? Jew, Polack, Negro, whatever . . . I know you, Werner, it's not something that generally concerns you."

"This gets more entertaining by the minute – please continue . . . "

"You wanted my opinion!"

He gulped down his champagne. "Give me the chance to pour another glass first then." He refilled, and noticed there were tears in her eyes. "I'm sorry. It's just difficult, okay, getting your life summed-up in a sound bite or two . . . "

"I'm telling you this because I love you, because I care. None of your friends will speak to you like this – they couldn't care less."

"Let's say that's true, then. What do you think *is* the issue? Or don't you even think it's a problem, my son and his lovely *kosher* wife."

"What I'm trying to say is, you're really upset about how this effects *you*. I agreed with your decision to stay here – God knows, you've done well, darling – and there are hoops that everyone has to jump through these days, but deep down, you know you've been a little *too* eager to please, and you know this business with your son is potentially . . . "

"Stop! Please stop . . . " He stared at his wife, searching for answers. "Then what can I do, Maria? Tell me, please! I'm up to my eyes in *Scheiße*, aren't I?"

"No darling . . . " she wiped his cheeks and started to stroke his hair. "There are always options."

"Like what?"

"Like moving away – getting out of here. You always said how much you loved being in the States. You could hook-up with some old friends out there – you've got contacts in Hollywood."

"If only it was that easy . . . "

"It *is*! You heard what happened to Conrad, he's making *millions* over there after that movie *Casablanca*."

"Don't exaggerate, darling."

"I'm not – it's true!"

"He was playing a fucking Nazi officer, Maria! Fucking traitor . . . I never liked him."

"Traitor – just listen to yourself, Werner. You're an *actor*."

"I'm a *German*, Maria. And being German has worked out quite well for us so far, wouldn't you agree?"

"At what price though, Werner? Most fathers would jump for joy at the announcement of their son's wedding. Look what it's done to you."

They sat up in bed, in silence. Maria finished her glass, and Werner finished the bottle. After a while, Maria settled down . . .

"Just think about America, okay?" she said, and closed her eyes. Werner tried to think of a riposte, but he was so tired, tired of talking and talking . . . what did he have to complain about? He was Werner Krauss for God's sake . . .

Werner checked himself in the mirror. He looked like a dancer at the Lady Windermere – with orbs of rouge daubed onto his cheeks and eyebrows painted on to give a permanent look of surprise. He even had a beauty spot drawn beneath his left eye. He looked down-ward to find he was wearing a basque – an enormous petticoat and high-heeled shoes. Outside the dressing room they were getting rest-less. He could hear them stamping their jackboots and slapping the table.

"Werner, Werner, Werner . . . " they chanted.

He broke into a cold sweat – what were his lines? Did he even have any lines? He needed help . . .

"Maria . . . " he called. "Please darling, come and help me."

"She's gone, sweetie." he turned to find another man dressed like him, staring into the mirror and painting on some red lipstick, " . . . but I'm always here."

"Well where is she? She knows I'm on in a minute."

"She's gone, darling."

"Gone where?"

"You know where, you sent her . . . "

He had to play along, he had to find out what was happening.

"Of course, so I did."

"But, you know, Werner . . . " the man leaned in closer, "I can help you right now . . . "

He dropped to his knees and disappeared beneath Werner's multi-layered underskirt.

"What are you doing? Get off, get off! Someone will see!"

"Just relax . . . " *he heard the voice say between his legs,* " . . . we're just pretending, right?"

"No! You're fucking disgusting. Get off!"

Werner stood and lifted his frock.

"Come on," *said the man,* "just once – no one will ever know . . . " *he clambered towards Werner on his knees, trying to grab him under the skirt. Werner felt sick. He lashed out with his leg, and caught the man square on the chin with his knee.*

"Fucking fairy, don't come near me again!" *Blood was pouring from the man's mouth. But Werner didn't want to stop, he felt so angry. He punched at the top of the man's head, and the man fell to the ground.* "Who are you, eh? Fucking queers disgust me . . . "

"It's just me," *spluttered the man,* "stop, please, you're hurting."

There was something familiar about him, a look, a neediness. Werner punched again, and kicked, and grabbed the man by the throat and planted a head butt. He didn't want to stop – he wanted everyone to know he wasn't that way, this wasn't who he was, he would show them, he would kill this little bastard . . .

4

He was awoken by a newspaper being slapped across his face.

"Cheating bastard dragging me to a fucking hotel!" He wrestled his arms free from the sheets and shielded his face in self-defence.

"What? What's going on?"

"Wife, Werner? Your fucking *wife*? Stick your hotels and fucking horses up your arse for all I care!"

The slapping stopped. The door slammed. The door re-opened.

"Better still, why not take your fucking *wife*!"

The door slammed again. His wife? Surely she couldn't be talking about Paula? He sat up, reached for the paper and began to flick through its pages. He couldn't see what the problem was, until he found a small article towards the back. Under the crude headline: *Werner Krauss – Modest Genius*, was a blurry photograph of him and Sofia in his dressing room.

"Fuck! Fucking idiot kid journalist, fucking fuck!"

It got worse. Beneath the photograph was the caption: *Werner Krauss and his wife relax backstage.*

"Scheiße!"

He quickly skimmed through the article itself, to find lots of syco-phantic drivel about 'the greatest Shylock of the age' and 'the leading light in the theatre of the Reich', but no further mention of that girl. He tossed the paper aside and lay back down for a moment, wondering what on earth he could do to calm her down this time. He had to go on the offensive – rumours would be starting, gossip . . . and what about Otto? Casually reading the paper, wherever he was, and finding his daughter *in flagranti* with a friend twice her age. Or was it three times? Anyhow, he had to act quickly and decisively. He crawled over to Maria's side of the bed and picked up the phone.

"I don't care what fucking time it is, you need to get here *now!* . . . The Quadriga Hotel on the Eiselberner Straße . . . well we could spend all morning talking about it over the phone *or* how about you get off your lazy arse and get here *now*! Which is it to be? . . . Suffice to say, it's damaging, okay? I'm not going to spell it out over the phone . . . The paper! Don't you read the fucking papers? Isn't it part of your job? . . . Sorry, sorry, just trust me, you need to get here and help . . . and bring your contact book if you've fucking got one . . . no she's not here and it'll be blatantly obvious why *if* you put the phone down and get in a cab . . . now, Stefan, now!"

He had to admit, it was quite cathartic to be able to shout at his agent. He quickly dialled again . . .

"Hello, Uta, is that you? . . . It's Werner, is Maria with you? . . . You've seen it then? Please let me explain . . . No it was some girl – she's the producer's daughter, I . . . Otto Weitner . . . he *does* have a daughter – *that's her!* . . . Okay, whatever you think, just do this for me please . . . Please, just listen, if you see Maria, tell her to call me at the hotel – it's all a stupid misunderstanding . . . the paper got it wrong – they'll be apologising in tomorrow's edition, I promise you that . . . Please remember what I said? . . . Goodbye . . . "

Uta was Maria's agent, and the only other phone number he knew by heart. She said *he* would be the *last* person she'd tell, even if she *did* know where Maria was. He decided to run a hot bath.

As he lay there unwrapping the fluorescent green hotel soap, he stared down at his penis floating in the water. Could this small appendage, this dumb acorn, be to blame for everything? He tried to go over yesterday's events in his mind: he hadn't invited that girl into his room, or, at least, he hadn't invited her *to* his room. She had, lit-erally, thrown herself at him. They'd barely had a conversation – she went straight for his zipper. And of course he was aroused, what man wouldn't be? She had stroked him and looked at him with those deep, dark eyes. He had touched her head gently – he wasn't guiding her – it just felt right, like a parental act of affection. Then there was the knock. And the news new-boy. And the flashing fucking camera.

Stirring up these memories had caused another stirring in the warm water in front of him. He considered touching it, but was disturbed, yet again, by a knock.

"Werner, it's me. Straight here, like you wanted."

"Give me a minute, Stefan . . . " He climbed out of the bath and took a deep breath. His penis shrivelled and cowered in the cold air. Was it to blame? Of course it was. He pulled on a robe and threw a towel around his shoulders. "This is when . . . " he opened the door, and Stefan ambled into the room, " . . . you earn your money."

"I knew you wouldn't resist a girl like that, Werner. You've always been a sucker for those young ones . . . "

"Stefan, grow up!"

"It's a shame you don't take the same attitude to your women."

"Okay, first job, you call the paper."

"And say what exactly? The girl *was* in your room, after all."

"But she's not my wife!"

"And you want to draw attention to that fact, do you?"

"Good point," Werner said. He hadn't even entertained the option of keeping quiet about this. "But what about Maria?"

"Did the journalist catch you doing anything?"

"No – because we *weren't* doing anything . . . "

"I can't help you if you don't tell me the truth."

"It *is* the truth – she burst into my dressing room and grabbed me!"

"Why doesn't that ever happen to me? Why don't girls ever just grab me?"

"It's either the way you look, smell or feel, Stefan."

The agent made a rather dramatic gesture, plunging his nose into his own armpit. He took a sniff, and smiled.

"So Maria saw the article?"

"Of course she saw the article – have *you* seen it yet?"

"I had a quick look in the taxi, *terrible* photo, Werner . . . "

"Okay, stop. This might all be a big joke to you. But think about it a second – it's serious, it could fucking *ruin* me."

They both fell silent. Werner had hoped Stefan would have ideas, take the bull by the horns and sort it all out. But he was only human, and the evidence was pretty difficult to dispute. It was all so stupid.

Stefan put an arm around Werner. "Come on, you'll get through this. Who should I call first?" Werner didn't reply. "Anyone, come on! Like you said, this is what I get paid for."

"Weitner."

"Are you joking?"

"Do I look like I'm joking?"

"Weitner . . . fuck! What the hell am I supposed to say? 'Did you see your daughter in the newspaper today?'"

"You said *anyone* – just find out where he is and have a chat. See if he's seen the article . . . give him an explanation."

"Okay I'll do it." He squeezed Werner's shoulder. "And the reason she was in the room?"

"Say anything . . . say she wanted some autographs for her friends."

"Ever thought of becoming a professional liar, Werner?"

"Isn't that what I do already?"

Stefan opened his tatty old red contact book and started to flick through. Tracing a name and number with his finger, he picked up the phone and began to dial.

"I'm going back to bed, I don't want to hear this . . . I'm not here, okay?" He walked through to the bedroom and collapsed. To think he was paying for this hotel as a way of getting closer to Maria . . . He closed his eyes and hoped sleep would take him. But his head throbbed with lies and problems. Perhaps she was right about America – they could make a fresh start together . . . he could call Conrad to find out what was involved. Would he even be welcome abroad? Maybe if he took Egon with him, and his wife . . .

"Hallelujah!" Stefan burst into the bedroom, and flicked-on the lights.

"What happened?" Werner sat up.

"Weitner's fine, absolutely . . . "

"What did he say?"

"That she's a terrible flirt and he hopes she didn't get in your way!"

"Did you tell him what it said, about her being my wife?"

"He had a good laugh about that actually. He's quite a gent when you get to know him."

"Next job, call the paper – we want a retraction and an apology – the girl was just an autograph-hunter . . . their mistake has caused considerable distress to my wife and I," he slipped out of bed and started to get dressed.

"Where are you going?"

"Home, to look for Maria. If she's not there, at least my contact book is."

"What about me?"

"You know what to do."

A different driver appeared at the reception desk. He was stocky and swarthy.

"Where's Lothar?" Werner asked.

"He won't be driving you any longer sir, my name's Gerard."

"Fuck, why, what happened?"

"You'll have to ask the agency, sir. I just got the call this morning."

"Yes, of course, sorry Gerard." He held out a hand. "Pleased to meet you, my name is Werner."

As he had expected, Werner returned home to find the place empty. There was no note, and no sign that Maria had even been there at all. He found her list of phone numbers and dialled them all, but by now everyone in town had seen the article, and some hung-up the moment he introduced himself. The thought of withdrawing from tonight's performance crossed his mind, but he decided this would only fuel the speculation about his private life, and make it look as though he had something to hide. So, with time to kill, and resigned to the fact that today was unquestionably a bad day, he poured a large brandy, and decided to drink until show time.

After three drinks, the telephone rang.

"Maria? . . . Sorry, how are you, Stefan? . . . Did you talk to someone at the paper? . . . Thank God – and they didn't question you at all? . . . So they should be . . . That's great, thank you, Stefan, I'm sorry I was so manic this morning, you understand . . . take a guess? No, the house is empty and she's not been back . . . Well, what can I do? . . . I've had *one* drink and I think I deserve it today, don't you? . . . What do you think – of course I'm not going to Marian's for dinner. I'll talk to him . . . The performance will be fine, I know that Jew inside out . . . would I ever let you down? . . . don't answer that, old boy . . . By the way, why isn't Lothar driving for me anymore? . . . Find out, will you, the new one looks like a shaved gorilla . . . thanks Stefan . . . oh, actually, sorry, there was something else I wanted you to get into the paper, about the Shylock Jewish thing . . . I suppose so . . . yes, okay . . . remind me another day, it is important . . . No, I'll be fine . . . okay, thanks . . . Goodbye."

"Yes!" he shouted. It seemed as though this whole mess might get sorted out after all. If only he could find his wife. He dialled Uta's number again, but this time there was no answer. Again, he reached for the brandy decanter and drank to a slumber.

A slamming door woke him.

"Thought you'd find me at the bottom of that bottle did you?"

"I've looked everywhere – where have you been? I've been worried sick."

"Saying good-bye, Werner. Good-bye to Mother and to everything . . . "

"Darling, please . . . "

"Don't bother, Werner. I've had enough." She waved a bottle of pills in the air. "You won't see me again. Enjoy your new life without me, Werner. New life and new wife."

"Can we at least talk?"

She ignored him, turned, and left.

"Please!" he shouted, "Maria!"

By the time Gerard arrived, Werner realised he had drank too much. As he searched for his coat, he stumbled from one foot to the other, and didn't even attempt to lock the apartment with his key.

"We have to stop for coffee on the way, dear . . . awfully sorry, forgotten your name already . . . "

"It's Gerard, sir . . . "

"Gerard – isn't that French? Please can we stop for some coffee on the way, Gerard."

"Of course, sir, although I was told to get you to the theatre for five thirty . . . "

"Dear boy . . . " Werner placed an arm around his driver's shoulders, "they can't start the play without me – I'm Werner Krauss!"

"Very good, sir."

"Do you have a wife, Gerard?"

"I don't actually, sir, no . . . "

"Good for you – more trouble than they're worth – honestly, you make one or two *little* mistakes – they haul you over the coals, Gerard, they want their pound of flesh . . . "

He arrived at the theatre thirty minutes before the show was due to start. He felt as though he had sobered up, and was confident he could still perform. Gerard helped him out of the car and was rewarded with twenty marks

"Welcome to the team, old boy – never a dull moment."

"Thank you, Herr Krauss . . . most generous."

"Now make sure you're here *the moment* I come offstage. I need to see my wife as soon as is humanly possible."

"As you wish, sir."

They were ushered to a side-door by a security guard, who got ten marks and from there, a member of theatre staff guided him backstage and was rewarded five.

"Herr Muthel, I'm sorry, it's been a hell of a day . . . "

"Don't worry, Stefan explained. Are you sure you can do this?"

"Positive, old boy. It'll be nice to transform myself into the old Usurer for a couple of hours – just what the doctor ordered."

"If you're sure?"

Werner nodded.

"So then everyone, it looks like we've got a show. I want costume here *now* to work on the glorious Herr Krauss – and somebody tell front-of-house we'll be running a few minutes late."

Muthel's authoritative tone was reassuring, and the assistants immediately sprang to life. Werner's attempts to strike up a conversation with these women were met with icy silence – the whole place had obviously been on tenterhooks as they thought cancellation was imminent. They appeared in and out of focus for Werner, who drifted off to sleep for a few minutes whilst having his make-up applied. In what seemed like an instant, he was waiting in the wings, hunched over in a heavy coat and with the giant prosthetic snout stuck to his face.

Why there, there, there, there! A diamond gone, cost me two thousand ducats in Frankfort! The curse never fell upon our nation till now; I never felt it till now. Two thousand ducats in that, and other precious, precious jewels. I would my daughter were dead at my foot, and the ducats in her coffin!

The virulent booing and hissing of the crowd seemed to vindicate his decision to perform tonight. He smiled as rotten fruit narrowly missed his head – Muthel had planted stooges in the audience to throw these things and whip the crowd into a frenzy. Behind the Semitic nose and bushy eyebrows he lost himself in the world of the greedy Yid. He had even granted himself a quick gulp of brandy during the interval. As the curtain fell for the final time, he headed straight to the stage door. He didn't change out of costume or even remove his make-up. Greeted by the familiar Berlin chill, he dashed to the front of the theatre, where Gerard welcomed him.

"Good show, Herr Shylock?"

"So – so. Now drive quickly. I've a marriage to save."

"Very good, sir."

It had played on his mind all through the performance. How seriously should he take her words? Maria had always been dramatic (of course), but in all those years of threatening to leave, threatening to call the police or, indeed, threatening to kill him, this had been her first threat of suicide.

But what could he say to her? Turning up, sweaty and inebriated, with a million other things on his mind – *what good could he do?*

"Stop the car, Gerrard."

"Yes, sir."

"I want to walk home, I need some time to think . . . "

"As you wish, Herr Krauss." He climbed out of the car. "But sir, your costume . . . "

Perhaps he could buy her roses . . . they could talk of holidays and children. She always *said* she didn't want children, but maybe that was because it's what she thought he wanted to hear. Stooped, and stumbling past the gaudy shop fronts of the Frederickstrasse, he wondered if he really wanted any of it – children, Maria, the whole idea of damn relationships. The shouting, the worrying, the fighting, the *energy*. Like when he was married to Paula, all Maria seemed to do was remind him of his inadequacies. Sofia, on the other hand, obviously thought he could do no wrong.

It wasn't as if this was the first time a beautiful young stranger had propositioned him. In the past, though, he'd always managed to dismiss these girls as silly, infatuated and most probably dull (after initial passion and wrecklessness, that is). He couldn't decide if it was Sofia he craved, or simply anyone other than his wife.

"Juden. *Juden!*" – a couple of youths called after him. Used to being beckoned by strangers, he didn't think about what they had said. He simply turned, smiled, waved, and returned to his thoughts. He couldn't deny that the thought of sleeping with Sofia was appealing. She obviously wasn't shy . . . and she was so young, so lithe . . .

"Where is your armband, *Jew*?" One of the youths spat, and shouted again. "Not welcome here, *Jew*. Not very clever, *Jew*." He turned again, and realised the youths – dark-haired boys who were well-built, but could only have been about fourteen – were following him.

"Stop this now!" his voice quivered. He maintained a steady pace.

"Or what, *Jew*? What will you *do*?"

"I am not a Jew, don't be absurd. Run away before I tell your parents."

Werner caught a glimpse of his own reflection in a shop window. He saw an old Jew, staggering along, as if imbalanced by the weight of his hooked beak.

"Father hates Jews, doesn't he?" said one boy. The other, shorter but stockier, grunted in agreement. And with that, they charged. He heard the quickening of footsteps, but knew he couldn't run in his heavy coat. He turned his back to them, his face flushed with outrage.

"You boys are in a lot of trouble."

"Yid thinks he can tell us what to do," said one. He pushed the actor in the back, causing him to stumble.

"You'll regret that."

"Says who, Jew scum?" The other boy took his turn to push, and this time he fell. The pain in his knees was sickening. It reminded him of falling from his bicycle as a child.

"Stop, stop!" he pleaded, and turned to face the boys. They were poised with stones in their hands, ready to throw. "I'm not a Jew, I'm a German. A German, I swear . . . " In one swift movement he tore the whiskers from his chin.

"What the . . . " said one boy, " . . . who the hell *are* you?" The boy flexed his throwing-arm once more, but began to back away. With great deliberation, the actor pinched his right nostril, and resisted the temptation to smile.

"I said 'who are you?' Are you fucking deaf?"

Suddenly, he tore the nose from his face. Both boys shrieked, and he threw the long Jewish snout in their direction. The taller boy flinched as the rubber appendage bounced off his shoulder. They both dropped their stones and ran. "*Sich. Sie ist Sich!*"

DEAR WERNER,

I sometimes wonder – what did you want to be? What did you really want to be? I remember all those years ago when Das Cabinet *was released: everyone in Germany went to see that movie, then people around Europe and finally America. You predicted it would happen and it did! Such happy times! You had the whole world in your hands – complete control over your destiny. But I wonder if maybe control was something you just couldn't handle – something you were never supposed to have.*

Most of your friends took control – they could see what was happening here and they didn't like it. People like Conrad – they could have stayed to become a hero for the government, a stooping, snivelling National Socialist icon like you. But they gave it up, because they knew what they believed in, knew exactly what they wanted. Did you know what you wanted, Werner? Or did you just drift from one state of affairs to the next, from one set of rules, from one luxury apartment, from one day, one drink, one fucking girl – to the next?

Perhaps it's a skill – something I'll never understand, this ability you have to just set fire to the past and take refuge in the present. When you drink, the past doesn't matter, does it? It's just a series of incidents, coincidences, mistakes, gestures – all gloriously and chaotically leading you to a bottle and a glass.

But to me, each sip is an insult – you're so desperate to get away from what we have, what we had, that you'll gulp and slurp and swallow until it's all gone. Just you, a drink, and maybe a giggling little whore, eh Werner?

Did you know that most men reach a point of realisation? They know they can't just pluck a new young thing off the street every once in a while. That's why people get married, Werner. Most people recognise that their looks, their charms or talents are all fleeting . . . they have to work at a relationship because they don't want to die alone. Like an investment, because they want someone to share life with and grow old with – their looks might deteriorate but their hearts . . .

Of course, you don't have to, do you? You only have to cast your net as far as the nearest star-struck schoolgirl. I bet you don't even make an effort anymore – at least when I was eighteen I'd get a few anecdotes, a quip and a whiff of the latest French fragrance. Look at you now, ushering girls into your dressing room with nothing but a robe to conceal the purpling veins and the paunch. I bet she's the envy of all her friends. Her parents must be so proud.

Before she died, Mother warned me about you. She said the only way anyone ever became famous was through selfishness. It makes perfect sense, because most people are too busy looking after their family, or are too burdened with doubts and fears, that only the truly conceited can rise to prominence. "How on earth do you expect him to treat you properly, when his job, his whole reason for being, is acting?" she said. Poor mother, stuck in that damn hospital, listening to me recount your empty promises . . .

You might think it a little ridiculous – not one note from me but several, not one death but many. But maybe when you read these (as you surely will) you'll finally get the chance to take a proper look at the dream world you live in. That what you do actually affects people, *Werner. This is the only way I'll ever make you see that.*

Goodbye –
Maria x

"Darling, you're home – thank God! . . . I've told you, the paper have promised to print my letter – I don't really trust Stefan so I did it myself, I've just got off the phone to them now . . . For God's sake, of course I care . . . I needed to know you were alive! . . . Do you remember what you said this afternoon? . . . I didn't know where you were . . . But Uta said she hadn't seen you . . . yes, *very* clever, hope you all had a good laugh at old Werner's expense . . . well, I suppose so . . . maybe we should forgive each other? . . . All right, but you'll at least give me a chance to explain? . . . And I'll see you at home tomorrow? . . . No, I'm staying with Freund, he's looking after me . . . Maria, stop being paranoid for once – I'm injured and can barely move . . . it's too late now and I'm tired, let me explain tomorrow, let's just say it's been a bad night . . . Yes . . . and you have to stop doing this . . . Promise? . . . I love you, darling . . . bye."

He replaced the handset, took a breath, and limped from the study to the bedroom.

"How could they do it to my sweet *Shylock*? Just lie down – don't move – I'm going to look after you. Make it *all* better."

He untied his nightgown and it dropped to the floor. Glancing in the mirror, he noticed thin, greying hair, a sagging stomach and grazed knees. Momentarily his heart sank, as a pale, naked Sofia joined him in the frame, and began to massage his shoulders.

5

His head was pulsating. He had to get back to Maria. A theatrical temperament was one thing, but feeling suicidal was quite another. He had to take this seriously, and try to do the right thing. As much as he had enjoyed the frantic, slippery glow of his late-night adventure, he was also racked with guilt, and perturbed by his lover's neediness. Having lay there for a couple of hours, he slid out of bed and started to dress.

"Where are you going?" She was completely naked, her head resting on a beige comfort blanket.

"Nowhere . . . " He buckled his watch and searched for his socks.

"You're not leaving, are you? After what we . . . "

"I'll call you tomorrow, okay?"

"Don't bother!" She jumped out of bed and headed for the bathroom. The door slammed. He finished dressing, and limped as quietly as he could down the stairs. It was three a.m. and he had no idea where he could find a taxi. He hobbled as far as the *Torstraße*, hoping there would be a café or dance hall open, but all was dark. He started to become frightened – what if he was mistaken for a Jew again? He was wearing the big Shylock coat, after all. He considered dumping it, but it was too good at keeping out the cold. He made a conscious effort not to limp, and walk in an upright, respectable, German manner. But maybe, he thought, *this* would draw attention, and he could get attacked in a more traditional fashion – beaten up for his wallet full of cash . . . "I'm going mad," he thought, "leaving a warm bed, an exquisite girl . . . for this."

He walked for what felt like miles until he noticed flashing neon salvation in the distance. It was a small hotel on the Koppenplatz. He did his best to get there quickly, and shed a tear of joy when he reached the reception.

"No vacancies . . . " said a deep voice behind the desk.

"Hello . . . that's fine, if possible, I just need to use your phone . . . "

"They don't pay for themselves you know, sir . . . "

"I'll make it worth your while." Werner slid ten marks across the counter, and the telephone appeared.

"What on earth happened? Oh, Werner come here!"

He limped into the arms of his wife. "I just couldn't be away from you any longer, I was so worried, darling, about what you might do . . . "

"I was upset. People say silly things when they're upset." She rubbed his back with motherly vigour.

"I know, darling, I know."

He held her tightly; gripping her emaciated shoulder, he could still smell the vinegar sweetness of Sofia on his fingers.

"Get into bed, I'll make us both a hot drink, and you can tell me all about it . . . "

He kissed her cheek. "Thank you, darling," he said, and, after washing his hands, he did as he was told.

He ran and ran as fast as he could. He somehow knew it was going to be bad news, but maybe if he could get there quickly enough . . .

Paula had been the first to warn him. She'd garbled some rubbish about his influence and responsibility, but he wasn't listening, he knew he just had to run. He reached the summit of a large hill in Tiergarten, and the scene came into focus. A wedding dress, a soldier, a gun. As he ran down the hill, he lost his footing and tripped. He rolled, only to stop at a mound of blood-stained silk. He shrieked. It was Hannah in her white dress – she had been shot dead. He found his feet, leapt over her, and continued to run, until he came to the officer poised with the gun. A man was kneeling and screaming in front of him.

"You bastards! How could you do it?"

"Turn around now, Herr Krauss, there is nothing to see . . . "

"Egon?" he called, "Egon, is that you?"

The kneeling man didn't answer, he just shivered and gasped.

"Herr Krauss, it is my duty to inform you that you have to leave, now please, I am under strict orders."

"Egon, what happened?"

"Father – tell them to stop!" Egon turned to face his father. There was blood oozing from his mouth. Werner turned to the officer.

"For God's sake put that gun away . . . "

"This is your last warning, Herr Krauss . . . "

"So you know who I am, then. If you've got any fucking sense, you'll put the fucking gun down!

The soldier turned to face Werner.

"I am under orders, Herr Krauss, under the laws of racial purity, whoever you are, this man is a criminal . . . "

"He was getting married you idiot, not robbing a bank . . . "

"I don't enjoy doing this Herr Krauss . . . "

"Doing what?"

The gun fired, and Werner fell.

"Father! No!"

A white light. Warmth. The soldier was under orders. A high-pitched buzzing in his ears. Orders must be obeyed. Was he urinating?

He woke up, and the first thing he saw was the large mug of cold cocoa on his side table. The space next to him in bed was empty. He rubbed his eyes, and tried to remember exactly where he was.

"Maria . . . " his voice was whiny and childlike, "Ma – ri – a!"

"You're awake. Time for some explanations." She breezed into the bedroom, and straightened the sheets, even though he was still in them.

"Darling, you were right."

"About what, in particular?"

"America. You were right, we should go. We *will* go."

"Are you serious?" She pulled open the curtains, causing Werner to shield his eyes from the morning son.

"Yes, of course. I've been so stupid – for the people who matter, for you and poor Egon, we could all start again, darling. We could all just start again."

"Tell me about the girl."

"Did you hear what I said? About America?" He slipped out of bed, and headed for the lavatory.

"What happened with the girl?"

Werner sighed, he hadn't planned to defend himself whilst urinating. "It was the same girl from the party, Weitner's daughter. I know, I know, but believe me, she's crazy. She turned up at the dressing room, asking for autographs for all her friends. I just wanted to get rid of her . . . and thought the quickest way would be to sign the damn things and get it over with."

"Enough lies – she was there during the interview, Werner, it's in the paper – she's in the fucking photograph!"

"Now, ah, you're wrong. I didn't even give an interview. You made me cancel, remember?"

"What?"

"Remember, you told me not to go for the interview. You told me I should meet Egon, 'he's your son, Werner', remember?"

"So?"

"So, it was *that* journalist. *He* turned up at the same time as the girl, asking why I didn't show up. I apologised and gave him *carte blanche* to just make up the whole story . . . "

"So he saw this girl, this girl so *desperate* for an autograph, and somehow deduced that she was your wife?"

"Pretty much – they were both in the room for three minutes, if that."

"Ridiculous . . . "

"It's the truth." He grabbed her hand. "Darling . . . " She pulled away.

"And last night?"

"I stayed with Freund, I told you, remember?"

"You did, didn't you? In fact, according to Freund, you're still there."

"What do you mean?"

"'He can't come to the phone now, Maria, he's taking a bath.' It's actually quite sweet, how many of your pathetic minions will lie for you . . . "

"All right, all right . . . I went to see her."

"I knew it!"

"But only to sort things out. Tell her there's nothing, of course there's nothing between us, it's all so stupid."

"And a midnight visit helped with that, did it? Sent out the right signals?"

"I didn't care what the time was – I wanted to stop her from hassling me, okay? Her father has a hand in most of the plays that get shown in this town. You have to do these things properly."

"Fine . . . " she seemed exasperated. Werner's head was spinning. His entire life was starting to seem like an interrogation.

"It's the truth, darling. I could see how much it had upset you – her stupid note and that fucking photograph. I had to put a stop to it."

"So why couldn't you just tell me that then, be honest with me?"

"Because I knew how you'd react. How you always react. You're suspicious at the best of times, am I really likely to tell you I'm visiting a girl?"

"I suppose not." She started to take clothes from her drawers, unfold then re-fold them. "For what it's worth then, what's your big plan for America?"

"There is no 'big plan'. We just need to get away. I want you to be happy and I want to get Egon out of danger. Berlin, Europe, we need to get away from all of it, at least until the war's over. I know it's strange, but I had this dream . . . "

"I heard. You were whining again."

"It was more like a nightmare this time. He was in terrible trouble."

"Who?"

"Egon. He was in trouble because of *her*, the Jew. It felt vivid, like a warning. I don't usually remember my dreams."

"Well do it for him, then . . . I'm serious, Werner, if you're doing this to please me, don't bother. But if you genuinely think you can help your son . . . "

"I will. Thanks." For the first time, he was starting to get the impression she really didn't care. "Darling?"

"Yes . . . "

"What about us? We didn't finish talking about last night, the newspaper and everything. I was attacked you know, by a gang of thugs, they thought I was a Jew."

"Really . . . maybe you can tell me about it another time."

He heard her shuffle around in the lounge, and the door was closed carefully.

He looked at the drinks cabinet, but decided to resist. Perhaps if he made some enquiries about America, just to find out if it was even possible, she would take him more seriously, and maybe start to forgive him. He slipped into his dressing gown and searched through Maria's drawers, where she had neatly filed all their bills and important papers. Her system was immaculate, and each piece of paper pristine. Eventually, he found what he was looking for – the old contact book from his time on *Das Cabinet*. He picked up the phone.

=== ❖ ===

"I told you to come alone!"

"Father, Hannah's going to be my wife – get used to it."

"Fine."

"Now, why the hell did we have to come here just to talk about – what was it again – a holiday?" Egon surveyed the derelict building site around them.

"That was just what I said on the phone. Egon, you need to start thinking about security . . . people listen-in all the time. People spy – that's why I told you to come on your own."

"Do you mean people like him?" Egon nodded in Gerard's direction. Werner's black Mercedes was certainly conspicuous amongst the dust and rubble.

"He's just my driver, he's . . . "

"Okay, okay – get to the point, Dad."

"The way I acted the other day, around you, Hannah, it was rude and stupid . . . " She gave a polite smile. "The truth is, I've known plenty of Jewish people over the years, they've never really caused me any problems. In fact, my mentor was the great Max Reinhardt – have you both heard of him?" Hannah nodded. "I know they're – you're – getting a rough time at the moment . . . "

"Took a while to catch on, did it?" said Egon.

"So, Hannah," he took her hand, "I'm sorry. Welcome to this family of ours . . . though God only knows why you put up with this one." He pointed towards his son. She smiled.

"Thank you, Herr Krauss. Egon has always said that you are a good man."

"Now, the reason I wanted to talk to you. You mentioned that Hannah had a lot of family in America . . . "

"They're going to America, or trying, at least . . . "

"Maria and I talked it over and . . . nothing's certain . . . but we'd like to move there too. Why don't you both come with us?"

"You can't be serious . . . "

"I am, why not? Let's be honest, this place isn't safe for you both, is it? I have heard how the Jews are being treated – I'm not *that* out of touch – and . . . " he swallowed hard, "I don't think it's right. Maria's really keen, and I need a new challenge, a fresh start."

"What about money, and work . . . we'll need passports and . . . "

"Hold it there." Werner interrupted, "nothing's for certain yet. But you're forgetting your old Dad has friends over there – producers, studio-types . . . that sort of thing shouldn't be a problem."

"Oh, Herr Krauss!" Hannah leapt forward and embraced him. "If you could help us, it would be so wonderful. You're a good man, Herr Krauss – we love you!"

He delicately patted her on the back. It was a relief to feel her close to him, and not collapsed in a pool of her blood, as she had been a few hours earlier. Noticing her armband once more, he checked that no one was watching.

"Like I said, nothing's for certain. But I'm looking into it – I think it's best for all of us."

"What about mother?" Egon asked.

"Of course, if she wants to come too . . . " Werner hadn't considered Paula, and knew the idea wouldn't exactly improve things with Maria. "Don't get your hopes up. I'll be in touch again in another few days when I've spoken to the right people."

"Father, thank you. I'm so . . . *we're* both grateful to you . . . " He hugged Werner and started to weep. For the first time, Werner realised that their lives must already be quite difficult. He felt proud of the fact Egon obviously loved this girl, and was prepared to endure anything to stay with her.

"I need to get going. But, like I said, I'll be in touch."

On the journey home, Werner shed a few tears of his own. He hated the thought of his son struggling – the worry and torment they must be going through. Whatever happened, he thought, between him and stupid girls or directors, producers, whoever – he should do all he could for Egon.

He felt a little in shock at having been so friendly with the Jew. His own words echoed in his ears "I know how Jews are treated and I don't think it's right." He'd never said anything like that before. Usually, if the subject of politics came up when he was amongst friends, he would go to the bar, or simply make a joke of the whole thing. Now, it felt as though he had committed to something, and taken a stand. He thought about the way those boys had behaved – the vile, loathsome looks on their young faces and their foul language.

"*Scheiße!*" he said, "the newspaper!"

He asked Gerard to stop at the newsagents. Werner dashed into the shop, grabbed a paper and left a five mark note on the counter. Frantically flicking to the arts section, he found what he was looking for. He read it aloud to Gerard:

THIS IS A SPECIAL ANNOUNCEMENT, REGARDING ONE OF THE REICH'S MOST RESPECTED AND ESTEEMED ACTORS.

DESPITE HIS SKILFUL AND ACCURATE PORTRAYAL OF DESPI-CABLE JEWISH CHARACTERS, WERNER KRAUSS, THE ACTOR, IS *NOT* A JEW. RATHER, HE IS A LOYAL ARYAN, SEEKING ONLY TO SERVE HIS ART AND HIS COUNTRY. HERR KRAUSS AND HIS WIFE MARIA ARE STRONG SUPPORTERS OF THE NEW REICH, AND PASSIONATE DEFENDERS OF THE NATIONAL SOCIALIST IDEAL.

"Very impressive, sir."

"You don't think it a little excessive?"

"Not at all, sir. I think it's to your credit – you don't want to be confused with that fucking Yid filth – if you'll pardon my language, sir."

"Yes, of course." With his rugged features and leery demeanour, Werner could tell that Gerard was clearly uncomfortable in his chauffer suit, and realised this would be a good opportunity to find out what the average man really thought about his new friends.

"So you feel strongly about the Jews then, eh?"

"Of course, sir."

"You don't mind me asking questions, do you?" Gerard shook his head. "It's just interesting to me. Ever have any problems with them?"

"Yes sir, got all the good jobs, didn't they? Doctors, lawyers, fucking bankers – and didn't deserve any of it. Thank God – and the *Führer* – it's all changing now."

"Indeed." There was an almost sarcastic tone to the driver's voice, which made Werner feel uneasy. "But, what I mean is, were you ever affected *personally* – did you ever have to work with them, or, God forbid, live with them?"

"No, not really, sir. We had some at the bottom of our street, but, never had anything to do with them, kept themselves to themselves."

He arrived home to find Maria writing a letter.

"So did you see the paper, darling?"

"I saw the piece about the paranoid actor not wanting to be mistaken for a Jew, if that's what you mean."

"Very funny – it said Herr Krauss and his wife *Maria* . . . "

"In the small-print was I? Well, what an honour . . . "

"Darling, I could hardly ask for two announcements – not in the same edition – that *would* be paranoid."

"Don't worry, I'll cope. So are you going to tell me what happened with this blood-thirsty gang of Jew haters, then?"

"It was my own fault I suppose, I was so worried about you – so confused – I left the theatre straight away, and started wandering home in the full Shylock costume."

Maria stifled a laugh.

"It's not funny. I thought you were going to kill yourself, I didn't know what to do."

"Oh, Werner . . . " She stroked his arm. He couldn't determine the extent to which she was being ironic, but was grateful for some physical contact.

"They started shouting at me, it was terrifying. "*Jud, Jud, Jud*" they said. They were chasing me, then they tripped me up . . . "

"So how the hell did you get away?"

The telephone rang.

"Sorry darling," he said, and lifted the receiver. "Yes, who is it? . . . I saw it . . . obviously, it was me who changed it – who did you think it was? . . . If you must know I was attacked, by a gang – they thought I was a fucking Jew . . . never mind 'why', they just did – I told you before there'd be trouble – anyway, what do you want? . . . I made a few calls, that's all . . . since when was I supposed to inform you of every call I make? . . . it's an idea, okay? Everyone needs a challenge, look at what's happened to Conrad over there . . . millions I heard . . . now's not the time, Stefan, not over the phone . . . where do you think you can meet me? The theatre! I'm there most days, in case you hadn't noticed . . . oh, did you find out anything about Lothar? . . . Stay on the case, though . . . Okay, see you later."

He replaced the handset.

"So you really are serious about America?" She sounded impressed.

"Yes, I told you . . . "

"I thought it would just be one of your fads that never amount to anything."

She scrunched up the piece of paper she was using into a ball, and held it tightly.

"What you said about Egon was right – if I can help him then I should . . . "

"I'm proud of you, Werner." She gave a warm smile. "Though what Hannah's family will think when they see your pronouncements on 'despicable Jews' remains to be seen."

Despite her tone, what he wanted most in the world, at that moment, was to kiss her. He knew he'd not been a great husband, and had behaved pretty appallingly of late. He also knew that a morning of phone calls wouldn't earn him the right to kiss her. But

if he could, perhaps she would just lose herself to him for a moment
. . .

"Don't you have another interview today?" she asked.

"Yes, I'm supposed to be there in an hour – he's renowned for his
– ahem – *inventive* questioning apparently. Stefan said he's amazed the
man's still in work. Of course, if it was up to me, I'd prepare for him
with a cocktail or two . . . " he smiled, "but one of your steaming hot
coffees would do just as well . . . "

She stood and headed for the kitchen.

"At least I'm good for something." she said.

"Well, I'd love to postpone the interview and remind myself what
else you're good at . . . "

"Don't push your luck, Werner. Coffee's more then you deserve."

"I was thinking about what you said earlier, sir, about the Jews."

"Ah yes . . . " Werner felt pleased to be broadening his driver's hori-
zons. "Pray, what conclusions did you draw?"

"Well, you were asking if they've ever caused *me* problems, sir, and
the answer really is 'no'. Of course, I still hate the fucking vermin –
excuse the language."

"Naturally . . . "

"But I was thinking I must be one of the lucky ones."

"Well, yes, me too I suppose. Though perhaps that's the point, old
boy . . . "

"What do you mean, sir?"

"They're clever. We might both have been manipulated by the Jews
for years, without even knowing it . . . "

"Really, sir?"

"Who knows? To be honest with you it's hard to know what to
believe, my friend."

The interviewer, Michael Gerber arrived an hour late.

"You do realise I have a show to do this evening?"

"Awfully sorry. Werner Krauss, isn't it?" Gerber was tall, and had
a bumbling, aristocratic demeanour. He held out a hand and Werner
shook.

"It is indeed, we met in Vienna that time . . . on the Führer's
birthday . . . "

"Of course we did, yes. Can I get you a drink?" He didn't wait for a reply. "Waiter! A bottle of your finest, whatever it is . . . " Gerber seemed to stare blankly at his interviewee.

"So are you going to ask a question?" Werner looked at his watch. Gerber didn't reply. "Herr Gerber? A question?" Again, there was a long pause. "I'm beginning to wish I'd brought a book along with me."

"You know you can tell a lot about someone by gauging their reaction to silence."

"Are you implying that some people are comfortable with being ignored?"

"I . . . "

"Or perhaps all you get is varying levels of annoyance." Werner interrupted.

"We're in a beautiful restaurant, in the finest city, in the greatest nation in the land." Suddenly, Gerber didn't seem quite so clueless. "Everyone has food in their mouths and everyone has a job. Our wives are dutiful, our children educated, and our brave troops win each battle they face."

"Amen to that," said Werner, obligingly.

"I suggest, Herr Krauss, that we should *all* take a few moments for silent reflection, once in a while. Don't you agree?"

"What exactly do you hope to achieve in this interview?"

Gerber smiled.

"It is your job to deal in identity, Herr Krauss. You wear a multitude of masks; you adopt different facades – a professional schizophrenia, if you will. Describe to me, if you can, your own identity."

"I'm a husband, a friend, a loyal National Socialist. I have acted for many years in many different roles. I've been lucky enough to travel the world – to see a great many things and meet many great people, all of which have helped to make me the person I am."

Werner smiled, satisfied with his patter.

"Very good, Herr Krauss, very good indeed . . . tell me, do you think an actor such as yourself has a role to play *off* the stage?"

"Yes, I take my responsibilities very seriously."

"What sort of responsibilities?"

"Firstly I think that anyone with a public profile has a duty to be a role model to young children, who are our greatest treasure, but who are also impressionable. It is vital that our children learn the values of respect and *have* respect for the social order."

"You've taught those values to your own children?"

"I think so," Werner said. "Yes."

"If your life were a play, which would it be?"

With over an hour to go before the show, Werner was pleased to be made-up, and in costume in plenty of time. He attached a 'Do Not Disturb' sign to the door of his dressing room and bolted it locked. There would be no impromptu interviews or illicit liaisons today. Rather, he would relax in his reclining chair with a pile of fan mail, and a bottle of Burgundy. A few years ago, he would have meticulously replied to each of these letters of support. He had been so thrilled to think of people generously spending their time just to contact him, it made him feel truly humbled.

Yet as time had worn on, and his reputation grew, the mailbag got larger; requests for autographs were supplemented by requests for locks of his hair, for him to visit sick children in hospital and, increasingly, for money. Indeed, some letters even had a desperate, threatening tone, calling him 'disgraceful' for sending theatre tickets rather than cash, and 'treacherous' for declining requests to visit dying geriatrics. It was unfathomable. Somehow these people thought that they owned him, that he owed them something. Wasn't he the one who had spent his adolescence travelling the country, performing twelve shows a week for no money? Hadn't he accepted every dumb, humiliating extra role the Deutsche film industry had to offer? Why the hell should *he* feel guilty? What the hell did he owe *them*?

Among the adoring and slightly disconcerting fan mail was a telegram from Veit Harlan.

MINISTRY COMMISIONING NEW FILM. WANT ME TO DIRECT. HISTORICAL DRAMA. YOU'LL PROBABLY BE ASKED OFFICIALLY. THOUGHT I'D ALERT. STARRING ROLE. MONEY GOOD. INTERESTED?

Harlan wasn't a man who took 'no' for an answer. He could do no wrong as far as Goebbels was concerned, and had a reputation for greed, amongst other things. Yet it would be impossible to make plans for America if he was tied in to a film project. He cast the telegram aside.

"Starring role. Money good. Not fucking interested!"

He smiled and refilled his glass. It felt good to have a plan, to say 'no' for once, and have control. America would be an adventure, and a way for him to finally earn the respect of his son and his wife. The thought of it made him feel nervous for the first time in years.

"Werner . . . " There was a knock on the door. "Open up, Werner!"

"Stefan?"

"Yes it's me, open up!" He started to beat on the door.

"Can't you read the sign?"

"Believe me, you need to hear this."

Werner stood, the pile of mail fell from his knees and scattered all over the floor.

"I just wanted a few minutes alone – for the love of God." he opened the door. Stefan barged into the room.

"It's happening . . . " He was gasping for breath. "We thought it might, but it actually is. It's happening . . . " as he entered the room, Stefan trampled on the fan mail.

"What? *What's* happening?"

"The gala reception for Mussolini's visit is tomorrow. The Führer is sending a private plane to take you to Vienna after the show tonight. *You* are the guest of honour . . . well, apart from the Führer, and Mussolini . . . *you* are special guest. It's really happening, Werner!"

Stefan grabbed Werner and embraced him. Werner peered over his shoulder and wondered what on earth he was getting himself into.

"But . . . what about the show tomorrow night?"

"Cancel! Chances like this don't come along every day – you'll be at the top table, meeting the great and the good . . . it's by order of *the Führer*, Werner, there'll be no problem."

"So what about Maria? Can't I talk to her first?"

"I did want to ask you about that actually."

"Go on . . . "

"The invitation *was* to Herr und Frau Krauss. But I got the impression . . . "

"You got the right impression, Stefan, she'll hate it. Tell them she's not well . . . " he groped around in his head for a lie, "but that she was honoured to be asked, *etcetera, etcetera* . . . "

"No problem."

"Now get out – I've still got a show to do . . . " Werner ushered his agent out of the room and closed the door. He sighed. "*Scheiße, Scheiße, Scheiße!*" he whispered. There was another knock. Stefan let himself back in.

"One more thing, Werner . . . "

"Make it quick."

"I found out what happened to that driver of yours, what was his name?"

"Lothar. What happened, where is he?"

"Arrested. No one knows why."

"You're joking?"

"According to the agency, they waited for him to arrive one morning . . . "

"Who did?"

"Troopers. Waited for him and dragged him straight off in a military car. They haven't seen him since."

The speed of his Mercedes made Werner feel nauseous. He had been allotted two motorcyclists to provide a cavalcade and clear the way for his route to the airport.

"Do we really need to go so fast, Gerard?"

"Afraid so, sir. General Schloss works to a tight schedule."

"How do you know the General's name? No one told me . . . "

"Must have seen it on the itinerary, sir . . . "

Werner was becoming increasingly wary of his new driver, after what had happened to poor Lothar. He was beginning to suspect that Gerard's stocky build wasn't that of a corpulent sloth at all – he looked like a soldier.

"In that case you need to talk to me, take my mind off the terrifying bloody velocity of this thing . . . tell me, when did you first start driving, Gerard?"

"With all due respect, sir, don't you think I'm better off concentrating on the road?"

The aircraft was impressive. Werner was unsure how to respond to each of the soldiers who saluted him, eventually deciding upon a polite "thank you." He quickly pulled on the distinctive black uniform, got handed a helmet and was strapped into his seat. The helmet carried the terrifying skull logo of the Deutsche army. Werner preferred to think of it as Yorick's skull from *Hamlet*. He chuckled at the thought of each soldier wearing a different theatrical symbol. "Imagine," he thought, "being shot-down by a man sporting the poodle from *Faust*!"

As the engines roared, his sickness returned, and he was grateful to find a bottle of sleeping pills in his bag. He gulped down three, and tried to sooth himself by listening carefully to the throbbing rhythms of the monstrous machine.

Dear Werner,

Do you know what's truly unique about you? Do you know the one quality that sets you apart from everyone else? I'll tell you . . .

For others, a lie is a slow, cancerous and fearful process. The very notion of hypocrisy, sends shivers down the spine. Of course, everyone toys with the truth at some point, but most people do all they can to conceal a misdemeanour – limit the damage – cover their tracks.

I once lied to you, you know. It was a brilliant lie – planned perfectly and executed with the sort of panache you'd expect from a talented actress (if I do say so myself). You're still none-the-wiser to this day, of course.

You see, I knew what a man like you wanted from a girl. You wanted innocence, virtue and naivety. You were so sure of yourself; you just assumed I'd never been with another man before you. You never asked. As far as you were concerned, I was just young and silly, and I didn't even exist until the day you decided to grace me with a wink and a kind word. I knew this, and I liked it. Men like you can't abide the thought of anyone else being with 'their' girl, and I let you believe that they hadn't.

But guess what, Werner; there was *someone before you. When I was fourteen I met this boy, Jens. He was a couple of years older, and he was allowed to drive around in his father's car. When he first asked if he could kiss me, I gazed into his eyes and fell in love. In an instant I saw the wedding, the house and the children. I would do anything for him. Only a few weeks after that first kiss, there were more things he wanted me to do. Each night he drove us to the park, and he told me what I should try – where my hands should go, my thighs, or my lips. In hindsight, of course, I know this was all he was interested in. The whole affair was quite functional. We'd meet, kiss, and he'd slip his thing out of his trousers and tell me what to do with it. Romantic, eh?*

So when you first came back to my room (it was the night we went out for a meal – do you remember?) I wanted to make you happy in the same way. I was older, and desperate to find out what it was like, with a real man who (I thought) cared for me, not a stupid boy. You see, I thought you loved me . . .

But I knew if you were to stay with me, you would want innocence and naivety. It would flatter you to be my instructor – I would be a challenge that you could return to again and again. And so, when I put my hand in your trousers that time, I knew what I was doing. I gripped and pulled and yanked like a stupid little girl would.

And that's my lie. And mine is like a million others that get told every single day. At the time, it felt horrible and desperately wrong. I was awake the whole night, crying over the way I'd treated you, wondering if I should tell you the truth. I lied because I loved you and I thought it would make you happy.

Now let's look at one of your lies. You wake up, feeling guilty about spending the night with some young hussy. (Your lies covering that particular episode up were, of course, laughable.) Then from the sweet blue Atlantic sky, you pluck this idea about going to America. You're prepared to surrender all your Nazi connections, and start a new life on Allied territory. You even had me believing you were on a mission to save your son's life, like a modern-day Noah – you'd pack us up, two-by-two and take us to salvation.

And this is where it gets interesting – this is where you come into your own. Because for most people a lie can last for days, weeks, years even. The conviction, the knot tied around the truth slowly becomes unravelled. Lies usually wither and rot over time. Not for you, Werner. No. Because within hours *of starting to believe in you again, within* hours *of thinking that perhaps you deserved another chance – it was* hours, *Werner, since you made a promise to your eldest son – within* hours *of seeing a glimmer, the slightest slither of decency in you, what happens? One of your flunkies calls because you've had the great honour, the wonderful fucking privilege of meeting some extremely important people. But, being you, of course, with your principles and your determination to do what's best, you wouldn't possibly go along to meet* one *psychotic fascist, one* savage, murdering, power-crazed monster. Oh no, not for you, Werner, no, one despot, one* insane dictator wouldn't be enough *– you have to grovel, squirm and suckle to* two *of them!*

"Frau Krauss, he so desperately wanted you to come with us, too, it's such a shame that the plane is leaving immediately . . . "

It makes me sick. You know, I used to blame myself. That was why I had these crazy ideas, that I should end it and leave you alone because, after all's said and done; you're a decent man. That's why I started writing these letters. Not any more, Werner. Now, I just want to fucking get away from you – you're a monster – no different to either of the moustachioed, insane fools whose arses you're kissing right now.

So congratulations, Werner! You're a terrible liar – something you should probably be proud of, if it wasn't for the fact that you told so many terrible lies, and so often. I hope you have a wonderful time with your new friends in Vienna *– perhaps you could ask them for help with your son's problems?*

Yours,
Maria x

The plane landed, and Werner was whisked to his hotel, again at high speed. Heinrich, the media co-ordinator for the event, joined him on the back seat.

"We will spend a few hours tonight on briefing, Herr Krauss . . . "

"Hours? I thought it was a gala reception, not a military operation."

"In fact, it is both. You will be required to use a false name from now until the dinner." he passed Werner an envelope, "and all your movements have been carefully planned so you must seek approval if you need to veer from the schedule."

"Is there an allotted time to take a shit? Or should I request someone's approval?"

"Not funny, Herr Krauss. Do you have any serious questions?"

"Yes, what's in here?"

Heinrich nodded towards the envelope. "Open up and find out." Werner opened the envelope and found a passport in the name of 'Egon Baum'.

"Egon? Is this a joke?" He thought of his poor son, and wondered if they were already onto him. Perhaps they wanted to see how he would react to the name.

"Why? What's wrong with the name 'Egon'?"

"Nothing, nothing . . . I'm sorry. I do suffer a little from travel sickness, I think the speed of this thing . . . Look, isn't all this a little pointless? It's my face that people know, that they recognise, not, necessarily, my name . . . "

"That's why we have brought you this." He reached over to the front passenger seat and produced a large-rimmed black hat. "Wear it whenever you're out in public."

Werner stifled a laugh. "Fine. Anything else? A false beard perhaps?"

"No, we're finished for now. I just need a list of the people who know you're here."

"Well that's easy – Stefan, my agent, Gerard, the driver . . . and my wife."

"Ah yes, your wife, the lovely Maria Bard. Such a shame she couldn't make it."

"It is, isn't it?"

"And she's been told of the secret nature of this whole assignment?"

"The dinner?"

"Yes, she knows not a word is to be said?"

"It was my agent who spoke to her before we left, actually, so . . . "

"Not a problem – you can call her as soon as we get to the hotel. Just make sure you're discreet on the phone."

"Darling, I'm glad I caught you in . . . how are you? . . . Stop, stop, please you must stop, you don't understand, we're being listened to . . . no I'm not paranoid, there's a man here with me, Heinrich, who's listening to the conversation . . . Now's not the time for this. Look, all I need you to do is say 'yes' or 'no', do you understand? . . . I said: 'yes' or 'no', *darling* . . . please?"

He held the phone away from his ear and covered the mouthpiece.

"She's just upset that she couldn't be here with us. Please excuse the language."

Heinrich nodded earnestly.

"I just need you to do something for me . . . please . . . the reason we're here – you know that, don't you? . . . So that's 'yes', you do, all I need you to tell me is, have you told anybody about what I'm doing, have you mentioned it to anybody at all? . . . Please just answer . . . Thank you, that's all I needed. I'll call you again later, darling. . . . and hope you feel better soon – bye."

He slammed down the receiver.

"Excellent, Herr Krauss. Now I'll leave you to get some sleep."

"What about the hours of briefing?"

"I think I have all I need for now. The room will be patrolled throughout the night so if there's anything you require just pop your head out of the door – these men are your assistants, use them as you wish."

"All quite unnecessary, but I will, thank you . . . "

"You will be woken at O-seven-hundred hours for breakfast."

"I look forward to it."

Werner surveyed the room. It was functional, plainly decorated, and the bed had a stale, musty odour. He was pleased to find a telephone by his bedside, knowing that he must contact Maria as soon as he could. He undressed, and whilst removing his watch, noticed the time was already two thirty a.m. He sighed, and climbed into the heavy sheets. He reached over for the telephone and started to dial . . . was it worth the hassle of having her shout at him again? He'd tried to do good things all day – meet with Egon and make plans for America, yet she still seemed angry. He replaced the handset and lay back down. He was tired, but had far too many worries swimming through his head to sleep. With no alcohol in the room, he embarked upon his other method of sedation. Sofia appeared in his mind, on her knees, as she had been the previous night. This gave him an idea. He crawled out of bed, wrapped a small towel around his waist, grabbed his wallet and opened the door to the room. His so-called bodyguard was slouched against the corridor wall, with his eyes closed.

"It'll be a fucking miracle if we win the war with soldiers like you,"

he said. The bodyguard, a young man wearing spectacles, was startled.

"Sorry, sorry sir. Can I help you at all, sir?

"Yes, what are the chances of getting some girls up here?"

"Sir?"

"Don't worry, I'll give you the money. Can you make it happen?"

"With all due respect, sir, I think you should go back to bed . . . "

"Come on, you must know where to go. There'll be a twenty in it
for you too."

"It's three in the morning, sir."

"I don't think that matters in their line of work, do you? They
weren't unionised the last time I checked . . . "

"Sir, please, I think you should return to your room. And please .
. . " he winced, and pointed to Werner's crotch, " . . . adjust your
towel."

Werner looked down and realised his semi-erect penis had emerged
from the towel. "Sorry, sorry . . . " he said, "perhaps you're right. I'll
just go back to bed." He handed over ten marks and retreated to his
room.

6

*"I've told you before, Werner, the rain always sounds heavier than it
is,"*

*Sofia whispered to Werner as she stroked his chest. They were both
wearing military uniforms, and Werner pulled the girl's hand from his
neatly ironed shirt.*

*"All I know is it sounds pretty heavy." Each drop tormented the
canvas covering of their tent, "the slightest leak in this thing and
we're done for – everyone will see us, everyone will know what we're
up to."*

*"You're such an old fuss, Werner, I know what will cheer you up."
She produced an old woollen sack, and from it she pulled a chequered
games board and some chess pieces.*

"I didn't know you played chess," he said.

*"I don't. You're going to teach me." As she carefully placed the
pieces on all of the wrong squares, Werner felt a rush of affection for
the girl. Like him, she had gone most of her adolescent life without a
father around to teach her games like chess. He re-arranged the pieces
and explained that as she had the white pieces, she should go first. She
tentatively moved a pawn forward, then started to unbutton her shirt.*

"What are you doing?"

"Nothing – you concentrate on your own game."

He cautiously brought out one of his own pawns, a move which Sofia replicated when it was her turn. This time, though, she removed her shirt completely, leaving just a vest to cover her chest.

"Sofia, come on, you can't . . . "

"I can't what? Do this?" She removed the vest, and started to unbutton her khaki trousers. "What about this?"

"Stop it. Stop it!" He said. "We'll get caught!"

"You wanted to play a game, Werner. This is what you wanted isn't it?"

"No, no, you don't understand . . . " he tried to cover her up, and leaning across the tent he knocked the board and all of the pieces started to roll away.

"You were going to teach me, Werner."

The rain got louder and louder. "Please, you have to get dressed – what if we get the order, what if they come for us?"

"They'll never come for us, Werner, they never do." She tried to kiss him.

"No. Please, leave me alone, Sofia. Just leave me alone . . . "

The telephone rang. "*Scheiße*! Maria, *Scheiße*!" scrambling over to the handset, he realised he had been dreaming. "Darling, I'm so sorry, how are you? . . . Oh, okay, yes, how embarrassing. Thank you for letting me know." He put the phone down – it was actually his morning call from reception. He took a moment to catch his breath – he felt confused and afraid – how was he going to entertain his host tonight? And how the hell would he begin to convince Maria he was serious about America? Or anything? He picked up the phone again and dialled the home number. It rang and rang but there was no answer. Eventually he gave up, washed, and dressed ready for breakfast.

The dining hall was deserted but for a scruffy waiter. Werner found a table and ordered coffee. He started to wonder about poor old Lothar. What on earth could the authorities want with him? He was a careful, law abiding man, with a wife and children. Werner made a mental note to make contact with Lothar's wife when he got back to Berlin. Maybe he could use some influence to make sure he at least gets a fair trial, for whatever he's done. And he would also get rid of that odious Gerard.

"Ready for your briefing?" Heinrich unceremoniously joined him at the table.

"*Und Guten Morgen* to you too . . . "

"Remind me of your name, Herr Krauss."

"Any idea how stupid that sounds?"

"Just give me your name."

"Charles Chaplin, pleased to meet you." He gave a salute.

"We don't have time for jokes."

"Egon, okay? My name is Egon."

"Egon what?"

Werner genuinely couldn't remember his allotted surname. "You'll have to give me a clue . . . "

"*Baum!* It's Egon-fucking-*Baum*, alright?"

There was silence. Apart from the people he had married, no one had shouted at Werner like that for years. He decided to remain calm.

"I think, Herr whoever-*you*-are, that you're forgetting who you're talking to."

Heinrich leaned in for a whisper, "We'll see about that, shall we?" It felt as though Werner could see each of the cracks in this cruel, ashen face all at once. Why was he being treated this way? Wasn't he supposed to be the guest of honour? "Let's start again, shall we?"

"Yes. Let's . . . "

"Here is your itinerary. You'll notice at sixteen hundred hours you have been summoned to an appointment with General Schloss. Under no circumstances must you be late for this. I suggest you look smart, and have your wits about you."

"Herr Heinrich, I'm sorry if I might have given you the impression I was a bit flippant . . . this all comes as a bit of a shock. Is any of it really necessary?"

"I am completely indifferent to *impressions*, Herr *Baum*. However, in light of your recent conduct, it has been decided that you should not be allowed to leave the hotel today."

"Recent conduct? What the hell are you talking about?"

"Don't think your behaviour last night went unnoticed. Trying to get hookers up to your room on a State occasion such as this."

Werner swallowed hard on the warm spit of sleep. "That was all a joke. I was teasing the boy. Testing him . . . "

"As I said, I'm indifferent. But you are not permitted to leave the hotel. The guards will be there for anything you need. Read the itinerary, and think carefully about your actions from now on."

"So they're *guards* now are they? I thought they were assistants."

Heinrich remained silent.

"And I'm *summoned* to appear at four?"

"Sixteen-hundred hours, yes. Now I shall leave you to enjoy your breakfast."

Werner's chest felt tight. He winced with pain and screwed up the documents he had been handed. He could understand the increased security, and that the pressure on these soldiers must induce a little paranoia. But he was being treated like a criminal. It all seemed so damn *personal*. Perhaps he had been stupid to try to get some girls last night. He didn't eat, just returned to his room and tried to call Maria. Even if she were mad at him, her voice would come as some comfort. The phone rang and rang – there was no answer. He tried Lothar:

"What the hell's going on? . . . It's awful . . . Damn right there's no niceties – I'm being shunted around like a fucking pig, I can't leave the hotel, there are soldiers guarding my room . . . You're asking me? I *don't fucking know*; but what I do know is, I don't like it one little bit – wasn't this supposed to be the great State occasion – 'Guest of Honour' you said . . . And what, exactly *were* you told about this thing? . . . They didn't mention interrogation, or anything? . . . I hope you're not laughing – there's no one laughing at this end, believe me . . . No I won't calm down – do you know *anything?* . . . Well if you want to keep your job you'd better fucking find something out, okay?"

He slammed down the phone. "*Scheiße*," he said, and picked up the receiver once more. He sighed, and re-dialled his agent's number.

"Sorry Lothar, sorry, I meant to say – I can't get hold of Maria, could you make a few calls and find out where she is? I need to talk to her. Yes, thanks . . . oh, and what I said before . . . you know . . . bye . . . "

His guard started to march, and Werner had to skip in order to keep up with him. The guard knocked briskly on the imposing wooden door and opened it immediately. Schloss was a fat, balding man, wearing a uniform smothered in multicoloured medals.

"Herr Krauss, take a seat, please."

"Thank you, sir."

"I'm going to come straight to the point because you must be a little confused about what's been going on."

"You could say that, sir."

"This was *supposed* to be a good day for you, Herr Krauss, a very good day indeed. A couple of months back the Ministry decided to award you with the Goethe Medallion. Apparently your services to the theatre and to the culture of the Reich have been exemplary."

"Thank you, sir. I've always put my country first and . . . "

"Save it, Krauss," the General interrupted, "these aren't my words."

"Sorry, sir."

"So, the Ministry felt what better occasion for you to receive this honour than an important State visit – the Führer was hoping to show

Mussolini the best of German talent – he wanted to wallow in our great achievements . . . "

"And he *can*, sir. Surely?"

"When all of this was decided, I was entrusted with the task of investigating your . . . personality. I had to keep an eye on your habits and behaviours, ensure there was nothing that could potentially embarrass us, when you were given the accolade."

"You spied on me . . . "

"You make it sound sinister, Krauss. Remember, we *wanted* to give you this award – at first it was just standard procedure. I had some men follow you, recorded a few conversations . . . nothing intrusive . . . "

"No, sir?"

"And increasingly we found your behaviour to be . . . erratic. There were the girls, and the drinking – we were willing to overlook these more *human* character flaws . . . "

"Am I supposed to be grateful?"

"No, Krauss, you're supposed to be sorry." The General's voice briefly reached a high-pitched yelp. "You'd do well to remember who you're talking to."

"Sorry, sir. Please continue . . . "

"You must know where this is going, Krauss. We had a few people tracking you, we gave you a new driver . . . "

"Gerard, yes – I knew it!"

" . . . and started to discover some very disturbing things indeed. Would you like to take a guess as to what these were?"

Werner combed his hand through his thinning hair. A photograph of Egon appeared in his mind. He was splashing around on the seashore at Cuxhaven. Taken when he was about twelve years old, on the cusp of adolescence. His son, his little boy . . . "No, tell me, please . . . "

"Let's start with this. You weren't thinking of moving anywhere, were you? A country we could soon all be at war with, by any chance?"

"No idea what you're talking about, sir."

"Perhaps this will help. A telephone call you made just yesterday morning: 'So what are the chances then, realistically, of getting over to the States without causing too much of a stink?' To which a friend of yours replies: 'It can be done, but maybe not if you're Werner Krauss.' To which you reply: 'How hard can it be? Come on, I need this to happen, can't Conrad help?' Would you like me to read on?"

"You seem to forget, I'm an *actor*. Actors have these sorts of conversation all the time – always looking for the next big job – we've got families to support and . . . "

"Are you suggesting the Reich's most celebrated actor isn't getting paid enough?"

"No, let me put it another way. It's bullshit."

"Excuse me?"

"*Bullshit*. All actors do it. We lie and . . . and we exaggerate all the time. If I *am* such a big deal in *Deutschland* then where is there for me to go? What is there left to, you know, show-off about? So, idly . . . just an ego thing really . . . I feed some friends this stuff about America. It means *nothing*, I swear, pure bravado, stupid fucking . . . conceit."

"Thank you, Herr Krauss. I think I get the idea. However, that fails to explain the other conversation we picked-up, and I quote: 'Would I need to have a false name for this? How about Maria, and the children?'"

"It was rubbish, I'm telling you. Obviously now I know I was being stupid, but . . . "

"You know I believe you." The General interrupted. "All actors do lie – it's what you're paid for. But how am I to know you're not *acting* right now? I put it to you that you *do* want to defect to America. Tell me why you might want to do that?"

"I don't . . . I . . . "

"A particular political view perhaps? Or, let's say, for instance, you were involved in . . . perverse sexual activity, with men . . . "

"How dare you?"

"It's been known in your profession, Herr Krauss. The theatre seems to be a magnet for that sort of depravity."

"That's disgusting!"

"Indeed. But it might explain this eagerness to emigrate."

"I can't believe this! You said yourself, you knew how many women I'd . . . you know . . . in the last few weeks . . . "

"Perhaps you're familiar with the theatrical line: 'The lady doth protest too much'? You were seen meeting with your friend Willem Wenzeslaus last week, after all . . . "

"Preposterous! Look, I told you. I know it sounded bad, but I was talking nonsense – complete bullshit . . . "

"I think we've had enough of that language, now."

"Sorry, but it was . . . just lies to make myself sound important. My life here in *Deutschland* is perfect. Look at my record; no other actor has garnered such State approval. Each night I get on that stage and . . . and give lessons about the villainous Jews and the . . . the lying, avaricious scum they are!"

"Exactly why you were supposed to be awarded this medal. But I'm interested in this apparent hatred of yours for the Jews . . . "

"What do you mean, *apparent*?"

"The other night, for instance, you were dressed in costume as Shylock, and we saw you wandering around on the *Frederickstrasse*."

"I wasn't thinking. I didn't realise I still had the costume on. There was a family emergency . . . and I panicked . . . "

"So what about those Jewish *friends* of yours?"

That was the one thing he didn't want to hear. He knew if the questions were about him, about women or being a drunken old fool, he'd be okay. But Egon had his whole life ahead of him, and the thought that Werner could actually make things *worse* for him . . .

"Now I really don't know what you're talking about . . . "

"The name Hannah Landauer doesn't mean anything to you?"

"Nothing. Apart from the fact it's a palindrome."

"A what?"

"The name 'Hannah', it's spelt the same backwards as it is forwards."

"Yes, so it is." The General actually seemed flustered. "Back to the point. You've not met this girl, not had any cause to deal with her family . . . ?"

"No, sir. But as I said before, please remember in my position, I do meet hundreds of different people all the time – fans, people from the press, *etcetera* – if you've been following me you'll know that no two days are ever the same. You ask me 'have I met this person', or 'that person' I can never really be sure. I've never heard that name before, though. No."

"Fine. Well we're running out of time, so I think I should sum things up. As I said, we've found your behaviour to be erratic, and were it not for your *special* role in the arts, we would have good grounds to arrest you and lock you up. However, I happen to think you pose no serious threat to the state, maybe just to yourself and those around you."

"Thank you, sir."

"Fortunately for you, the world's press were already briefed about your appearance tonight, so we still want you to attend . . . "

"I see. But the medal . . . "

"You won't be getting any award tonight. Let's say it's under review, shall we? Don't forget, you've only got yourself to blame, Herr Krauss."

7

"Time to go, Herr Krauss, or the plane will leave without you."

Werner stirred, and looked at his watch. Six a.m. "It's a private plane. It's private to me. It can't leave without me, that's why it's called a private plane." He wasn't sure if he actually said this, or just thought it. Either way, he smacked his lips together and got comfortable for sleep to take him again.

"Herr Krauss, we're waiting."

"Just fucking leave me alone, will you?" He definitely said that. The sheets were pulled off him and he cowered in his underpants.

"*Now*, Herr Krauss," the voice shouted. He turned to find two young soldiers, who were obviously very pleased with themselves for bellowing orders at the famous actor. Reluctantly, he sat up.

"Do you know who I had dinner with last night? Because if you did I think you'd change your fucking tone."

"Yes, Herr Krauss, you had dinner with the Führer – the same man who you're sharing a flight to Berlin with this morning, in approximately fifty minutes' time. Now I'll ask you to get up one more time, and after that you'll only have Adolf Hitler to answer to."

On the journey home from the airport, Gerard was unusually talkative. "Saw you in the newspapers, Herr Krauss. What an honour! You must have had quite a time down in Vienna."

Werner wondered if Gerard knew he was aware of his spying. There was certainly something more relaxed in his mannerisms.

"It was. Truly an honour, Gerard. The Führer make you feel so comfortable in his presence, and yet he still maintains . . . I don't know what the word is, 'authority', I suppose . . . "

"It's greatness, sir. Greatness and charisma."

"Indeed."

"So come on then, sir, do tell all! What did he say to you?"

"He said he hoped to catch one of my performances soon . . . that he's sure Herr Goebbels will be offering a host of new film roles in the near future, that he hoped I would accept these offers."

"Of course you will, sir."

"Quite. He asked about the family, the children, Maria."

"Children, sir? Didn't know you had any . . . "

Werner maintained a considered silence – what was this man trying to prove? His job was done, wasn't it? Why couldn't they just send Lothar back to be his driver? Or someone else?

"Yes. They're grown-up now, I don't see them as much as I would like."

"Understandable – a busy man like you. So what about Mussolini, what did *he* say?"

"He referred to me as 'a lion'. Otherwise we just exchanged pleas-antries. There's not much an actor like me can really say to these world leaders, is there?"

"But hasn't he written plays, Herr Krauss? One was called 'Julius Caesar' wasn't it?"

Eventually Gerard's inane banter ceased, and Werner could stop worrying about exactly what he should and should not say. He looked forward to seeing his wife again, and hoped she would understand that, in the circumstances, a trip to America was now completely out of the question. He dozed on the cool leather in the back seat.

"Home and dry, Herr Krauss! Up you get . . . "

"Thanks Gerard," he stirred, and reached into his pocket for a twenty. "Treat yourself," he said, "you've earned it."

With a wry smile on his face, Werner emerged from the Mercedes and entered the apartment block. He collected a large pile of unopened mail and climbed the stairs. He used his key for access to the top floor, "I'm back darling!" then he entered. "Oh no! Fuck! No, no, no, no, please no! Please!"

He dashed towards Maria, whose body was hanging from the rafter across the hallway. The thick rope had cut into her throat, but by now the blood it produced was dark and dry. Werner grabbed her pale calves and hoisted her upward, and while she lay slumped across his shoulder, he struggled to free her head from the noose with his left hand. "Darling, please! My God, please be okay." He knew it might be futile, but he laid her down gently and attempted to revive her. The moment he touched those clammy, rubbery lips with his own, her death felt a reality. He blew into her mouth and gave firm compres-sions to her chest for at least twenty minutes, but, however hard he blew, her expression was always the same: a look of indifference, of dissatisfaction.

Eventually he called Doctor Ritter, who in turn called the under-taker. The two men arrived at the same time, and seemed uncomfortable reciting the standard phrases of sympathy, knowing full well they didn't quite apply when the deceased had taken her own life. Werner too was uncomfortable, because by admitting he hadn't seen or heard from her for a couple of days seemed like an admission of guilt – he literally wasn't there for her when she needed him most. The undertaker worked swiftly, summoning the two young apprentices he had left in the car outside to come up and help. The doctor ushered Werner away from the hall and into the kitchen, engaging him in a meaningless exchange of clichés while his wife was taken away.

"And is there a local Priest you'd like to call? Even for those who don't practice a particular faith, it can be comforting to have a man of God around at a time like this."

"No Doctor, thank you. I'd like to deal with this in my own way, if I may. Besides, the church doesn't look too kindly on . . . " he didn't want to feel the word 'suicide' in his mouth, not yet, "you know, on this sort of thing, do they?"

The doctor grabbed Werner's arm tightly.

"He would be here *for you*, Herr Krauss. When things like this happen, it's nobody's fault. It's inescapable – certain paths people take in life; they sometimes lead to . . . " the doctor was also reluctant to deal in specifics. Werner patted his hand in appreciation.

"Thank you Doctor, I know what you mean. But I really don't want to see a Priest or anyone for that matter."

The undertaker took his wife away, and Doctor Ritter left him with a large supply of sleeping pills. He called Stefan and told him the bad news. He said he didn't want to be bothered by anybody for the rest of the day. He told him he could let everyone know. He wouldn't be performing tonight, or for the rest of the week. Stefan agreed to everything, said, "yes, yes, yes, yes, yes" in a tone that suggested scepticism. "If there's anything I can do, Werner . . . " he said, a phrase which echoed, a phrase which was already becoming tiresome.

He put the phone down, and paced the room. Despite their success, he and Maria had always kept this small apartment on *Alexanderplatz*. When they first moved in together it was all they could afford, and although over time they had bought and sold holiday lodges, penthouse suites and even rented a medieval castle in the Bavarian forest, this place was their home. Werner felt at a loss as to what to do. He couldn't cry, even though he felt he should. Perhaps there was something about suicide that denied the usual processes of grief. His instinct was to reach for a cognac, but he felt some vague sense of duty to remain sober. He decided to look at the place in a fresh light – pay attention to its crevices, its floorboards and wooden skirting.

He sat cross-legged on the cold tiles surrounding the fireplace, and started a small fire. He was momentarily mesmerised by the mysterious shades of yellow and orange, which swallowed the rolled-up pieces of newspaper and licked the pieces of coal. He found comfort in the nihilism of the fire – each news story that shrivelled, each photograph burnt, each opinion singed – it felt healthy. As he rolled up another page, he noticed the flustered expression of his own face peering up at him, along with the devilish glare of his young mistress. *Werner Krauss and his wife relax backstage before the show* the caption read. He felt a warm tear slide down his cheek. "What a fool, what an absolute fucking idiot!" he said, and threw the rest of the paper into the flames.

He felt a cold shiver as he stood up and wandered into their bedroom. It was pristine – the bed linen was fresh and folded neatly, the curtains pulled-back in their matching ties, the dresser still had a whiff of furniture polish – this was Maria's domain. She had always refused to have a housekeeper, and even after the most gruelling working day, she would strip to her underwear and clean the apartment meticulously. By leaving no physical trace behind in this way, it felt as though she was everywhere. Werner pulled open the draw of her bedside table and discovered a stack of papers. He noticed the phrase: *Of course, you're always friendly and polite to everyone else* and shut the drawer instantly. The sight of her careful handwriting just increased his feeling of nausea. Nausea and anger. Surely things weren't that bad, were they? Whatever his failings as a husband, she was never hungry, never short of money, never denied anything. There were plenty of other people with reason to complain, he thought. But what did he know? He hadn't seen it coming. Even though she'd threatened, even though she'd shaken pills and promised she would do it – it never really occurred to him that she would. He fetched some pills of his own, and swallowed two.

He returned to the bedroom and opened the drawer again. *I could be out there too, Werner, ever think of that?* It was torture – these words were *horrible*. He closed the drawer again, sunk to his knees and lay down in the doorway between the bedroom and the hall. The hard-oak floor felt good on his back, which ached from the awkward, turbulent flight. He knew that when the news of her death filtered through to every friend and relative, every news agency, every actor and actress, producer and director, his whole life would become one long denial, one carefully rehearsed and defensive strategy. "Maria had her demons," he would say, "and no matter how hard you try, no matter how much you might love someone, there is an inward process . . . " no, he thought, not 'process', too mechanical, "there is an inward, downward spiral," yes, a 'spiral', 'from which Maria was never to return'. That would do. Perhaps he should write that down – let a succinct, prepared statement do all the work for him. But, there in the doorway, he was too comfortable; in fact, he was surprisingly close to sleep. He wondered if he should contact her mother . . . surely she had a right to know . . . perhaps Stefan could do it for him . . . or what about Uta, but she fucking hated him – she believed everything Maria told her about him . . . even if *most* of it was true, she only ever saw things from her perspective . . .

The clatter of the letterbox made Werner sight upright. The warm spit in his mouth told him he must have fallen asleep, but he didn't remember dreaming, which was a relief. He felt giddy as he walked along the hallway to find a postcard. It was an official telegram from the Propaganda office, offering Werner their sincerest sympathies and assuring him that his wife's tragic death would be publicized 'only with the greatest degree of sensitivity'. They assured him that her obituary would be handled with a great deal of care. "Stupid, stupid bastards . . . " he muttered. There was a conspiratorial tone to the note, which he resented. He returned to the living room and threw the card onto the fire.

Part Three

1

'"Krauss was the unashamed anti-Semite whose prejudices would draw him to the Nazis, whose luminary he would become . . . ' fucking unbelievable! I *liked* him as well – Gottfried – can you believe that? I *liked* that grovelling shit." Sat up in bed, Werner cast the newspaper aside. It had become quite normal for Willem to let himself into the house and bring the newspapers upstairs to Werner, who held court from his gothic four-poster'.

"He's probably been misquoted or something. Take no notice – people don't read this stuff anyway. Don't worry about it, Werner."

"Don't worry? They get to throw this shit around and I can't do anything to defend myself. And how the hell can you misquote this: 'drawn to the Nazis', 'their luminary', it's outrageous. But what *can* I do? Nothing. Impotent – that's it, that's what I am, I'm *impotent*, old boy."

"Your day will come again, Werner, trust me. Just try to keep your head down and ride it out . . . "

"Why should I, Willem? Why the hell should I?"

Willem poked his cigarette into an ashtray on the dressing table.

"Well I might be able to help you, Werner. But only if you want to help yourself?"

"What does that mean?" Werner laughed. "That doesn't *mean* anything – help myself do what, exactly? I wake, I eat, I drink – what else do you want me to do?"

"Tell me what happened with Stefan."

"What do you think happened? The moment things started to get difficult; he didn't want to know. Good riddance, I say. I'm better off representing myself."

"I'm not so sure. Tell you what, I'll be back tomorrow morning – I've got an idea . . . "

As far as Werner was concerned it was quite simple. He was not a member of the Nazi Party, and had never been a member. He wondered what more evidence anyone could need. He thought about the people who were members, and all the terrible things they were supposed to have done: forced labour, torturous treatment of Jews and gypsies, mass murder. Yet because the clear majority of them didn't have a famous name, they could carry on with their lives – continue in their jobs, form relationships, laugh and fucking joke. Yet he was sat in bed, so confused and wracked with worries he could barely breathe.

Bosweldt gave his customary rap at the door, and let himself in. A chubby, bespectacled man – to Werner he looked more like a bank manager than the sharp lawyer he had heard so much about.

"Sorry I'm a bit early, Herr Krauss, back in court this afternoon."

"Not a problem, old boy, I imagine you've got everything you need from me now anyway," he pulled out a chair for his guest, and cleared some space on the dining room table.

"We're nearly there, Herr Krauss, yes. But there was one thing I wanted to go over in some detail." He dropped his briefcase onto the table, flipped open the lid and produced a stack of papers. "I need you to tell me about your relationship with Frau Kopenik."

"And what's that got to do with the case?"

"I don't want to alarm you, Herr Krauss, but this could be something the trial pick-up on. Your dealings, shall we say, with Frau Kopenik put you in direct contact with senior party members, as well as foreign diplomats."

"You don't understand . . . "

"If I might finish, Herr Krauss," he interrupted. "I want you to tell me about it, informally, so that I can start to understand how the circumstances arose, with the diary, and your dealings with Herr Goering."

It felt as though Werner couldn't think quickly enough. He knew he had to give his lawyer a version of the story, but which one? Wasn't this a man whose job was to see through lies and conjecture? Werner cleared his throat and took a deep breath.

"It was the winter of thirty-nine. I don't remember many of the details – didn't seem too important at the time. A soldier, who I had become friendly with over the years, was working on one of my houses. In the past he had built a garage for me and landscaped the garden. It's important to only use people you trust."

Bosweldt looked at his watch.

"One evening, he happened to mention this girl. He said that she was well-known to a lot of the higher-ranking officers, and that as she was interested in the film and theatre world, it was hoped that I could show her around a set, or backstage at a play."

"And did you?"

"Yes, I didn't see why not. We were shooting *Jud Süß* as I recall, and I told him she was free to drop by anytime."

"So what happened?"

"Nothing much; she showed up at the set, shook hands, said everything was 'wonderful' and went home. It was the *second* time I saw her when things got interesting."

"Perhaps you could tell me about that then?"

"Not without a drink inside me first, old boy! Can I get you anything?"

"I'm fine, thank you."

Werner wandered into the kitchen, continuing to tell his story.

"You know, not six months had gone by since Maria, and she sucked me in. That girl. A week or so after we met, I was at the launch party for Schweikart's new film, *In Flagranti*, when the Party men and diplomats turned up – Goering was there, Hoess was with some important Italians. Then I saw her. 'Looks like I have the honour of your company again, Herr Krauss,' she said, 'shall we go somewhere to talk?' All I could do was try to judge the right time to put a hand on her thigh – you know how it is."

Again, Bosweldt looked at his watch.

"Then, she said the magic word: 'Of course, we knew *Adolf* would be there . . . '

'Adolf?' I said. 'Adolf who?'

'Hitler! Who did you think I meant?'

Again, I'd had a little too much to drink to remember many details, but suffice to say, she moved in the right circles. I'd always assumed everyone referred to Hitler as '*Mein Führer*'."

"Yes, quite . . . " Bosweldt started to scribble notes.

"It was surprising to hear someone talking so openly about the Fuhrer, in public no less. 'Have you ever been to his Bavarian place, Herr Krauss?' she said.

'Call me Werner, please,' I'd say, 'no, I've never been. I'd imagine it's pretty spectacular,' which of course it was. In fact, everything to her was 'spectacular', 'splendid', 'stupendous', 'divine'. I was starting to wonder if getting her into bed would be worth having to listen to all that wheezing. Eventually I whispered in her ear:

'You know we could take our drinks up to one of the rooms.'

"Right then," said Bosweldt, agitating at his forehead with his pen lid, "so was that when you first had, let's say, *relations* with Frau Kopenik?"

"Actually, no. 'You know what I just have to do,' she said, 'is go and find some of the other girls. They'll all be dying to meet you!'

'Even better – the more the merrier . . . ' I said, and off she went. I assumed it was some sort of brush-off, and didn't think I'd see her again. But sure enough, she came back and introduced me to three more young-looking girls, whose names I forget now. You know what, Herr Bosweldt, I stared at their puppyish pale skin and realised they probably weren't even born when *Das Cabinet* was released."

"I'm afraid I don't have that much time today, Herr Krauss. If you could just give me the facts . . . " Bosweldt interrupted, but Werner continued regardless.

"I answered all their silly questions with the degree of truth they deserved – inventing some bizarre stories for them, some elaborate tales. These girls were lapping it up, and – I don't mind telling you – the possibility of taking them *all* upstairs entered my mind. 'More drinks everyone?' I asked, but they all declined apart from her. She seemed to be able to match me, drink-for-drink. Eventually she sat close and we started to kiss."

"So this was the point at which you left the party, Herr Krauss?"

"Exactly."

"And you got a room?"

"Yes, there at the *Esplande*. She got out of bed as soon as we were finished, and started to dress.

'Why the hurry?' I said 'We have the place all night, you know . . .'

'You *know* why not, Werner,' she said, 'I'm married.' I just laughed, I mean, what else could I do?"

"And this was the first you learned of her marriage?"

"Of course. She didn't even look old enough to be married. And anyway, there was no husband actually *at* the party."

"So it's fair to say you were deceived?"

"I suppose it's up to her, isn't it? What she decides to tell me."

"You're missing the point, Herr Krauss. If we can suggest to the court that you were tricked into this relationship in the first place, it might help to explain your subsequent actions."

"If you think it'll help. You're the lawyer. In fact, I don't remember actually seeing a wedding ring – although, as I've said, I don't tend to remember much these days."

"No, now you're thinking, Herr Krauss. The more manipulative we can make her seem, the better. So, what happened next?"

"I asked her again – *told* her – 'come back to bed'. But she started screaming 'get me a taxi now' and 'this was a mistake'"

"And you acquiesced to her demands?"

"Of course. I was pretty tired, anyway, 'if she wants to go, let her go' I thought."

"And as far as you were concerned, was that the end of this . . . affair?"

"Well, I made sure I got her telephone number, I mean, who wouldn't?"

"Alright, you'll have to accept my apologies, Herr Krauss, I really must go. This has been interesting, though, I think I have something to work with . . . "

Wasn't the right number though, was it? She just wanted to get away, fob me off with fictional digits. I tried calling it in the morning but it was just a buzz. I couldn't explain to the buzz that I was 'sorry', that I'd maybe got a bit carried away – getting to touch her breasts and between her legs and then finally . . . hot, frantic, I just got carried away, a playful hand on her throat, and I think she said 'don't' but it was all just a game, drunken fun. Stupid, stupid. She was trying to get away but there was no stopping me, gripping and pushing and squeezing. Lost in the moment, they call it. Who can stop that once it's started? When I was done I noticed tears and a crimson face. I was disgusted. I spat. It wasn't me, it wasn't me.

There was another knock at the door. It roused Werner from his sleep and gave him the momentary realisation that he hadn't left the house in days. People just came to him: Willem, Bosweldt, it was as if they were visiting a patient in hospital, or an elderly relative. He opened the door.

"You said I could come tonight if I wasn't doing anything better." Liselotte was carrying a battered suitcase.

"It's *so* nice to feel wanted, dear."

Liselotte had been a regular visitor since the end of the war. An actress whose career had been hampered, both by poor choices of theatrical roles and of the men she brought into her life. She met Werner at a screening of *Annelie* and seemed to believe that keeping close to such a famous actor might result in a starring role of her own. Although they slept together occasionally, over the years Werner had spent more time talking, crying and drinking with her than actually making love. She was short, with muscular thighs and a pale face.

"Is it okay for me to start a fire? It's freezing out there."

"Be my guest, dear. I'll get the drinks."

Werner prepared a large gin for his guest and a slither of tonic water. He poured a neat brandy for himself.

"I'd offer you something to eat, but . . . " he gestured towards the piled-up pans and greasy surfaces.

"I know. Don't worry. A drink will be fine."

"So what's in the suitcase?"

"Just some clothes. My friend's getting married and she wanted to get rid of all of her negligees . . . "

"Been keeping secrets from husband-to-be?"

"He hasn't got a clue, which is probably for the best, being a preacher's son!" They laughed.

"That's not true . . . " Werner said.

"Well he's from a rich family, anyway, and she got scared that stuff would give her away."

"Well, you'll have to try some of it on for me later . . . "

"You're an old devil, Werner. Only ever one thing on your mind, isn't there?"

"Don't know what you're talking about, dear," he sipped his drink.

"Besides, most of it wouldn't fit me. She's a tall girl, there's no meat on her at all. I'll probably end up selling most of it on."

There was a cheerful innocence to Liselotte, an unassuming nature that could, at first, be mistaken for inanity. Werner was very fond of her candour, and was starting to entertain the idea of proposing to her, as soon as his court appearances were over.

"Let me ask you something, dear."

"What is it?" She put two cigarettes in her mouth and lit them both. She inhaled, and then passed one of them to her host.

"When we've . . . you know, *been* together . . . "

"Spit it out, Werner!"

"I've never mistreated you, have I?"

"That's a funny question to ask."

"Seriously, though?"

"You're a perfect gentleman."

"Okay, but what about other men you've been with? Do they ever *push* you? *Make* you do things . . . "

"It happens. You get the sort who just think you're a piece of meat – just there to be thrown around, think they can do what they like to you . . . " she stared at her feet, and took a gulp from her drink.

"And what do you do? Specifically, when that sort of thing happens?"

"Werner! For God's sake, at least let me have my drink."

"Of course, sorry, dear. I'll get you a top-up." He stood, stooped, and ambled back to the kitchen. This time he grabbed the whole bottle.

"Why are you asking all this, anyway?"

"Just curious."

"Come on, Werner, you can tell me.."

"No reason. I don't know. I've got a suspicion that Willem has a woman lined-up to work for me."

"Really?" Liselotte had the terrible habit of finding the innuendo in any sentence.

"Nothing like that – she'll act as my agent, represent me. I doubt it'll ever happen, but Willem does have his funny ways. It got me thinking about the differences between men and women. You know, however bright a girl is, or however strong – they're still physically inferior, still at the mercy of men."

"Never really thought about it before, Werner."

"It must be frustrating though. You must feel helpless sometimes."

"Women are stronger than you think, Werner. We have ways of getting what we want."

"I suppose so."

An image of Maria flashed through his mind. The more time that had passed since her death, the more Werner felt he had a sense of exactly who she was. In her own way, Maria had been strong, and had obviously exercised control over own life in the most extreme manner possible. Perversely, he was starting to admire her conviction.

"So tell me about this girl. Let me guess: she's tall, attractive, a brunette, 'and just delighted to be working with the great Herr Krauss.'" Liselotte adopted a high-pitched whine for her impersonation.

"Not jealous are you, by any chance?" Werner smiled.

"Of course not."

"Because you know there's really only one girl for me . . . "

"And who might that be?"

"Come over here and I'll tell you." Liselotte got to her feet, crossed the room and clumsily sat down on Werner's lap. They laughed as both their drinks spilled.

"Get off, woman!" Still laughing, Liselotte sat beside him, the started to rub his crotch outside his trousers.

"So does the new girl do this for you?"

"Give it time."

"What about this?" Expertly, she unbuttoned his trousers with a click of her fingers, then unzipped. Her hand slipped inside his underpants, and she started to kiss his neck. Werner pawed at her breasts and legs.

"Let's go up to bed." he said.

"Not 'til I've finished here," she replied, stroking vigorously. "You know, if you're interested in getting rough with me, we could give it a try?"

"What?"

"You were saying earlier, about *pushing* me . . . "

"No!" he cried, and grabbed her wrist. "Stop that!" He stood, tucked his shirt in, and re-buttoned his trousers.

"Jesus, Werner, what's the matter?"

"*You* woman, *you're* the matter – are you fucking stupid?"

"I thought you'd like it, what are you making such a fuss about?"

Looming over her, he grabbed Liselotte's shoulder, and moved his face so close he cold smell the gin on her breath.

"I would *never* do anything like that, *never*. Do you hear me?"

She nodded, and started to whimper "Get off . . . please, Werner . . . you're hurting me."

He relinquished his grip on her shoulder. She stood quickly, and ran to the door. "I'm going to bed."

Wondering exactly how this had all happened, he finished first his own drink, then hers. He sank into his chair and tried to masturbate, tried to think about that girl, the lovely Peta, but it wouldn't happen, and he was soon asleep.

2

He woke alone, at seven a.m., in his chair. Liselotte had left a note, saying she was sorry, and that she had taken thirty marks from his wallet. He wandered around the house looking for something to do. Eventually, he climbed upstairs and slipped into his bed, which was still warm, and smelled of her lavender perfume. Willem, along with his radical plan, soon woke him up.

"I'm really not sure about this."

"Because she's a woman, I suppose?"

"It's just not right, I . . . "

"Put it this way. What was the first thing you thought when you saw her? And be honest."

"I thought, 'nice legs', and 'I wonder if she might have a thing for older men.'"

"Exactly! Doesn't that just make her perfect? You need someone who's going to convince the theatres and the studios you still have something to offer. She'll *charm* them, Werner. She's bright, and pretty – producers and agents will lap it up – they'll all find it impossible to say 'no' to her, I promise."

"She needs experience, Willem, *credentials*. Otherwise my credibility will be . . . "

"Wake up, Werner!" he interrupted. Credibility's not exactly something you have in abundance right now. And frankly, as things stand, none of the agencies want to take you on. As for experience, she's handled all my accounts for years and done a damn good job. She's done plenty of public relations, and she did front-of-house at the *Metropol* for years. Plus, you know her contacts book is good, *because it's mine!*"

"Maybe it's not such a ridiculous idea then." Werner couldn't help but feel that the whole plan reeked of desperation.

"It's a brilliant idea! You need a new image, right? The caring, sensitive Werner Krauss, open-minded, misunderstood – then be a pioneer, be the only actor in town to have a woman representing him."

Willem was desperate. This woman, Peta, was his wife's cousin, and Willem had always seemed peculiarly obliging where his wife's wishes were concerned.

"She can have a trial. Two weeks. If I like her ideas, she stays."

"You won't regret this, Werner."

"If it doesn't work out, I'll just have to go crawling back to Stefan."

"I'll get her to come round this evening – you'll hit it off, just wait and see!"

In truth, he was just paying lip service to Willem's request. Willem was a good friend, one who still returned Werner's calls and wasn't ashamed to be associated with him, and had said so in *Deutsche Zeitung*. Plus, the thought of getting that girl into the house was too good for him not to, at least, give her ideas a token hearing. He scampered around the room, desperately trying to tidy it, but only moving the mess from one place to another. Until recently he employed a cleaner, but she left after a series of misunderstandings. Werner couldn't stand women with no sense of humour.

With the room in a fairly acceptable state, he climbed the stairs to begin a lengthy operation in the bathroom. It must have been a fortnight since he last washed properly, and he was determined to be ready for Peta's arrival. He turned on the tap to the old bath, and started to undress. A sweaty, stale aroma filled his nose. Like the house around him, it was the stench of bachelorhood. He looked in the mirror and saw a gnarled, stooped old man staring back at him. In the man's eyes, he saw the look of one of his characters, a Paracelsus or a Shylock: startled, slovenly, confused.

As usual, the water was far too hot, but having grown-up regarding hot bathing water (on tap, no less) a flagrant luxury, he was reluctant to dilute it with cold. Having tentatively stepped in the tub, scalding and cursing, he started to lower himself down, feeling the burn first on his posterior, then on his testicles. Eventually he lay there fully immersed, and began the cleaning ritual. His toenails were yellow and far too long. The feeling of them scraping against the enamel bath surface made him cringe, and he vowed to cut them later, if he had time. He scrubbed his legs and groin, forced, as he was, to heave his stomach out of the way in order to properly clean his genitals. "Bom bom bom bom" he liked to hear his deep voice resonate around the tiled room, and continued to sing fragments of old ballads:

"Sleep! sleep! beauty bright, / Dreaming o'er the joys of night; / Sleep! sleep! in thy sleep / Little sorrows sit and weep. / Sweet babe, in thy face / Soft desires I can trace, / Secret joys and secret smiles, / Little pretty infant wiles. / As thy softest limbs I feel, / Smiles as of the morning steal / O'er thy cheek, and o'er thy breast, / When thy little heart doth rest. / Oh, the cunning wiles that creep / In thy little heart asleep! / When thy little heart doth wake, / Then the dreadful light doth break"

He considered masturbating, but didn't have the energy, so just hauled himself up out of the bath and towelled dry.

He chose one of the few remaining clean shirts, it was deep blue with white cuffs, but went back to the underwear and trousers he had been wearing for the last week. He crept slowly back down the stairs, and poured a whisky. As was happening more and more of late, he had started to talk to himself. 'Would a girl like her *really* be interested? Perhaps if she's desperate enough for the job . . . ' There was a knock. He limped to the door, and opened it to find *those* legs.

"Well, I must say you look most fetching, my dear."

"That's very sweet of you. Now I've got plenty to say, Herr Krauss. I can either give you my long list of ideas, or a summary . . . " She swept past him, down the hallway and into his study.

"I was never one to 'beat around the bush', as the English say," he closed the door.

"Fine. Okay, firstly, your court appearance is soon, and that has to be your main priority."

"Agreed. Don't you want to sit down first, though?"

"Yes, yes . . . thank you. The way I see it, we have to turn this messy business to your advantage."

"It's a de-Nazification trial, my dear, not a matinee."

"No." She carefully removed the pile of newspapers from one of the chairs and sat down. As she sat and crossed her legs, her skirt crept up her thighs. Werner tried his best to concentrate. "But it *is* a moment in the spotlight – a chance to defend yourself and give your side of the story."

"I know this, I know this, woman! For God's sake – what's your idea?"

"A memoir. Think about it. In the court you'll be cross-examined, scrutinised – maybe even tricked into saying something you don't mean. But if we can get a book out – and soon – it'll be perfect: regretful, reflective, but above all positive."

"You really think I have time for writing books? Didn't Willem tell you – I want to get on the stage, *I want to act.*"

"You don't have to write it, as such. All we have to do is schedule some interviews, I'll borrow a tape recorder and ask some questions – doesn't matter where we are, backstage, in a restaurant, wherever . . ."

"Taking me to a restaurant, are you?"

"The point is, the book will be minimum effort and maximum reward. You can make people love you again, Werner." The girl was almost convincing. There was a purpose to the way she spoke, 'she'd be an absolute *animal* in bed too,' he thought.

"So what about the acting, dear? I am also an actor in case you'd forgot."

"There's talk of Hauptmann's *Vor Sonnenuntergang* coming back, nothing definite planned, just talk."

"Since when? Why did no one tell me?"

"What matters is that I spoke to a couple of the producers this morning and we might be able to arrange a meeting."

"What sort of role?"

"I thought just supporting at first, Erich Schellow or maybe Claus Biederstaedt. Just get you back on the stage without too much fuss. Think of it this way: Mr. and Mrs. Average in – I don't know, Cologne – they see the name 'Werner Krauss' in small print and they think 'oh, he's back then' and don't give it another moment's thought. If you want the lead – the backlash and the headlines – I'll support you, but in my opinion it's a mistake."

"Makes sense." It really did make sense. Perhaps a woman agent wasn't such a ludicrous idea after all. She had spirit and energy. "I'm most impressed. This isn't going to be easy for either of us, God knows. But, I'll go along with these ideas of yours, if you think it'll help." He held out a hand, and Peta took it. He scooped her hand up to his lips and kissed her cold skin. "Now, how about a drink?" He let go of her hand and shuffled towards his drinks cabinet.

"It's strange you should mention that actually."

"I beg your pardon?" he reached for a decanter of cognac, and started to search for a clean glass.

"Well, part of my plan was also to help you *personally*, get your life back on track, so that you would be focused and . . . " she took a deep breath, "focused and sober, when all of this attention comes your way."

"What exactly are you insinuating, girl?"

"It's my job to show you in the best possible light, Herr Krauss, and Willem mentioned you'd taken to drinking quite a lot . . . since your wife . . . "

He slammed down the decanter, and walked away from the array of drinks.

"You've quite a nerve, coming to *my* home and insulting me this way."

"I've always thought, Herr Krauss, it's better to be honest and open with people. It's how I behave with you, and with anyone I do business with."

"Is that so? And I suppose your shit doesn't smell either?"

She stood, as if she was about to leave. Then she spoke softly.

"In my experience, it's the person who has the problem who's often the last to know about it. Their friends just patronise them, laugh about it behind their backs; their family become either bitter or afraid."

"And here I was thinking I was hiring an agent, not a psychiatrist."

"Of course, if you don't think it's a problem, just say now, and I won't mention it again. But if you *do* want to change, and for things to start working out, say so now, and I can try to help."

He knew she was right. Of course, she was right. But what else did he have, other than a few brandies every now and again? His name was mud, all around the world – why should it matter if he was pissed out of his mind?

"You know, my wife, Maria, hated drinking. Absolutely *hated* it. She could never understand what was to be gained from it – how people could enjoy themselves when they were drunk, 'idiotic' she called it."

"And do you think you drink too much?"

"Don't give me that, dear. Please. According to Willem you've worked in the theatre all your life."

"I have!"

"Then you'll know what it's like! Rehearsal – lunch – wine – matinee – restaurant – wine – show – dressing room – drinks . . . " It felt like sparring with Maria again, all those years after what she did.

"Not for everyone, Herr Krauss." She played with her hair in the embarrassed silence. Werner felt vulnerable, as though he were a charity case. Wasn't he a *star* for God's sake? "I don't want to upset you," she said, at last, "but at least we're talking about it, and that's a good start. Now why don't I make us both a nice cup of coffee?"

"Fine, why not?" he said. She wandered off to find the kitchen.

"Very first thing I'm going to do is hire a cleaner, Herr Krauss. This is no way for a great actor to live."

As they drank their coffee, Werner decided to take the girl on, and go along with some of her suggestions. He needed to bring a woman's touch back into his life, and he needed fresh ideas if he were to ever rescue his reputation. "So the bastards think they've seen the last of Werner Krauss?" he thought, "The agents and so-called Intendents. They can think again."

"Are you listening, Herr Krauss?"

"Yes, yes, of course, dear . . . " she slipped into her long coat, and picked up her handbag.

"Then shall I do it?"

"Do what?"

"Write that letter – the response to what Gottfried said, in the paper . . . "

"Yes, yes thank you. Sounds like a good idea."

Upon leaving, she presented Werner with a file.

"This is for you. It's a list of things I want you to get done."

"And when do I have for this, exactly?"

"You'll make time. I'll be back again tomorrow – I want everything on the list done by then. Goodbye, Herr Krauss."

He followed her to the door, but she left swiftly, without turning back. He returned to the house and opened the file. He felt a pang of guilt upon reading the carefully typed sentences, her lists with well-intentioned headings: 'Charming the Media', 'Two Years to the Top'. He turned to the page headed 'Priorities':

1. Make an appointment with the doctor.
Public success must begin with personal well-being. We must ensure that you're fit and healthy – ready for court, and subsequently, a long theatre run.

2. Make a list of your friends in the business.
We can call upon these people to defend your character and maybe contribute to the memoirs. I need to know whom we can rely upon. The support of a well-known figure would be advantageous.

3. Make a list of instances where you were disobedient/not complicit with the Nazi regime. This will help your defence.

4. Write a description of exactly how you'd like your life to be in five years time.

He decided to start work on demand number four on Peta's list. He could see the merits of two and three, but this task seemed to require some creativity – it implied a sense of hope and of possibility. He poured a drink, found some paper and a pen, and cleared some space on the dining room table.

DEAR PETA,
How does one start a letter like this? I must give you credit, dear, it is an interesting exercise. Believe me, I welcome any opportunity to talk about myself! (Just joking).
In five years time I would like to have all of this silly political stuff finished with. I was an actor then, I am an actor now, and, while I still draw breath, I would like to continue acting. The extent to which I did or did not help to influence any particular political cause is of no relevance to me. Anyone who closely examines my record, anyone who truly knows me, will support that judgement. In my humble opinion, if anyone is so stupid as to be influenced by a play or a film, it is they who should be tried in the courts, not me. They can accuse me of pragmatism, even opportunism, but hatred? It's silly, my dear, very silly.
Although I was, of course, awarded the Goethe medallion, I've often been asked about other merit awards, recognition of a lifetime of achievement and such like, but none of this really interests me – especially in the short term. As much as I hate to go crawling back; it is essential that the theatrical community once again accepts me. Perhaps then, with all of these problems behind me, it would be nice to receive some sort of recognition. If nothing else, it should also serve to draw a line under this invasive (and entirely unjustified) Nazi business.
Needless to say, if I do make it back on the stage, or back in front of a camera, I hope to have made shrewd decisions as to which roles I accepted. It would be particularly satisfying to end my acting career the way it began, with an international success. In hindsight, I never truly appreciated the pleasures that came with that first flush of acclaim after "Das Cabinet". They say that success is wasted on the young, and I'm inclined to agree. Although when I was younger I felt that money was wasted on the old, a point which might be equally valid.
I bet you wish you hadn't asked me to ramble on at you now, don't you, dear?
A glib answer to your question would, of course, have been: in five years time I would like to be happy. But why shouldn't I

want that? All of my life I've worked hard and have done my best to bring joy to those people around me. I could have been a better father; I could have been a better husband. It is months since I spoke to either of the children, and even that was over the telephone. Perhaps spending my life in service to the public was at the expense of those closest to me. But these things are too complicated to reduce to a few sentences. In scripts, in novels, stories are always so neat, coincidences so convenient, emotions so simple to gauge. Isn't life just a series of misunderstandings, broken promises and disappointments? This court business, for instance, in a play it would be the centrepiece, the showdown, the climax. In truth, (according to Willem) the proceedings could take months, even years. In fact, he said he wouldn't be surprised if there was more than one trial. You can't see that happening in a novel, can you? It'd be even worse in a script. Imagine an audience sitting there while old men shuffled papers, secretaries typed and translators yapped. I wholly expect the courtroom to be as mundane as any other room.

I fear I have drifted from the subject somewhat, but reading back over my words I think you'll agree that my ambitions are largely based in the short-term. I need to get these stupid accusations dealt with – swiftly and properly. How can anyone be happy with all this nonsense being written about them? I read another report today, quoting a man called Hudder, who said that my work in Jud Süß *was a "dark stain" on my reputation, that it was an example of my "fascistic collaboration." These things need to stop if I am ever to find any peace, if I am ever to find any happiness.*

I do hope you can help me to achieve this, my dear. You are an extremely capable and intelligent girl, and I predict huge success for you in the career you pursue – with me or anyone else. Perhaps it would be possible for us to talk about this "plan" at greater length sometime, over dinner. I can fill you in on my glorious history (just joking) and you can tell me more about yourself.

Sincere wishes,
Werner

He looked over the letter, and worried that his parenthesised reassurances might be a little too informal, a little too . . . desperate. He thought that this was probably how young people addressed each other – informally, suggestively – but he really wasn't sure. It was this same desperate feeling, of scrabbling to win the affections of a younger woman, which compounded Werner's difficulties with Frau Kopenik. The day after their encounter at the *Hotel Esplande*, he had insisted that Stefan found out her address and her (correct) telephone number.

"You're still getting used to life without Maria, is it such a good idea to get involved with this woman now?"

"I'm not getting *involved*, I just need to talk to her."

It didn't take long for Stefan to track her down, and that evening Werner was standing on her doorstep in the freezing cold.

"I've got nothing to say to you," she said.

"Please, can I come in? I just want to apologise. What happened wasn't right and I don't want you to think . . . "

"You don't want me to *tell*, you mean? What do you think the press would make of this? The great Werner Krauss – a predatory beast."

"You couldn't – nobody would believe you – please, I . . . "

"You really have no idea who I am, do you, Werner? I'm friends with every newspaper editor in *Deutschland*."

"Darling, it's getting freezing, who are you talking to?" A deep voice came from within the house behind her."

"Nobody, darling," she replied, "a tramp looking for somewhere to stay." And with that, she closed the door.

At the time he blamed Maria for his subsequent behaviour. If she hadn't been so stupid, so selfish, doing what she did, writing those letters . . . but with hindsight, he can see that his drinking was getting out of control, and that no matter how badly he behaved, he seemed to still be praised: praised by the Party, praised in the press and adored by the public. No one ever said 'no' to Werner Krauss.

Having parked his Mercedes at the top of her street, he decided to sleep there, in the back seat. He woke early in the morning, and kept watch on the elegant three-story town house, until eventually her husband left. Werner took a gulp from his bottle of whisky. There was no way she should get the better of him, threatening his reputation with her blackmail. He could get some ammunition of his own. He walked back to the house, and knocked. As soon as the door opened, he thrust his foot into the gap.

"What the hell are you doing?"

"We need to talk." He barged past her, entering the hallway. "I wanted to say 'sorry' for the other night."

"You stink! I was right, you're no better than a tramp!"

"Please – you've got the wrong idea about me."

"You've got one minute to explain yourself before I call the police."

"Fine. Thank you." He tried to put a hand on her shoulder, but she pulled away. "The other night, I'd drunk far too much, it's no excuse, I know, but I shouldn't have done those things. I shouldn't have . . . "

"I get the idea. Now will you leave?"

"Don't you have anything to say?"

"Like what? 'You're forgiven, Werner. Please come in for breakfast.' Is that what you want?"

"I want you to understand – I liked you, I still like you, and I want you to get to know me. You'll see that I don't treat people, women, in that way."

"I couldn't care less what you're like. Now just get out, and don't come back here again."

"Can I at least use your lavatory? Please? Then I'll go, I promise."

She nodded her assent. Werner climbed the first flight of stairs, and opened the first door on his left. It was their bedroom. He quickly closed the door and shuffled away, but not before noticing a black diary on one of the pillows. He tried the next door, and proceeded to use the toilet. Catching sight of himself in the mirror, he realised how pathetic he must look to her. Unshaven, bleary-eyed and sweaty. He had considered hitting her when she complained about his smell. He had to focus, get out of this strange house and go home. He started to urinate, and considered his options. He could just try to forget about this silly business and hope that the girl kept her mouth shut. Or, he could pose a threat of his own. Perhaps he could tell her husband about their indiscretion. Or, he could find out about her so-called 'influential friends' by contacting a few of his own. She wasn't the only one who could start a rumour, after all.

Almost without thinking, he finished in the bathroom and calmly strode into the bedroom next door. He slipped the diary under his shirt and made his way downstairs.

"I mean it, Werner. Don't come back." Frau Kopenik held the door open for him.

"I'm sorry," he said, not breaking his stride out of the door and into the street.

He stared at Peta's words, not knowing how to interpret them.

3. Make a list of instances where you were disobedient/not complicit with the Nazi regime. This will help your defence

Of course, she was only doing her best. There was no way she could understand the pressure he had been under at that time: the constant sense of compromise, of simply getting by. Life hadn't happened in hours and days back then, but in promises and gestures, appearances and obligations. The cessation of war hadn't brought a sense of jubilation or of loss, for Werner, it had simply brought an unavoidable awareness of *time*. Now on the cusp of a new decade, and undeniably on the verge of 'retirement age', he could feel the spotlight being thrust on the nineteen forties, and his place in them, from the high-minded detachment of another age.

Time now arrogantly insisted that he completed Peta's tasks before her return, and though he could easily usher-in another day with a bottle and bed, he was determined to stay awake in the hope that his efforts would garner her luscious approval. He knew he had the perfect answer to her question, but by describing an isolated example of his resistance to the Nazi regime, was he somehow highlighting its exceptional nature? He poured a small glass of *Rottwein*, and set about describing his most public affront to the Hitler Reich.

I choose to tell you this story, for the simple reason that above the desk at which I write is a poster for a particular production, a memento of one of my most accomplished performances. It reads: Grand premiere, 2nd March, 1937, Werner Krauss stars in a Jürgen Fehling production of . . . Richard III. Staatstheater, Berlin, Commencement 7 p.m.

As Richard, I limped around the stage, creating the illusion of desperation, depravity and deformity. In the second scene of the play, my slobbering approach to young Anne, coupled with the hobbling, reminded some in the audience of the notorious antics of our Propaganda Minister. I couldn't possibly comment on such hypothetical interpretations, of course. Nor could I comment on the costumes deployed in that play, particularly those worn by Clarence's murderers, clad as they were in black uniforms, with shoulder straps and highboots. Some saw parallels between their brutality and that of the SS. Indeed, the actors guarding me in the court scenes were wearing trooper-style helmets. I have photographs if you'd care to see them some time, my dear?

If you were to be at all convinced by these allusions, you might wish to seek further associations in the production. I heard, for instance, that some commentators compared the ghosts which appeared before Richard with the dead of the Night of the Long Knives in 1934. Richard III ran for twenty-one performances and was later revived for a further run of seven. I can't begin to describe the thrill of appearing in such a production – each night onstage felt dangerous, necessary and pertinent. When asked by the Party, in 1938, to choose a perfor-

mance to celebrate my twenty-fifth year on the stage, I chose this one, much to the chagrin of certain 'officials'.

Of course, you could argue that such nuances of performance and staging are too subtle to have been seen as a protest in any tangible sense. But I have faith that a great number of audience members made those connections with the political situation, and engaged with the allegorical nature of Fehling's production. Furthermore, I recall a review by Karl Ruppel of the show, which spoke of the play's depiction of the 'intellectually outstanding political criminal'. Poor Fehling was threatened with the sack, and only maintained his job because Gustav Grundgens told Goering he would resign if Fehling went.

What you must understand about this, my dear, is that such understated protests really were as radical as it was possible for us to get, without directly endangering our lives, as well as those of our family and friends. Such productions were staged throughout the Reich, albeit with more restrained metaphors and allusions.

He felt exhausted. On the one hand, it was a laborious task, trying to articulate events that were already clear in his mind. Yet he couldn't deny there was a cathartic quality to writing, and he was starting to think that an autobiography would indeed be a good idea. For the first night in weeks, he made the decision to go to bed, rather than drunkenly slumbering in whichever room he happened to be in. "Whatever I'm paying that girl," he thought, "it isn't enough."

3

He woke feeling lucid and refreshed. Reading over his words from last night, he felt he had made a pretty convincing case, and that perhaps there was hope after all. He decided to try to get some exercise, starting with a run around the park. He had no suitable clothes for this venture into the cold morning, and within a few strides, the run became a jog, which subsequently became a walk. Nevertheless, it felt good to leave the house. At the other side of *Rosensteinpark*, he found a small café, where he enjoyed a rich, frothy coffee and a Danish pastry. Hesitantly, he turned the pages of *Stuttgarter Zeitung*, which someone had left behind. He couldn't bear the thought of the words 'Werner Krauss' leaping from the page to spoil his day. But it was fine. All the headlines talked of Konrad Adenauer, the Marshall Plan and VFB's chances in the forthcoming cup match. There was something quite reassuring about the fact that life was going on without him. *Westen Deutschland* itself, though devastated just a few years earlier, seemed to be functioning quite normally.

Walking back through the park, he was stopped by a woman with two Alsatians.

"Excuse me . . . " she said, "are you Werner Krauss?"

He paused. His heart sank. He just wanted to get home, without having to argue or explain himself. The dogs were leaping up at him, their panting producing steam in the cold air. Tentatively, he held out a hand. "Yes I am, pleased to meet you!" He hoped a friendly gesture would at least be met with civility. She took his hand.

"How wonderful!" she said. "My sister, Louisa, she won't believe me when I tell her who I've met."

"And your name is?"

"Angela."

"Such a pretty name. Send my best wishes to your sister. It was splendid to meet you Angela, truly."

He strode away from her, not wanting to dwell and invite small talk. In the past he had issued such platitudes with cold, military precision. Today though, it *was* splendid to meet Angela and her dogs.

The icy stethoscope bell made Werner's heart jump.

"Diet good, Herr Krauss? Regular exercise?"

He wondered why the Doctor always had to talk in such a clipped, curt manner. "Terrible diet. I did try to go for a run this morning, but I haven't really exercised in years, old boy."

"We'll have to do something about that. Any chest pains, shortage of breath?"

"Tell me, doctor, do I look pretty good for my age, in your experience?"

"Like most of us, you could do with losing a bit of weight, but, yes, I suppose you do."

"So any habits I've got: smoking, drinking – they're not causing me any problems?"

"Nothing I can detect, Herr Krauss, no. But of course, any ill-effects of such habits do not necessarily manifest themselves physically."

"Meaning?"

"It's just common sense. Heavy drinking, in particular, can take a psychological toll – years before the liver gives way."

"Well thanks, Doc, that's really cheered me up."

"If you're concerned, it would be a good idea for me to take a sample of urine and do some tests."

He reached into his bag and produced a bottle. "If you could do me the honour, Herr Krauss?"

Although it was all very well preparing letters for Peta, pissing for doctors or recounting anecdotes to Bosweldt, Werner knew that sooner or later the focus of everyone's attention would be the film he had made with Veidt Harlan: *Jud Süß*. The initial filming, on this occasion, was relatively straightforward, and the script was apparently faithful to the novel by Lion Feuchtwanger (Werner hadn't actually read it himself, for fear that his own interpretation might become stifled by an author's solipsism). However, the production and final editing were fraught with problems. Werner had never known such intense interference from the Propaganda Ministry. Harlan had encouraged the actors to take their cues from an authentic Yiddish film, *Dybuk*. This strive for authenticity was attractive to Werner, who was keen to address his pantomimic portrayal in *The Merchant*. His friend, Ferdinand Marian was starring as the eponymous Josef Süß, and Werner played several, minor Jewish roles, most significantly, Rabbi Leouw.

However, on seeing the production, Goebbels was furious. He insisted that the script underwent a complete re-write and that several scenes had to be re-filmed. It was this process that Werner found so torturous, yet he imagined it would be those very scenes on which he would now be judged.

"The ascendants are favourable, Rabbi." Leouw and Süß were sat at a modest dining table.

"Because they have to be."

"There's no have to be."

"Can you determine the course of the stars?"

"We cannot determine the course of the stars, but surely the actions of men – if we convince them the Lord has sent this."

"My son Josef . . . The Lord looks down on you, and sees you have grown vain and proud, like a peacock. Stern is the Lord's punishment, upon the Jew who forgets who he is."

"What can I do, Rabbi?"

"Don't you live in a palace like Solomon? Don't you sleep in a gilded bed? Are your walls not covered in books which you should not read? Don't these drapes cost 12 thalers a yard?"

"But Rabbi?"

"The Lord wants his people to walk in sackcloth and ashes, to be scattered throughout the earth, so they may rule in secret, over the peoples of the earth."

"How can I rule if I do not show myself?"

"Rule over the pockets of the goyim, but keep away from the affairs of princes."

"*Halt!* Lovely stuff, Werner." Harlan had said. He joined Werner and Ferdinand at the table. "I wonder, though, if you might just consider trying again with the Jewish nose? The Minister is adamant that we should show the real Jew."

"No. Never! There is more to acting than silly noses – it is out of the question. I want people to know that I am Werner Krauss, the actor, and not a hook-nosed Jew puppet!"

"Fine, that's perfectly understandable. I'll pass on your comments to the Minister."

"As you wish." Werner had felt exhilarated by his defiance.

"We're going to pick it up from there then, but this is the point at which things turn sinister, can you do that for me, Ferdy?"

"Surely, Süß wants to please the Rabbi?"

"To an extent. But we've been told to assume that he's just paying lip-service to old-fashioned sensibilities. Süß is hungry for power. Gaze into Werner's eyes with conviction, but let the audience know you have ulterior motives."

"No problem, Veidt."

"Good, when everyone's ready . . . " he stood and skipped back to his place behind the camera, "*und Aktion!*"

"By ruling princes I rule the people."

"A prince is pardoned, a Jew hanged."

"It cannot be the will of the Lord to prevent me from making Wurttenberg into the Promised Land for Israel. I'm nearly there, about to grasp it. Already, I can see the milk and honey flowing – for Israel. Am I now to stop on the banks of Jordan? Is that not the will of the Lord?"

"You read the Lord's will as it suits you."

"We should read the will of the Lord as it suits Israel. That is the will of the Lord, Rabbi."

"What should I do? Lie to him?"

"No, don't lie. Tell him the "second truth" in our version only. Remind him of his motto: attempt"

"What does it mean?"

"To him who dares."

"My son, you must wait."

"I haven't time."

"You must speak to me for our brethren."

"If you lack the peace of mind for prayer, you will fail."

"Peace of mind is all very well, but now I need 5 times 100,000 thalers.

"Are you insane?"

"Listen, I've come because they're all assembled now. The Estates want to expel all Jews from Stuttgart, but the Duke is prepared to bring in soldiers to crush the Estates. He will be absolute ruler, and then he will protect the Jews!"

"Do you want the Yids to fight?"

"No, pay! Soldiers cost money!"

"If you want to fight against the goyim, you have to dress like a Yid again, you will have to wear a caftan again, you will have to grow your beard back, like a son of Israel."

"Rabbi, don't you see? This is important! I know because I am at the source. If the Jews give the 500,000 thalers, I'll see to it that the Duke will never forget that it was Jewish money. But if the Jews are close-fisted, skulk behind their fine Talmudic sayings, they will lose everything. Maybe their lives."

The final cut was ghastly, drawing upon base stereotypes and transparently attempting to instil a sense of fear in the audience. Yet Werner knew it would be this film that determined his fate. This would be the point at which court hearings, interviews or even damn autobiographies had to be dealt with carefully. He needed to talk of 'universal themes', 'human qualities,' he needed to talk of the manipulative post-production, the dubbing and re-editing. People *must* recognise the coercion involved, they must *not* associate him with . . .

He poured a drink. The day had started so well, why did he have to dwell on this damn trial? He couldn't remember when Peta was due to arrive. Clutching his brandy with one hand, he made a tentative effort to tidy the lounge, but it was no good. He just wanted to sit and sink and swallow. He needed that burning feeling in his throat, he wanted to turn down the volume on the world around him, give himself a sense of perspective, a sense of absurdity. He needed to drink just to make the world *tolerable*.

Walking along the railroad track, he waved 'auf wiedersehen' to his wife and daughter with a heavy hand. Their shelter, like the track, was covered in tightly-weaved snow. This walk seemed so familiar now, hopping from one wooden sleeper to the next. His ears were trained to detect even the faintest of sounds, in order to allow plenty of time to make way for an oncoming train. After about a mile, he saw the signalman sat reading a newspaper in his hut in the sidings. He said 'hallo' and the signalman nodded, without looking up from the paper. Despite what he had heard, he trusted his daughter, and was determined to harbour no ill feeling for this man, just because of some silly rumours.

He continued to walk until a couple of miles into his journey; he noticed a deep claret stain in the perfect snow. Not far from the stain were two sets of footprints, one shallow, and the other deep. He decided to follow the footprints to the siding, and out into a neighbouring field. There were further drops of blood, and the tracks went right into the centre of the field. He trudged in the ever-deepening snow, ever wondering if he ought to just turn back and continue his journey into town. As he reached the other side of the field, he noticed that the footprints stopped. He started to dig, using only his hands. Frantically he scraped away the snow, until he found a small mound of freshly dug earth. He plunged his fingers into the mud . . .

A knock at the door. Werner couldn't be sure if he heard correctly, and wanted to sink back into his dream. He was on the set of *Scherben*, he was a young father, a romantic lead. The knock came again. He scrambled to his feet, and swigged the slither of remaining brandy. "On my way, dear!" he shouted. He wiped his eyes, noticing an unusual build-up of tears. He tucked his shirt in, and made his way to the door.

"Looking splendid again, dear."

"Thank you, Herr Krauss." Confidently, she strolled past him and entered the lounge. "Now let me guess, you had no time for my little tasks?"

"On the contrary, dear. Give me a moment." He searched around the scruffy dining table and eventually found the two documents he was looking for. "Here's the letter you requested, some notes on my performance in Richard III and, you'll be pleased to know, the doctor gave me a clean bill of health."

Peta made a point of straightening out the crumpled papers, and brushing off the dust with the back of her hand. "I'm impressed, Herr Krauss, and surprised, I must admit. Although, there doesn't appear to be the list I asked for."

"List? What list?" . . . "Of friends. People we can rely on. People we might have to call upon."

Werner tapped his forehead. "That list is all in here – no need to worry your pretty face about it."

"Very well. As I said, I'm impressed with your efforts."

"Then perhaps you'll join me for a drink to celebrate? I've had a particularly good day."

"It's only six o'clock, Herr Krauss."

"Come now. We've been colleagues, *partners* for two days – surely it is bad luck not to toast our new arrangement?"

"A small *weisswine* then. Thank you."

Werner stumbled into the kitchen, pouring a brandy for himself and a large glass of wine for his guest.

"I have some news, Herr Krauss, a role . . . " he was irritated by the way she raised her voice to him. He wasn't deaf. "But it might not be what you expected."

"Come on then, girl, out with it!"

"It *is* a production of *Vor Sonnenuntergang*, but – and this is the clever bit – it's in the West End."

"London?"

"Yes. I know I said it would be wise to stay low-key, but don't you see? You'll be sending a message out to the world – Werner Krauss was not, *is* not, a Nazi. Frankly, the sooner you can get onstage in one of the allied nations, the better."

He thought of his previous trip to London, and a disastrous attempt to act in English. Despite his best efforts and tireless rehearsals, the performances fell flat, the words falling awkwardly from his mouth.

"That's all very well for you to say, dear. You won't be the one facing crowds of rabid Englishmen, baying for blood."

"Like I said, it's a risk. But I think it's going to be bold gestures like this that can be the solution to all your problems. If you can successfully face the London press, the rest of Europe will be simple. Then maybe America . . . "

"I'll think about it."

"Good. In the meantime, we need to contact one of these friends of yours. Care to divulge one of the names in your head?" She smiled.

"Well if I'm going to be an honorary *Englander*, then why not start with George Bernard Shaw?"

"Isn't he Irish?" Peta smiled. "I take it you have a typewriter I can use?"

"You're doing it now?"

"Time is of the essence, Herr Krauss."

"It's Werner, please. And anyway, the letter will need to be in perfect English – surely we should hire a translator, which will take time and money . . . "

"*My* English is very good, Herr Krauss. Perhaps if you could dictate to me, I'll do my best to translate, and we'll send it off to Herr Shaw tonight."

Werner felt overwhelmed by her grace and clarity of thought. Whereas he could only see one, huge, tightly woven mess of trouble – she had the ability to see several, small problems, and they were apparently easy to solve. He fetched his typewriter, and even found a pile of the headed notepaper that Maria had insisted he ordered. He hovered over her as she typed, wondering what it would take for him to be able to embrace her, tear her clothes off, and make love right there in the lounge.

"So where did you last meet Herr Shaw? How will he remember you?"

WERNER KRAUSS

Stuttgart W,
Zeppelinstr. 47
(14a) US – Zone
Germany

MR. GEORGE BERNARD SHAW
London

Dear Mr. Shaw!

I take it that my name is not quite unknown to you, because I have acted in many of your plays in German Theaters. During my stay in London in the year 1933 I had the pleasure on the 5th October to be your guest together with Siegfried Trebitsch and Maria Bard.

During the nazi regime I was put under pressure to act in the antisemitie film "Jud Süß".

Although this cooperation was forced up on me at the time, the authorities here will now for-bid me any further activity in connection with my professional calling as an actor.

I now ask you to kindly answer the following question:

Do you consider such an interdiction as justified?

Trusting to receive a reply in due course I remain

yours very sincerely
Werner Krauss

"Do you still think about Frau Bard?"

"Of course. In fact, you remind me of her a little – she was also very intelligent, and she kept me in my place. You know, a lot of girls would've given up on a bad-tempered old man like me by now."

"Just doing my job, Herr Krauss."

"Hold that thought, dear." Werner turned on the gramophone, Louis Spohr filled the room. "As your employer, I insist that you join me for a dance."

"We have work to do, Herr Krauss."

He held out his hands. "Dance with me for a few moments, please, *Die Jahreszeiten* is my favourite."

She took his hands. "I hope you're taking me seriously, Herr Krauss?"

"Of course I am, dear, of course. And I told you, call me *Werner*." He held her close, and they started to spin around the small room. "A young girl like you must have gentlemen clambering for dances with them all the time."

"I'm not sure about that, Herr Krauss. And I'm not so young."

"Nonsense!"

"I'm thirty-six, and *you're* an old charmer."

"You don't look a day over twenty, my dear."

They both smiled. Werner considered pulling her closer, but there was something stopping him, somehow things seemed fine as they were. He took a deep breath.

"And is there a husband I should be manically jealous of?"

"No. Not any more."

He felt a rush of relief and excitement. "I could kiss her now," he thought, "and she probably wouldn't mind." Then came a knock at the door. Peta stepped away from him, and turned down the volume on the gramophone.

"Ignore it, dear!" he pleaded.

"It could be something important – your lawyer, perhaps."

Werner stormed towards the door. There was another knock. He jerked it open. It was Liselotte.

"What is it?"

"What a welcome!" Again carrying a suitcase, she climbed the step as if to let herself in. Werner put a hand across the doorframe to stop her.

"You can't."

"Stop being silly, Werner." He could smell the gin on her breath. "If this is about the other night, let's just forget all about it. Sorry if I did whatever it was I did. Just let me in, I'm dying for a drink . . . "

"No. Sorry. I'm busy," he said, "maybe call round tomorrow."

"I want to come in *now*." She hoisted up her suitcase. "Do you know how heavy this is?"

"I've told you, I'm busy!" He grabbed the case and placed it outside the door. He then seized Liselotte by the shoulder, and tried to force her away.

"You've got a woman in there, haven't you? It's that new girl who's working for you I bet – got your teeth into her already, have you?"

At that moment, Werner felt Peta brush past him, and out of the door.

"I must get going." She said. "I'll come back tomorrow."

"No, wait, please . . . " said Werner. She gave a polite smile and briskly walked away.

"*Auf Wiedersehen*, my darling – Werner will have you again tomorrow!" Liselotte called after her. Then she turned to Werner. "She's gone now, so can we please have a fucking drink?"

"You're disgusting!" Werner said. He spat at her feet, and slammed the door shut.

The Minister was stood with his back to the wall. His hands held out in front of him, tied tightly with thick rope.

"*You might be a man of God,*" *Werner said,* "*but God wanted my people to go free.*"

The Minister's lips seemed to be muttering a last prayer.

"*Tell me what you're saying! Tell me!*" *Werner yelled.*

"*I was asking for for for . . .*" *his lips started to quiver,* "*forgiveness.*"

"*And why do you want forgiveness? Admitting that you're wrong?*"

"*I'm asking God to forgive you.*"

He pulled the trigger, and the minister collapsed. The audience gasped.

Werner wheezed. He was sweating and wet. He had obviously fallen asleep after masturbating, having conjured images of himself and Peta. He thought his dream was of the staging of I.N.R.I., from 1923. It was a glorious run, fresh from the success of *Das Cabinet*, it was this play in particular where he noticed people were attending just to see him. He was young and virile back then, but he still remembers feeling anxious about his age, even in his early thirties.

He considered calling Peta, but wanted to make sure he knew what he was going to say first. How would he explain Liselotte? The truth of their 'arrangement' would make him seem tawdry and desperate.

4

He woke early. If this was to be the day he seduced Peta, he wanted his home to be clean and welcoming. He gulped coffee as though it were keeping him alive, and rampaged through the house with a refuse sack, throwing away anything that wasn't of immediate necessity. He found piles of old press clippings, diligently collected by the various agents and assistants he had employed through the years. He was particularly intrigued by a review by Potkamin who described *Die Hose* as "a blend of grand burlesque and satire." Werner apparently "excelled" as "a petty official with all the traits of the German Philistine."

He started to realise that the vast majority of these reviews were positive. Even in his early career, relatively minor roles would be noted for their "great promise." It had never occurred to him before, but perhaps such universal praise was largely responsible for his decision to stay in Germany, regardless of the political situation. For if he were to be judged on reviews and contemporary press acclaim alone, history could only view him positively. Perhaps what he had needed for all those years was some criticism and doubt. Who had ever been there to say 'no' to him?

He soon found an answer to this question, in a box that had been taped-up tightly for almost ten years. It wasn't even opened when he moved to Stuttgart, he just dumped it in one of the spare bedrooms, and marked it with one word in lower-case: 'maria'.

He considered throwing the box away, but thought that perhaps he could turn Maria's spite and loathing to his advantage after all. If he could bring himself to read one of her letters, he might learn what he needed to change about himself, in order to win Peta and keep her. With great difficulty, he tore open the box, and once again faced the pristine poison of Maria's handwriting.

> DEAREST WERNER,
> *It is either a great testament to my discretion, or to your ignorance, but it has been two weeks now, and you still haven't noticed the angry scars on my arms. Perhaps you will never notice, because I'm no longer a naïve girl, no longer 'forbidden' to you – you're no longer interested in my body. Nowadays I'm just another piece of property, like the garish vases and orna-*

*ments that arrive each day from that wonderful Party of yours.
The cracks have appeared, so eventually I'll be thrown out and
replaced.*

*I often think about your poor wife. At least when I'm lied-to and
abused, I can be grateful for our nice apartment and comfortable lifestyle. That poor woman must've worked and lived in
poverty, bringing-up your children and cooking your meals. And
while she did all this, you spent your time preying on the next,
younger, prettier girl.*

*I used to despise your wife. Some days I would walk up and
down your road, just to get a glimpse of her, to see what she was
really like. There were times when I even considered confronting
her in the street, or knocking on the door. What drove me so
mad was the thought that although I got to see you showing off
– acting and charming your way around Berlin – she got to see
you at peace, at ease, quietly reading or playing with the children. It drove me wild, the thought that with me you were just
acting. Now, of course, I realise how lucky I was. Take away the
acting and there's hardly anything left.*

*You probably promised your wife and I the same things, and
you're probably promising those things to girls now – young
actresses or impressionable teenagers, just desperate to meet the
famous Herr Krauss.*

*I wonder if that ever bothers you, Werner? The thought that now
you are famous, the attention that you get might not be anything
to do with your looks or charm, but might be solely due to your
fame itself! How does it feel to hide behind your name, hide
behind your face, never quite knowing if a girl likes you, or if
she likes the idea of you? Perhaps it is to give you too much
credit, to even consider that such thoughts might have crossed
your mind. Mother was right about you.*

*I'm not going to be here to find out – you'll see. Gone are the
days when I just indulge your selfishness with smiles.*

Goodbye, Maria x

He screwed up the letter, threw it back into the box and carried the
box down to the dining room, whilst trying not to weep. He now
realised that not only were these letters harmful to him personally; if
found they could also seriously harm his defence in court. Every other
letter seemed to bemoan his 'Party friends' or 'fellow Fascists.' If
someone so close to him could draw such conclusions, how would a
jury react?

He tried to start a fire with the remaining wood and coal that was left in the grate, but this soon became too much effort so he simply took a match to one of the letters, and piled the others on top. Black smoke soared from the individual words that caught his eye: 'loyal', 'careless', 'drunk', 'promised'. Werner vowed that this would not hamper his clean-up operation, nor would he let it affect his chances with Peta. When the letters were reduced to an amber glow, he climbed up off his knees, and returned upstairs.

Several of the boxes contained the ornaments she had referred to. Although they couldn't be burned, he must also dispose of them due to their Nazi connections. There was one statue of a bronze eagle, in particular, which was unmistakeably a Party artefact, not least because of the gaudy swastika it perched upon. He wondered why he had ever accepted such gifts, let alone displayed them. Perhaps he had hoped, rather naively, that the more he *appeared* to be supporting the Party on a symbolic or even a professional level, the lower the risk of his actual affiliations ever becoming scrutinised. He had always naturally assumed that, at heart, he was apolitical. Yet the evidence to suggest otherwise was literally piled up in front of him.

There was a knock at the door. His frantic effort to impress Peta had entirely dwarfed in his mind any other important business, including an appointment with his lawyer. He opened the door and did his best to postpone the meeting.

"So you see, although I am keen to get this done, it really isn't the best time . . . "

"I'm afraid it will have to be, Herr Krauss. Your trial is imminent and there are still some very important issues that we need to discuss. In fact, it's possible that the court sessions could begin as soon as next week."

"I suppose you'd better come in then."

Werner fetched himself a brandy and prepared a coffee for his guest.

"When we last spoke you told me about your first meetings with Frau Kopenik. How you started a relationship . . . "

"If you can call it that, Herr Bosweldt! We met a few times, different hotel rooms, different pseudonyms – I believe once I even checked in as Herr Churchill, would you believe?"

"So how did you come to retrieve this diary?"

"Boyish curiosity I suppose. It doesn't reflect well on me, I know, but one evening Frau Kopenik left the bedroom to take a bath and I saw a book in her bag. Quite unable to resist, I expected to be leafing through womanly whims, and hoping to find my own name mentioned."

"And what did you find, at first?"

"I was surprised to find lists. There were long lists of names and particulars and peculiar notes in shorthand. I remember one page which noted troop movements in the Netherlands and details of military personnel."

"And did you know that the Secret Service were looking for this diary at the time?"

"Of course not! The last I heard they were supposed to keep their work a secret."

"Very well. So, did you take the diary into your own possession straight away?"

"If you'll excuse me, Herr Bosweldt, nature calls."

He rushed upstairs, locked the bathroom door and breathed deeply. He felt angry at himself for not preparing more carefully for this session. He had to stop embellishing and just give the bare facts. He flushed the toilet and washed his hands, so as not to arouse suspicion from his Lawyer.

"I do apologise, Herr Bosweldt."

"It's quite all right. Now, was this the point at which you actually took the diary?"

"No, it was not. I was fortunate enough – or unfortunate enough, you might say – to meet Herr Goering the very next day. He was attending the *Cavour* premiere and I asked if I could speak to him in private. I said how unusual it was for a woman to be keeping such things in her diary. Of course, it was at this point that he told me who she was – closely linked to the Belgian ambassador, and privy to the most intimate State secrets, including detailed aspects of the Führer's private life."

"And Goering's reaction was?"

"He said the situation was too delicate for any arrests, but if I could *procure* the diary, and give it directly to him, it would be advantageous. After all, there could be troops lives at steak, if this were to fall into the wrong hands."

"Did he offer any sort of reward?"

"No. I said I'd be happy to do it – it was the only thing I could do, when this diary included such sensitive information. My loyalties were to our soldiers."

"Good, good, yes, of course, you should remember that argument when it comes to court – you were simply serving the soldiers, rather than garnering Party approval."

"It's the truth."

"So when did you actually take the diary?"

"I went to her house the next morning. She didn't want me to be there – said her husband could come home at any minute. I asked if I could at least stay for coffee, and when she moved into the kitchen, I discreetly found my way into her bedroom and took the book. After that, I made my excuses and left."

"Hello operator, I wonder if you can help, I need the number of somebody who can cook me a meal . . . No, dear, you don't understand, I don't need a restaurant, I need someone to cook dinner for me here – then leave me when it is done . . . You're the operator, I thought you would know . . . It's very simple, I wish for someone to buy the ingredients at a shop, come to my house and cook those ingredients, I will then pay whatever it costs, and they can leave me to enjoy the food with my guest. Do you understand now? . . . Hire a chef from a restaurant? . . . If that's what I have to do, then I suppose . . . give me the number of the *Steigenberger*."

"Come in, my dear!"

"Something smells good. I thought it would be a good idea to start work on your memoirs today, Herr Krauss." She was struggling to carry the recording device, which seemed quite cumbersome and primitive. He felt a pang in his heart at the thought of her exertions in getting it on the train.

"I've prepared a special treat – let me take your jacket." As he stepped behind her and helped remove the thick black coat, he shivered with anticipation.

"Herr Krauss, I'm supposed to be here to work, there's no need at all for treats."

"Nonsense! And besides, I've just spent all morning going through memories and damn details with my lawyer."

"Just doing my job, Herr Krauss."

"Yes, speaking of your job, we still haven't discussed your salary yet, have we my dear?"

"Willem said it was a two-week trial . . . "

"It is dear, but I should at least be responsible for your expenses. Shall we say three hundred marks, for this week?"

"Three hundred? Yes, that's wonderful – I was only expecting . . . "

"That's on the condition," he interrupted, "that you join me for dinner before we start ploughing up the past again."

"It's a deal."

She followed him through to the dining room.

"I wanted to apologise for the behaviour of that awful woman who was here last time."

"There's no need – it's really none of my business."

"Of course it's your business, dear." The table was laid immaculately and he grabbed a bottle of champagne from its ice bucket. "That crazy woman knocks on my door all the time – she's completely insane! Somehow she found out my address and ever since she goes round telling people we're an item."

"Really, Herr Krauss, it didn't bother me."

He carefully pulled back one of the chairs, and invited her to sit.

"How many times must I tell you, it's *Werner*!"

She smiled, nodded at him, and proceeded to place one of the serviettes on her lap. She studied the embossed gold lettering on the napkin.

"This says '*Steigenberger Graf Zeppelin*', how on earth did you manage to get their table linen?"

"You ask too many questions, my dear."

"Isn't that my job?"

Again she smiled. Werner was convinced that she was flirting with him. Nervously, he offered a top-up for her champagne, even though she was yet to take a sip. They sat for a moment in silence, before he realised what was missing.

"Food! Of course! Sorry dear, just give me a moment."

The maid from the hotel had carefully left notes, instructing Werner when to use his oven to heat the main course dishes, and when to remove the desserts from the refrigerator. He found the note marked *Aperitif* and carried the respective plates into the dining room.

"Really, Herr Krauss, you didn't have to go to all this effort. If I had known you were making dinner I wouldn't have eaten earlier."

"What we eat is unimportant – it is the company we keep."

He sipped the soup, doing his utmost to avoid slurping, and delicately nibbled the baguette. Unable to think of any other topic, he asked if she had any more ideas for his professional rehabilitation.

"I'm really excited about London," she said, shuffling the food around her plate. "If things go our way, we could change everyone's perception of you overnight. In fact, if it goes really well, you could even move to England. It's the last place anyone would expect to find a so-called Nazi."

"Indeed. I wish I shared your optimism, dear."

"Couple that with the autobiography and your reputation will be restored."

"Is it really that easy though, dear? Will anyone take any notice of a book?"

"Normal people might not, but the press will lap it up – some attacking it, some defending – what's important is that your side of events will be out there in black and white. It certainly can't make things worse, Herr Krauss."

The meal ran smoothly, with the exception of an undercooked piece of lamb. Yet Werner had still been unable to turn the conversation round to their relationship. Somehow her voice had a steely, professional tone, which gave nothing away. He had been so sure yesterday, as they danced, that a kiss was inevitable. As he cleared away the plates, he decided to be more direct.

"Yesterday you mentioned a husband, dear."

"Did I?"

"You said that you were married, but not any longer."

"That's right."

"Any particular reason?"

"It's quite personal, Herr Krauss. And besides, it's getting late, I really think we should get to work on your memoirs."

"As you wish." He knew there must be another way of winning her affections, but he couldn't concentrate, he started to feel drowsy.

"Let's start by talking about the film *Jud Süß*. I did some research yesterday and was perturbed by the film's notorious reputation. Apparently, it's a blatant work of Nazi propaganda. So why exactly was it that you agreed to play so many Jewish roles? I haven't actually seen the film for years, but weren't you five or six different Jewish characters?"

"Shall we just take this one step at a time, dear?"

"Okay, well, how did you become involved with the film in the first place?"

In 1939 I decided to retreat to the Bühler heights. It was a place I had always gone when I felt that I had eaten or drunk too much and needed some space in which to recover. It was there I received the letter approaching me to be part of the film Jud Suß. At first I had refused . . . no, not really refused, I simply said to myself "I don't want to!"

Following this I received a second letter, informing me that it was the express wish of the Propaganda Minister that I must under all circumstances play the 'Lion Rabbi'. I deliberated greatly, and came to a decision without consulting Marian, knowing that this is the kind of matter that one has to approach alone. Then I had an idea. I said to myself: "if I am to play a Jewish role in this film, it will naturally cause people to speculate as to whether or not a Jew would be more capable in the role than a non Jew." I did not want to be part of such a political debate, so I made a demand: I would do it, but only if I, bar the title role, could play all the Jewish roles.

I later mulled over this decision and thought upon it many times, finally deciding that one should not just accept this challenge, but rather, one should go into it with great delight.

In the end I played a Jewish Chairman, I briefly played a Jewish woman, who peers in through a window, a grandfather and a Jewish Butcher. The woman looks through the window at those who pass below holding them in her gaze. For each of these roles I refused to wear a prosthetic nose, but rather, only a beard. My face stayed as it was.

Whilst in Poland the German army discovered a film, a wonderful film that had been shown by the Habima. They brought the film back to Germany. It was called 'Dybuk', and, in my opinion, it was an artistic masterpiece. It was set in a small town in Poland where all the residents were Jewish. The story itself was similar to Romeo and Juliet. One family had a very beautiful daughter and another had a son. However, he was a little stupid, and sought the money to marry by going to her parents to ask for her hand with suitable dowry. The beautiful girl, meanwhile, is in love with a student, a hansom man, and her parents cannot bare this. So, by playing tricks on the boy, everything explodes and he ends up dead and buried.

'The Dybuk' itself is a ghostly apparition. In one scene, a rich Jew is walking at a brisk pace through the town, when the Dybuk appears on the roadside and pleads to be taken along. It taunts him as he keeps on going, travelling for miles and miles. However, the Dybuk travels fast, and whichever way he goes, the Dybuk is waiting for him.

It is said in a common proverb, that when someone stands and waits by a grave during a full moon, the dead contained within will rise, and so it is in another scene of the film. With this mind, the girl goes to the graveyard and waits. As expected, the one who had died rises out of his grave and makes love to the girl. As a result of this encounter, she becomes pregnant, and then through her marriage to the other, she too dies and they are united in marriage and death.

It was a wonderful film – all those who played the central roles in Jud Süß *had seen it. This film that was so transcendent, that at the time Hitler had forbidden anyone to see it.*

"Surely that's enough for one day isn't it, dear? You must have three pages already."

"Possibly . . . why don't we talk more about the actual filming?"

"Whatever you say, if you promise to join me for a drink before you go home."

"Do you always work in bribes and blackmail?" She laughed.

Then came the call from the film studios:
"Goebbels has requested that you use a false nose",
"I won't do it" I said, "I have other means or expression than false noses!"

The human quality in this film was such that those who are repre-sented as the bad characters are the Duke of Württemburg, who puts on a ballet, and Oppenheimer of Frankfurt who Württemburg invites to his ballet, in order for them to barter away their fellow countrymen. Until the film was finished I had not seen it, but I must have seen it myself later at least three times purely in order to pass judgement on it . . .

"What's the matter, Herr Krauss?"

"Nothing. Can we just stop this now, please? I'll talk another day; this stirs up too many bad memories. After what happened to the Jews, I . . . "

"It's okay. I'm sorry, we can take it one step at a time." Peta put an arm around him. He resisted the urge to smile. "You poor thing."

"It's not easy, dear – these questions. It's all very well for you, but when you leave me I'm alone here until the next day, no one to talk to or share things with . . . " he tried to muster a tear.

"Maybe I can stay for a while. There's no need to get upset."

"Thank you, dear."

"It's the least I can do after such a nice meal."

"You must think I'm a silly old fool . . . "

"I'd think less of you if you *didn't* show some emotion. After all that's happened, it must be quite painful."

He took her by the hand. "You seem to be the only one who under-stands me, dear. Without you, I don't know what I would do."

"Happy to be of service, Herr Krauss." She gave his hand a reas-suring squeeze, then pulled away. "Now why don't I make us a nice drink?"

"Now you're definitely talking my language!"

"Brandy?"

"Only if you'll join me, dear. Help yourself to the rest of that cham-pagne."

"I can have a glass I suppose."

As much as he disliked having to illicit sympathy from Peta to get her to stay, there was some truth in his reluctance to talk about that film. Goebbels' first visit to the set had really established the tone for what was to come. Werner felt helpless as his co-star felt the wrath of the diminutive minister.

"Herr Goebbels, I usually play bon-vivants and lovers. However, this Jew Süß, the way you want him, is a truly unpleasant character. I don't want my fans to see me like this . . . "

Goebbels went over to Marian and shoved him against a table, speaking quietly, he said: "Your public would not like to see you in this role? Who casts you in your roles? Your fans or me?"

Marian shook his head. What reply could he offer? The minister continued, "I have just recently seen you as Iago in a German theatre. You were excellent. Was he a nice Bon-vivant?"

"But that was Shakespeare, Herr Minister!"

"And I am Joseph Goebbels!" he screamed in Marian's face. He then turned to Werner, "How about you, Herr Krauss? Surely a former vice-president of the *Reichstheaterkammer* will have no objections to a little more . . . drama, a little more malice, in your portrayal?"

"So what *would* you like to talk about then, Herr Krauss?" Peta passed him a drink, and placed a motherly hand on his shoulder. "Take your mind off that dreadful film."

"How about you?" He said. "I feel like I hardly know you, dear."

"There's really not much to tell."

"Nonsense! Willem said that you had all sorts of jobs at the *Staatstheater*."

"I suppose I did. The most interesting were for the film Ministry, though."

"You worked on film too?"

"I was employed by the RMVP as an editor for a while. I even learned how to create animations for one film . . . "

"I didn't think women had such jobs!"

"Of course. With so many men drafted, especially towards the end of the war, they had no choice. There were lots of us involved in post-production. Women were trusted to be efficient and diligent. It was just the creative element – script editing or directing – that we were prohibited from. You must have met plenty of women on film sets, Herr Krauss?"

"Yes, I did, dear."

"But you didn't know what sort of work they were doing?"

"I just assumed they were all make-up girls." He laughed and sipped his drink.

It was joyful, having her talking, relaxing in his presence. "So, in a way, you worked for the Party in the same way that I did. Would you agree?"

"I dare say you had more choice than I, Herr Krauss. But the question has obviously occurred to me, how far I might be responsible in my role . . . " Werner struggled to keep his eyes open. He was determined to listen to her, " . . . of course, it's impossible to say what might have happened if one had refused, or even migrated . . . "

Dressed only in his silk robe, he took the familiar walk along the upstairs hallway from his bedroom to the bathroom. He entered.

"*Don't you ever knock?*"

It was Peta, laying in his bath. The warm water was clear, so, momentarily; he could see her supple, pale body. He turned his head with embarrassment.

"*Just wanted to brush my teeth, dear. But I can come back?*"

"*It's your place, Werner. Do what you have to.*"

He squeezed the paste on his brush, and tried to concentrate on the scrubbing, although he soon realised that his shaving mirror, if adjusted slightly, would give him a perfect view of his guest. He poked the brush around his mouth, and tilted the mirror accordingly. She didn't seem afraid of him, or even embarrassed to be naked in his presence. She simply moved the soap around her arms and face. He could feel himself becoming aroused, and knew he would have to stop the brushing soon, or else cause his gums to bleed.

"*You know I'm not getting any younger either, Werner.*" *She said.* "*I'm sure a famous actor like you could have all the young girls he wanted.*"

He put down the brush and rinsed his mouth. His gums were stinging, and he noticed slithers of brown blood disappearing into the plughole. "*Why are you saying this, my darling?*"

"*Because you're scared, aren't you, Werner? You know I don't mind – I can be patient.*"

"*What are you talking about, woman?*"

"*You're scared about what might happen. You think you might not get it up. You think . . .*" *he noticed in the mirror that she pushed her hand between her thighs,* "*you think I'll laugh and tell all of your friends, that the great Werner Krauss is finished.*"

He felt his erection pushing against the cold ceramic of the washbasin.

"*I don't think anything of the sort, dear. In fact . . .*" *He turned to present himself to her, and untied his robe. But there was nothing there. He grabbed his crotch, but only felt a small stump. He tried to shout but no sound was produced.*

The lounge door closed. He woke up.

"Where are you going, darling . . . my dear?" he called after Peta.

She came back into the room. "I was trying not to wake you, Herr Krauss. It's late, I really need to get going."

"No, don't. Stay. Please . . . " He wiped his eyes. His mouth was so dry, but somehow he felt a rush of adrenaline. "There's something I want to tell you, dear."

"It'll have to wait, I really do need to go."

"No!" He shouted. Peta seemed shocked. "Sorry, dear. What I meant to say is: 'stay with me', please. What I have to say, it really is most important."

She placed her recording equipment on the floor, and joined him on the sofa, still wearing her coat.

"What is it now, Herr Krauss?"

"I wanted to tell you, Peta, darling, that I love you." She took a deep breath, and was about to speak, but he continued. "If you would give me one kiss, you would make me the happiest man alive."

"Herr Krauss, you don't understand – it is impossible."

"Why, dear? You're not married anymore – I'm also on my own – we could make each other very happy."

"I'm not married, this is true, but it is impossible for me to be in a relationship with you. It's very flattering, of course, but . . . "

"'Impossible, impossible,' why do you keep saying 'impossible'?"

She sighed. "Because there is someone else, Herr Krauss. I am in love with someone – I didn't think I would have to tell you this – our relationship should be a professional one. I'm sorry, I really must go."

She stood, but he grabbed her arm. "Tell me about him. Whatever he can give you; it isn't enough, my dear. He can't possibly understand your . . . " he began to stutter, "your beauty, the way I do."

"Let go, please." She pulled away from him. "If you want me to be honest with you, then I will. Though I don't think it's anyone's business."

"I pay you to *make* it my business, dear! Come on, who is he?"

"If you must know, there is no 'he'." She took a deep breath. "I'm in love with another woman. She is called Kate, she's from England, and she lives in the apartment below mine."

"You're saying you're a . . . "

"Yes. I'm *Lesbier*. I'm gay. Whatever you want to call it. We've been together for three years and we love each other. I trust you can understand that, Herr Krauss. Now that you know, may I be permitted to leave?"

"Of all the filthy, disgusting . . . is that why your English translation was so good? Because of a fucking *woman*?"

"I'm going." Leaving the recorder behind, she turned to leave.

"You're not going anywhere." He stood and, again, he grabbed her. He pushed his face close to hers. "The way you treated me, wiggling your pert little arse around my house – you knew exactly what you were doing – and all along you had these sick ideas . . . "

"Get off, Herr Krauss. I'm sorry if you got the wrong impression." She tried to pull away, but this time he grabbed her tightly, just below each shoulder. "Let go, please!"

"There's no way you're getting the three hundred now!"

"You bastard – get off me."

"Kiss me," he said. "Then you can go."

"You don't know what you're saying, Herr Krauss. You're too drunk, maybe. Let me go and we can forget all about this."

"Kiss me! If you know what's good for you, you'll do it."

She kicked his ankle. He shrieked with pain and let her go. She ran for the door.

"You bitch!" he shouted, and limped to try and catch her, but he was too late. The door slammed and he heard the clap of her heels running down the street.

5

Sat up in his chair, he didn't remember falling to sleep, but suspected he might have done. At first he wondered if seven a.m. was too early to call Peta, but he decided that it wasn't – if he was to prove to her how serious he was, time should not be an issue. He searched around the room for his diary, and found her number, underlined and circled with naive, teenage enthusiasm. He dialled the number, and waited.

"*Hallo* . . . who is this? . . . Never mind who I am, I'd like to speak to Peta, please . . . I know what time it is, is she there or not? . . . All right, yes, it *is* Werner Krauss. You must be Catherine? . . . Kate, whatever – can I talk to her? . . . I actually just wanted to apologise . . . *hallo? Hallo?*

He replaced the receiver, and re-dialled immediately. She shouldn't be allowed to think the worst of him, as she was bound to be doing right now, in bed with that woman.

"*Hallo*, if you could just let me speak to her? . . . Then at least pass on a message? . . . Please? . . . If you could tell her I'm sorry. I know I was wrong to say those stupid things – if we could just go back to the way things were . . . I really don't think it's any of your business . . .

you're enjoying this, aren't you? You fucking bitch. Just pass on the fucking message. Okay? . . . *Hallo?*"

He calmly replaced the receiver. Then wrenched the telephone from it's socket, and launched it across the room. It smashed into several pieces.

"Bitch, bitch *fucking* bitch!" he screamed.

He climbed back upstairs, turned on the wireless in the hope that the voices would relieve his loneliness and settled into his bed, wrapping the blankets over his shoulders and tucking them under his feet. He started to cry. His head was throbbing with the prospect of resuming life without her. He just wanted the world to carry on, and not notice the absence of old Werner Krauss. This wasn't the first time he had been rejected, but usually he could laugh off his disappointment and concentrate on the next girl. But there was something special about Peta, which wouldn't allow him to purge her from his thoughts. Perhaps the fact that she was so unobtainable actually made her more alluring. Curled up in this warm foetal huddle, he wept until his headache eased, and the soothing swirl of sleep started to take hold.

Why didn't they tell me? Why don't any parents warn you, before you go to school? "More news now from the trial of Franz Rademacher . . . " *At that age you just don't realise – if the kid sitting next to you has a bruise on their arm with the texture of a mouldy apple.* "Rademacher was the head of D III, head of the so-called 'Jewish desk' of the Nazi Foreign Office between 1940 and 1943 . . . " *All you can do is find it interesting – interesting! – as if the bruise makes them exotic in some way.* "Today the court heard detailed accounts of his alleged crimes . . . " *Even worse, if the kid smells bad, smells musty in the way that excites the saliva in the back of your throat, convincing you that you'll be sick.* "He was described as being 'at the heart' of plans to re-settle the Jews to Madagascar . . . " *Your instinct is to poke fun. Tell everyone about the smelly kid. Why didn't they warn me? Mother and Father, just a few words to make me wonder where the bruise, or, even worse, the smell came from.* " . . . but after this plan could not be realised, he was relocated to Serbia to help the local authorities find a solution to their so-called Jewish problem . . . " *Is innocence really so important, that we should be able to inflict it on others?* "Witness testimony describes the use of firing squads, who took direct orders from Rademacher. The trial continues this afternoon." *The perfect circle of childhood, turning, turning regardless . . .*

Werner leapt out of bed and fumbled with the wireless. "Shut up! Stop, just stop!" It wouldn't turn off, so he yanked the volume control, leaving just a low buzz.

"Herr Krauss . . . " Bosweldt was out of breath and sweating profusely, "I've been trying to call you all morning – what's happened to your telephone?"

"Nothing . . . that I've noticed. Why, what's so urgent?"

"It's your trial . . . " he took a deep breath. Werner thought the tubby lawyer might collapse at any moment. "As I suspected, it's been moved forward . . . "

"Well, when to?"

"I'm sorry Herr Krauss . . . it's actually tomorrow." Werner stood aside, allowing his lawyer to enter the house. "If I could have a glass of water . . . I'd be most grateful."

"No problem. I might pour something for myself too."

"From what I can gather, the courts seem to be mounting a stronger case against Herr Harlan. Although we had good reason to believe his trial would come before yours, in fact, they'll effectively be using your trial to bolster their case against him."

"So you're telling me this is *good* news?"

"In a manner of speaking, Herr Krauss, yes. Although obviously there are still serious repercussions if you are proven to have know-ingly aided the Nazi cause, I suspect it's actually Harlan, as director, that they want to get."

"So *Jud Süß* is very much the focus of the trial?"

"I suspect so. But your history of related activities, such as your performances in *The Merchant of Venice*, will also be scrutinised."

Bosweldt was thorough and methodical. He talked Werner through the court process, and seemed genuinely sympathetic to his client's cause. He spoke of the need to describe any instances of coercion. He should emphasize the fact that he had never formally joined the party, and that he had been made vice-president of the *Reichstheaterkammer* without his permission, or indeed his knowledge. Werner tried to concentrate, but he had become so nervous that he resorted to concealing shots of whisky in his morning coffee. Eventually, he ordered his lawyer to go.

"I'm sure you'll do a first-rate job, Herr Bosweldt, it's just that I can't take any more of this."

"I do hope you'll have more stamina tomorrow, Herr Krauss. There's still lots to discuss – you need to focus."

"What I need is some time to think. As I said, I'm sure you'll perform perfectly well, whatever we do today. One thing I must insist upon, though, is increased security outside the courtroom. There's no telling what might happen if a group of Jewish activists get wind of my appearance."

"This is quite short notice, but I'll do what I can, Herr Krauss."

"Good. Now, if you'd be so kind as to leave . . . "

Ten minutes later, there was another knock at the door. Werner just yelled from the lounge:

"I'm not talking anymore – you've heard what I had to say. Just leave me alone. Please. I'll see you tomorrow."

"Werner?" came the response. It was a male voice, but it didn't sound like Bosweldt.

"Who is it?" He made his way to the front door.

"I'm looking for Werner Krauss, the actor . . . "

He opened the door. It was Hessler.

"Looks like you've found him, doesn't it?" They laughed and embraced. "Hessler, you old *hund*! What are you doing here?"

"I came to town last week, I heard your trial was coming up and thought I'd come to show my support." He handed Werner a bottle of *Asbach Uralt*.

"Hessler – I can't believe it! Do come in. How long has it been now?"

"Must be twenty years. I took that job you arranged for me, with Wiene in Vienna, and our paths never really crossed again. You're not an easy man to find these days though, Werner, I always assumed you'd stay in Berlin."

"Not since the war. Too many memories."

Hessler seemed to hover uncomfortably. Werner picked up a pile of clothes, clearing some room on his couch.

"Do take a seat, old boy, I'll get you a drink."

"A small one, thanks. I'm meeting Rebecca for lunch."

"*Rebecca*. This your latest girl then, you old rogue?"

"We've been married for twelve years, actually. Three children, two houses and a dog called Pavlov." Werner fell silent. For some reason, he had hoped that Hessler hadn't changed at all. It was reassuring to think there was someone out there who he had once been a civilising influence upon. "By the way, sorry to hear about Maria. I remember being in New York when someone passed on the news – didn't really believe it – she always seemed so happy. You both did."

"She had a lot of problems."

"You still must have some good memories though. I remember when you first got married – you were *Deutschland's* golden couple.

Two famous actors at the height of their theatrical powers. It was the stuff of fairy tales, Werner."

He shrugged. Although just minutes earlier he had been delighted to see his old friend, he soon wanted to be alone again. He fetched the drinks.

"Memories, memories. I'm starting to wonder if they're a blessing or a curse, you know. My lawyer, my agent – they've been relentless these past few days. Picking through my memory like old women at a fruit stall, trying to discard all the rotten and bruised apples to find something more palatable. 'When did you do this, Werner?' 'Where were you when this happened?' 'Why did you let this happen?' It makes you sick after a while. Why can't the past just be left alone? What good will it do, trudging through all these problems and mistakes?"

"Don't let it get to you, old boy. So you get a slap on the wrists by the courts – they've got real criminals to deal with, Werner. What we do is just entertainment – open to interpretation and, yes, maybe misunderstanding, you can't be responsible for every madman in the world who sees a film then does something crazy."

"Thanks, Hessler."

"No need to thank me, it's true. I'm right in assuming you've never killed anyone?"

"Of course!" Werner laughed in amazement.

"Then that makes you less guilty than hundreds, even thousands of men who took part in that war. And you can use that in court if you like, because I believe it."

"So why didn't you stay in *Deutschland* when the Nazis took power."

"I'd just got a great agent, Kaufmann, a Jew. He was convinced that there would be a place for me in Hollywood if I worked hard and took a few dud roles. Artistically, as much as anything else, he said that *Deutschland* was dead. He'd seen the way the Nazi bully boys behaved right through the twenties – said it would be no place for real artists."

"Good to know you've lost none of your famous tact, old boy."

"You know what I'm saying, Werner. Surely it crossed your mind too, you either had to stay and accept their interference, or start again somewhere with more freedom."

"That's all very well for you to say. I was already established here. Once you get to a certain age, you feel as though you've earned the right to not have to worry about when the next show will come up. I hadn't attended an audition for ten years before the Nazis came in, you know. *Ten years.* That makes you feel very comfortable, Hessler. After years auditioning for bad parts, *any parts*, to reach the point where the theatres and the studios were making me offers. It hardly felt real. Do you think I wanted to give that all up, just because of the failings of a set of stupid politicians? Perhaps if I was younger, like you, with more energy, more sense of adventure. But what you said is right – I never committed a crime – and I never wanted anyone to get hurt."

"So when is the trial, old boy? You ready for it?"

"It's tomorrow, would you believe? Obviously, it'll be good to get it over with, but, as for being ready . . . "

"I suppose it all boils down to what they consider to be 'collaboration.'"

"Exactly. As if it was ever simply a case of saying 'no' to them, and carrying on with your life. Fear became implicit, do you understand? Fear was such a part of everyday life, that it actually stopped being a consideration, you just got used to it. You never have to remind yourself to breathe, do you?"

Hessler just laughed.

"Do you though, seriously?"

"Of course not!"

"Right. And I never had to remind myself to be afraid of them. You did what you had to. And that's the case for the defence."

When Hessler left, Werner decided to indulge his drinking habit in earnest. With Peta gone, there was no reason to make an effort, or even to consider curtailing his thirst. Uncharacteristically, he also smoked several cigarettes, and even crushed one packet to fit into his shirt pocket, so that he wouldn't have to leave his bed in order to smoke at night. If this was to be his last evening of freedom, before the sober rigours of his trial, he would act accordingly. He ambled over to the socket with the remains of his telephone, plugged it in, and, miraculously, there was still the faint hum of a dialling tone. He was lying on the floor, which seemed to be spinning beneath him. He took a breath and dialled Liselotte's number.

"*Hallo,* darling, it's Werner . . . *Werner!* You'll have to speak up it's a terrible line . . . just forget . . . darling, please . . . just forget about the other day . . . that woman – she left me you know – just fucking went and left me . . . why don't you come round? . . . I'll send a taxi to pick you up . . . come on, Liselotte, you know me . . . come round I'll treat you like a queen . . . there's a bottle here with your name on it. A nice long glass too, with ice . . . Liselotte, darling – you know I didn't mean it, you caught me at a bad time . . . Fine, well how does fifty marks sound? . . . I don't *expect* anything – I just want to see you . . . a hundred? You already owe me thirty from the other day, which you helped yourself to . . . Good. I'm sending the taxi now. Okay, darling. *Wiedersehen."*

6

It was dark, but for a shaft of light which came in through a crack in the door at the far end of the room. He was alone in a double bed, but felt cold, and could hear a commotion outside the room. He pulled the duvet round his shoulders and tried to bury his head in the pillow, but could find no comfort. After a while, the door opened, and a familiar figure wandered in.

"*Who is it? Turn the light on . . .* " Werner sat up.

"*Shh! It's only me, don't worry.*" It was Willem. He pulled back the duvet, and lay down next to Werner.

"*What the hell are you doing? I've got to get to sleep, my trial's tomorrow.*"

"*I thought you wouldn't mind.*"

"*Where's Liselotte?*"

"*Come on now, Werner, don't play games with me . . .* "

"*I don't know what you mean. Look, if you have to sleep here, then fine, but please be quiet, I need to get some rest to prepare for the trial.*"

"*You can trust me, Werner. No problem.*"

Werner lay still, staring up at the ceiling. He tried to imagine himself in the courtroom. What on earth was he going to say? Did he really have any defence? To some people he would just appear to be a Nazi co-conspirator, a pathetic Mitlaufer. *He started to sweat, as he felt a warm hand on his thigh.*

"*Willem!*"

"*Just relax, Werner. No one will know.*"

"*Get off! I'm sorry, Willem. You'll have to go . . .* " Willem obliged *and left the room. Instantly a girl with blonde hair replaced him. She was wearing a gold-coloured, silk negligee. She too climbed into bed with Werner.*

"*Can you believe those men out there?*" She said. "*I thought this would be the safest place. Is it okay for me to join you?*"

"*I suppose so,*" he said. He turned on his side to look at her, and soon realised it was Sofia. "*What are you doing, dear? It's been so long. I always meant to call you, but my wife . . .* "

"*I know about your wife. I read about it in the newspaper. You shouldn't worry so much. People are bound to accuse you, Werner, but I know you had nothing to do with it. You were too busy paying attention to me at the time, do you remember? There was that time in your dressing room – perhaps we could carry on where we left off?"* She held his hand and pressed herself against him.

"Any other time, dear, of course. But my trial is tomorrow – I really need to sleep. God knows. What's the time now? I probably only have a couple of hours before I need to wake." He checked his wrist, but found no watch. He sat up, and searched the room for a clock, but to no avail. He had to know the time . . .

It was six a.m. He daren't go back to sleep, and got out of bed carefully, so as not to wake Liselotte. He knew that a brandy would help to settle his nerves, but he had to resist. He must do all he can to get Peta back. When she was around there was a purpose to his life – she actually believed in him, and he liked her ideas and her energy. He found some paper and a pen, and decided that one way to impress her would be to continue work on his memoirs. It might also bring some clarity to his thoughts before he faced the questions in court. He tried to concentrate on *Jud Süß.*

Harlan gave me an example of a prayer that I was to recite by heart. It was written by a Negro, and was entitled 'Schema Israel'. I was instructed that one only prays this prayer when one is truly alone, whilst striking oneself about the chest. Harlan assisted me with it himself, and it is this prayer that is featured in the film. Harlan had also helped me with the beard in order to enable me to play the part without the false nose. He had yet another input to the film – a curse. At the point when the "Sweet Jew" is being lead into captivity, he utters a terrible curse, after which he is taken away, whimpering. This too came from Harlan.

To talk of all the problems that arose during work with Harlan and Marian, is really quite pointless. We had to work together and were happy as we felt we were ready. I also had the role of a prayer leader, I played the role, with the chant being dubbed in, the chanter being a Jew from Prague. I must also now say, without any deception, that it was only later that questions about the film emerged.

It has been said that the film was "conceived in the Warsaw Ghetto, where Krauss had once been". Astounded, I said "I have never in my life been to Warsaw!" but I had no means to prove that I was not there, and it was alleged that I travelled there to see how Jews were mistreated, in order for me to study it. I did not; I simply took inspiration for all of my Jewish characters from the film "Dybuk".

He stared at the page. Just these three, simple paragraphs had been extracted excruciatingly from his memory. He had drunk three cups of coffee and eaten four pieces of toast. Peta had made the process of writing seem so easy – she had transcribed his words lucidly and accurately. Re-reading his scribbles, he wondered if it might actually be wise to await the outcome of Harlan's trial before writing any more about him. Without necessarily trying to, he seemed to be simultaneously defending and attacking the director. On the one hand, he was highlighting Harlan's quest for authenticity and the relatively sensitive way in which he handled Jewish traditions in the film. Yet on the other hand, he was shifting responsibility away from himself, and illustrating Harlan's ultimate control over the project. It felt as though writing to satisfy a particular agenda wasn't really writing at all – just a series of unconvincing answers to a set of impossible questions. Somehow, Goebbels' skill for ruthlessly executed propaganda seemed inspired in comparison.

He was just about to make a tentative attempt at a fourth paragraph, when there was a knock at the door. He welcomed the distraction from his writing, and limped over to the door.

"Herr Krauss?" It was a homely looking old woman, wearing an apron and clutching a bucket.

"What can I do for you?"

"I'm your new cleaner. We got a call a couple of days ago."

"You must have the wrong address, dear."

"No, it's this address. It was arranged by Frau Peta Viertel."

"I see. Well, I'm afraid I'm actually rather busy today. Perhaps if you came back next week?"

"As you wish, Herr Krauss."

The woman seemed quite disappointed, turned, and walked away rather slowly. Perhaps she was hoping he would reconsider. Having been selected as the cleaner for the famous Krauss residence, perhaps she was hoping to discover the secrets of her eminent new employer. Werner chuckled to himself at the thought, and closed the door.

He returned to his page of writing, deciding to focus on his other notorious Jewish role. By explaining how he had first taken on the role of Shylock under the tutelage of his (Jewish) mentor, Max Reinhardt, his later performances could be given context.

I came back to Berlin, to Reinhardt, and there again Schildkraut played Shylock, and then Basserman, and only when both were away on guest appearances, could I play Shylock. I was playing the role of a navy soldier in Kiel in the town theatre when the piece came my way early in 1921. Max Reinhardt was to direct. Reinhardt asked me when we were nearing the beginning of rehearsals: "How do you, yourself, visualise him?" and there I told him, I wanted to make a move away from Schildkraut's representation, as "a broad muscular man, more like a Butcher than a trader or money lender, or whatever". To this, Reinhardt said "Yeah, Yeah . . . I think that's a good idea".

On the next day the rehearsals began, and there he demonstrated something to me and said "when you get to this part 'as Jakob Labans sheep bleated – he was the third heir of our Holy Abraham,' . . . yes, that's right, the third . . . I really want to see that from you, its all in the eyelids, the impact of that look, contains one thousand years of Judaism".

He had explained the part to me in that way and I played the part as close to his wishes as I could, and so on the next day, when the part came round he listened to it and did all that he could to help me. Then he turned around and said:

"As I suspected . . . it can only be done by a Jew! That flashback six thousand years into the past."

Of this remark I admit I was not too pleased, as I had always said, Jewish actors have already played non-Jewish characters, why not the other way round? Reinhardt went away in the following days with his ensemble on a journey to Sweden and Denmark, to play a guest role and passed the responsibility for the rehearsals over to Berthold Held.

I sat now at home, rehearsing that 'look' and thought: 'How can I come up with a resolution?' I mulled it over all night, until shortly before four, looking into the mirror – but all I saw was myself. So I would smoke and drink a bottle of wine, pondering: "How would Max Pallenberg play the role of Shylock?"

Disturbed yet again by a knock, he threw down his pen and hobbled to the door, his ankle was still quite sore. He was delighted to find it was Peta.

"My dear, I'm so glad you came, please accept my apology . . . "

"I'm really not interested, Herr Krauss."

"But please, I have to go to court today and if you could only come with me . . . " It was such a relief to see her. All his frustrations seemed to come to the fore. He began to weep uncontrollably, whining phrases that were barely audible, "I didn't mean . . . " "I only wanted . . . " "It's just not fair . . . "

"I'm actually busy today, Herr Krauss – applying for jobs . . . "

"Where will you go, dear?"

"It doesn't matter . . . "

"Come back to work for me – four hundred a week."

"I don't want your money. I came to give you this." She handed him a letter. "It arrived at my address this morning. I thought you should have it."

"Thank you – why don't you come in for a coffee – sit down, relax, dear."

"Werner!" Liselotte's voice called from upstairs. "I thought you said that bitch had left you? Just tell her where to go, and come back to bed!"

"*Auf Wiedersehen*, Herr Krauss. Good luck with your trial."

"You don't understand – don't listen to her, she's a madwoman!"

"I really don't care, I'm going, Herr Krauss. Farewell."

She stepped back from the door, and pulled it shut. Werner sank to his knees, he felt breathless, as though he had no control over anything or anybody. He'd offered four hundred a week, and still the girl didn't want anything to do with him. As he tried to regain his breath, he focused on the piece of paper he was clutching. Below the original letter Peta had carefully typed out for him, was a handwritten note.

All civilisations are kept in existence by the masses who collab-orate with whatever government are for the moment established in their country, mature or foreign.
To treat such collaboration as a crime after every change of government is a vindictive stupidity which cannot be justified on any ground.

G. Bernard Shaw

Though he knew such an endorsement should be great cause for cele-bration, he couldn't help but feel sorrowful; that here was a testament to Peta's great diligence and hard work, qualities that he had squan-dered, simply because of his rapacious libido and stupid mouth. Such support from Shaw made him believe, for the first time, that he could be found 'not guilty', and that the theatrical fraternity might not have turned their backs on him after all. Yet at precisely the moment he felt confident about the trial, he also realised precisely why he was being tried at all. With Peta, as with much else in his life, he had *assumed too much*, and jumped to the conclusions that were easiest. He really wasn't too bothered, that a girl could be in love with another girl. Yet the language to condemn her had been too readily at hand, prejudices too well rehearsed in his mind, that it was actually difficult *not* to spit and shout at her.

He took a bottle of *Asbach Uralt* from the cupboard. Grabbing a dirty wine glass from the draining board, he poured carelessly, over-flowing the stemmed glass. Preparing himself for a shock, he gulped it down. Tears rolled from his eyes, but he resisted the urge to vomit. He took a cigarette from the box that had been to bed with him, and, with an unsteady hand, placed it in his mouth. Sinking to his knees, he lit it using the gas flame of the oven hob, which had been burning all night. He stole an hour of sleep, there on the kitchen floor, with the cigarette butt still in his mouth. Waking with a start, he dressed thoughtlessly, and, realising he was too late to arrange a ride, headed for the court on foot.

Postscript

BERLINERS STORM A THEATRE
Herr Krauss Resented

From our own Correspondent
BERLIN, DECEMBER 8

Several hundred demonstrators compelled the Vienesse Burgtheater Company to suspend their production of Ibsen's "John Gabriel Borkmann" to-night because a member of the company, the Berlin actor Werner Krauss, had taken a leading part during the Nazi regime in Dr Goebbels's anti-semitic film "Jud Süss." About eight hundred policemen using a loud-speaker van as a special truck equipped with high pressure hoses, were unable to prevent the demonstrators from penetrating into the forecourt of the theatre where the play was being performed. There were numerous hand-to-hand encounters between the police and the demonstrators, several of whom were injured.

For at least two hours there was constant bickering and intermittent scuffling in the forecourt of the theatre in the foyer, and in the road outside. The police made sparing use of their truncheons and the demonstrators replied by throwing tear-gas bombs into the police trucks. Several of the theatre windows were broken by stones, and the placards announcing Herr Krauss's appearance were torn down. The whole turbulent scene was illuminated throughout by the magnesium flares of the newsreel and press photographers.

The controversy which led to this evening's demonstration began when it became known that the Vienese Burgtheater Company, which includes Herr Krauss and Max Reinhardt's widow, Helene Thinig, had been invited to perform in the Berlin Municipal Theatre. The Jewish community protested at the time against the city authorities' decision to invite a man who had taken a prominent part in Herr Veit Harlan's film "Jud Süss," a production which the Jewish community feels was designed to encourage anti-Semitic feeling. In spite of reports to the contrary this protest, according to the Jewish community, was allowed to stand.

Manchester Guardian
9 December 1950

BERLIN OPPOSITION TO
WERNER KRAUSS
—
PERFORMANCES CANCELLED

FROM OUR OWN CORRESPONDENT

BERLIN December 12
Because of continued opposition to the acttor Werner Krauss the Vienna Burg-Theater Company has cancelled the two remaining performances (to-night and to-morrow) of its season here. The company came here at the invitation of the Magistrat and it had not been expected that Herr Krauss's erstwhile Nazi affiliations, for which he has gone through the process of German law, would be held against him now. The weight of responsible opinion in Berlin is opposed to the demonstrations against Herr Krauss, which were first staged by non-German Jews and students last Friday night, but which have since been sponsored in immoderate and even threatening language by the leader of the local Jewish community. This evening Herr Reuter, the senior Burgomaster, expressed regret that after the company's initial success here political passion should have clouded the atmosphere of the city.

The Times

13 December 1950

GERMAN FILM ACTOR
HONOURED
Nazi Victims Protest

From our own Correspondent
BONN JUNE 25

The award of the Grosse Verdienstkreuz, the Federal Republic's only deco-ration, to the actor Werner Krauss has provoked violent protests from sections of the community who suffered under the Nazis. Herr Krauss played the title role in the film "Jew Suss" which had no connection whatever with Oppermann's novel but was a piece of Nazi racial propaganda.

The first protest was made yesterday when it was learned that Herr Krauss had been honoured by President Heuss on the recommendation of the Berlin City Senate. Herr Krauss was 70 on Wednesday, and this was considered a fitting occasion to make the announcement. The protest was made jointly by the Jewish community in Berlin, the Organization of the Victims of Nazism, and a number of liberal students and journalists.

The Society of Racial and Political Victims of Nazism declared that the award was an insult to the dead and living who had suffered under Hitler. Democratic Action, a group of young Liberals, stated the award was a piece of shocking tactlessness and a slur on other holders of the decoration. The effects of the film "Jew Suss" are not easily forgotten, for it contributed to the stirring-up of hatred against the Jews.

Manchester Guardian
16 June 1954

Obituary
HERR WERNER KRAUSS

A DYNAMIC ACTOR

Herr Werner Krauss, the actor, who was a dominant figure in the German speaking theatre for almost half a century, and almost certainly the most controversial personality in it during his later tempestuous years, died in Vienna after a serious illness in the early hours of yesterday. He was 73.

By the age of nearly 50 he had made such a position for himself in Central Europe by his stage and screen work that he felt he had a right to be seen and heard in London. This was legitimate, but his performance in the West End in 1933, when he appeared with British actors, himself speaking English, was a disappointment. The virtue seemed to go out of him and there was more virtuosity in its place. Yet Krauss's performances in his native language and in the wordless language of the silent films had, theatrically speaking, great virtue. In his work and in the storms he aroused in public life Krauss had something about him to remind Englishmen of Edmund Kean.

He was born at Gestunghausen near Coburg in 1884 and made his first appearance at the municipal theatre at Guben 20 years later. By the time the First World War ended and a period of violent change and experiment set in on the German stage Krauss was an actor with a sound record in classical parts behind him. Something in the air of the new Expressionistic theatre, in the influence of the Russian stage in the Post-Revolutionary period, in Shakespeare in modern dress, and – not least – in the rise of the German film industry acted upon Krauss in such a way as to turn him from merely a good actor into an actor seemingly possessed. He, more than Jannings, Veidt, Moissi, or Kortner, was felt to be representative of the essential Germany, of the colossus that had been defeated but could not be destroyed. He was the living ghost, the walking reminder, of the great past.

Curiously and regrettably this quality in him that first showed itself within the framework of bizarre, Expressionistic, "decadent" productions later became identified with Nazi mythology in the classical revivals and films of the Goebbels regime. Whether he consciously lent himself to it or was tricked into it, the King Magnus of *The Apple Cart*, the modern dress Falstaff, the Spielmann of Reinhardt's *The Miracle*, was transformed into a Napoleon (the

Napoleon of Mussolini's play), a Julius Caesar, a King Lear of the Nordic Superman variety. After the war, in 1948, he acquired Austrian nationality, but his membership of the Burgtheater Company that visited West Berlin in 1950 led to violent demonstrations on the Kurfurstendamm and to the premature closing of the season.

In London in 1933 the first night of his appearance in Hauptmann's *Before Sunset* had only been saved by Dame Peggy Ashcroft's appeal to the demonstrators to be fair. Thirty policemen in the house on the second night ensured the run of the play – for a few weeks; Krauss's career continued – for many years. He was big enough to withstand even the storms of his own raising and, if not to direct them, to sway hither and thither and to ride them till his life, not theirs, was spent.

Krauss turned his attention to the cinema during its early silent days and found the new medium particularly well suited to his own style of acting, as did other famous German actors of the period, such as Emil Jannings and Fritz Kortner. This immediate post-war period of the German cinema has been described as the golden era of German film production, for it was then that the German film became absorbed with its preoccupation with the macabre, the supernat-

ural, with folklore and the fantastic – an atmosphere well suited to the Teutonic mind, and one which was brilliantly exploited by the great German directors such as Wiene and Pabst.

The film by which Werner Krauss will chiefly be remembered – particularly by every serious student of film history – was Robert Wiene's *The Cabinet of Dr. Caligari*, which was made in 1919. This film was an expressionistic study in madness, strangely and unforgettably distorted, with Krauss himself playing the mad doctor. Lili Dagover as the girl, and Conrad Veidt as the Somnambulist. He also appeared in Paul Leni's *Waxworks*, the only occasion on which Veidt, Jannings and Krauss were seen together in the same film. Later Krauss played in *Secrets of a Soul*, which Pabst made in collaboration with Freud, and in 1925 with Greta Garbo in the same director's film, *The Joyless Street*. A year after he appeared again with Conrad Veidt in *The Student of Prague*, a sad and poetic film: but it is certainly *The Cabinet of Dr. Caligari* with which his name will always be associated.

Manchester Guardian
21 October 1959

Source Attribution

In-keeping with conventional practice for fictional novels, source materials have not been directly cited within the main body of this fictional re-imagining of Krauss' life. However, below is a list of sourcing information for the more explicitly referenced texts. For the definitive list of sources that were influential to this project, please refer to the bibliography.

Listed according to first reference within the novel

Quotation from: Etty Hillesum, *An Interrupted Life: Diaries 1941–1943* (New York: Henry Holt, 1986).

Translated dialogue from *Das Cabinet Des Dr Caligari,* Director: Robert Wiene, Screenplay: Carl Meyer and Hans Janowitz (Decla-Bioscop AG, 1920).

Lines from William Shakespeare, *King Lear* (London: HarperCollins, 1994).

Lines from Johann Wolfgang Von Goethe, *Faust: The First Part of the Tragedy, Part 1* (London: Penguin Classics, 2005).

Description of scenes from *A Day's Pleasure*, Director: Charles Chaplin, Screenplay: Charles Chaplin (First National Pictures, 1919).

Otto Horny review in Richard Geehr, *Karl Lueger, Mayor of Fin de Siècle Vienna* (Detroit, 1990), p. 361.

William Shakespeare, *The Merchant of Venice* (ed. by John Russell Brown), (London: Routledge, 1985).

Quotations from Emily Brontë, *Wuthering Heights* (Oxford: Oxford University Press, 1995)

Paraphrased public request by Werner Krauss, adapted from source in David Welch, *Propaganda and the German Cinema 1933–1945* (Oxford: Oxford University Press, 1983). Original source: W.A. Boelcke, *Kriegspropaganda 1939–41. Geheime Ministerkonferenzen im Reichspropagandaministerium* (Stuttgart, 1966).

Quotation from Gottfried Reinhardt, *The Genius* (New York, 1971), p. 242.

Lines from 'A Cradle Song' from William Blake, *Selected Poems* (ed. by P.H. Butter), (London: Everyman, 1991), pp. 16–17.

Assimilated extract describing Krauss' performance in Richard III from William Grange, 'Ordained Hands on the Altar of Art: Grundgens, Hilpert and Fehling in Berlin' from *Theatre in the Third Reich, the Prewar Years* (ed. by Glen W. Gadberry), (London: Greenwood Press,1995), pp. 85–86.

Dialogue from *Jud Süss*, Director: Veit Harlan, Screenplay adapted from the novel by Lion Feuchtwanger by Veit Harlan and Ludwig Metzger (Terra Filmkunst, 1940).

Letter to George Bernard Shaw, taken from Werner Krauss, *Das Schauspiel Meines Lebens* (Stuttgart: Henry Goverts Verlag, 1958), p. 228.

Translated extracts from Werner Krauss, *Das Schauspiel Meines Lebens* (Stuttgart: Henry Goverts Verlag, 1958).

George Bernard Shaw reply, taken from Werner Krauss, *Das Schauspiel Meines Lebens* (Stuttgart: Henry Goverts Verlag, 1958).

Bibliography

Primary Sources

Listed alphabetically by author, unless otherwise stated

Films

Listed alphabetically by title

Das Cabinet Des Dr Caligari, Director: Robert Wiene, Screenplay: Carl Meyer and Hans Janowitz (Decla-Bioscop AG, 1920).

A Day's Pleasure, Director: Charles Chaplin, Screenplay: Charles Chaplin (First National Pictures, 1919).

Die Morder Sind Unter Uns, Director: Wolfgang Staudte, Screenplay: Fritz Staudte, Wolfgang Staudte (DEFA, 1946).

Jud Süss, Director: Veit Harlan, Screenplay adapted from the novel by Lion Feuchtwanger by Veit Harlan and Ludwig Metzger (Terra Filmkunst, 1940).

Mephisto, Director: Istvan Szabo, Screenplay: Peter Dobai (Mafilm, 1981).

The Merchant of Venice, Director: Michael Radford, Screenplay: Michael Radford (Spice Factory, 2004).

Rotation, Director: Wolfgang Staudte, Screenplay: Erwin Klein and Fritz Staudte (DEFA, 1949).

Schindler's List, Director: Steven Spielberg, Screenplay: Steven Zaillian (Universal, 2003).

Sophie's Choice, Director: Alan J. Pakula, Screenplay: Alan J. Pakula (ITC, 1982).

Newspaper Articles

Listed chronologically

'Berliners Storm A Theatre', *Manchester Guardian*, 09/12/1950.

'Demonstration Outside A Berlin Theatre', *The Times*, 09/12/1950.

'Berlin Jews Win Their Fight', *Manchester Guardian*, 11/12/1950.

'Berlin Opposition to Werner Krauss', *The Times*, 13/12/1950.

'German Film Actor Honoured', *Manchester Guardian*, 26/06/1954.

Memoirs and Diaries

Anne Frank, *The Diary of a Young Girl* (ed. by Otto H. Frank), (London: Puffin, 1997).

Etty Hillesum, *An Interrupted Life: Diaries 1941–1943* (New York: Henry Holt, 1986).

Werner Krauss, *Das Schauspiel Meines Lebens* (Stuttgart: Henry Goverts Verlag, 1958).

Primo Levi, *If This Is A Man, The Truce* (London: Abacus, 2003).

Novels

Martin Amis, *Experience* (London: Vintage, 2000).
Martin Amis, *Koba The Dread* (London: Vintage, 2002).
Martin Amis, *Money* (London: Vintage, 2005).
Martin Amis, *The Rachel Papers* (London: Vintage, 2003).
Martin Amis, *Time's Arrow* (London: Penguin, 1991).
Emily Brontë, *Wuthering Heights* (Oxford: Oxford University Press, 1995).
Philip K. Dick, *The Man in the High Castle* (London: Penguin, 2001).
Umberto Eco, *Misreadings* (London: Harcourt, 1993).
Lion Feuchtwanger, *Jew Süss* (London: Martin Secker, 1926).
Stephen Fry, *Making History* (London: Arrow, 1996).
Johann Wolfgang Von Goethe, *The Sorrows of Young Werther* (London: Penguin, 1989).
Günter Grass, *The Tin Drum* (London: Vintage, 1998).
Christopher Isherwood, *Goodbye to Berlin* (London: Vintage, 2007).
Franz Kafka, *Metamorphosis* (London: Penguin, 1988).
Franz Kafka, *The Trial* (London: Penguin, 2000).
Thomas Keneally, *Schindler's Ark* (London: Sceptre, 1982).
Klaus Mann, *Mephisto* (London: Penguin, 1995).
Friedrich Nietzsche, *On the Genealogy of Morals* (Translated by Douglas Smith) (Oxford: Oxford University Press, 1996).
Marcel Proust, *The Way By Swann's* (London: Penguin, 2002).
Philip Roth, *The Plot Against America* (London: Vintage, 2004).
Art Spiegelman, *The Complete Maus* (London: Penguin, 2003).
William Styron, *Sophie's Choice* (London: Vintage, 2000).

Poetry

William Blake, *Selected Poems* (ed. by P.H. Butter) (London: Everyman, 1991).

Plays

Johann Wolfgang Von Goethe, *Faust: The First Part of the Tragedy Part 1* (London: Penguin Classics, 2005).
Christopher Marlowe, *The Jew of Malta* (ed. by James R. Siemon), (London: A & C Black, 2001).
Moritz Rinke and Katharina Gericke, *Two German Plays: The Man Who Never Yet Saw Woman's Nakedness* and *Warweser* (London: Oberon, 2001).
William Shakespeare, *The Merchant of Venice* (ed. by John Russell Brown), (London: Routledge, 1985).
William Shakespeare, *King Lear* (London: HarperCollins, 1994) .
Arnold Wesker, *The Merchant* (London: Methuen, 1983).

Miscellaneous Promotional Material

Hundert Tage: Film written by Mussolini, staring Werner Krauss. Promotional magazine, plus six contemporary newspaper reviews.

Secondary Sources
Arranged alphabetically by author or editor

<u>Serials</u>

Carmel Gaffney, 'Keneally's Faction: Schindler's Ark', *Quadrant 29* (1985, Vol. 7, PT 213).

Richard Johnstone 'The Rise of Faction', *Quadrant*, Vol. 24. (1985, Vol. 4).

Wayne Kvam, 'Grundgens, Mann and *Mephisto*', *Theatre Research International*, Vol. 15, No. 2.

Gerwin Strobl, 'The Bard of Eugenics: Shakespeare and Racial Activism in the Third Reich' *Journal of Contemporary History*, Vol. 34, No. 3.

Gerwin Strobl, 'Shakespeare and Racial Activism in the Third Reich', *Journal of Contemporary History*, Vol. 34, No. 3.

Gerwin Strobl, 'Shakespeare and the Nazis', *History Today* (47:6) 1997, 17–21 (1997).

Susan Tegel, 'Veit Harlan and the origins of 'Jud Süss', 1938–1939: opportunism in the creation of Nazi anti-Semitic film propaganda', *Historical Journal of Film, Radio and Television* 16 (4) Oct. 96, pp. 515–31.

Ulrike Weckel, 'The Mitlaufer in Two German Postwar Films: Representation and Critical Reception', *History and Memory*, Bloomington: Fall 2003, Vol. 15, Issue 2, pp. 64–93.

Hayden White, 'Figural Realism in Witness Literature', from *Parallax*, Vol. 10, No. 1 (London: Taylor and Francis, 2004).

<u>Post-War Studies, Essay Collections and Critical Theory</u>

Theodor W. Adorno, 'Working Through The Past' in *Can One Live After Auschwitz?* (ed. by Rolf Tiedemann) (Stanford: Stanford University Press, 2003).

Jay W. Baird, *The Mythical World of Nazi Propaganda, 1939–1945* (Minneapolis: University of Minnesota Press, 1974).

Andrew Bennett *et al.*, *An Introduction to Literature, Criticism and Theory* (London: Prentice Hall, 1995).

Haim Bresheeth, Stuart Hood and Litza Jansz, *Introducing The Holocaust* (Cambridge: Icon, 1997).

Brian Cheyette, 'The Uncertain Certainty of *Schindler's List*' from *Spielberg's Holocaust; Critical Perspectives on Schindler's List* (ed. by Yosefa Loshitzky) (Indianapolis: Indiana University Press, 1997), p. 228.

Survivors, Victims and Perpetrators; Essays on the Nazi Holocaust (ed. by Joel E. Dimsdale), (London: Taylor and Francis, 1980).

Robert Eaglestone, *Postmodernism and Holocaust Denial* (Cambridge: Icon, 2001).

The German Unemployed (ed. by Richard J. Evans and Dick Geary), (London: Croom Helm, 1987).

Barbara Foley, *Telling The Truth; The Theory and Practice of Documentary Fiction* (London: Cornell University Press, 1986).

Michel Foucault, 'What Is An Author' in *The Foucault Reader* (ed. by Paul Rabinow), (London: Penguin, 1984).

Jo Fox, *Filming Women in the Third Reich* (Oxford: Berg, 2000).

Theatre in the Third Reich, the Prewar Years (ed. by Glen W. Gadberry) (London: Greenwood Press,1995).

Richard Geehr, *Karl Lueger, Mayor of Fin de Siècle Vienna* (Detroit, 1990).

Martin Gilbert, *The Holocaust: The Jewish Tragedy* (London: Guild Publishing, 1986).

Hugh Grady, 'Modernity, modernism and postmodernism in the twentieth century's Shakespeare', from *Shakespeare and Modern Theatre* (ed. by Bristol, McLuskie and Holmes), (London: Routledge, 2001).

Sabina Hake, *Popular Cinema of the Third Reich* (Austin: University of Texas, 2001).

Holocaust Remembrance: The Shapes of Memory (ed. by Geoffrey H. Hartman), (Oxford: Blackwell, 1994).

Geoffrey Hartman, *The Longest Shadow; In the Aftermath of the Holocaust* (London: Palgrave Macmillan, 2002).

Introducing Foucault (ed. by Chris Horrocks and Zoran Jevtic), (Cambridge: Icon, 1997).

David Irving, *Hitler's War* (London: Focal Point, 2002).

Siegfried Kracauer, *From Caligari to Hitler; A Psychological History of the German Film* (Princeton: Princeton University Press, 1974).

Lawrence L. Langer, *Pre-empting the Holocaust* (London: Yale University Press, 1998).

Lawrence L. Langer, *The Holocaust and the Literary Imagination* (London: Yale University Press, 1975).

Deborah Lipstadt, *Denying the Holocaust; The Growing Assault on Truth and Memory* (London: Penguin, 1994).

Theatre Under The Nazis (ed. by Jack London), (Manchester: Manchester University Press, 2000).

David Lowenthal, *The Past is a Foreign Country* (Cambridge: Cambridge University Press, 1985).

Donald L. Niewyk, *The Jews in Weimar Germany* (Manchester: Manchester University Press, 1980).

Sharon Oster, '"The Erotics of Auschwitz": Coming of Age in *The Painted Bird* and *Sophie's Choice*', *Witnessing the Disaster; Essays on Representation and the Holocaust* (ed. by Michael Bernard-Donals and Richard Glejzer), (Wisconsin: University Press, 2003).

Gottfried Reinhardt, *The Genius* (New York, 1971).

Richard L. Rubenstein, *The Cunning of History; The Holocaust and the American Future* (Toronto: Harper Colophon, 1978).

Lars Sauerberg, 'Fact Into Fiction; Documentary Realism in the Contemporary Novel' (London: Macmillan, 1991).

Daniel R. Schwarz, *Imagining the Holocaust* (New York: St. Martin's Press, 1999).

Peter D. Stachura *The Weimar Republic and the Younger Proletariat: An Economic and Social Analysis* (London: Macmillan, 1989).

George Steiner, 'The Hollow Miracle', in *Literature in the Modern World* (ed. by Dennis Walder), (Oxford: Oxford University Press, 1990).

Richard Taylor, *Film Propaganda: Soviet Russia and Nazi Germany* (London: I.B. Tauris, 1998).

Sue Vice, *Holocaust Fiction* (London: Routledge, 2000).

Richard Wagner, 'Judaism in Music', from *Richard Wagner; Stories and Essays* (ed. by Charles Osborne) (London: Peter Owen, 1973).

David Welch, *Propaganda and the German Cinema 1933–1945* (Oxford: Oxford University Press, 1983).

John Willett, *The New Sobriety: Art and Politics in the Weimar Period 1917–33* (London: Thames and Hudson, 1978).

The Operated Jew (Translated with Commentary by Jack Zipes) (London: Routledge, 1991).

Film, TV and Documentary

Extras, Written and Directed by Ricky Gervais and Stephen Merchant (BBC/HBO, 2005–2007).

Lutz Hachmeister and Michael Kloft, *The Goebbels Experiment* (First Run Features, 2004).

Propaganda: The War of the Mind, Contributors: Chris Read, Robin Lenman (Pegasus, 2006).

The Sopranos, Created by David Chase, Series 1–6 (HBO, 2002–2007).

Selected Websites

Jan Frans van Dijkuyzen, 'A Universal German Classic; Shakespeare in The Netherlands during the Second World War', website: http://shakespeare.let.uu.nl/kultur.htm Accessed: 01/11/2004

Cary M. Mazer, 'My Problem With Shylock', website: http://www.english.upenn.edu/~cmazer/mvnews.html Accessed: 08/11/2004

Thomas Staedeli, 'Portrait of the actor Albert Bassermann', website: http://www.cyranos.ch/smbass-e.htm Accessed: 08/11/2004

Thomas Staedeli, 'Portrait of the actress Maria Bard', website: http://www.cyranos.ch/smbass-e.htm Accessed: 08/11/2004

Thomas Staedeli, 'Portrait of the actor Werner Krauss', website: http://www.cyranos.ch/smkrau-e.htm Accessed 08/11/2004

www.ingramcontent.com/pod-product-compliance
Lightning Source LLC
Chambersburg PA
CBHW071603110726
47908CB00007B/2222